Praise for Helen Whitaker

'Funny and frank'
Dawn O'Porter

'So well-observed, with a kind eye and an open heart'
Laura Jane Williams

'Emotionally smart and thought-provoking'
Clare Pooley

'A triumph!'
Mike Gayle

'Truly brilliant'
Emma Gannon

'Hilarious'
Woman

'Packed with wry humour'
Woman and Home

Helen Whitaker is a journalist and author living in London. Formerly the Entertainment Director of *Glamour UK,* her day job is currently Editor of *High Life* magazine. She writes books in her lunch hour, in the evenings and in any free time she has around parenting. Her writing has been published in *Grazia,* the *Telegraph, Fabulous, Stella, Red* and on BBC Three. Helen has written three previous novels, *The School Run, I Give it a Year* and *Single in the Snow. Flying Home for Christmas* is her fourth novel.

Also by Helen Whitaker

Single in the Snow
The School Run
I Give it a Year

HELEN WHITAKER

Flying Home for Christmas

HODDER

First published in Great Britain in 2023 by Hodder & Stoughton
An Hachette UK company

This paperback edition published in 2023

1

A CIP catalogue record for this title is available from the British Library

Paperback ISBN 9781399713047
ebook ISBN 9781399713023

Typeset in Plantin Light by Hewer Text UK Ltd, Edinburgh
Printed and bound in Great Britain by Clays Ltd, Elcograf S.p.A.

Hodder & Stoughton policy is to use papers that are natural, renewable
and recyclable products and made from wood grown in sustainable
forests. The logging and manufacturing processes are expected to
conform to the environmental regulations of the country of origin.

Hodder & Stoughton Ltd
Carmelite House
50 Victoria Embankment
London EC4Y 0DZ

www.hodder.co.uk

For my family

Chapter One

23RD DECEMBER

'**B**ut I have to get home for Christmas.'

Thea looks around Portland Airport. The departure hall is rammed. The queue for every airline desk stretches back to the kerbside drop-off zone, where security guards are instructing people that there's no more room inside the building and they need to go back to their cars, but the gale that's ramping up with every passing minute is making it hard to be heard.

Inside, it's chaos. Babies cry, and a guy Thea recognises from an HBO show about cops-turned-drug-kingpins pushes to the front of the queue next to her and demands to know where the VIP line is, while passengers grab onto anyone looking remotely official and plead to be let onto planes. Planes that, Thea is being categorically told, are not going to be taking off tonight.

Robyn, the perfectly made-up ground crew member standing in front of her, shakes her head, lips pressed together sympathetically. She has a veneer of professional concern cloaked in an aura of weariness, most likely caused by reading from the same script many times this afternoon. With every, 'Unfortunately, severe weather conditions have caused all flights to be grounded, both international and domestic,' she probably wants to say, 'Look outside, there's a hurricane warning. Are you crazy enough to want to get on a plane in these conditions?'

The problem is, Thea *is* crazy, or at least ultra-impatient to get home to London. She hasn't seen Mum, Dad, Kit and Nan for six months, the longest she's ever gone. Her heart squeezes when she thinks about getting home to Nan. She *cannot* be stuck here.

'The storm is forecast to pass overnight and all being well, flights will start taking off again around six a.m.,' Robyn is saying, her long nail art pecking at the keyboard in front of her. 'Tomorrow's noon flight should be up and running.'

'OK.' Thea tries not to well up. With the eleven-hour flight and an eight-hour time difference, flying home tomorrow means not landing until Christmas morning. She knows the zillions of other people surrounding her are also stranded, but they all seem to be travelling in pairs or groups. The thought of going back to her tiny studio apartment alone tonight brings the sting of tears to her eyes. As she'd prised the remaining takeout cartons from her fridge that morning, there had been a sense of extreme relief that she wouldn't have to think about Portland, or iDentity Creative, for seven whole days. In the world of American annual leave, getting a full week off is like being granted a paid sabbatical and one that Fuchsia, her boss, would definitely have reneged on if Thea hadn't negotiated it in writing when she was offered the job.

'You'll need to be here *early* tomorrow,' Robyn warns. 'Because everyone here this evening—' she gestures around the departure hall – 'is now going to be travelling tomorrow, along with everyone already booked to travel tomorrow. And as you probably know, there are only two direct flights a day to London.' Thea nods, her heart rate increasing. She doesn't need reminding.

'OK, thank you,' she says, moving her overstuffed backpack out of the way so the next person can hear the same bad news. They barely let Thea stand aside before they hurl themselves over Robyn's check-in desk. She starts her patter with the same practised line. 'Unfortunately, severe weather conditions have caused all flights to be grounded, both international and domestic,' Thea hears her say as she negotiates the crowd.

She hauls her backpack onto her shoulders and tries to navigate through the crush, picking her way to the exit with the symbol for the taxi rank above it. Why did she say Teddy could borrow her crappy car while she was at home? Because his equally crappy car is in the shop for its latest bodge job, she reminds herself. Her friend was heading straight home to his parents in Seattle after dropping her off and hopefully will be halfway there now, storm permitting. She'll have to suck up the cost of a cab she can't afford.

At the automatic doors, so many people are trying to get in, they're stuck half open, with the roar of a tempest behind them and freezing rain sheeting down. It's already dark outside, but beneath the shaking floodlights she sees unsecured suitcases whip off into the road and crash into travellers already struggling to stay upright in the wind. Security is trying to close off the entrance with the excessive use of weighted cones, and Thea finds herself being corralled around a newly created one-way system that takes her past the airport bar. Giant screens that usually show American sports games with rules that Thea barely understands are set to rolling news.

STAY AT HOME ORDER ISSUED

The ticker tape scrolls across the bottom of the screen as images of twisted fallen trees and houses stripped of their roof tiles flash up.

PORTLAND RESIDENTS WARNED NOT TO TRAVEL UNLESS UNAVOIDABLE

Thea stops dead in the one-way lane, people grumbling as they're forced to flow around her. 'Sorry, sorry,' she mutters, aware that she never sounds more British than when apologising for other people banging into her. Attempting to go back to her downtown apartment tonight is a stupid idea – if there's even a taxi to be found to take her. Plus, it's best she stays in the airport so she's first in the check-in queue in the morning. She *has* to be on the next departing flight to London. Has to. Spending Christmas Day alone in the USA isn't an option.

She runs through her choices, landing on the idea of booking a cheap room at a budget hotel in the airport, and looks up again at the signage. Along with the arrivals and departures, there are arrows directing people to the rail transit system, the bus station and the hotel shuttle bus pick-up area. She weaves her way over, pulling up a hotel booking site on her phone at the same time. On the budget end, there's a Days Inn, an Econo Lodge and a Best Western – any of those would do. She thinks briefly about her bank balance, as she taps in her booking parameters, praying that the room prices aren't surging because of the situation and that her iDentity salary has actually been deposited into her account this afternoon as promised.

Fuchsia had made such a big deal about the staff – exclusively struggling twenty-somethings with crippling student loan debt and no savings – getting paid early 'for the holidays', as though it was a massive favour. She sees no irony in the fact that iDentity's relationship to regular paydays is commitment-phobic at best. No one ever has any idea when their wages will show up in their account and thanks to the haphazard system, Thea is perennially in her overdraft anyway, meaning the wages barely register when they do eventually turn up.

She hits enter.

Your search has returned no results.

'Shit!' she says, refreshing the page. The same thing happens. Thea's stomach lurches as though she's just missed a step going down the stairs. She sees a woman hunched over her phone next to her, who says, 'There are no vacancies,' to the guy she's standing with.

'Try another,' the man replies.

Thea unticks all the price options to widen the search. There's a Marriott at four hundred dollars a night. Does she have that much of her overdraft left? She checks her balance, and no, no she does not.

Nan's credit card.

The thought floats up and she agonises over it for a second. Meanwhile, the page times out and she has to re-enter the search. The Marriott is gone. As is the Hilton, the Hyatt and the Ramada. There's only one search result in the airport left, the five-star Opulent, a place that bills itself more as 'an experience' than a hotel. The room is a thousand dollars. 'Only one room left for this date', the listing trills. The combination of time-pressure and price makes Thea think she might be sick.

'You cannot wait in this area.' An announcement comes over the Tannoy. 'Passengers with cancelled flights should find accommodation for the night or take refuge in their cars in the indoor parking lot.'

Thea stops ruminating and pulls out her emergency credit card, the one in Nan's name that she gave her before she came to America, along with the warning not to use it unless strictly necessary. For that reason, and knowing how Nan has scrimped her whole life, Thea has never taken its fifteen-hundred-pound credit limit less than seriously. She's never even removed the sticker and checked it works. Now, she works fast, scanning the card in, knowing this is going to pretty much max it out in one transaction.

Your reservation number is PTLD274558.

Thea gasps out a breath, putting her phone away with shaking hands, and picking her bag back up. The only time she's ever dropped that much money in one go, it involved first and last month's rent, not just *one night* of accommodation. Her stomach is still roiling. She sees that the shuttles for The Opulent don't depart from the same zone as the budget hotels. She has to go back through the airport and past the corridor that leads to the First and Business Lounges, where there are separate entrances and exits for people with enough money not to have to mingle with the masses. On the way, she's stopped twice by airport officials asking to see her documents, before her reservation number unlocks the route. The airport is quieter, sleeker here, and there's a special seating area that she's led to by an airport representative, so she doesn't have to stand and wait for the shuttle. The driver will come in and fetch her, she's told, and would she like water, coffee, wine while she waits?

'No, thank you,' Thea replies, feeling more self-conscious by the second. She's the only person here, surrounded by attentive staff. She sinks into a seat, listening to the weather raging outside, and the clatter of what sounds like metal on concrete above the howling gale. She's relieved when a middle-aged man wearing an Opulent badge and uniform arrives, saying, 'Ms Bridges?' The shuttle driver, she presumes.

They tussle briefly and awkwardly over who will pick up her battered bag, and after he wins, he leads her outside where the strength of the wind slaps into her and almost knocks her over. Rain plasters her hair to her head. The driver grabs hold of her arm to steady her and shouts above the roar, 'Let me get the car door for you. I'll hold it so it doesn't blow shut.' Thea is so busy fighting the gusts that it's not until she's on the back seat that she notices that the hotel shuttle isn't a bus at all.

It's a limo.

And there's an incredibly hot man already sitting inside it.

Chapter Two

Thea drags her wind-tangled hair from across her face to smooth it into something less matted, but her hand gets stuck as she uses her fingers as a makeshift comb. She gives up, leaving a knotty snarl halfway down her long brown bob that she knows will be painful to brush out later. She smiles at the stranger sitting on the opposite seat – riding backwards as the limo pulls away from the terminal building – and pulls her puffer coat around her. He nods in greeting and twists his mouth – a very cute, full-lipped mouth, she notices – into something that's not quite a smile, but friendly all the same.

If she'd known she was going to be staying at a five-star hotel she'd have worn something other than her long-haul travelling clothes – an oversized grey hoodie and matching jogging bottoms that might have passed muster as 'loungewear' when she bought them five years ago, but don't now that they've bobbled and stretched and picked up an oily takeaway stain that only ingrains more deeply with every wash. It's all topped off with a slightly-too-big North Face puffer jacket that she inherited from her brother Kit, who constantly upgrades his coats and trainers, preferring them to be box-fresh in a way that everyone else in the family considers a total waste of money. Her look – or lack thereof – makes her only more aware of the good-looking man sitting opposite her. She scrutinises him as he peers out the limo window at the storm, where rain is lashing against the glass and the wind is going berserk, making her feel anxious for the long length of the limo.

In a bulky charcoal-coloured woollen coat and a black beanie hat that hides his hair, he looks like someone who knows how to 'dress for the weather'. His eyes are behind thick-framed glasses that are part hipster, part tech nerd – so far, so Portland – and the requisite dark brown bushy beard covering the bottom half of his face tops off the look. He's dressed simply with no visible labels but that doesn't mean his clothes aren't expensive. And if he's staying at The Opulent he must be rich. NFTs she decides, or crypto. Something she doesn't really understand and allows you to dress like a humble lumberjack while coining it in. He's probably *really* into coffee, Thea thinks idly, as though six months in Portland haven't inducted her into the ways of caffeine snobbery that she used to snigger at back in the UK. For reasons she can't put her finger on, she's trying to come up with ways to do him down. Maybe because she's feeling self-conscious, in both appearance and social class, that she needs to dismiss him before he can do the same to her. Nan would have a field day with the psychology of that one.

Nan.

God, she hopes she makes it onto tomorrow's flight. 'Christmas is a season, not a day,' Nan told her before she left, when she'd looked into return flights and realised it was double the price to fly pre-Christmas than leaving the USA on Boxing Day. 'Save your money and we'll see you when we see you.' As though Thea was doing her a favour by trying to get back earlier when really, Nan is her anchor. To England. To home. To herself. Nan might not mind if she's late for Christmas, but Thea wouldn't be able to stand it if she didn't see her.

Guilt twangs. She'll have to warn Nan about that credit card payment before she checks her balance and reassure her that she'll be paying it off. Likely in interest-inflated instalments for the rest of her life, but still, she will.

'Oh my God!' Hot Limo Guy's deep, American-accented voice pierces the thought. He sits up a little straighter in the seat and peers out of the window, his eyes wide. They're dark blue, almost navy, she notices now. She feels a fizz, as though someone has lobbed a bath bomb into her stomach.

'Look,' he says urgently, pointing to a runway in the distance. A jumbo jet is wonkily coming into land, its wings tipping madly one way and then the other as it's buffeted by the wind. It gets closer and Thea leans forward to track its progress. 'The pilot is probably loving it,' she says. 'I bet these sorts of conditions count as fun for them – all their training kicks in.'

'Not so fun for the passengers,' he replies, as the plane tips again. They both keep their eyes on the plane, which is getting closer to the runway but no steadier. Metres from the ground, it abruptly ascends again, its lights rising and then disappearing back into the dark sky. 'What was that?' Thea yelps.

'It's making a go-around,' the driver chips in. 'It couldn't level off so will come back for another try. They're still trying to land all the planes due at the airport but it's taking a while because of the weather.'

Thea's gaze instinctually seeks out Limo Guy and their eyes lock. They grimace at each other, mirror images of the gritted teeth emoji face and then burst out laughing.

'I was desperate to get my flight out tonight, but I think I've accepted that I'm better off down here for now,' Thea says.

'Ditto,' Limo Guy replies. 'Where are you headed?' She can't tell if he's just making polite conversation after their shared wobbly plane experience, but his voice is warm.

'London,' she tells him. 'Back home for Christmas with my family. How about you?'

'East Coast. Boston. And same. For Christmas. Do you live in Portland?' His voice is deep and he takes his time with what he's saying. Thea is used to the snappy rattle of voices in the iDentity office, everyone talking so fast to get their ideas out or to issue demands. She finds herself slowing her own speech down to match his.

'Yes. Well, I have done for six months now.'

'And how do you like it?'

Thea's mind flicks through every negative emotion she's felt over the past six months – loneliness, imposter syndrome, almost constant financial anxiety – before the positives bubble up behind them: the sense of potential, the joy of discovery, incrementally feeling that she's making inroads with friends and in a new city.

'I love it,' she says truthfully. 'Even when I kind of hate it.'

Limo Guy crinkles his eyes and gives her an inscrutable close-mouthed smile. 'I know what you mean,' he says. The air seems to crackle and not just because of the whipping wind outside. 'I've only been here a year myself.'

The limo door seems to explode open, and they both start. Thea hadn't realised they'd pulled up at the hotel's forecourt. The roar of the storm renders any further conversation impossible, and they climb out, Limo Guy gesturing for Thea to go first. Bellboys are standing with enormous golf umbrellas emblazoned with the hotel's logo under the entrance awning, and one rushes forward to shelter her, almost taking off when a blast of wind batters at his right-hand side. The umbrella doesn't flip inside out – no cheap umbrellas for The Opulent – but he has to fight to hold on to it.

'Head inside,' he yells, giving up on escorting her while doing battle with it. 'I'll get your bags.'

Thea rushes through two sets of sliding doors and she finds herself in the hushed sanctuary of the lobby, feeling more bedraggled than ever when confronted with its understated glamour and chic Christmas decorations. There are several six-foot-high Christmas trees dotted around, all decorated with red baubles and twinkling gold lights. Each one has a large gold bow at the top, which is repeated in decorative accents around the rest of the lobby and perfectly complements the velvet sofas and bucket chairs that are arranged around high-shine tables. Her boots bounce along the springy, carpeted floor as she seeks out the check-in desk, her nose filling with the scent of pine and cinnamon as though they're being pumped in directly from Lapland. There are so many uniform-clad people hovering around that the guest/staff ratio screams 'expensive' even if she'd somehow missed the décor. It's insane that this level of luxury exists right next to the faded ceiling panels and utilitarian seating areas of Portland International. A woman appears beside her with an iPad in her hand and a welcoming smile on her face.

'Checking in?' she asks. Thea nods, trying not to look too much like a hillbilly who's never seen the inside of a five-star hotel before, even though she's a hillbilly who's never seen the inside of a five-star hotel before. When she sits down on one of the velvet sofas, Thea realises she's been subtly led there without registering it. It's an excellent skill. Out of the corner of her eye, Limo Guy is being led to a sofa on the opposite side of the room and she sees him at full height and build. Standing up, he's around five foot ten and solid without seeming too slight or built. Average on both fronts, if she were to describe him to the police, but also anything but by the way her heartbeat drums when she looks at him. He's pulled his hat off, revealing a floppy tangle of curly hair, a shade or two lighter brown than his beard. Busy watching him walk, she's missed entirely what the elegant staff member has said to her.

'Sorry, sorry,' she garbles, turning her attention back to the check-in lady's face.

'That's OK. I was just explaining that we find a traditional check-in desk is restrictive. It creates too much of a boundary between us and the client, so we make the process more relaxed.' Her voice is soothing. Perky without being false, and undercut with a tone of reassurance that makes Thea feel as though she's being taken care of. *This*, she thinks, *this* is what people pay for.

'Firstly, can I get you a drink?'

Thea's mouth feels very dry from the anxiety of the whole situation, but what if they bring her a mineral water and she has to pay? She shakes her head and murmurs thank you. She'll have tap water when she gets to her room.

'OK, then. Could I have your name and confirmation number?'

Thea fumbles for her phone and pulls up the confirmation email before handing it over, glancing away as the front desk agent rakes her gaze over it.

'Fabulous. I just need a few extra details, and to take a copy of your passport. You'll be with us for just one night?'

'God, I hope so,' Thea says automatically. 'I mean, yes, that's correct. I'm flying back to the UK tomorrow, the second this storm lets up.'

'I know, right? It's brutal out there.' She hands the tablet to Thea. 'If you could just check the address, contact and billing details are all correct and sign at the bottom.'

Thea obliges.

'Is the card on file the one we should use for any incidentals? We place a hundred-dollar hold against any room charges, which will be released upon checkout.'

'I guess so,' Thea replies nervously. There will definitely be no incidentals. She brought her own supply of snacks for the flight to avoid having to buy anything at inflated airport prices and thank God; there's no way she can afford to start raiding the minibar in a luxury hotel.

'Would you like me to make you a reservation in the restaurant or spa?'

Thea almost laughs. 'No. No thank you.'

'In that case, you're all set.' The check-in agent stands up elegantly, pushing her knees up at an angle and ending in a finishing-school pose. 'Leon will take you to your room.' She gestures to a bank of lifts, where the bellboy – now recovered from his battle with the umbrella – is waiting with her backpack. It looks in even worse shape juxtaposed against the flawless soft furnishings and the gleaming lift doors.

'Thank you.' Thea holds her hand out for the room key, but the check-in agent just glances at her hand lightly. 'Leon's going to sort you right out with your key.' They're now beside the lifts, having moved again without Thea noticing. The check-in agent smilingly withdraws. Meanwhile, Leon calls the lift and installs them inside it in one fluid movement. As the doors ease closed Thea catches sight of Limo Guy again, still working through the check-in process with his own agent. His head is bowed slightly and he's nodding while wearing that same close-mouthed smile from the car. She wishes she'd had the nerve to at least ask his name, but really, what would be the point? It's not like she'll see him again.

The bellboy doesn't say anything as the lift ascends, leaving Thea to panic about whether to make chit-chat and, more pressingly, what to tip when they reach the room. Six months in the States have taught her that whatever she thinks is a suitable tip is usually way lower than is deemed correct, according to Teddy. And now here she is in a posh hotel where she's sure most guests press twenties into the palms of the staff as though they're single-dollar bills. Never mind twenties, does she even have any single-dollar bills in her purse? Who even carries cash any more?

Rich people. Rich people carry cash. Probably. And if they don't, they're not agonising over appearing tight in front of a bellboy.

Thea does care, but she's too broke to do anything about it. Should she warn him, she might not have any money? Give him the opportunity to slink off without wasting his impeccable customer service on her? At the ninth floor the doors glide open, and the bellboy leads the way, his jaunty walk unhindered by the uneven straps of her bag across his back. At Room 985, he demonstrates how to use the contactless key and opens the door, placing her bag on a stand next to an enormous king-sized bed. She gazes around a bedroom – a seemingly 'standard double' according to her booking. It's approximately the same size as her whole studio apartment in Portland.

'How's the air?' says Leon, the first words he's spoken throughout their journey.

'Fine I guess,' Thea replies, realising that it's actually perfect. Americans are obsessed with air-con, but as a Brit, her relationship to temperature has always been more of the 'put a jumper on, or take one off' side of things.

He strides to a panel on the wall. 'You can adjust it here, or using the handset next to the bed. Speaking of—'

He gestures to the king-size bed, topped with layers of pillows of varying sizes and textures, and a duvet that Thea can't wait to sink into. 'If you download the app you can heat-control the bed and set it to your preferred temperature. It works with your circadian rhythm, optimises sleep and helps to prevent jet lag.' He pulls out his own phone to demonstrate, chattering about connecting to the machine via Bluetooth and then shows her where to find the app on her own phone.

Thea makes all the right noises knowing that perfect temperature or not, there's no way she'll sleep well tonight. Nerves about missing the next flight home almost guarantee she wakes up every twenty minutes in a panic that she's overslept, and she'll end up shattered and jittery when she checks out. However . . .

She eyes the freestanding bath that stands proudly next to the floor-to-ceiling window. It's like every fancy hotel shot she's ever liked on Instagram. A big, pointless bath *in* the bedroom. No worrying about wet floors or privacy when you can afford a giant room to yourself, and there are staff to clear up any sloshes. She will definitely make the most of it and use every single one of the luxury, eco-friendly toiletries that she clocks are lined up along its wooden bath shelf. The window, which she assumes is one-way glass, has a view of the runway a few hundred metres beyond. If it wasn't for the dark and lashing sleet she'd have a prime view of the planes coming and going. Of course, if it wasn't for the weather, she wouldn't be here at all.

She realises Leon has finished talking about the magic bed. 'Is that everything?' he says expectantly, and Thea fumbles for her purse, praying there's something in there.

Her eye snags on a crumpled bill. A five. Is that too much or not enough? She doesn't have time to debate, and besides, it's all she has. 'Here you go.' She thrusts it at him clumsily, and he pockets it, smiling and nodding in a way that in no way answers her question.

The second Leon leaves the room, Thea turns the bath taps on to full blast, tipping into it a generous helping of some rose-scented bath oil from a luxury 'scent apothecary' downtown that she's always been too intimidated to go into. It smells divine. She runs to get one of the dressing gowns – robes, she's sure they'd be referred to here – from the bathroom, and strips off her clothes before hugging the ultra-soft material around her body. Is this moment worth a thousand dollars? Maybe. Or it will be, once the bill is paid off and it's a funny story to tell Teddy at work or Nicole back home.

She remembers Nicole's questioning message sitting guiltily in her inbox.

I'll see you on Boxing Day, right?

She hasn't replied yet, knowing that as much as she wants to see Nicole at their uni group's biennial Boxing Day drinks, she wants to see Christian less. The only upside to potentially missing Christmas in London is that it'll take the decision about going to the drinks out of her hands. She'll let Nicole know what she's decided once she's blissed out from the bath and she can separate what's stress from losing her flight home and what's perfectly rational stress at not wanting to face her ex.

She lets it fill as much as she dares before turning the taps off. The temperature is perfect: hot enough to sit here for a good hour, her skin pruning. She undoes the belt of her robe.

Just then, the bedroom door opens and another bellhop enters. She catches the phrase 'temperature controlling app' before he realises the room is occupied and trills, 'Oops, apologies.' He stops abruptly, causing the guest behind to crash into the back of him.

'*Shit*,' says Limo Guy, tripping over what must be his suitcases. He looks straight at where Thea is about to disrobe as he falls on the floor.

'Shit!' Thea shouts in response, pulling the robe belt so tight around her to avoid flashing them that she almost folds herself in two. 'Are you all right?'

'I am *so* sorry,' says Limo Guy's bellboy, trying to back away but getting himself caught on Limo Guy's luggage and Limo Guy's legs, as well as the self-closing door. 'This room isn't supposed to be occupied.' He shoots a look at the door number. 'Room nine eight five, right?' he says. Limo Guy has his eyes trained on the floor, which isn't helping either him or the bellboy untangle themselves from the person/luggage pile.

Thea takes a couple of deep breaths, ensures the dressing gown is secured around her person, and tries to muster up some dignity.

'Yes, that's right. I was just about to . . .' she gestures at the bath, and the bellboy nods, mortified. He extricates himself from the suitcases, which are those sturdy, ridged aluminium-coloured ones that look like they're for camera equipment. It's all matching. Expensive, Thea notes.

The bellboy's eyes narrow nervously. He taps at the tablet in his hand. 'I'm going to step out and get this cleared right up. He holds a hand out to help Limo Guy up, who then grabs at his suitcases, trying to manoeuvre them out of the room. They get caught again on the closing door before it shuts in his face. In his haste to leave, the bellboy hasn't held it open for him, and Limo Guy becomes increasingly flustered. Every time he pulls the door open, a wheel gets stuck. Every time he pulls it free, the door starts to shut again.

'It's OK!' Thea calls, rushing towards him to help. She kicks the comfy bra she's just taken off under the bed, and adjusts the robe, so there's no chance of it adding to this comedy of errors by falling open when she gets to him. She grabs one of the cases and yanks it firmly back into the room. Very heavy, she notices, wondering what's inside. 'He'll only be a second, so you can wait here. It's all right.'

'Are you sure?' Limo Guy looks to her for reassurance, and when she nods, he takes a tentative step back into the vestibule area, letting the door click softly shut. Thea parks the case to one side and returns to where she was, near the bath, leaving him where he is.

She and Limo Guy exchange edgy smiles across the expanse of the bed. The room, which moments ago seemed enormous with perfectly temperate air, is now a little too warm, and a little too small. Or is it just that the king-size bed is *right there*, simmering between them?

Thea perches on one corner of it. What's the etiquette in this situation? 'Would you like to sit down while we wait?' she says. She guesses that technically it's her room and her offer to make, but her words are infused with awkwardness.

Limo Guy comes a little further into the room and lowers himself onto the opposite corner – he's still in his thick winter coat, which she suspects must be boiling – before sliding a hand through his curls. 'Thanks. I'm probably next door or something. Sorry about all this.'

Thea nods. Silence descends and her stomach flutters. First the cancelled flight, then the expense of booking the hotel and now this. He seems all right, but then, don't most people until you know otherwise? He could be a murderer. Just because he's rich doesn't mean he's a good guy. Probably the opposite in fact. That's usually how it works. And what's in his incredibly heavy suitcases? Weapons? Body parts? It could be anything. She fiddles with her phone for something to do but her fumbling only serves to knock the temperature app. She hears a low hum come from the bedside machine and the bed starts to heat up under her bum. She jumps up.

'Tea?' she asks, heading towards an alcove that seems to have been built for the express purpose of laying out the minibar contents in an appealing shop-front style. Tubes of artisan crisps – or chips here, she guesses – nuzzle up to small-batch brand chocolate and locally-distilled gin. Tea and coffee must be free, right? She grazes an eye across the price list. A half-bottle of red wine starts at forty dollars, but she can't see a cost per teabag, which she takes as a good sign. 'I'm having one. If I can find some teabags,' she mutters. She can't stop fiddling with the robe. How can something so thick and fluffy somehow at this moment feel so revealing?

Limo Guy gives her a slow crinkly smile. 'That's the Brit way, right? Tea for every occasion.'

She breathes out a nervous laugh. 'What can I say, I'm a cliché.'

She spots the fancy coffee machine immediately, with a shiny hardwood box of varying strength grinds next to it, but there's no sign of a bog-standard electric kettle. She's found this in peoples' homes too. Americans favour a stovetop kettle, which though aesthetically pleasing, is a total pain when all you want is to flick a switch without faffing with the hob or being whistled at when the water boils.

And there's no stove here. Maybe there are no teabags *or* kettle. She rifles through the items in front of her. Pringles, M&Ms, pretzels, a velvet pouch she discovers contains a 'sensuality kit' before blushing and throwing it back down. Finally, at the back, there's a collection of teabags – mostly herbal, but there are a couple of black teas in there too, even if they are Lipton, AKA the most pointless tea in existence.

'Do you think I can boil water in this?' she asks, gesturing at the shiny De'Longhi coffee machine.

'It probably won't go all the way to a hundred, but should get warm enough. Let's see.' Limo guy joins her at the alcove and starts pressing buttons. The machine lights up. He pulls out a few drawers and levers. 'It's sparkling clean so there's no old coffee residue.' He holds out a clear plastic container that he's pulled away from the side and frowns at it. 'I bet if we fill this with water and don't put any coffee in, we can heat it up. What do you think?'

The way he says 'we' – twice – makes Thea glow. She takes the container off him and busies herself filling it up in the bathroom, while also taking the opportunity to slip on some leggings from her bag underneath the robe. Now she's fifty per cent less likely to have a wardrobe malfunction, she feels better. She runs the tap and gives herself a moment's pause, admiring the walk-in rainforest shower and flattering light in the mirrors above the sinks, if not her slightly spotty, make-up-free face, before she returns.

Limo Guy has found two crackle-glazed kiln-fired mugs. More local craftsmanship with an extortionate price tag, she assumes. He drops a teabag into each.

'I went for a camomile,' he tells her a little sheepishly, clicking the holder back into place and pressing a button. 'I don't get the milky dishwater you Brits call tea.'

'More of an artisan coffee guy?' Thea can't help saying. Coffee snob, she knew it.

'I live in Portland,' he replies with the ghost of a smile, before pulling a 'what can I say?' face. He looks goofy. And cute. His toothy smile is at odds with his dark beard. 'You know where the best coffee in the city is?'

Thea suppresses a groan. She has this conversation almost weekly with people in her work's co-working space, all of whom claim to know the best 'spot' for beans or brew. Fuchsia is evangelical about it. Not that she ever buys her own, but she always wants it from a place that charges about seven dollars a cup. To Thea, they all taste like variations on . . . coffee. She arches an eyebrow. 'Let me guess. Bean and Gone? No? How about Roasters Paradise? Or Brew-ha-ha.' The machine clicks off and Limo Guy pours steaming water into each of their cups.

'Is the last one even real?' he says, throwing a dubious look. He opens the fridge beneath the machine and pulls out a tiny, perfect reproduction of an old-fashioned milk bottle, holding it up to offer it to her. Thea skims the menu again to see if milk is on there with a price next to it. She'll have her tea black if she has to pay. Listed alphabetically, the menu goes from malt whiskey to Milk Duds with nothing in between. Thea nods and he pours milk into her cup. She watches him, wincing. He hasn't taken the bag out yet or even let it brew properly. If this is how he makes tea, then no wonder he thinks he doesn't like it.

'Thank you.' She accepts the mug when he offers it, and discreetly takes over, squeezing the bag as hard as possible with a spoon until it goes from anaemic to the correct deep mahogany colour. Only then does she fish out the bag.

'Brew-ha-ha totally exists,' she continues. 'It just opened near Hawthorne.'

Limo Guy nods, as though another coffee house in that area is no surprise. 'I wasn't actually going to say any of them though.'

'Go on,' Thea says in encouragement, before taking a sip of her tea. It's the perfect temperature and strength. She does make an excellent cup of tea.

'Are you ready?' he says.

She rolls her eyes slightly at him and nods, before taking another sip of tea.

'It's Dunkin' Donuts.'

Thea barks out a laugh, spitting tea back into the cup.

'I'm not kidding!' Limo Guy says. There's a cheeky look on his face. 'I've done extensive research into all of these so-called best spots, and concluded that good old DD is as good as any.'

Thea's still smiling, her hand covering her mouth where she can't believe she just spat her drink out in front of him. 'I'm surprised you've lasted a year here with fighting talk like that,' she says. 'You must have very few Portlandian friends. Even *I* have chosen a coffee house allegiance and I drink tea most of the time.'

They grin at each other as a soft knock at the door interrupts them. The elegant front desk lady, trailed by the bellboy, enters the room.

'Hi,' they both chorus at her. At seeing that the bellboy has returned with backup, Thea feels a prickle of uncertainty.

'I'm so very sorry about this situation and the inconvenience,' she begins.

Not good.

'So, I have a reservation for this room under Theodora Bridges,' she continues.

Thea nods.

Elegant front desk lady turns her attention to Limo Guy. 'But I also have a reservation for this room under Logan Beechwood. A glitch in the system meant that when bookings surged due to the storm, it got double-booked.'

'That's OK,' says Limo Guy – Logan – cheerfully. 'I'm happy to move.' He puts down his mug and makes to leave.

'That's just it.' Front desk lady's professional mask slips for the first time, revealing an anxious look beneath. 'There are no free rooms to move you to. The entire hotel is fully booked.'

Logan's face is now far less cheerful; his dark brows furrowing together. 'So, what are you saying?'

'There's room at our sister hotel in downtown Portland, so we could move you there – with a significant upgrade of course. Although we'll have to wait for the shelter-in-place order to lift before we can shuttle you over, which is likely to be in the early hours of the morning.'

Limo Guy's face crumples in comprehension. 'But that's no good to me. I need to be back in the airport as soon as flights start taking off. And what am I supposed to do until then?' He looks at Thea pleadingly. 'Maybe you could take it instead?'

She shakes her head, even as she wonders what a 'significant upgrade' on a room that's already the best room she's been in in her life would be. 'I'm in the same situation. There are only two flights a day to London and with the flight time and then the time difference, tomorrow is my only shot at getting home for Christmas Day. Sorry,' she adds, although she's not really sorry. The front desk lady said it was her room first, so it's her room. Now is not the time to concede out of a misplaced sense of politeness. She hopes he's not the type of guy to kick off when he doesn't get his way. After all, what does she really know about him?

'So, what should I do?' is all Limo Guy asks instead. 'Am I allowed to spend the night in the terminal?' The hotel staff look at him slightly blankly.

'We will of course look into that for you,' says front desk lady.

'They seemed to be sending people away from the airport buildings when I left,' Thea says slowly. 'They were directing them to their cars in the indoor car park.'

Logan nods slowly in resignation. 'I guess that's where I'll be, then.' He takes a wistful look around the room. Front desk lady turns to lead the way out, mentioning the possibility of a food and beverage voucher for the inconvenience, as well as a discount on a future stay. 'Not to mention a full refund for tonight, right?' Logan asks as he starts to follow her.

At that moment there's an almighty crash as something thuds into the floor-to-ceiling window and bounces off. All four people in the room rush over and peer out into the gloom, seeing an object – perhaps a food tray from an aeroplane, but it's too dark and chaotic to tell – drop nine floors to the ground, before it's whisked up again by the wind and dances off.

'Reinforced glass,' says the bellhop uneasily. 'And pretty well soundproofed. To block out the noise of the planes. When there are planes . . .' he trails off.

'You can't go back out in that,' Thea blurts. 'Even just back to the terminal building. What if you get hit on the head by, I don't know, a piece of propeller or something?'

Limo Guy flashes that twitchy smile again. He's standing right next to her and it makes Thea want to give him a flirtatious nudge of the hip.

'A piece of propeller?' he says in an amused voice. 'I didn't realise we were going to be flying out in the 1940s.'

'OK, maybe not a propeller, then,' Thea says with a laugh. 'But debris. Suitcases, branches—' she throws up her hands – 'I don't know, storm stuff.'

He nods as though absorbing what she's said. 'Maybe I can hang out in the lobby for a while.' He shoots a look at the front desk lady whose expression has returned to its elegant impenetrable mask. Technically he is still a paying customer, but Thea suspects this is an unprecedented situation and front desk lady doesn't have the authority to make that call. They can't boot him out into a potentially deadly storm, can they?

'Unless it's not the sort of place you'll let me sit all night,' Logan continues lightheartedly when he gets no immediate response. 'Not least because I might get mistaken for an escort. High class, of course.' He smiles again, and takes his glasses off as he thinks. His eyebrows unknit and she gets a face-on look at those dark blue eyes. Kate Middleton's sapphire engagement ring pops into her head. They're the same colour.

'We could share,' she blurts without thinking. 'The room. And split the cost. To be honest, I can't actually afford to stay here anyway.' She turns quickly to the front desk lady, who is silently watching the exchange. 'To be clear, I *have* afforded to stay here, but only by maxing out my credit card and I already feel sick about the bill. If we split the cost, it would really help, and it's not like I'm expecting to get much sleep anyway.' Her eyes wander to the bed.

In this room with Limo Guy – Logan – all night. Getting no sleep.

'Because I'm too wound up about catching my flight home, that is, not for any other reason. I see this more as a waiting room really.' She looks at the hand-painted, gilt-leaf wallpaper. 'A very fancy waiting room. So you could stay. I don't mean *stay*, I mean wait here as well. If it's not too weird. Although it *is* weird, but the whole thing is weird if you really think about it.'

Thea, the bellhops and the front desk lady all look at Logan. His forehead wrinkles again as he absorbs her offer.

'Let's do it,' he says slowly, nodding. 'There's plenty of room and I'm happy to split the cost if you need to.'

The way he says 'if you need to' is mild and he likely doesn't mean anything by it, but Thea notices. The subtext is that he hasn't pushed himself past his financial limit to spend the night in this hotel the way she has. But even if she were rich, she wouldn't want to pay full price for a room that she's now sharing with a stranger. And she's not rich. So a five-hundred-dollar refund is five hundred dollars she's just clawed back from her future sporadic pay cheques.

She doesn't say any of this. 'Great!' she says instead.

Logan clears his throat and addresses front desk lady. 'We're going to split the room, so just to confirm we'll both get a fifty per cent refund on the rate we paid?'

She agrees, looking beyond relieved that the situation has been settled despite its unconventional resolution. 'I'm so sorry for the inconvenience,' she keeps saying.

The cheeky look returns to Logan's face, as though something has just occurred to him. 'It really has been an inconvenience,' he says in a very reasonable but also a very confident voice. He definitely has money. You can just tell. He sweeps another hand in Thea's direction. 'For both of us.' He flashes a wide, charming grin. 'And you did mention food and beverage vouchers. To make up for it, how about you throw in dinner for us in the restaurant downstairs?'

Chapter Three

Like everything at The Opulent, the restaurant is supremely tasteful and as Thea walks in, she's absorbed into a room that has got the understated-but-expensive festive memo. On the way to her table, she passes a hard-lined architectural tree covered in enormous, oversized baubles that the maître d' informs her has been designed by a renowned artist, and there are strings of white lights and deep green garlands strung from the ceiling and along the mantelpiece of a fireplace that stands at one end of the room. There's even a real fire blazing away in it. Thea marvels at it all as she sinks into the embroidered cushion of her dining chair. In whose universe is having a Michelin-starred restaurant the dealbreaker when choosing an airport hotel, she wonders, a place that you only pass through while en route to somewhere else? She's so far out of her comfort zone, it's apt that she's in a different continent to her hometown.

'You look nice,' Logan says as she sits down opposite where he's already seated at the table. Now out of his coat, he's wearing a dark grey, brushed-cotton shirt with black jeans. His voice is polite and his striking blue eyes are friendly.

Thea goes red at the compliment, even though she put the dress on in the hope of getting one. 'Thank you,' she says. She smooths down the front of it, a swingy-skirted, vintage, red velvet dress that she'd spotted at a Portland flea market a few months back.

After the hotel room refunds were issued and a voucher for a complimentary meal presented ('To a value of three hundred dollars,' Logan had informed her, shortly before she realised that would barely get them an appetiser and main course each at the Michelin-starred Tête-à-Tète), Thea had asked Logan if he could leave while she took a shower. She reluctantly drained the bath, acknowledging that even having booted him out, there was no way she would feel comfortable enough to enjoy it knowing he could walk back in at any moment. She needed a room with a manual lock and some space to try and expunge the horror of almost flashing him. Of course instead, she'd stood under the showerhead and relived the embarrassing moment over and over before giving up and getting out. She'd decided there was no way her long-haul sweatpants were making another cameo at this hotel, so she'd detangled her wind-battered hair, and blow-dried her long brown bob into two polished curtains. Then she'd truncated her make-up regime into ten efficient minutes and pulled on a dress that she knew made the most of her figure, skimming her boobs and hips, before settling mid-thigh. She'd added thick black tights and biker boots to make the look more nineties riot grrrl than Mrs Christmas and was pleased with the result. She'd been looking forward to wearing this outfit to the pub over the Christmas break and being able to tell people at home that the dress was something she'd 'picked up in a little second-hand place' she knew in Portland, but sitting in it here, now, with a cute guy she's just met in the back of a limo, feels even better. She allows herself to think about telling *this* story in the pub over Christmas instead, to all the old uni friends that she knows will be there – including Christian – and has to focus on the menu in front of her to stop herself getting carried away. It takes all her concentration to read the starters in the leather-bound menu, and not just because she doesn't know what half of them are.

She flicks a look around Tête-à-Tête. The restaurant's eight tables are all occupied, but they're spaced out in a way that gives the veneer of intimate seclusion. There's plenty of room for the waiting staff to stand in coordinated teams behind diners, so dishes can be placed down in gentle synchronicity. Ambient music plays in the background, neither loud enough to hinder conversation, nor quiet enough to make the place devoid of atmosphere. Again, the temperature is perfect. A lot of effort has gone into making everything seem serene.

Being rich is basically like being Baby Bear, Thea thinks. Everywhere you go, everything is just right.

'Do you know what you're having?' Logan asks, gesturing to the menu. Thea doesn't want to admit she needs to Google two thirds of the starters.

Waitstaff glide by with appetisers for their nearest neighbours and they watch the choreography.

'Ooh I'm going to have that,' says Logan, pointing to a passing plate. 'Do you think it's the scallop? It looks amazing.'

'It does,' Thea agrees, quickly looking for something she recognises. 'In that case, I'll go for the shellfish and pork fat, followed by . . .' she says, scanning the menu.

'Steak,' Logan says, just as she says it herself. They catch each other's eyes and laugh self-consciously. She glances quickly away.

'This is probably my only opportunity to see if an eighty-dollar steak is worth the price tag,' she says, before going red again. For all she knows, Logan eats eighty-dollar steak all the time.

'Good idea,' is all he says though, smiling in agreement.

His fingers, long and tanned, skim the stiff cardboard of the menu as he tots up the cost of their choices. 'By my reckoning, we'll have enough for a side to go with the steak and a drink, as long as we don't get carried away. What the hell, I'll throw in twenty dollars of my own if you want fine beans *and* dauphinoise potatoes.'

Thea laughs. This is starting to feel very much like a date. But not like a real-life date, where you 'grab a drink' as a prelude for deciding whether or not the person is worth the time or financial investment of dinner, but like a date in a film, where people skip straight to a formal sit-down meal without any back and forth of deciding which neighbourhood is convenient for both parties or which venue best reflects your personality, without being *too* exposing – because no one wants their favourite restaurant to become the new favourite hangout of someone awful you went on a date with once.

'Are you ready to order?' Another groomed Opulent staff member appears beside them. Thea and Logan repeat their choices, just as a sommelier materialises. He's young, but formal, with the confident air of someone who knows what he's talking about.

'Let me talk you through the wine journeys we have on offer this evening,' he says smoothly.

Thea's eyes widen. 'I think we're just going to have a glass of something each. If that's OK?'

The sommelier nods while closing his eyes as though she's just made an excellent decision. 'Of course. I'd be happy to suggest what pairs best with your meal choices.'

Thea looks at Logan for backup. She has no doubt that the sommelier's choices would be perfect with steak, but she doubts he will also tell them the price up front and she's far too self-conscious to form the sentence, 'It needs to cost less than the remaining forty dollars we have on our voucher.'

'What can you suggest for two strangers who've been doubled-booked into the same room?' Logan says with a twinkle in his eye.

His joke unlocks something in the stiff sommelier. 'Are you those guys?' he says with a grin. Word has clearly spread among the staff. 'In that case I propose a glass of Champagne. On the house, of course.'

Thea feels a burst of in-it-togetherness, as she and Logan exchange a conspiratorial look. Another small piece of us-ness that this surreal situation has facilitated. Her heartbeat drums.

The sommelier withdraws and the waiter re-appears, complimenting them on their choices sincerely enough that Thea almost believes he wouldn't have made the same appreciative noises whatever they had chosen.

That done, Thea smiles at Logan again, but more shyly. After all the attention from the servers it feels strange to be alone again. The pre-ordering small talk came easily: it was all about what to order. With that over, sitting directly opposite each other for an entire dinner will amplify any awkward silences.

'What do you do?' Logan asks, seeming to have none of the same apprehension. All the Americans she's met are so good at talking. At work Teddy immediately latched onto her, announcing he needed a British friend to facilitate his dream of moving to West London and marrying a 'younger Hugh Grant in *Notting Hill* type'. She hadn't had the heart to tell him that where her parents lived in the East End was very different to the pastel-housed streets he was thinking of. And now Logan is confidently overcoming the weird situation to make conversation, and with jokes, she thinks, as he adds, 'Unless the very British activity of making tea in an emergency *is* your job?'

What *does* she do? She readies herself to wheel out the practised lines she always does when people ask about her job at a creative marketing agency and her scrappy-but-bold journey to the role. About how, having worked for four years at a London agency, nine months ago she saw a job for iDentity, and after seeing how cool and dynamic it looked on Instagram, she applied, not for one moment thinking she would get an interview ahead of what must have been dozens of other applicants. About the three interviews and demanding project, which led to the American embassy for an in-person visa application that would mean she could live in Portland for as long as she was employed by iDentity. About flying out six months ago, despite not knowing anyone in the USA, and throwing herself into the challenge of working for a company that described itself as a 'start-up with soul'. About the long hours, demanding clients, but rewarding work.

But something about Logan's curious expression and steady gaze makes her veer off message. Maybe it's because he's a stranger, or maybe it's because he seems so open, but keeping up the façade doesn't seem to be an option. The truth starts to pour out.

'I work at a creative marketing agency for a woman who describes herself as an "industry disruptor" but is incapable of updating her own laptop login password without a tantrum,' she says. 'Lots of badly paid, increasingly cynical twenty-somethings walk around saying things like "sonic social" and "architecting a brand identity" with zero sense of irony, managed by a woman with no charm and not enough business nous to get away with her lack of social skills being seen as a Mark Zuckerberg-type quirk.'

Thea sighs, on a roll now. 'I'm learning a lot,' she goes on, and then frowns. 'But not all of it is positive, especially when it comes to my boss.' It all comes tumbling out. How she loves words and telling stories and making them connect with an audience, but her role seems primarily to being Fuchsia's lackey. How despite her title of Account Executive, under which she worked with clients all the time back in London, all she seems to do here is email ideas to Fuchsia for meetings she's rarely allowed to attend. That she knows from the others that Fuchsia harvests her best ideas and passes them off as her own, while dismissing everything else. At some point during Thea's tirade, Champagne has appeared on the table in two delicate flutes. She picks one up and takes a sip. The bubbles fizz in her mouth. It takes all her willpower not to neck it in one go.

'The only feedback I ever get is that my ideas are schmaltzy and uncool,' she says with a sigh, putting the glass back down. That particular criticism will never not hit harder than it should. It's too interwoven with her history – and her break-up – with Christian. He was always telling her how naff her ideas were, even as he used her work to get ahead. 'I never get to work on the pitches we win doing the creative work. If I'm honest, I don't always think she comes up with the best ideas, which is a new feeling for me. In my last job, I always respected my boss's decisions, even when her take was completely different to mine, and even when it meant I had to redo something I'd spent ages on. It would be something clever that I hadn't thought of, and I could see the end result was going to be worth it. I always felt as though I was learning. At iDentity—'

She stops, feeling she's said too much. She lowers her gaze, fiddling with the weighty silverware so she doesn't have to absorb the look of boredom that she's sure will be on Logan's face. He signed up for a free dinner with polite chit-chat, not a blow-by-blow of a stranger's dream job that has failed to deliver. But when she glances up at him from under her eyelashes, he doesn't look bored. His expression is attentive and thoughtful.

'Schmaltz is my bread and butter so that's not a criticism in my book,' he says with a sip of his own Champagne. 'But your boss sounds hideous.'

Thea sees a waitress silently file behind Logan, holding his starter. Then she senses a presence looming at her own back, confirmed by Logan stifling an awkward smile. Yet another member of staff then appears, this time where they can both see him. He gives a brief overview of their dishes' voyages from farm to fork before they're set down simultaneously in front of them. After a flurry of smiles, nods and admiration, everyone leaves.

Logan's plate contains one large, lone, scallop, topped with gold leaf. He slices through it with the side of his fork and takes a bite.

'That is *good*,' he says with a contented sigh.

Thea eyes her langoustine, realising that in terms of table manners, she may have made a mistake. De-shelling it is going to be a complicated job. She tries to do it with her cutlery, succeeding only at spurting oily liquid across the tablecloth as she removes its head. Logan either doesn't notice or doesn't care, as he's too busy demolishing the rest of his scallop.

To hell with it, she ditches her knife and fork and pulls off the shell with her hands. With the oily sauce still running down them, she tries it. The taste explodes in her mouth. In two bites, it's gone.

'That is one of the best things I've eaten in my life,' she says with a happy moan. 'I can't believe it's over.'

'The more expensive the food, the less there is of it,' Logan agrees, tipping his plate up to scoop up his remaining sauce with a spoon.

'What did you mean about your bread and butter being schmaltz?' Thea asks, mopping her hands with a napkin. He doesn't seem half as sensitive about it being levelled at him as she is. A small bowl of warm, lemon-scented water appears at her elbow and she dips in her fingers.

Logan pauses, the spoon in his mouth. 'The reason I moved to Portland was to grow the business I started with my college buddy Felix. I think your boss would definitely think it was cheesy.'

'What's the business?'

Logan's nose scrunches up slightly, less in embarrassment and more as though he feels exposed. 'It's a memory-preservation video company. We make bespoke films, usually for families who want to make sure elderly family members' memories are recorded before they pass on.' His face opens up again. 'Not very cool. But I love it.'

'That sounds lovely!' Thea says with feeling. She thinks of Nan. She wishes she could store her memories, from her life in the sixties ('Mick Jagger asked me for a light,' Nan once told her. 'What happened then?' Thea had asked eagerly. 'I told him I didn't smoke and he moved on to the next person') to the voice notes they leave each other several times a week. 'How did you get into that?'

'The usual,' he says. 'Studied film at college, went through a black polo-neck phase of thinking I was going to be the next Martin Scorsese or Christopher Nolan but then realised that if I wasn't prepared to intern for the next decade, I probably wasn't going to make it as an auteur director.' His face clouds over with sadness. 'At college, Felix and I put together a film about my grandfather after he was diagnosed with Alzheimer's. He wanted a way to record his memories and pass them on to my mom, and he'd always been so supportive of my wanting to make movies.'

'That's such a wonderful idea,' Thea says, her own eyes pricking with tears as she sees Logan's fill up.

'My grandpa passed away just before I graduated, which made me even more grateful that he'd given me the idea.' He clears his throat, looking away for a moment while he collects himself. 'And after that, my mom's friends started asking if we could do films about their family members. We made some more, while working other jobs, and it sort of went from there.'

'I'm sorry about your grandpa,' Thea says. 'It must have been so hard.' Her throat gets tight and her foot instinctively knocks the wooden leg of the sturdy table just thinking about Nan being diagnosed with such a cruel disease.

'It was,' Logan nods. 'I still really miss him.' He takes two quick sips of his drink in succession. Thea can tell he's feeling uncomfortable. 'But I owe my whole business to him, and I think about him every day because of that. I like that my job helps other people hold on to their memories.'

Thea smiles. 'You sound like you love it.'

'I do.'

'And your parents must love that your grandpa inspired your career.' And it must be doing pretty well, if you can afford to stay here without blinking at the cost, she adds in her head.

An ambiguous expression crosses Logan's face for a moment, before lifting. 'Sometimes,' he says. 'They had other ideas for me, and I think they thought I'd eventually get tired of *messing about with movies*.' The emphasis and accompanying eye roll tell Thea there's a backstory there. 'It made me think maybe I would too. But I didn't, even when I had to work other jobs to support the movie company as a side hustle. Then it really started to take off about eighteen months ago.' That same unreadable look crosses his face again before it clears. 'By then I needed a change. Our clients are from all over the States so we can pick any location as a base. Felix is from here, so I decided to move over.'

'So that's me. Why did *you* choose Portland?' Logan asks as their empty plates are silently removed and their main courses replace them. There's another reverential moment as they slice into their steaks, while making exaggerated faces of delight at each other.

Thea pauses. 'I've always wanted to live in the USA,' she says carefully. It's true, she has. She always meant to apply for one of those Camp America summer jobs when she was at uni. But every year, she didn't. She hadn't wanted to spend so long so far away from Christian, even though, at that point, they weren't even together. She'd always felt that if she were out of his immediate orbit, their special connection would break. Now, the thought that a few weeks in different countries would have been what made or broke them makes her hot with embarrassment – but that's how it felt at the time. 'I didn't really have the opportunity until I got this job.' She means to leave it there, but something about Logan's open demeanour makes her unable to stop herself. 'Plus, I'd been through a rough break-up,' she admits, 'and being a ten-hour flight and an eight-hour time difference away was an appealing prospect.' They'd been broken up a year by the time Thea got the iDentity job, but in London she'd never shaken Christian's voice out of her head – usually expressing disapproval. The physical distance, and him having no idea what her day-to-day life looked like, had helped it recede. Snagging a job at a hip Portland start-up – exactly the sort of thing he'd have told her she wasn't edgy enough for, when he was working for an East London agency while she was working for a mainstream company that represented supermarket brands – also helped.

'I hear you about putting some miles between you and your past,' Logan replies. Again, her senses prick up. Is there a messy break-up in his recent history too? The possibility is enough to make her keep speaking.

'Being on a different continent at least lessens the possibility of running into someone your ex was sleeping with behind your back.' It's supposed to be a joke but the second it's out of her mouth she realises it probably sounds bitter. She has no desire to tell this near stranger about the humiliation of going to an 'account exec mingler' set up by a few of the larger London agencies and sealing an immediate friendship with a woman at the open bar – only to discover that her new BFF had slept with, and subsequently been ghosted by, her boyfriend after a similar event a few months previously. Thea had stumbled out of the conference venue and confronted Christian on the phone, but even as they were breaking up, with her telling him she'd seen the messages he'd sent before he disappeared, he claimed it had never happened and accused Thea of being paranoid 'like she always was'. That's what convinced her for certain that the other times he'd accused her of being 'suspicious', he actually had cheated on her. And there were plenty of those times. She physically shakes her head to rid herself of the memory, before realising Logan is scrutinising her.

'If London is too small for that, it's definitely time to leave,' he says, screwing up his mouth in agreement. 'Space is good,' he says. 'Space has been very good,' he repeats softly. He looks like he might continue, but at that moment red wine is brought to the table served in large, fine-glassed domes. 'Just a small taste,' the sommelier informs them with a wink, 'but you cannot eat the steak without trying it with this Cabernet – complimentary of course.' They gulp it back and the conversation moves on, flowing so perfectly it's as though it's been co-ordinated by the hotel, along with the temperature and the food. The Baby Bear of chat. Thea discovers that Logan has two brothers in Boston, one three years younger and the other over a decade, and Thea tells him that after a – mild, thankfully – stroke Nan moved from her flat into Thea's family home, so Mum and Dad can keep an eye on her, along with Kit depending on where in his home-to-flatshare boomerang cycle he's at.

By 10 p.m., Thea still hasn't uncovered Logan's flaw. Because if there's one thing Christian taught her, it's that there always is one. Usually more than one. Her few dating forays in Portland have only confirmed this hypothesis. The Flaw can be anything from outright meanness, to guys stating they're 'curious' about 'both sides' of an issue like climate change or women's rights; throwaway insults about people in the bar, or an unhealthy obsession with their ex's shortcomings.

Christian only had the one flaw. It's just that this happened to be all-encompassing egomania.

That moment doesn't happen with Logan. He says he mostly gets on with his family, without the caveat of anything creepy like 'I call my mom three times a day'; he's passionate about his job without seeming to be defined by it, and he's disarmingly open, without any sort of an agenda, during their dinner.

It's easy because it's not a date, Thea reminds herself as a tangy crumble, served inside a fondant dome shaped like an apple, is placed between them. A shared dessert – all they can afford with their voucher.

She looks at Logan, who has his spoon poised over it. His face is friendly, but there's definitely something more there. A frisson.

So why does it feel like one?

Chapter Four

Back in the room, the bed is still enormous, invitingly bed-like and *right there*. And so is a bottle of Champagne, resting in an ice bucket, along with a note from The Opulent's General Manager, who apologises once again for the horrendous mix-up and hopes they will accept it with her compliments.

'Why is it that the richer you seem to be, the more free stuff people want to give you?' Thea says, reading the note aloud.

Logan holds up the bottle and cold water drips off the bottom. 'It would be rude not to open it, right?'

The big meal and the drinks have caught up with Thea, dulling senses that are usually on high alert. She feels jittery from Logan's proximity, but it's undercut by calm, as though his very presence is reassuring. She could stay up all night talking to him. The way the evening is going maybe she will.

'Definitely,' she says. 'Besides, it's over one hundred mil, so neither of us can take it home in our hand luggage. Although Nan would love it if I walked in with a bottle of fancy Champagne.'

Nan.

Thea hasn't told her about the credit card. She's suddenly dying to fill Nan in on what's been happening.

'Excuse me a sec.' Thea heads into the bathroom and turns on the taps as she opens WhatsApp so Logan won't hear her talking. Nan has never really got to grips with texting – she finds tapping at the keyboard too fiddly – but she loves a voice note. Thea looks forward to waking up in the morning in Portland, eight hours behind the UK, and seeing Nan's name on her home screen, along with her latest instalment about what's been going on back home in East London.

'Nan,' she starts, pressing her thumb to the phone. 'The storm must have been on the news so I'm sure you've seen what's happening, but I'm stuck in Portland Airport tonight and won't be landing on Christmas Eve after all. I've got to be back at the airport first thing to try and get a flight tomorrow, well today now for you. The other thing is—' Thea stops and then blurts it all out in a rush to get it over with – 'I'm really sorry, but I couldn't leave the airport because of the weather. I had to use your credit card to book a room and the only one available was in a five-star hotel. It was a lot. *A lot.* Please don't freak out. It was an emergency. I'll pay it off, I promise.'

Thea drops her voice, feeling unable to keep the events of the evening from Nan, even for a few more hours. 'Plus, it's going to cost half as much as it originally was supposed to. Because staying in a posh hotel during a hurricane isn't the only thing I wanted to tell you about. Wait, don't panic, it's not a hurricane. It's a category three storm, which I'm told is at least two below a hurricane. Anyway, I met someone. At the hotel. *In* my room. A mix-up that feels less like a mix-up as the night goes on. I'll explain when I get home, but it feels as though we were meant to meet. Is that really naff?'

Outside, in the bedroom, she hears the pop of a cork. 'I've had some Champagne. I know! And there's more waiting for me right now so I better go. It's six a.m. where you are and I hope you're still asleep. I love you. I'll be back as soon as I can.' She watches the message wheel turning as it uploads her voice to their chat, and sees the two ticks appear. She waits for a second to see if Nan is awake, but the ticks remain grey.

She checks her reflection in the mirror and wipes a little rogue mascara from the crease of an eyelid, feeling a little nervous about where the evening might go next.

When she emerges, Logan has arranged the pillows on the bed so they can sit side by side. It makes it seem less beddy, but only marginally, so when he holds out a glass of Champagne for her, nerves compel her to sit down as far away as she can while still technically being on the bed. She absorbs herself in the light switches above her bedside table, testing out a range of lighting options from full beams to up-lighting individual areas. She settles for turning on all the lamps and sidelights, which gives the most flattering effect without looking like she's coordinating a seduction. She would like to coordinate a seduction.

'Everything OK?' Logan asks, taking a sip of his drink.

Did he hear her talking to Nan? Or just talking? What if he thought it was to herself?

'I was just leaving a message for my nan,' she says in explanation. 'It's her credit card and name this room is booked under so I needed to give her a heads-up about the charge.' She clocks his look of confusion. 'She's Theodora Bridges too. But everyone calls her Dora while I've always been Thea. Anyway, I thought I'd better explain why a massive amount of money is on there before she has a chance to see the bill, and also why I'm still in America rather than landing in London right now.'

'Are you guys close?'

'Yes,' Thea replies. 'I miss my parents and my brother, but Nan is—' she ponders it for a moment – 'she's my champion, my cheerleader and my conscience all in one. My best friend, really.' Thea feels her eyes well up a little just thinking about Nan. Her straight white bob, and the bright blouse that seemed to hang off her already bony frame the last time she'd FaceTimed. 'It probably sounds a little sad that my best friend is over seventy, doesn't it?'

'Not at all.' Logan's face, in the flattering sidelighting, looks melancholic. 'I miss my grandpa all the time. All my childhood memories are wrapped up with him. He used to take me camping and hiking, first to get me out of my parents' hair with two younger kids to look after and then it became a tradition all through middle and high school. I wish I'd had time to know him properly as an adult, but he got diagnosed in my first year of college and soon needed too much care for us to be able to carry on. Then he was gone not long after.'

'What was his name?' Thea asks.

'Henry. But everyone used to call him Hank. He was my mom's dad and lived just a few blocks away so we saw him all the time. My other grandparents died either before I was born or when I was small. I know I'm lucky to have had that relationship with a grandparent at all, but I'm sometimes envious of the families I make movies for, when there's four or sometimes even five generations involved in filming. My family is just me and my brothers and my parents now. Two generations.'

'Until one of you boys makes them the grandparents anyway,' Thea says to lighten the mood, realising as she says it that it might be interpreted as digging. Weighted. It's the kind of comment Christian would have absorbed and then twisted back on her as 'pressure'. He hadn't always been like that, but by the end of their relationship, she'd interrogated every thought she had before she said it out loud, checking it for anything that could annoy him. It hadn't worked. There was no predicting what that might be.

She can't think about Christian now. So far, aside from the incoming, quease-inducing credit card statement, the whole night has been a dream sequence. She refuses to let memories of her ex-boyfriend hijack it.

'Hopefully it'll be either me or Jackson first,' Logan replies lightly, taking it for the surface comment it is. Thea breathes out, not realising until then that she was holding her breath for his reaction. 'Not sure Mom and Dad will be thrilled if seventeen-year-old Keaton makes a pregnancy announcement any time soon. Anyway, cheers to a great evening.'

He holds out his glass to clink with hers and Thea finds herself inching closer to him on the bed so she can do it without stretching her arm to its maximum length.

'Cheers,' she says, holding his eye contact. It feels loaded, but she's too buzzy from Champagne and butterflies to know if it runs both ways. Misinterpreting the moment will make the next six hours too awkward to stay in the same room. She breaks the contact before he can.

'Tell me more about your nan,' Logan says, filling the silence. 'Is she like a grandmother in a British film? Swearing in a Cockney accent and delivering no-nonsense advice while smoking cigarettes?'

Thea bursts out laughing. 'You're not actually far off. Aside from the cigs. If she had smoked, my grandad might have been a Rolling Stone rather than a pub landlord.' She thinks for a second. 'Where to start with Nan?'

'Your grandad was the landlord of a London pub?' Logan interrupts. 'I'd definitely start there. That's a pivotal role in any British film.'

Thea laughs. Maybe it's his experience in family film-making, or the fact that she knows about his own beloved grandpa, but he's just so easy to talk to, and so enthusiastic. Before she knows it, she's telling Logan Nan's potted history and he's chipping in with stories about his and Hank's hiking expeditions, which all seem to involve a funny, minor disaster like a flooding tent or losing their supplies to raccoons. He laughs as Thea does impressions of Nan talking to her pub regulars, and keeps their glasses topped up, while asking questions. As they talk, they get closer and closer together, before they're comfortably cocooned in the middle of the bed against the nest of pillows, their sides resting lightly together. Thea's entire left-hand side buzzes with little waves of adrenaline that she's sure he must be able to feel radiating off her.

Before long, the bottle is empty, and the ice has turned to slush in the bucket. They're still talking but sleepily now. Thea yawns, which sets Logan off. The bed is so warm, and the room is so cosily lit.

Baby Bear again.

How many drinks have they had now? Four, five? Part of Thea wants to make a tea, which she knows will wake her up a bit, but she's too snug to move, with Logan's thigh pressed against hers and her head intoxicatingly close to resting on his shoulder. It feels reassuringly like the right place to be right now and she doesn't want to puncture this moment. She's not sure she's ever felt so close to someone in such a short amount of time.

More than anything, she wants to keep talking.

'What's your favourite part of making memory movies?' she asks.

She'll definitely stand up in a second, go and brush her teeth and then if, when she sits back down, he instinctively gets close to her again, she'll ask if he's feeling how she's feeling.

Logan thinks about it for a moment before answering. 'I like the ones for landmark wedding anniversaries, when I'm doing the story of someone's relationship. We like to do talking heads with each partner telling the story from their point of view – I know, it's a total lift from *When*

Harry Met Sally.' The lights cast a warm glow across his face. Thea's eyes feel heavier and heavier but her skin is tingling where their fingers are touching slightly. She wonders if he's tingling too. 'But I like hearing how they met.' The last thing Thea hears before she falls asleep is, 'Even when it's the most mundane how-we-met story in the world, there's always a story. And if you're a happy couple, it's a meet cute to you.'

Chapter Five

The muted sound of a plane taking off wakes her. Pressed against Logan like he's an island in the sea of the king-size bed, her neck is cricked at an uncomfortable angle with her chin tucked into her armpit and the side of her head resting gently against his chest. It takes her a moment to register where she is, and then she smiles to herself, enjoying the sensation of being next to him. The air is thick with booze and sleep, but as she comes round, the sound registers properly in her brain and contentment gives way to panic.

'Shit! Logan! Planes are taking off.'

She jumps up, her hair getting snagged on the buttons of his shirt. She wrenches herself free, ripping strands of her hair off in the process, and she rushes across the room to pull the curtains open. Logan joins her at the window, pulling his glasses on and raking his hands over his beard. It's still dark outside, but the taillights of a plane can be seen steadily ascending. It goes straight up, no wobbles and nothing else is disturbed in the air around. The storm is over. Planes are taking off.

'What time is it?' Logan asks.

'Six a.m. We need to get to the airport.' Thea circles the room, picking up the few things she removed from her backpack and stuffing them back inside. She runs into the bathroom, spends a millisecond contemplating the flat-haired, panda-eyed version of Thea that stares back at her from the mirror, and then splashes water on her face, pulls her hair back into a ponytail–bun hybrid and trades the slept-in red dress for her sweats. She rejects the idea of a shower, no time, but does brush her teeth, before rushing back into the room to find Logan spraying himself with deodorant, a flash of toned torso visible as he lifts his shirt to do it. He hurries into the bathroom after her, speeding back out a minute later trailing the smell of toothpaste and antiperspirant. The previous night's spell is broken as they switch to autopilot, concentrating on getting ready and out of the room as efficiently as possible. If she had time to dwell on it, she'd be crushed, but there isn't. They have to go. Thea checks her bag for her passport, unplugs Logan's phone charger from the wall and does a visual sweep of the room, her gaze landing on Logan who is zipping up his bag. She hands him his charger and their hands touch briefly, the contact high remaining when he doesn't pull away, and sparking a physical memory of how their bodies were twined together in sleep just minutes ago. His beard is wild, and his hair is all over the place. She wants to smooth it down just to feel it spring back up again.

Is he going to acknowledge this unspoken thing between them? Should *she*? He strides around the bed, holding his bag, and stops in front of her, looking at her. Really looking at her. As though he's going to say something important.

She looks at him expectantly. But then he just says, 'We better leave,' and opens the room door, letting her out first. They hustle down to reception, eschewing any help from hovering bellboys in favour of speed. This time they sit together as the desk agent works through their process, charging fifty per cent of the bill to each of their credit cards before printing out two copies, slipping them into stiff, logo-embossed envelopes and handing one to Thea and one to Logan.

With it, Thea feels their shared night transition back into two halves. Two strangers, with two credit cards, paying their individual portions.

No longer 'us'.

They're both quiet during the short limo ride back to the airport, where they automatically sit in the same seats as on the way there. Opposite the other rather than side by side, and anxiously looking out at the runway where another plane takes off cleanly as they pass. No winds batter the side of the car and it's quiet enough to hear each other speak, but neither of them do much, instead exchanging small, nervy smiles as they check their phones.

'All flights are up and running,' Thea tells him, reading from the airport website.

'Now we just need to get seats,' he replies, tapping out a message, to who, Thea can't see. 'Fingers crossed.'

The driver deposits them at Departures, and Logan dispatches a tip without a trace of Thea's awkwardness. Ten dollars, she notes, should she find herself in a limo in the future. They head inside, the doors swooshing open to a scene as busy as the previous day, but without the howling weather. Around them long queues are moving purposefully along the concourse, and the atmosphere feels both over-excited and overwrought. Everyone is bustling, aside from Thea and Logan who stand motionless in front of the signs on the wall. One arrow points left for domestic departures, and one right for international. They both make to follow the direction they need to go in and then stop, turning back to each other. Thea is a mass of feelings. Nervy about getting on a plane, but just as anxious that whatever was between them last night will evaporate the second they say goodbye.

'I guess this is it,' Thea says, wanting to say so much more. The thought of him disappearing into the throng without acknowledging their perfect evening together layers melancholy onto the adrenaline that's pumping through her veins. She has to try and get her flight, but she also doesn't want to leave this spot. The way his face looks now, as he looks away from the sign and towards her face, she thinks he's feeling the same way.

Thinks, but isn't definite. And now they're back in the real world, there's an uncertainty. She wasted years pining for a guy in London. Once she got him, he turned out to be so wrong for her. How much does she know about Logan, really?

Maybe he's just tired and anxious to get going.

But maybe he's not.

'I hope you make it home,' he says, his gaze fixing on her face.

'You too.' She takes a deep breath and carried by an inner velocity, she fumbles for the right words, the right way to put herself up for potential rejection. 'Maybe we can meet up—' She realises halfway through that he's talking too.

'—when we're both back in Portland?' he finishes. 'Couldn't have put it better myself.'

Thea laughs. 'I'd like that. Coffee?'

'Sure, if you're open to Dunkin' Donuts.' He grins back, wispy beardy bits dancing in the over-ventilated airport building.

'You're on,' says Thea, not moving her eyes from his face. There's maybe a metre between them, but without having to vocalise it, they start edging back towards each other.

'Well, I guess this is goodbye for now, and Happy Holidays.' Logan stretches his arms out as though to hug her and she's drawn towards them.

'Hey, look.' He points above their heads. Attached to a strip-light fitting is a bushy sprig of mistletoe, along with a few baubles spinning madly on their threads each time the doors slide open or closed. Thea's tingles are back.

'I'm glad to have met you, Theodora Bridges,' Logan whispers as he wraps his arms around her and she rests her cheek on his shoulder, returning the hug. She breathes the smell of him in, feeling herself relax the way she had on the bed last night. Around them, people rush past with determined looks in their eyes. Besides them, everyone is moving.

'And you too, Logan Beechwood.'

She's glad she spent the extra thirty seconds this morning brushing her teeth. Because in a second, she's going to look up and he's going to kiss her. Or she's going to kiss him.

They're going to kiss each other.

She looks up, and he's looking right back at her. And then their lips are together and the kiss banishes any thoughts of the cold-but-clammy airport building. It's soft and tentative, and then firm and confident, and then completely and totally consuming, as they press against each other more tightly.

The Tannoy crackles and they jump from the noise, pulling away from each other breathlessly. Thea holds a hand up to her mouth as though she's been shocked. 'All passengers for Boston Logan International, please make their way to Gate Nine now. The next departure for Boston Logan International will be from Gate Nine. Boarding will commence shortly.'

'That's me,' Logan says with a note of panic in his voice. His eyes dart around as though he's unsure what to do.

'Go,' Thea urges. Her synapses feel wild from the kiss, it's as though she's made entirely from nerve endings. But she doesn't want him stranded here for Christmas any more than she wants to be stranded herself. She hugs him again, and, reluctantly, pulls away, her pulse thundering. 'Go to Boston Logan, Logan from Boston. I'll see you after Christmas.'

He smiles, his navy-blue eyes shining at her and still holding loosely on to her hand. He takes a couple of steps in the opposite direction to her, trailing his fingers down her arm, before he finally lets go, and then turns back to wave, walking backwards and only turning away when he's far down the concourse. She keeps her eyes on him as long as she can, before the crowd swallows him up and her ankle is banged by the wheels of someone's suitcase, shocking her into remembering why she's here.

She turns away and she runs towards international departures with the memory of Logan's heat next to her body. And the kiss.

Perfect, but unfinished.

It's only when she's queued for two hours, is early enough to be assigned one of only a handful of unreserved seats on the noon flight from Portland to London Heathrow, and clears security, that she realises that before they parted, they forgot to swap numbers.

Chapter Six

Bone-penetratingly cold drizzle greets Thea as she heaves her backpack through Arrivals at Heathrow. Despite it being 5 a.m. on Christmas Day, Dad's here to get her, even if he isn't *here* here, waiting with the excited groups of people surrounding the Arrivals exit, trussed up in tinsel and making *Love Actually* jokes. This is because to park up and come into the airport costs money, whereas waiting in a layby near Heathrow and only setting off to fetch her when she texts that she's in the queue for passport control doesn't. Instead, he meets her at the rapid pick-up zone, where you have five minutes to greet and load before you get charged. As Dad's a cab driver, he's a pro at both. Although today he's in the family car rather than the black cab.

'Merry Christmas, darling,' Dad says, hoisting her bag into the boot before folding her into a hug. Like her, he's wearing one of Kit's cast-offs, a shiny black Barbour gilet, over his own bobbly fleece. She hasn't seen him for six months but Dad smells exactly like Roy Bridges always smells: apple-scented shampoo and soil, from the allotment he goes down to almost every day, whatever the weather.

'Merry Christmas, Dad,' she says, the sound muffled into his shoulder. Dad is big and solid, and the quilted bodywarmer adds to his bulk.

'Mum'll think you're not eating enough,' he says, pulling away to look at her with a critical eye. 'You're all skinny. I thought they supersized all the meals in America.'

'That's if you eat out.' Which she doesn't that much. She takes packed lunches to work and relies on the freebie table – snacks provided by clients from protein ball brands to artisan doughnut makers – to top them up.

She wants to tell Dad about the tiny but delicious portions of food in the hotel last night though – or wait, was it technically two nights ago now? – but instead yawns so hard her jaw feels like it's going to dislocate.

'Mum and Nan have barely slept, worrying about you getting back, and you must be tired too,' Dad says.

Thea watched back-to-back films on the plane, first because she was buzzing from making it onto a flight, and then because she was too wired from her night in the hotel with Logan and from *analysing* her night in the hotel with Logan, to even think about sleeping.

As well as replaying the kiss.

Over and over again.

Nine hours of non-stop comic book adaptations, weepies and action movies, none of which she really absorbed because everyone and everything reminded her of him. At one point, she'd even thought about springing for the extortionately expensive in-flight wi-fi just so that she could look him up on social media. She'd managed to distract herself for long enough with Harry Styles's superhero debut to let the urge pass, but the itch to dissect every last moment had remained under her skin, preventing her from relaxing enough to drift off.

Now, in the pre-dawn London outskirts, and leaning against her dad, who must have been up since 3 a.m. to get here, she starts to wilt with exhaustion.

'Get in, get warm,' Dad tells her, sensing it but also aware they need to hustle. Thea sinks gratefully into the front seat of his Volvo, the heaters noisily blasting. She feels her eyelids droop the second she hits the seat, her nose full of the scent of an aggressively strong pine air freshener dangling from the rear-view mirror.

'Sorry for dragging you out here at this time. It'll take ages to get home,' she tells him.

'Don't be daft. And it won't take long at this time on Christmas Day. The streets are empty.' Dad rubs his hands together to shake off the damp and pulls away tidily, making a noise of satisfaction when he registers at the barrier that the whole process has taken a mere four minutes and twenty seconds, and cost them nothing, when it's five pounds per half-hour for the short-stay car park.

Thea smiles, watching the suburban houses near the airport, with their Christmas trees and decorations sliding past the car window as they make their way home, before falling asleep. She only wakes up when they pull up outside her parents' terrace in Leytonstone – bought long before the gentrification that meant that they wouldn't in a million years now be able to afford the house they've spent their thirty-year marriage in. Thea has always lived with Mum and Dad when in the UK, aside from one year in a horrible, damp flatshare so far on the outskirts that it barely counted as London. She'd stuck it out until the lease released its strangling fingers and gone home. Sometimes when she thinks about it, she's a bit embarrassed to have spent most of her twenties there, but her uni friends who stayed in London after finishing their degrees were all jealous that she had a low-rent option within decent commuting distance of her first, badly paid jobs. Besides, crucially, she also liked living with them, until the push to start afresh and leave London – and Christian – behind, catapulted her almost five thousand miles away.

It's just shy of 7 a.m. when they arrive, but Mum rushes out of the door in her fleecy dressing gown, with a tea towel flung over one shoulder, holding the squeezy turkey baster she was obviously busying herself with before they arrived. The narrow path is strung with fairy lights that throw a twinkling glow over her as she bustles up to the gate that Dad is carrying Thea's bag through in the opposite direction, with Thea following. They all meet in one crush and Mum intercepts her, clinging onto her in a bone-crunching embrace. Over Mum's shoulder, Thea sees Nan standing in the doorway peering out, looking a bit wobbly on her feet but with an enormous smile on her face. 'Merry Christmas!' she calls from behind the front step. 'You made it. I'm so pleased!'

At the sight of her, Thea feels her energy return, but the temperature is frigid. 'Go in, Nan, you'll get cold.' Nan doesn't move.

Dad shifts the backpack onto his other shoulder. 'What you got in this bag, ornaments made from Oregon rock?' he grumbles good-naturedly, squeezing past Nan and dropping it into the hallway.

'Mum, let's get in the house,' Thea finally says in exasperation. She suddenly feels overwhelmed. Being back here makes her feel as though both everything and nothing has happened in the last six months. Or even in the last forty-eight hours. 'All the cold air will be getting in.'

Her mum links arms with her as they go up the path and through the door, where she hands her off to Nan, to repeat the manoeuvre down the hall and into the living room. She deposits Nan into her remote-control-operated reclining chair, which is surrounded by Christmas decorations that have been put up every year that Thea can remember. Cards dangle from strings threaded on the bookshelves, while mismatching lights and tinsel twist around the TV unit and the family pictures displayed on the walls. The dining table at the far end of the room is already set with a silver-and-purple Mrs Hinch-inspired tablescape that she knows Mum has admired on social media. Despite how early it is, Nan's already fully dressed in a silky emerald-green blouse and navy trousers, white bob encased in Elnett and with mascara on. She feels light as a feather next to Thea, and while they used to be the same height, five foot seven, Nan has definitely stooped to at least an inch or two below that. Has that happened since she went to the States? Or does it just feel like that because she hasn't seen her for so long? Has she always been this fragile?

'Where's Kit?' she asks to rid herself of the thought. She plops down on the arm of Nan's armchair, still feeling jittery and strange from the hour of fractured sleep she had in the car.

Mum sighs in pretend annoyance, and adjusts her dressing gown, retightening the belt around her waist. She's wearing Christmas pyjamas underneath with 'Sleigh Queen' written across the top. 'Bed. He only got back from Christmas Eve drinks about two hours ago. He came crashing in just as your dad was getting up to fetch you. I wouldn't expect to see him for a bit.'

At three years younger than her, and as a tech whizz who 'does coding' (that's about as far as Thea has managed to understand it) Kit's earning potential by far outstrips Thea's, but because he can't be bothered with full-time permanent work, and spends all his wages on clothes, he's pretty much continued to live at home since university too. Mum secretly loves having him here, as much as she complains about him needing to be more sensible with his money.

'I'm so sorry about using the credit card,' Thea whispers to Nan, as Mum keeps talking about Kit and the permanent position he was offered at the company he's been freelancing for, who were so impressed with him, they gave him the same Christmas bonus as the permanent employees as an incentive for him to accept. Instead he told them he was going travelling, so wouldn't be back after Christmas (a lie), and promptly spent the bonus on a Burberry coat.

'At least it'll keep him warm,' she's grumbling as Nan leans in and says, 'Don't be. I know you wouldn't have just spent it on something daft like your brother.' She looks up at Thea's mum. 'Will I be getting this Blueberry one when he's bored of it, then, Shelley?'

Thea's mum snorts. 'Probably. We'll see how long it keeps his attention for.' She seems to remember the turkey baster in her hand. 'I need to sort out the timings for dinner. When Kit gets up, we'll do presents.' She grabs Thea's hand. 'I'm so glad you made it home. When we saw the storm on the telly, your dad was convinced you'd be stranded there for the whole holiday. I hope it wasn't too pricey to get a room.'

Thea catches Nan's eye and they share a secret look. Thea hasn't told Mum and Dad about the cost. Kit fritters money away, but she can't criticise him too much because at least it's *his* money and he only spends what he has. It's another thing Thea getting Nan into debt for such an indulgence.

'How about we have a cuppa while you get back to your Christmas dinner schedule?' says Nan smoothly. 'Me and Thea can catch up while we wait for his lordship to make an appearance.'

'I'll make the tea,' says Dad cheerfully, disappearing with Mum into the kitchen.

'Shift over there, you,' says Nan to Thea. 'I want to adjust my chair.' Thea pushes a pile of magazines onto the floor and sits on the pouffe that they use as a second, unofficial coffee table next to Nan's chair. Nan presses a button and sighs in relief as the seat goes back and the footrest lifts her legs.

Thea shoots her a look of concern.

71

'Are you in pain somewhere?' she asks, eyeing the packets of tablets spilling out of a Tupperware box on the sideboard next to her.

'Just old and tired,' Nan says, brushing her off with a laugh. 'I'm paying for not being able to sit still until I found out you were on your way. I'm a long way from when I'd stand behind that bar for twelve hours at a time. Now, tell me everything – describe the hotel and the man – I want to hear it all.'

Thea digs into her bag and pulls out a clutch of toiletries from the hotel bathroom. 'Well, I made sure I brought these back for you for a start,' she says, handing over the mini moisturisers and shampoo, 'and I've got a picture of everything I ate in the restaurant on my phone.'

Nan struggles with the lid of the shampoo for a second, before Thea takes it from her, unscrews it and passes it back. Nan sniffs. 'Ooh sandalwood, lovely. Have you got any pictures of . . . hang about, you haven't told me his name yet.'

'Logan,' Thea replies, instantly reddening. 'And no, I haven't. But what I do know about him, is he's twenty-nine, he runs a business with his friend making films about peoples' families and he's gone back to his parents' home in Boston for Christmas.' An electric current pumps through her bloodstream even just talking about him. 'Nan, it was so amazing. We talked for ages then fell asleep in the room together. Nothing happened,' she adds quickly. 'Well, aside from a goodbye kiss at the airport.' Her pulse quickens. 'But we're going to meet up when we're both back after Christmas.'

'Look at you. You're head over heels.' There's a cheeky glint in Nan's eyes. 'Boston's East Coast, isn't it, so that's a five-hour time difference. Have you texted him since you've been back?'

'It was all so much of a rush to get on our planes that we didn't swap numbers,' Thea wails.

'So, look him up on social media.' Nan gives her a 'duh' look, as though Thea is the tech-clueless septuagenarian, not her.

'I was going to. I was just waiting until I was settled at home.'

Nan widens her eyes. 'Well, go on then.'

'Now?' Thea isn't sure she wants to do it with an audience. She's planning on a deep dive when she can zoom in on the photos and take note of details.

'What else have you got to do?'

'Here we are.' Dad comes back in humming and carrying two mugs of tea. He passes one to Thea and places the other down next to Nan. 'When you go up for a shower, wake that brother of yours, will you?'

'Will do,' says Thea, taking an appreciative slurp. 'No one in America makes a tea like you, Dad.' Logan's 'dishwater' flits through her mind. Maybe *that's* his flaw? She can live with that.

'I know,' Dad replies, even though he's never been to the States. He and Mum have just talked about going to Las Vegas for their wedding anniversary for five years on the trot.

He goes back into the kitchen where he starts singing 'When the red, red robin comes bob, bob, bobbin' along' out of tune and at the top of his voice, which in about two days will be getting on her nerves but today seems welcoming and perfect. Mum joins in with some similarly tuneless harmonies.

'Come on,' Nan says, prompting her again.

Knowing there's no getting out of it, Thea pulls her phone out of her bag. When she turns back to Nan, she's already got her readers on, the ones that magnify her eyes to about three times their usual size. 'Increase the display size. I can't see anything on a tiny screen.'

Thea can't help but laugh as she does as she's told. 'Right, in the hotel, his room was under the name Logan Beechwood. Can't be that common.' Which is true in London. However, it turns out there is a highly successful NFL star called Logan Beechwood, with his own account, plus fan accounts and hashtags, all of which hog the top search results.

'Oh. Well, that's not him,' she says, holding the phone in front of Nan to show her a photo of an enormous, thickly muscled shaven-headed man holding a trophy.

'Shame,' Nan says, with an almost dreamy look on her face. 'The size of his arms!'

'As he has two million Instagram followers, I doubt we'd be the only people trying to slip into his DMs. Hopefully, the less famous Logan Beechwood isn't so in demand. If we can find him. OK, he didn't tell me the name of his company but he said his business partner was called Felix.' She types 'Logan Beechwood Felix' into Google, and is rewarded with the first hit being 'Memento Movies'. She clicks hungrily on it, a montage of clips auto-playing as she opens their home page. An ancient woman at least twenty years older than Nan is talking about being separated from her fiancé by the Second World War as a black-and-white photo of a young man in an Air Force uniform flashes up. Thea pauses to watch it, a small knot of anxiety in her stomach forming in case the business he told her about actually *is* naff rather than as charming as he described. She's quickly eased of her concern. She knows less than nothing about film-making, but in the couple of minutes she sees, it's like watching a trailer for a documentary on Netflix, layering close-up shots of talking heads with archive footage and photos. These are not hastily thrown together home movies, they're professional, high-quality films made with care and talent.

Nan interrupts impatiently, making a grab for her phone. 'That's not him, is it?'

There's a fifty-something man on screen talking about summering on 'the lake' with his parents.

'No! These are clips from the films he and his friend make. They're good, right?'

'I don't know, darling. You know the only films I like have that Tom Hardy in them.' She waves her hand. 'So where do we find him?'

Thea clicks on the 'About' tab and another video starts to play. Suddenly, he's there, on screen, sitting on a sofa in front of a backdrop of camera equipment and next to another artfully cool guy with rusty-coloured hair, who she assumes must be Felix. Logan is dressed more casually than he was at dinner, in a short-sleeved shirt with his forearms showing.

'That's him,' Thea squeals.

'He has nice arms too,' Nan says, 'even if they're not as muscly. Must be hoisting all those cameras around.'

Logan's gentle voice is explaining why they set up Memento, and how they see their role as more than cameramen splicing together existing footage, but more as familial anthropologists, digging into peoples' lives to capture the history they want to preserve. A photo of a much younger Logan beaming next to an older man with curly grey hair and a very bristly moustache flashes on screen as he talks about what inspired him to set up Memento. His grandpa.

'I wanted to capture his memories, and my family's memories of my grandfather, before he could no longer recall them himself. Memento is all about bringing families together,' he explains on screen. They watch it to the end.

'Right, let's see if he's on Instagram.' She pulls up the Memento feed, which has a link to both Logan and Felix's personal pages, and she clicks on Logan's, which has an underscore in the middle to differentiate him from his more famous NFL name twin. It's all very artful, and clearly designed to promote his business. Thea thinks of her own account, which is a mishmash of professional achievements, nights out with friends, slightly crappy attempts at restaurant flatlays and family photos. In comparison, Logan's is expertly curated, meaning she can't harvest any personal information about him from it. She scrolls down a couple of screens, and sees all the captions are quite long, with accompanying stills or mini-clips from his videos. She clicks randomly on one and reads the caption. Even though he's talking about someone she's never met and likely never will, the way he writes sounds like him. It has the same tone as when he was telling her about his life and work. She resolves to dig into them later. At least she'll be able to hear his voice in them, even if the photos are infuriatingly neutral. He last posted something on his grid in mid-December. She checks the business account and when it was most recently updated – two days ago. The square has a 'Happy Holidays' message, explaining that they're out of office and making their own family memories until 30th December.

'Well?' says Nan expectantly. 'Aren't you going to like him or request him or follow him or whatever it is you do?'

Thea flips back to Logan's page. At least there's a photo of him there, even if you can only see one of his navy-blue eyes because the other is clamped to the viewfinder of a camera. His bio reads 'East Coast guy on the West Coast. Probably trying to make a movie.' Her thumb hovers over the follow button and a thought thumps through her. What if he was just being polite and forgot about her the second he was handed a bag of mini pretzels on his flight? What if the kiss was a spur-of-the-moment response to the heightened, but false, intimacy of the storm and the room?

Or maybe, like her, he thinks it's the start of something?

She presses it before she can second-guess herself again. It's 3 a.m. in Boston so it would be kind of weird if he *was* online to register the notification, but she waits for a minute all the same.

'Back home five minutes and already glued to her phone,' Dad grumbles, coming back in with a plate of mince pies. 'I hope it's not work. That mad boss of yours agreed to a week off so she'd better not end up contacting you all the time.' They've heard Thea's regular complaints about Fuchsia, a woman who comes with her own climate. One which is usually set to 'raging tempest'.

'I was just – Never mind.' Thea puts her phone down and eyes the plate. 'I'm not actually sure what mealtime my body clock is on, but it's Christmas Day, so a mince pie can count for any of them, right?'

Dad holds out the plate and she leans forward to intercept it, catching a whiff of 'eau de plane' as she does. She grimaces. Snatching one as she stands up, she says, 'I'll take this for the road and have that shower. *Don't* start playing the Christmas playlist without me.'

The morning has started to take on an unreal quality and feels a bit like she's a character in a play. Happy to be home, but not quite comfortable yet, and as though she's on show. She needs a shower, and to decompress and re-acclimatise to being back in the UK, especially after the rollercoaster of the past couple of days.

She squeezes Nan's bony shoulder and heads up the stairs, where dozens of family photos line the walls in a higgledy-piggledy pattern following Mum's recent obsession with gallery walls on Pinterest. She helps herself to a towel from the airing cupboard, breathing in the familiar smell of washing powder, and decides maybe she needs a bath rather than a shower. She never did get to try the one at The Opulent. Her parents' bathroom might not rival the hotel's set-up but compared to the bathroom in her tiny studio, which was billed as a 'wet room' by virtue of the shower drenching the sink and toilet every time you use it, there at least *is* a bath and that's a luxury.

Plus, while she's waiting for it to run, she can read a few more of those Instagram captions and see if she can find out a little more about Logan.

By the time they have Christmas lunch – and it *is* lunch in Thea's parents' household; all of them, including Kit, are around the table by 1 p.m. sharp – she's come full circle through tired and jet-lagged to buzzy and energised, and is starting to tip back into tired and jet-lagged again. A glass of Buck's Fizz sits in front of her and she's telling everyone how her job at iDentity is going. Or at any rate the bits that will least alarm them. Fuchsia being a nightmare taskmaster is fine, as are the long hours – graft has always been respected in her parents' home – but her increasing sense that she's going nowhere in her role is not. Nor is the lackadaisical attitude to payday being on a set and pre-determined date, which would horrify her working-class parents and grandparent.

She plays most of Fuchsia's demands for laughs, outlining the way she wanted one of them to immerse themselves in Portland's nascent nude dining scene – on their own dime of course – in order to research it for a pitch they were doing to a restaurant client.

Mum and Dad shake their heads in disbelief that such a thing even exists. They may have both grown up in the UK's capital, but aside from the odd stage show, they don't 'do' central London that often. That London most likely has its own nude dining scene, and much more besides, will have passed them by completely. They make all the right shocked noises at both the dining concept and Fuchsia's audacity.

Only Kit says, 'Aren't you bored of it yet?' He's in a hoodie and jeans that Thea can't give any attention to because if she does, she knows she'll sound older than Nan by saying 'Did you buy them ripped like that?' The label suggests they are designer but Thea doesn't recognise the brand. As ever, Thea is unsure if Kit is much cooler than her, or if he's a complete and tragic fashion victim, and the jeans are, in fact, just terrible.

'I've only been there six months,' she replies, rolling her eyes at him. 'Not everyone gets itchy feet as soon as they've passed their probation period.'

Kit shrugs, helping himself to more roast potatoes. 'Just the idea of being saddled with an awful boss and still *staying.*' He visibly shudders.

'The area I work in is so competitive that I don't have the option of walking out of a job in the morning and picking up some get-rich-quick freelance work by the end of the day. Besides—' she says, snatching the roast potato bowl off him before he takes them all – 'I really like it in Portland, and iDentity sponsor my visa so I have to stay there if I want to stay in the country.'

Mum sighs dramatically and Thea eyes her while dropping three more potatoes onto her plate. 'What?' she says.

'I was just hoping . . .'

Thea knows what she was hoping: that she would hate it in the US and after having a bit of an experience and adding a year at an American company to her CV, she'd toddle back to the UK. She thought that might happen too, or that the kneejerk of leaving an entire country to get over a break-up would make her so homesick she'd have to come back, but it's more complicated than that. She misses home and her family, but she likes Portland at the same time. Even if she feels as though she's going nowhere in her job right now, she can see the opportunities, just out of reach, but *there* all the same. The sense of possibility is along every pavement – sidewalk – she treads, and having spent her whole life in one place, she's enjoying discovering a new city by herself and without her nan or parents, or even Christian, having trodden the same streets before her. Not that she could tell Mum that.

She reaches over to squeeze her mum's arm. 'I'm here now, Mum. And you can all come and visit me. There's so much to do – nice food, cool shopping, outdoorsy stuff like waterfalls and lakes. You could hire a car and drive all the way down the West Coast to California, or even fly to Vegas – like you've always planned.'

'I'd love to come,' Nan announces and Thea grins at her.

'And I'd love to have you.'

Mum and Dad exchange a private look, one Thea can't quite decipher. 'I know it's expensive, but you can stay in my studio and I'll stay with Teddy and Jake while you're in town. You've *always* wanted to go to Vegas. Trip of a lifetime and all that. You deserve it.'

'Wonder how much it costs to fly business,' Kit muses. Thea rolls her eyes. He's the only person present who wouldn't have conniptions at the cost of her hotel room last night.

'Maybe you'd be able to afford to move out properly if you stopped frittering all your money away,' Thea tells him. 'Do one of those part-ownership schemes.'

'Pfft,' Kit says, a noise between a dismissal and derision. 'Then I really would be stuck in some job. No way.'

'Think about it, Mum, won't you?' Thea presses.

She nods, but distractedly. 'We'll look into it, maybe for some time next year. More turkey, Dora?' she says, changing the subject, and loading up Nan's plate even though she's barely made a dent in what's already on there.

Thea's phone buzzes in her pocket, and she can't resist a quick glance.

Logan Beechwood followed you back.

She grins again, shoving it underneath her thigh on the chair, and catching Nan's eye across the table.

'That him?' she mouths, and Thea nods. Nan's eyes twinkle back at her. She feels her phone vibrate again, and then again. She itches to pick it up, but Dad is asking her about her work commute and she's forced to talk him through the different routes she takes to iDentity's downtown office depending on the traffic, and which car parks nearby offer the best rates. From Dad's responses and seeming knowledge of the busiest roads, it's clear he's been studying Portland on Google Streetview. She suspects he'd quite like to quiz Portland's cabbies to see if they have an equivalent of The Knowledge.

'Looks like it would probably get quite congested around rush hour on the road outside your apartment.'

'Yes, it does. And there were roadworks for three weeks in October right outside, which meant I kept getting stuck in the temporary traffic lights. Nightmare.'

He nods sagely, genuinely interested.

Another buzz.

After what feels like a thousand years, and several more buzzes, they finish their lunch and settle back into the living room, Nan back in her chair, Mum and Dad on the settee and Kit and Thea lolling on the carpet in front of a Christmas tree that is groaning with mismatched and home-made decorations made by Thea and Kit in primary school, along with the chocolate decorations they insist Mum buys even though they're adults. They've been sitting in the same positions on Christmas Day forever. Thea chances a surreptitious look at her screen as the search begins for the TV remote and the *Radio Times*. Her screen is full of Instagram DM notifications, all from Logan.

'Shall we do presents?' Mum says, interrupting just as she's about to swipe into them.

'At *last*,' Kit shouts. Sometimes Thea thinks his spiritual age is closer to five than twenty-five.

'You were the one who didn't get up until midday,' Mum replies pointedly. He pulls a face.

'Do mine,' Thea says, pulling her gift from under the tree and thrusting it at him. Everyone's presents from her are slightly battered after being buffeted around the baggage scanners at the airport, but she is confident that Kit will be impressed with what's inside. She enlisted Teddy to go shopping with her, who, after listening to her endless parameters for what Kit considers acceptable (he was appalled that the designer vintage items he waxed lyrical about were rejected, even though Thea explained it wasn't the items themselves but that they were *used*), came up trumps with the suggestion of a wallet from an up-and-coming designer that he knew well enough to get a hefty mates-rates discount from. Of course, she personally thinks the plastic, neon, triangular-shaped item itself is both impractical and heinous, but that's always the case with things Kit likes.

'Nice one, Thea!' he shouts, unwrapping it and delightedly holding it aloft for them all to see. 'I love this guy's stuff, and you can't get it shipped over from the States yet. Thanks!' Nan and her parents look at the wallet politely. She can almost see the cogs whirring in her mum's mind, that if he likes *this* wallet, something that looks like it's covered in cartoon character stickers, then perhaps she can get him similar items next time she's in Primark. Thea will tell her later that this is a bad assumption to make. Meanwhile, Kit's already taking photos of the wallet to show his mates.

'Now me for you all,' he says, handing over an envelope to their mum. She opens it and gasps, before flashing it in front of Nan and Dad's faces. Their eyes all widen.

'What is it?' Thea asks. 'Let me see.' Mum holds it out to her.

'Bloody hell, Kit,' she says. 'This is too much.' It's day passes to a fancy wellness centre on the outskirts of London that has a golf course Dad has mentioned longingly more than once and a spa that Holly Willoughby was once papped coming out of, causing Mum to say, 'Lovely skin,' when she saw the photo.

He shrugs, looking pleased but embarrassed. 'You lot never treat yourself to anything,' he mumbles. 'There's an afternoon tea included. Thought Nan would like that bit.'

'Are you coming too?' Mum asks, pleased at the prospect of a family day out.

'Nah, bit old-fashioned for me, that place.'

Her face drops slightly. 'I'll give you a lift though. I want to go to the Acne sale at Bicester and it's on the way.'

More presents are exchanged, an ill-judged hoodie from mum and dad to Kit ('It wasn't even cheap,' she huffs when his rictus grin instantly gives the game away, before conceding she has the receipt), some vintage American road maps from Thea to dad, and some small-batch Portland gin from Thea to Mum.

'And this one is for you,' Thea says to Nan, lifting a thick square package onto her lap. Nan opens it and tears instantly pool in her eyes as she turns the page of the annotated photo album Thea spent ages putting together. It's pictures of her time so far in Portland. 'You're always saying you hate looking at pictures on screens, so I printed them all out for you, and there's room left to add some more. Like pictures taken when you all come and see me,' she says, looking at them one by one. 'Feels like a bit of a cheat because it's a present for me too, really.'

The photos include everything from shots of her studio and the exterior of iDentity, to shots of her and Teddy with his boyfriend Jake in their favourite neighbourhood bar. She doesn't actually look great in that one, but that's because Teddy insisted on picture approval, so he looks amazing while she looks just OK.

'You went for reality over Instagram, then,' Kit teases, pausing on a slightly blurred photo of a gaggle of dogs in the park with a beaming woman holding on to their leashes.

'That dog walker is there every time I cut through that park. I've told Nan about her, so I wanted her to see all the dogs. Besides . . .' She thinks of Logan and his films. She watched a dozen clips from his feed while she was in the bath and the memories people talk about in them aren't the grand gestures. They're the lived day-to-day reality of knowing someone: the quirky way they eat a chocolate bar layer by layer, or the phrases a person can never hear without thinking of a particular person. Nan knows that Thea has named all of those dogs without actually knowing what any of their real names are.

'This one's got to be Lieutenant Fluff,' Nan says now, pointing to a bichon frise with two bows in its hair.

'Yes!'

Nan continues to leaf through the album as they stick the Christmas Day film on. One by one, they nod off in front of it, finally giving Thea the opportunity to read Logan's messages without being accused of ignoring them. He's one of those people who writes a sentence on each line so Thea now has ten unread messages.

Logan: Merry Christmas! I'm guessing (hoping!) you made it back to London.
Logan: All hell has broken loose here.
Logan: Mom decided that now Keaton is almost 18, she didn't need to do Christmas stockings anymore.
Logan: Big mistake.
Logan: Huge.
Logan: Everyone, including the cat, is outraged.
Logan: (The cat gets a stocking too.)
Logan: She says it's because no one ever does one for her.
Logan: Except this year, we did.
Logan: Mom is the only person with a stocking.
Logan: 😬

Thea laughs. She can imagine his face in front of her telling her the story, his eyes crinkled in mirth and his lips – those lips – talking in his quiet, deep voice. She taps out a response.

Thea: I hope you haven't all stormed off to separate rooms. We're watching the latest Bond movie ('watching' involves me and Kit answering all Nan's questions about who everyone is and what they were in before while the actual plot passes us all by).
Thea: My brother loved his present from me. Hated his present from my parents (a 50% success rate is good), and bought us a

day trip to a place on a par with The Opulent in the fancy stakes that my mum is already fretting about.

Logan is typing . . .

Logan: Fretting why?
Thea: You may have noticed that 5-star hotels are not my natural habitat. For my mum, multiply the awkwardness by ten and you're not even close to how out of place she feels in posh places. By the time we go, she'll have talked herself out of it.
Logan: You better get there quick, then!
Thea: Now I know how the other half lives I can show her the ropes. I'll be disappointed if there's not a constant stream of free champagne though 😊
Logan: It's hard to come back to normal life after Champagne on tap.
Thea: Must admit I was disappointed I still had to turn right on the plane.
Logan: Haha, 'Don't you know who I am?' Internal flights are more like buses so no first class option for me. Just a guy next to me eating three Big Macs he'd brought on board for the journey in quick succession. At 7 a.m. It was a sight to behold.
Thea: Breakfast of champions.

With every bit of banter, Thea's stomach swoops. Not least because Logan speaks in full sentences and can spell. Another tick in the plus column. It erases the memory of every bad Tinder exchange she's had in Portland, where more than once a stream of emojis has been expected to pass for a conversational opener and an unsolicited dick pic has been a substitute for the suggestion of an actual date.

Thea: What are your Christmas Day plans? (Apart from sulking over stockings.) I get all my American Christmas intel from films so I'm assuming matching sweaters, charades, and maybe setting booby traps for some burglars after your parents go on holiday without you?

Logan: Correct, although instead of the latter, it's traditional for my dad to be attacked by a squirrel that's hiding in the tree.

Logan: For the UK, I get all my Christmas intel from TV, so a brawl in a pub?

Thea: We like to refer to it as a 'festive punch-up' but yes, exactly. Or maybe someone finding out that their father isn't their father, or that their wife is having an affair. It rotates.

Logan: So really, we usually go for a big walk while Mom makes dinner (before you assume we're awful misogynists, making the only woman cook, she will not let us in the kitchen. I've tried! She usually says something about it being the only place she can get away from that damned game of charades).

Logan: Then, after dinner, our next-door neighbors come over for drinks. They're more like family – we've lived next door to them my whole life.

Thea: Sounds wholesome!

Logan: Craig had to be 'helped' home last year after a few too many Snowballs, so not so much.

Thea: My nan is also a fan of the advocaat.

An hour passes this way, with them exchanging little snippets of information and jokes, before Logan says:

Gotta go for that walk. Screens off by royal (dad) decree (also it's
sub-zero out there, so my thumbs will freeze if I try to keep
texting). Enjoy the rest of your day x

Thea registers the kiss. It means everything and nothing,
signing him off for the day but injecting Thea with
hope.

One kiss interrupted at the airport, now a virtual one
completed. It could just be a reflex.

Or it could be a promise.

She leaves it there, hanging, wanting it to be the last
thing he said to her, and also not wanting to be the one to
have their message unanswered. She puts her phone down,
and flicks another film on, shaking her parents and Nan
awake to see if anyone wants a drink. She wants to wring
everything she can out of today.

But by 8 p.m., and after another couple of glasses of
wine, her eyes are burning again with tiredness.
Knowing she'll probably wake up in the middle of the
night, she admits defeat and goes up to bed. She's in
her pyjamas and about to turn off the light, when
emboldened by those glasses of wine, she decides to
reply to Logan.

Hope you've seen off the squirrel by now. Jet lag has defeated
me. Happy Holidays (and stay off the snowballs!)

She adds a kiss and hopes it has the same effect on him as
his had on her.

Flying Home for Christmas

A notification arrives almost instantly and she swipes open her phone eagerly. But it's not Logan. It's Nicole, whose message she never did reply to.

Merry Christmas! Are you coming tomorrow or what?!

Thea's stomach lurches, before she puts the question in a mental box marked 'tomorrow', snaps off the light and gives in to the jet lag.

Chapter Seven

'You don't have to go, you know.' Nan's look the next morning is shrewd, piercing directly to what Thea is thinking. 'If I ever see that bloke again it'll only be to point him out to Derek.'

Derek worked for Nan and Grandad at the pub, as barman and occasional bouncer. He often alluded to his underworld connections, but there was no evidence that they actually existed aside from his occasional mutterings about 'knowing a bloke who could kneecap someone and make it look like an accident'. However, the fact that she's invoking Derek shows how much Nan hates Christian.

'There should be a special type of punishment reserved for love rats,' Nan mutters, a theme she has returned to several times over the last eighteen months. Thea's theory is that it has stirred up Nan's past and it isn't entirely about Christian at all. Thea's pub landlord grandad, the man who her father called 'dad', wasn't actually her real grandad. When Nan discovered she was pregnant, the man responsible turned out to be already married with three children and living a double life. He then promptly disappeared, before Nan met and married 'her Brian', who became the beloved father and grandfather they grew up with, and who brought Roy up as his own. Nan loved Brian fiercely until he died from a heart attack when Thea was ten, but she always said the experience transformed her from a romantic into a realist, with a highly tuned bullshit-ometer. Thea suspects Nan's hatred of Christian is less about his behaviour and more about the fact that Nan was taken in by him, along with Thea. Or maybe she just straightforwardly hates him for cheating on her granddaughter. Or because of the time, just before their break-up, he told her in front of everyone at a family meal that she ought to dress more like a cool, branding executive if she wanted to work her way up the ladder, and less like a nerd. He wasn't joking.

Thea has a text already composed to Nicole, sending her excuses for tonight's meet-up, and her thumb hovers over the 'send' button. Nicole will understand. Christian will be there, and she doesn't want to see Christian, ergo she shouldn't go. But she's annoyed that his presence will prevent her from seeing her friend for the first time since she moved to Portland. She's not back long enough to arrange a solo meet-up, so her only chance to see Nicole is at the Boxing Day drinks that she has been organising since they all graduated from their Communications Studies course.

And the drinks mean seeing Christian for the first time in eighteen months, the first time since their break-up. Nicole would rather he wasn't there either – as one of the only people who never fell for his charms, she would have been happy if he hadn't attended even when they were together – but he's in the WhatsApp group. And for some reason, even though university reunion drinks are the epitome of something Christian finds lame, he always goes. Nicole's lengthy side texts to Thea have all been about emphasising that she will support her through the whole evening but to please *just come*.

When she met her in the first few weeks of their course, Thea began as a peripheral character in Nicole's world. Nicole belonged to so many societies that she was constantly surrounded by other people, but slowly, over the three years, Thea had grown closer to her. There were plenty of things Thea wouldn't have tried without Nicole there to tell her that no one was looking at her anyway, so who cared. A night in the pub with her, catching up on the past six months is so tempting.

But she *really* doesn't want to see Christian.

When he and Thea were together, he'd told her he only went to the drinks to show the others how much more successful he was than them. Thea assumes she's now part of the contingent he wants to prove he's better than. It makes him a dick, she knows it does, but he's always been able to make her feel in some way wrong. Even though she dumped him in the end, she still emerged from the wreckage feeling as though she was the one who had been rejected. After all, he'd spent most of their relationship fine-tuning how to do it.

Oh God, she doesn't want to see him.

Thea flips to her DMs and re-reads Logan's latest messages to delay making a decision. The final one was sent at 2 a.m. her time.

Logan: Thea, I *didn't* stay off the snowballs.

Logan: But that's not why I'm messaging you now.

Logan: Even if I hadn't consumed my bodyweight in advocaat, I'd want to tell you I'm glad the hotel messed up our reservations.

Logan: I'm glad I met you.

She beams like an idiot, and she catches Nan shaking her head at her with a knowing look on her face.

'Don't be sending any of those sexties to this bloke, Thea.' She winks. 'Or at least cut your head off if you do.'

Thea laughs. 'How do you know about sexting?'

'I see *Hollyoaks* now and again, I know how it works.'

'I think I'll stay at home tonight,' Thea says.

'If you're sure,' Nan says, eyes a little narrowed.

'What?' Thea asks, catching the look on Nan's face.

'You don't *have* to go, but also don't let *him* being there stop you either. They're your old friends too. *He* doesn't get custody of them.'

Nan's words galvanise her. She's right, these people were once their mutual friends and acquaintances, ones that she had never been derisive about as Christian had. Plus, a small but insistent voice inside says that now is actually the perfect time to see him. As far as all her former course mates are concerned, she has a sexy job in the States, and now she has a proper prospect with an equally sexy American.

Last year she wouldn't – couldn't – even have contemplated it. Six months in and the break-up was still too raw. But luckily it was, as Nicole insists on referring to it, a fallow year, and the drinks didn't happen (Nicole is of the mind that if it's too regular it's not special, and Thea defers to Nicole in all matters of this type). But this year it's different. She's not the more forgettable half of the Christian/Thea duo, and she's not torn up with heartbreak.

She deletes the pre-prepped message and replies to Nicole's message from the previous night.

I'm coming. Don't judge me on the try-hard message I'm about to send the group.

She flips to the 'Re-UNI-on' WhatsApp group to reply to Nicole's official message asking for numbers so she can hold enough seats.

I can pop in for a bit – trying to catch up with family as I'm only back in the UK for a few days. Still totally jet-lagged and US annual leave is a *joke*!

Perhaps it's a little *too* obvious and show-offy, but as the whoop emojis and 'can't wait to hear about it' messages roll in, she's not thinking about that. Her mind is on the fact that it's 10 a.m. and so she only has eight hours before the drinks to make herself look as casually attractive in front of her ex-boyfriend as possible.

Chapter Eight

'Casually attractive' has been usurped by 'conscious and dressed' by the time Thea pushes the door open to the Coach and Horses near Waterloo at 8 p.m. Having been felled by a jet-lag 'power nap' on the sofa at 4 p.m., she woke up at 7 p.m. and was already so late that she only had time to unflatten her hair and apply make-up over the creases in her face from the settee cushions.

Her body temperature is all over the place as she enters the pub; from Nan-pleasing, too-hot central heating at home, to the bone-saturating December mist outside, then onto the muggy Central and Northern Lines, back out into the cold, and finally the pub, where the combination of other bodies, booze and clanky old radiators makes her instantly sweaty again. The pub – always the same one – is always busy on Boxing Day, and there are layers of tinsel on every surface and flashing lights that compete with the fruit machines for attention. She strains to see someone she recognises through the loose groups of people dotted around the U-shaped bar and then scans the tables in the main room. Even Nicole's negotiating skills can't secure them a private area on Boxing Day, because the ebb and flow of peoples' Christmas commitments can't guarantee an exact number of people or bar spend. Whoever arrives first (Nicole) has to stake out territory until backup arrives, and that could be in any one of the pub's three rooms.

'Thea!' Nicole shouts to her as she looks over the bottom half of the stable doors that separate the main bar from an oak-panelled side room. She's being served from the side of the bar and hidden behind another wooden panel. 'What took you so long? I've been texting you. Have you got an American accent yet? Do you say "arugula" instead of "rocket"?'

Thea steps through to join her and laughs. 'Neither, as they're both gross. I do say "water" as though there's a "d" in the middle now though, otherwise waiters don't know what I'm asking for.'

'Well, no cause for you to say that tonight, because strictly no soft drinks allowed.' Nicole proffers a glass flute towards her, before picking up a silver bucket from the bar with a bottle of something in it.

'Prosecco?'

Nicole shakes her head. 'Crémant. All the bankers gave bottles of it to us lowly comms people for Christmas because apparently, it's "better" than Prosecco and "much more affordable than Champagne". Turns out they're right. Twats could have given us Champagne though.' At work, as a communications manager at a finance firm, Nicole orbits a world where hundred-thousand-pound bonuses and ostentatious displays of wealth are the norm. Because she's technically within finance, she earns the sort of salary Thea can only dream of but compared to the bankers, and judged as such *by* the bankers, it's pitiful, because it won't comfortably support even one child's journey through private education. Having hit her own earning goal (within publishing, not finance) Nicole doesn't care and holds a cheerful disdain for the hedge fund managers, bankers and finance CEOs she sends press releases about, in no way jealous of them or bitter that she can't keep up with the Joneses because, in her words, 'the Joneses are such tossers'.

'Love your dress by the way,' Nicole says now. Thea has dug out the vintage velvet for the second time in a few days. Putting it on, she hoped to conjure up a bit of the spirit of the last time she wore it, an aura of contentment that would rise above any churning feelings about seeing Christian.

'Yours too,' she replies. 'You look magnificent.' Nicole is in a form-fitting gold dress with cut-outs down the front that show tiny bits of skin. Her personality is pure practicality, but her fashion sense is the opposite. Monday to Friday, nine to five, she has to wear nondescript office wear deemed appropriate for the financial world. Off the clock, she succumbs to every trend she fancies, from floaty coastal grandma dresses to nineties-inspired crop tops. Her current thing is early noughties bodycon, even for an old man pub on a frigid bank holiday.

'We're over here,' she says, ignoring the group of pensioners in the corner that look as though they might have a stroke at the sight of her high-street knock-off Hervé Léger bandage dress. She leads Thea over to a group of small round tables that have been pushed haphazardly together to create a longer one, where she sees Holly, Emma, girl Jo and boy Jo facing out from one side. Opposite them, she recognises the back of Mal, Harry and – here her stomach thuds – Christian's heads. Everyone's already arranged themselves into small gossipy groups-within-groups.

She needs to get it over with. Then she's seen him and it's done.

As they approach, Nicole discreetly squeezes her hand and lowers her voice to say, 'He's here, but you look great and he doesn't matter. He's the same. *Exactly* the same. Still telling that story about the bloke from Kasabian complimenting him on his guitar playing when we were at uni. I mean—'

As usual, Nicole knows how to get her heart rate down far enough to slap a smile on her face and hit the right vocal pitch with her 'Hello everyone!' Another swig of the Crémant gives her face something to do while the others trill greetings back. Christian turns around, painfully slowly. He gives her a tilt of his chin rather than an audible greeting.

Thea throws him the biggest, fakest smile she can muster and then squeezes her way around to the other side of the table, sitting down next to boy Jo, with Nicole sitting on her other side. Everyone is talking animatedly but she can tell from the self-conscious flickers of eye contact around her that they're all wondering how this scene will play out. Thea and Christian's will-they, won't-they trajectory was their course's three-year soap opera, so when they finally got together after graduation, it was widely assumed that their course mates would be getting an invite to their wedding a few years down the line.

But those that didn't know Christian had a rotating cast of flings on the side anyway. Thea still isn't too sure who knew what, and part of the reason she wanted to leave is because from five thousand miles away it's harder to interrogate your occasional friends about what they suspected and/or knew about your former boyfriend.

Thea steals a quick look at Christian while she sips her drink, trying to maintain the illusion of nonchalance while on high alert. She's tuned in to exactly where he is and who he's talking to, which right now is girl Jo.

He looks good. From Nicole, who has absorbed the information from the others, she knows that he's now social media lead at an agency with lots of cool fashion and lifestyle clients, and his signature look must fit right in there: black jeans, boots and fitted T-shirts in a palette of colours that runs no further than from ice white to gunmetal grey. His naturally blond hair, that is – although he has always denied it – 'helped along' by a few highlights, is curling at his ears, and his tightly maintained stubble is still in place, but Thea can see two new artful tattoos on his right biceps and a few earrings threaded up his ear that weren't there eighteen months ago. He's also sipping whiskey, while the rest of them drink pints or share the bottles of Crémant that Nicole has sold everyone on. With a year and a half's distance she can see that he's curated the best bits from all of his pop culture icons, filtered them through an internal algorithm and projected out his ultimate distillation of cool.

Even knowing all this, Thea finds herself feeling hideously uncool in comparison. Same as she's always felt since she met Christian at eighteen.

'Sweet little geek,' he would say in a sing-song tone when they first became friends. By the time they broke up, 'geeky' was no longer an affectionate compliment; instead, it was a way to dismiss her opinion, whether about an activity to do at the weekend (most museums fell into this category) or the music Thea liked.

'Are you all right?' Nicole asks, nudging her.

Nicole and Christian had never got on. From week one of their course, he'd referred to her as 'mum', a putdown that didn't stop him from mooching off her organisational skills when it suited him. But it did make things tricky when Thea nursed a crush on him for their entire degree, and would have been downright awkward when they got together two years after graduation, if Thea hadn't pulled the classic arsehole move of distancing herself from Nicole during the three-year relationship so she didn't have to deal with her boyfriend and her best friend in the same room that often. Or manage Nicole's reaction when Christian started to regularly put her down in front of people. That Thea thought the solution was to see less of her friend than to get rid of Christian is one more thing she's ashamed of from their relationship.

Thea nods that she's fine, even though she's feeling on the back foot. Christian is making a much better job of not looking in her direction than she is with him. Instead, he's telling girl Jo about a Brazilian hip-hop band his agency is collaborating with for a sneaker launch. Nicole rolls her eyes as she hears Christian say 'sneakers'.

'You're the one who's been living in the States. Why is *he* talking with a mid-Atlantic drawl?' she hisses.

'Shhhhh,' Thea hisses back, but Christian doesn't or is pretending not to, hear them.

'And stop looking at him. He's irrelevant.'

'I'm trying I promise, it's just an adrenal reaction. He's so *there*, right in my face, and I end up feeling so much lesser, like I always did.'

'You are *not* lesser,' Nicole snaps. 'Why everyone thinks he's cool I have no idea. It's so obviously all front.' She swigs her Crémant angrily.

'I know all of this, I know,' Thea agrees. 'And I don't feel like this all the time. It's so much easier when I'm in another country.'

'Speaking of,' Nicole says leaning in, gossip pose engaged, 'tell me *all* about Portland. I'm living my vicarious alternative life through you right now. Is it all small-batch beers, work mixers with people who have better tattoos than Christian and hiking to waterfalls at the weekend? Because it looks like that on Instagram.'

Thea can't help but laugh. 'Nic, you literally hate all of those things. You're the only person I know who didn't force themselves to like beer at uni just to fit in.'

Nicole shrugs. 'That's the beauty of a vicarious life. You're doing it so I don't have to. I bet you're in loads of meetings with high-powered content people, aren't you, and because they're American they appreciate you being direct, rather than slapping you down because a public schoolboy called Tristan didn't think of it first?'

'Is that guy still busting your balls?' Thea asks.

'Urgh, I'll tell you about Tristan and Charles later. You first.'

Thea takes a breath, and contemplates telling Nicole the truth, that the job isn't what it's cracked up to be and that Instagram isn't real life. But even though she's facing boy Jo and the pub is getting louder, she can't risk Christian being in earshot of any negativity.

'The agency is *a lot*,' she says instead, not lying exactly but flapping a hand to make Nicole interpret it however she wants, 'but I love Portland.' That part, is at least true. 'I've barely scratched the surface of getting to know the city, but the parts I've explored, I've loved. You've got to come and visit, Nic. And it's so close to so many other places we could go to – Seattle, San Francisco, Yosemite – if I can save up *any* money. I've booked every routine medical I can for while I'm back because even with health insurance through my job I can barely afford to go to the doctor's.'

Nicole nods in understanding. 'Those American hospital invoices showing the cost of having a baby that go viral are terrifying. But enough of that. Tell me more stories about Teddy. Are you still at happy hour all the time?'

'Too often,' Thea says, helping herself to some more Crémant. 'Teddy's supposed to be saving up for his and Jake's wedding but we spend all our crappy pay at the bar downstairs from the office.'

Teddy rescued Thea at the end of her first week at iDentity when Fuchsia had cut her dead while presenting in her first brainstorm and called her strategy for a social campaign 'kind of sweet, but disappointingly small scope'. Mortified, Thea had managed to hold out for thirty minutes after the session before going to the unisex toilets to cry. Teddy had been waiting for her next to the sinks when she came out.

'Fuchsia,' he announced, while surreptitiously checking they were alone, 'is a bitch. She has no good ideas in her head, and she will repackage seventy-five per cent of your ideas as her own during the time you work here. Not that one obviously, because it was too small scope.' He'd grinned at Thea's collapsing face. 'JOKING. She will definitely steal that one. However, seeing as you've been foolish enough to abandon the UK for a job that pays nothing and has terrible benefits, I can only assume you feel about the US the way I do about the UK and you desperately want to be here, so you need to stick it out long enough to get what you need out of it. And rule one is—' he handed her a wad of tissues – 'never let her see you're upset.'

'How many rules are there?' Thea had sniffed, accepting the tissues and pressing them against her eyes.

'Good question,' Teddy had replied, frowning slightly as he did the maths in his head. 'I'd say about fifteen, all of which I will explain to you tonight, at happy hour, where we will go the second Fuchsia leaves for the evening. Stay at your desk until I give you the sign.'

Thea had nodded, twisting the tissue in her hands, and feeling hopeful that even if the boss was a nightmare, not everyone at iDentity was like that.

Teddy had glanced at himself in the mirror and adjusted the collar of his shirt slightly. He was wearing a Hawaiian shirt over a vintage band T-shirt with tailored chino shorts. His reddish-blond hair was styled into a rockabilly quiff. 'You're from London, right?'

'Yes, East London. My whole family is there.'

'Then I think we will be friends. I love London. And I love people who can provide me with sofas to surf on when I finally make it over there even more.'

True to his word, when Fuchsia had slammed her laptop shut at 6.30 p.m., Teddy had waited exactly two minutes ('sometimes she gets to her car and realises she's forgotten something') before gesturing for Thea and the three other content executives to get up, before they ended up in Moon Hare, the bar next door to their office building, that did 2-4-1 cocktails every weekday from 4 p.m. until 8.30 p.m.

Three rounds in, he'd listed all of his iDentity Fuchsia survival rules, as the three other minions nodded along and added their own details.

'Do everything you can to get into a room with the clients,' Teddy had told her sagely over the woo woos that had formed their third round. 'Because then they can see your ideas in person, and she has to let you speak. It's harder for her to take credit after the fact, even if she will insist that it's "something you've been brainstorming together for some time".'

'Urgh,' said Kim, slurping the last of her drink up her straw. 'If you want to see cut-throat in action, remind me to tell you about the time Fuchsia told me the case studies in my deck for a palliative care provider weren't glamorous enough.'

Teddy had cackled and informed Thea that she was now in the circle of trust, which meant that she had to both keep quiet about everything she heard at happy hour while also coming to happy hour at least once a week. That was six months ago and Thea estimated that since then a good quarter of her sporadic salary payments had been spent at Moon Hare.

'You get used to Fuchsia,' Thea finishes, realising that the people around her and Nicole are also listening, including girl Jo, much to Christian's annoyance. 'Bosses, right?'

'I'm *so* jealous that you've got a US work visa,' Girl Jo says. 'I'd love to spend a couple of years working in California.'

'I'll probably be doing more overseas work trips from next year onwards,' Christian cuts in.

'Thea's there right now though,' says Nicole smoothly, thwarting his attempt to pull focus. 'The first one of us to get a job abroad.' She raises her glass in celebration.

'Not sure I'd fancy the USA full time,' Christian says in an offhand way. 'From the news, it looks like non-stop MAGA rallies.'

Nicole gives him a withering look. 'In Portland? One of the most liberal cities in America? Also—' she throws a covert look at girl Jo who'd told her – 'I thought you applied for a job over there and didn't get it.'

'The company was pretty boring and mainstream,' he fires back instantly. 'Not the sort of place I want to work.'

'More like, you didn't have Thea to steal ideas off for the application,' Nicole mutters. Thea kicks her under the table. She'd only told Nicole after they'd broken up about the ideas that Christian had used to get promoted, which had come entirely from a conversation he'd had with Thea. She wouldn't even have minded, except that Christian had belittled her ideas at the time – and never even said thank you.

Nicole had minded. She minded enough for both of them.

She gives Thea a look to say 'OK, I'll stop'. 'Do you think the US could be permanent, Thee?'

'I don't know.' The only permanent thing right now is the sense of always feeling like she is hanging on to her job – and therefore her working visa – by a thread. 'I hope so. It's nice to be home for a few days though and see my family. And obviously to watch some British telly with a decent cup of tea,' she adds.

'Ooh, what do they say about Harry and Meghan over there compared to how the papers cover them over here?' Nicole asks.

'Celebrity gossip,' Christian drawls in a derisive tone. 'Really?'

With one sentence, Thea is transported back to the final few months of their relationship, when everything she was interested in was dismissed as cheesy or frivolous. She'd feel anxious and sick trying to think of a topic that was acceptable, and she feels anxious and sick now as he pulls the same move on Nicole.

She senses him trying to catch her eye, as though he wants her to do what she'd have done in the past, which is look to him in agreement. It takes all of her willpower not to. For the three years they'd dated, it was a reflex to slide her eyes to him for approval, or, more likely, disapproval. By the end, he barely approved of anything, communicated by a stony expression or an imperceptible-to-anyone-else shake of the head.

Her heart starts to drum. She should stick up for Nicole and tell him to shut up, or roll her eyes at the others to show what an idiot he's being, but for some reason she can't. She's back to being the meek person she became around him.

'I'm sorry it's so beneath you,' Nicole says sarcastically, without any of Thea's concern about how Christian will react. 'But people – *I* – like celebrity gossip and I especially like hearing about celebrity gossip in different countries.' She turns back to boy Jo, who has a story about his mother's friend's French polisher who works for one of the palaces and what he said about the latest royal fall-out. Christian laughs slightly and takes a self-conscious swig of his whiskey at being dismissed.

Thea is still holding her breath waiting to see what will happen next, trying to remind herself that Christian's feelings are no longer her problem.

She listens to the rest of the anecdote, inwardly trying to get herself back on firmer footing. Nicole squeezes her hand and when boy Jo stops speaking, turns back to her.

'Ignore him,' she says in a low voice. 'What he thinks about anything doesn't matter. It never did, but it especially doesn't now. You've done so well in moving on so far, so keep going. Eventually you might even meet a hot American. Then you definitely won't want to come home.'

Thea thinks of Logan and her face starts to turn the colour of her dress. Nicole's eyes widen. 'You *have* met a hot American,' she shrieks in excitement, getting the attention of everyone around them. 'Who is he? Is he called Chip or Chuck or Chet or Chad?'

Thea doesn't want to say Logan's name. It feels too much like tempting fate. But she *has* met a hot American, and just because it's new doesn't mean it's not a thing. It also feels important to show to everyone here – including yes, Christian – that she's not still mooning after someone who made her feel as though she should count herself lucky to be with him and she'd never find anyone else.

'Logan,' she says, unable to suppress a smile. 'His name is Logan.' She makes the mistake of glancing towards Christian to see how he's reacting to it. He's smiling at her the way they teach you to in 'active listening' sessions at work. Phonily. Thea smiles back, harder.

'He's great,' she says. That seems like too few words to describe him, and she's dying to tell Nicole everything, but not here and not now. As she looks at Christian again she realises she doesn't want to use their story as a weapon against her ex. Logan is already more important than that. The secret knowledge that it's something, and it's hers, is better than any attempt at proving to Christian that she's won.

She arrives home just the right side of drunk at 11 p.m. Everyone is in bed. She fills a pint glass with water and takes it up to her room. Mum isn't one of those people who keeps their children's bedrooms intact as shrines to her offspring, even though her offspring haven't ever moved out for more than a few months at a time. As such, Thea's childhood bedroom has been decorated several times since that year in the flatshare. Since going to America, Mum has got caught up in the craze of small-space home office conversions – despite the fact that she's a nurse and doesn't work at home – so Thea's bedroom is now a tribute to tasteful storage solutions complete with labels made using one of those special machines. All of her stuff is still here – along with a narrow console desk and floating shelf housing the books that Mum deemed worthy of display (orange-spined Penguin paperbacks and a complete set of Jilly Coopers with nineties covers that Thea, Nan and Mum re-read endlessly) – it's just that it's mainly stored out of sight. The unfamiliarity means she feels a little bit like she's in an Airbnb, even if it's one of superhost standard.

Sipping her water, she gets into bed and goes over the rest of the evening. She and Christian didn't speak much more to each other directly, only ever as part of the wider group, before she and Nicole disappeared to buy a round and spent forty-five minutes catching up with each other at the bar. Still, the evening has left her rattled, knowing how easily Christian can get under her skin and make her feel as though she needs to curate her opinions before sharing them out loud. She feels basic around him in a way she doesn't in other situations. Well, aside from when Fuchsia is giving her feedback on her ideas.

'The solution is to *not* be around him,' Nicole had told her back at the pub. 'Well, that and to embrace basic-ness as the positive attribute that it is. I'm basic and I don't care!' She'd held her Crémant glass in the air, striking a pose in her skin-tight dress and pouting.

'You're drunk, is what you are,' Thea had replied, laughing.

'Being a lightweight is *so* basic, and I still don't care. I like my middle-of-the-road, but well-paying job and I love my uncool boyfriend—'

'Seb isn't uncool.'

'Ah bless you. He's so uncool, which almost makes him cool.' Nicole's voice had raised at the end as though she was asking a question. 'No, definitely not cool, but I don't think the best people are. All praise my totally basic, utterly lovable boyfriend.' Nicole had grimaced at her glass. 'Shall we go? I've had enough and soon everyone's going to start expecting me to sort out their Ubers.'

As they'd hugged at the tube station, heading in different directions, Nicole had reassured Thea that she now wouldn't have to see or hear from Christian for a minimum of two years.

'By the time the next Boxing Day drinks roll around you might have lived in Portland for almost three years, put down roots, maybe even with this *Logan* guy.'

She allows herself to think about Nicole's throwaway comment and then pulls up Logan's Instagram again. Earlier today she'd read some more of his posts, and those essay-length captions. There had been a lot to get through, and though he mainly talks about the clients' videos, sometimes he includes a snippet about his own family, which is an instant dopamine hit. She thumbs the screen back to the post she'd reached earlier, and then decides to go back further, curious to see his very first post.

It takes a while and keeps buffering, but as she goes further back, the grid loses its business feel and gives way to a few selfies and nights out with friends. His first post is an adorable university graduation photo where he's young, clean-shaven and preppy-looking. There are others from the same day and she spends a little time analysing the people in the photos, tapping on them to see who's tagged, including the guy she recognises from the Memento site as Felix. Back then he looks quite clean-cut, compared to the brooding hipster type she saw with Nan yesterday. His look is straight from Christian's cool playbook. A very attractive woman, @coco94, is also in the pictures, with her arms around Logan and them snuggled into each other in his gown, before some pictures of them plus other people at a meal. As she works her way forward in time, she's a recurring character. Coco94 is at every birthday, gig, a few holidays, and even Thanksgiving with his family. They're not all lovey-dovey pictures but they're clearly an item, usually leaning intimately together like two people who are more than comfortable with each other. The last shot she appears in is five years ago, when the business posts start, so it's hard to know when they broke up, because there's nothing personal once he moves onto business promo.

Was it around the same time? Or is it just a coincidence?

He sort of, maybe, alluded to a break-up at the hotel, didn't he? Or did she just project her own situation with Christian onto him?

Thea deleted her photos from her relationship with Christian the moment they broke up. She'd felt a bit dramatic at the time, as though she was an A-lister making a deliberate point for the superfans to pick up on – but she didn't want any trace of him while she tried to get over him. Plus, she knew that the carefully selected photos on there only showed half the story: one where she was happy and confident and didn't spend nights worrying about her boyfriend not answering his phone even though they'd arranged to see each other that night. Thea never appeared in Christian's social posts at all. He claimed it was because he wanted his page to be professional in case employers looked at it, but it didn't stop him posting moody selfies at things he regarded as spiritual pilgrimages: outside John Lennon's childhood home or Poet's Corner in Westminster, despite that, to Thea's knowledge, Christian never read poetry. She'd accepted it at the time, but through the lens of the break-up she realised it was so other women didn't know there was a girlfriend on the scene.

Remembering this, lodges a splinter of doubt under her skin.

Logan's page *is* professional and he's open about Coco94 right until he switches to a more businesslike profile, she tells herself. He made it clear he wants to see her again. She shouldn't be digging around in the archives of his social media at all, looking for what exactly?

But she's here, half-cut, and with the memory of Christian and all that he did in her mind.

Thea looks again at a picture from some sort of Superbowl party six years ago, scrutinising Logan's family members in turn. There are two boys – one who must be barely in secondary school at this point, and one aged about twenty. They must be his brothers. There's also an older woman with eyes the exact same colour as Logan's who must be his mum. And yes, there's Coco94 again. She has glossy blond hair and is wearing an American football shirt with a streak of black face paint under each eye as though she's one of the players.

Thea clicks on Coco94's handle, telling herself the whole time that once she can see for herself that the other woman's feed is full of her current boyfriend, girlfriend or other evidence of Logan's absence, the fluttery panic will subside. She'll put all memory of her psycho behaviour behind her and message him to pin down their coffee date.

Coco94 is stand-up paddleboarding in her profile picture. She looks tall and athletic, and Thea hates herself for determining that both of those things are victories against her own average-sized body. She reads her bio. It turns out Coco94's full name is Courtney Montgomery.

Sports scientist. Pilates instructor. Boston marathon completer. Love, light and Lululemon for life.

Bit cringey, but she shouldn't judge.

She scrolls down and clicks on Courtney's latest post, her heart hammering because Logan is *not* absent. He's in the shot, which was posted yesterday, on Christmas Day – and it's one of those pictures Thea thought only existed in American movies or reality shows about incredibly rich people.

It's a shot of an enormous, real Christmas tree in an entrance hall, decorated in tasteful white lights and baubles, the antithesis of the wonky tree with handcrafted decorations at Thea's parents'. Coco94 is standing in front of it with her right arm around Logan, beaming at the camera, and looking older than in the previous picture Thea looked at, but no less stunning. These days she wears her hair in a sharp bob. Logan is wearing the same jumper he wore to dinner with Thea, his smile beaming out, and his hair as scruffily dishevelled as she remembers. The sight of his handsome face and the crinkles around his eyes that she knows he gets when he's happy registers as a thud in her stomach.

Her insides prickle with suspicion, panic spreading like a red-wine stain into a carpet.

She reads the caption.

'Obligatory childhood sweetheart shot!' There's a row of hearts next to it.

In Coco's left hand she's holding a glass of fizz, which, from the general vibe of the photo, Thea assumes is Champagne and not Crémant. Clearly visible on her fourth finger, is the most enormous diamond ring Thea has ever seen.

And worse than *that*, if it could get any worse at this point, is the first comment beneath the photo, from @logan_beechwood.

It reads, 'Love you Court!'

Chapter Nine

Blocked.

Both of them. Even though Coco94 has no idea of her existence. Thea's hands shake as she does it, sick humiliation swirling around in her stomach, blending with every memory of Christian taking her for a mug as his phone pinged with messages from a new 'friend' she'd never previously heard of.

Logan doesn't just have a girlfriend – he has a fiancée. And a childhood sweetheart no less. One with an engagement ring so big it resides in a different postcode to the rest of her hand, and a shared history with Logan and his family that reaches back years. He's doesn't just make movies about people's treasured memories, he's living in one of his own films.

How could she be so stupid? *Again.*

She'd been searching for Logan's flaw during dinner, but she hadn't expected him to be actively keeping something like that from her. OK, it wasn't a date, but who doesn't 'drop in' a mention of their partner if they have one. All it would have taken would have been a 'Sure, let's share the cost of the room, but I just have to text my

FIANCÉE quickly to tell her my flight doesn't get in until tomorrow'. Thea has worked with men who won't walk alongside her to Pret without ensuring she's aware they're taken, lest she gets the wrong impression.

Tears bubble up. Not just of hurt but ones that burn with a bitter anger. Why hadn't he just *said* when they were in the double-booked hotel room that he was with someone? Or when she'd babbled on about her break-up? That was the moment to drop in a smug mention of his perfect coupledom. But he said nothing. Because he didn't want her to know.

And then he kissed her.

Or she kissed him.

Same difference.

She thinks about the picture again. Was it taken at Logan's parents' house or hers? Not that it matters. It all oozes money and breeding, and on that front they're most likely well matched. Logan was *much* more comfortable in The Opulent's luxurious surroundings than Thea was.

Rich, she realises, feeling inadequate as well as idiotic. He's rich.

Thea contemplates her own family home. She knows that three bedrooms, with the little study room off the living room converted into a room for Nan, is *huge* by London standards, and she also knows that her parents' corner of Zone 3 has increased exponentially in value from the working-class, first-time buyers' price her parents had paid for it in 1989, when pre-gentrification East London was considered 'a bit rough' and houses cost about fifty pence.

Dad's a cab driver and Mum's a nurse, both solid, reliable incomes but not ones that would stand a chance of being able to buy this place now. If they were to sell it, they'd be able to downsize somewhere in the suburbs with money to live off during their retirement. In property terms they're more than comfortable, and Thea and Kit are lucky to have a low- to no-rent option at their disposal.

But she doesn't know anyone with a hallway big enough to house a *Real Housewives*-sized Christmas tree, or who can buy an engagement ring rock so large it looks like costume jewellery. Nan and Grandad rented the pub and Dad is the first generation of his family to own his home. Having grown up in count-every-penny poverty, Nan's always been careful with money and is allergic to any sort of debt. Kit's profligacy makes her physically uncomfortable – Thea has more than once seen her sit on her hands when he's taken something new and wildly expensive out of its box to show them.

She and Logan are obviously from different worlds. If she felt off-kilter when she was with Christian because he was several echelons cooler than she was, then trying to fit in to a family so much further up the class ladder would have been even more alienating. It probably wouldn't have worked anyway.

The knowledge is no comfort at all.

Thea contemplates unblocking Logan for long enough to send him a 'gotcha' message, telling him exactly what she thinks of him and his lying, cheating, kissing face. Instead she sags against the four thousand scatter cushions her mum has arranged on her bed, defeated. If he feels cornered, he'll only tell her she's got it all wrong, and he'd meant they should meet up as friends, before implying she's crazy, or worse, actually wanting to meet up as friends.

She doesn't want to be his friend.

She wants to feel the way she did when they kissed at the airport, as though there's potential for something new, after the disaster that was Christian. For a couple of days she got to feel as though she could connect with someone else, someone straightforward. She should be grateful for that, but it's no consolation.

He dislodged Christian, yes, but the trouble is, now Logan is wedged in her brain instead. His face comes back to her: the curve of his jaw through the bristles of his beard, the cheeky glint in those dark blue eyes; the look on his face as they said goodbye at the airport. All infused with hope. Until it was shown to be an illusion.

It was *one* night and it'll fade, she assures herself, as her tipsiness trips over into the beginnings of hangover dread. And a hell of a lot faster than she'll pay off the instalments to Nan's credit card.

Chapter Ten

Four days later, on Friday afternoon, Thea waits in Portland Airport's pick-up zone for Teddy. It's minus one and she's shivering, but it's not just from the cold and jet lag. Passing through the arrival zone and seeing the signs directing passengers to the taxi rank, the MAX Light Rail station and the airport hotel pick-up zones triggered a physical response, a muscle memory of the last time she was here, when a chaotic situation had briefly become one of the happiest episodes of her life.

Before it had curdled.

For the remainder of her Christmas break at home she had kept her phone in a separate room to stop her from compulsively checking it or being tempted to unblock Logan.

The trip to the spa had helped. Their 'digital detox' package involved having to hand over their phones in the morning upon arrival, before being pummelled and buffed by strong, smiling massage therapists and then handed over to the afternoon tea team. To stop the looping thoughts of Logan, Thea had swum lengths in the pool until she was physically incapable of doing any more and then steamed and sweated him out of her head. As predicted, Mum was wound so tight on the way there about the prospect of being 'waited on' that she had somehow come out of her 'de-stress massage' tenser than when she went in ('I was worrying about whether I was supposed to talk or not and then about the poor woman having to deal with my floppy bits, and then that she was getting tired massaging my back and shoulders'), while Nan spent most of the day looking tiny, wrapped in her enormous fluffy white robe and prostrate on a lounger in the relaxation room listening to her audiobook. 'No, thanks. I'm just chilling out, darling,' she'd say when Thea asked if she wanted to come in the jacuzzi. She'd managed to persuade her to come in the sauna for a few minutes, her too-loose swimming costume emphasising her birdlike angles, but she'd felt woozy after only a couple of minutes. Thea had helped her out, cursing herself later for being so pushy when Nan barely touched the cakes during the afternoon tea.

As Kit had driven them all home – Dad chattering about the quality of the golf course, Mum worrying if she'd tipped everyone enough and raving about the ostentatious Christmas decoration displays in the lobby – Nan had fallen asleep almost immediately, waking up disorientated as they reached the house. Thea had asked Mum if they should be worried, but Mum had instantly replied that not everyone could gallivant to different continents without getting a bit tired, which simultaneously made her feel guilty for living abroad and deflected attention from the question.

'TB!' Teddy winds down the driver's window and screams over the sound of the music blaring as he pulls in in her car. As ever, his hazel eyes are glinting with mischief. He leans over and opens the passenger door for her to get in.

'Bad news,' he says, 'I can't get the trunk to open from the outside, so you'll have to load your bag via the backseat.'

'Urgh, this car,' Thea groans, momentarily forgetting about both Logan and Nan. She'd bought the ancient Toyota Corolla from a web listing by a family who was offloading their late grandfather's effects. The only thing it had going for it, besides its relatively low mileage, was that she could afford to buy it. Everything else was gradually going wrong, some in more urgent need of fixing than others (a stuck boot, no; an engine that kept cutting out while she was driving, yes), something Teddy knew all too well as he owned a similarly decrepit rust-bucket VW. Living only a few blocks from each other, they had taken to carpooling, with the designated driver decided by whose unreliable ride was functioning at any given time.

'On the bright side, the doors are still working,' Teddy reminds her, while pulling away from the kerb. 'And that weird rattling noise stopped completely once I was an hour away from Seattle.' He turns the French hip-hop down so she can enjoy the engine's relative quiet. Teddy prefers music in languages other than English, so he doesn't get hung up on 'the unreservedly terrible lyrics'. Thea has suggested instrumental music before, but he thinks that's pretentious.

'Nice. Hopefully it's not an ominous silence,' she adds.

'Mine's out of the shop tomorrow so we're covered,' he shrugs. 'Anyway, tell me about your holidays. Did you see the evil ex? More importantly did you walk around in the snow in Trafalgar Square and go to Hamleys?'

'Teddy, only an idiot would go to Hamleys over Christmas. Especially if they don't have kids. And there was no snow. It was just dank and cold, exactly like it is here. When you come over, I'll take you to all the places that haven't appeared in a Richard Curtis film so you can see the real London.'

'Deal, but only if you also take me to all the places that *have* appeared in a Richard Curtis film,' Teddy huffs, merging onto the freeway.

'I'm going to have to. Otherwise, you'll just be gutted that it's nowhere near as magical and otherworldly as you think it is. The stuff you don't see in Richard Curtis movies includes a guy coming out of the pub on the corner of my parents' road and taking a piss right in front of their wall a couple of days ago. He just waved when my dad banged on the window.'

'This is exactly the sort of stuff I *don't* want to hear. I can see randoms pissing in Portland. However, you are swerving the real question. The evil ex, how did it go?'

Thea sighs.

'That good, huh?'

'Intellectually, I know my life is a hundred times better without him in it.'

'But . . .' Teddy prompts.

'But then I see him and somehow he manages to make me feel as though I'm lame and that if I was somehow better, cooler and less me-like I'd have kept him interested.'

'The guy is toxic male narcissism at its absolute most base form,' Teddy mutters. 'And that is the oldest but most effective trick in the book. Prick. You need to just not be around him. Ever.'

'That's what Nicole said.'

'I for one would have banned him from my seasonal drinks.'

'It's not Nicole's fault. I probably shouldn't have gone. I thought I'd be Christian neutral by now and was going to prove it to myself.'

'I get it. Proven indifference is *the dream*. Did I tell you I once swiped onto my worst ex on Grindr and I was so over him that I sent a message saying "lol". I didn't even feel the need to tell him that his profile picture was truly heinous. Emotional maturity at its finest.'

Thea laughs, which morphs into another sigh. 'I think meeting that guy Logan at the airport lulled me into a false sense of Christian security.' Thea had filled Teddy in on the highlights before her night at the pub, but as she's been avoiding her phone, and her phone contacts ever since, she hasn't updated him about the fact that he's engaged.

'A hot guy, a five-star-hotel meet cute and an arrangement to pick things up when you're back would definitely do that.' Teddy swerves around the car in front. Thea winces, grabbing on to the dashboard. Teddy drives as though he's being pursued, which is even more terrifying in a car that is averse to sudden manoeuvres. 'So why the sigh?'

'Because it turns out the hot guy isn't actually available and any arrangement to see each other will be behind the back of the fiancée he has stashed back home in Boston.'

'Nooooo!' Teddy turns to her to display the full breadth of the disapproval on his face.

'The road, Teddy, watch the road!' Thea shrieks. He snaps back to attention before Thea dares continue.

'Plus, his betrothed looks like the lovechild of Hailey Bieber and Gwyneth Paltrow, and she has an engagement ring that's probably worth as much as both our apartments put together. To buy, not to rent, in case I need to make that clear.'

'Fuck.' Teddy bangs the steering wheel with one hand. 'FUCK,' he says again. 'And he kissed you at the airport? How could he do that? I knew it was too good to be true. I *knew* it.'

'Did you?' Thea asks miserably. 'You didn't say that at the time. Anyway, you were right, it was. Logan is another arsehole who can't be trusted. What if *all* guys are like that and I'll be alone forever?'

Teddy overtakes a truck on the inside. 'Thea, you're spiralling. While, yes, this would have been an amazing, if sickening, story to tell everyone about how you met – it's *one* guy. Not all guys are liars and cheats. You've just had bad luck. It's the perfect time to reinstall the apps and get back out there. Have some fun. Meet some guys. Nice ones.'

Thea's heart sinks. 'By nice you mean boring, beige flag men.'

'NO!' Teddy brakes hard, as a car pulls in front of him. 'Nice guys are not necessarily boring. That's years of being conditioned by pretentious Christian who has made you internalise that nice is uncool. Honestly!'

Christian *was* pretentious, but he also had an energy that made you want to be in his gravity field.

'He never said nice was uncool,' Thea argues stubbornly, though she admits 'normal' was one of his biggest insults, usually said with just enough humour to make people think he was joking. He wasn't.

'And yet somehow you have absorbed it as a truth. We need to exorcise his influence. Anyway, fine. If you have already written off *everyone*—' he shoots her a not-angry-but-disappointed look so lingering that Thea panics again – 'on the apps, then at least let me set you up. Jake knows a tonne of straight guys from work. Tech nerds, yes, but cute, and not as spectrum-y as you'd expect. Well, not all of them.'

He clocks the look on Thea's face. 'Oh, come on, one date. Consider it a palate cleanser. So that the last date you went on wasn't with a no-good cheat who turned out to be engaged.'

'It wasn't a date,' Thea says automatically, but there's no bite to it. 'Fine. But no one that thinks knowing a lot about Radiohead is a substitute for having a personality. Or Marvel. Or Star Wars. And no one that wants to go to an immersive theatre experience. Or in fact anything immersive.'

She thinks back to the night with Logan again. She can't help it. The perfect dinner date that wasn't a date.

She wonders if he's even realised that she's blocked him yet, or if the reunion with Coco94 blasted away any residual memory of her. Tears prick at her eyes. She swipes at them angrily.

It's the long-haul flight making her over-emotional, nothing more.

'Agreed,' Teddy says happily, his eyes on the road for once. 'Now, do not mope. This is an anti-mope plan. Jake and I will narrow down the contenders when I get home. Just to be clear though, *Game of Thrones* fan, yes or no?'

'Define "fan" and I'll see,' Thea snaps, already weary at the thought of this apparently palate-cleansing date.

She fiddles with her phone as a distraction and sees a voice note from Nan. Saying goodbye to her had been awful, and Thea had felt even worse for knowing she'd been rubbish company since Boxing Day and the Logan revelation. She turns Teddy's music off completely and presses play, filling the car with Nan's East End burr. It seems all at odds with the American landscape zipping past outside: wide highways dotted with mini malls and giant billboards advertising divorce lawyers and life-changing liposuction; businesses with 'HAPPY HOLIDAYS' signs blinking on and off that seem incongruous now Christmas is over and there's nothing to look forward to.

'*Hello darling, hope you got back all right. We miss you already.*'

Nan's voice sounds wavery and thin. Old. Or is she just trying to disguise the fact that she's missing Thea? Either way, it's threatening to tip Thea over the edge.

'*I'm just sending this message to tell you that this fella—*' there's nothing wavery about that part; she says 'fella' the way someone else might say 'Donald Trump' – '*isn't worth getting yourself all upset about. I know you and it must be stirring up how you felt when you found out about Christian, but remember: this is just some chancer and he didn't get one over on you. You found out about him before it went any further, and you don't need him, or* any *bloke. Put it behind you and concentrate on your job and your friends. Don't let this spoil it. You've got a great opportunity living in America. Get Teddy to take you to happy hour and forget about it.*'

'Yes, Nan,' Teddy agrees gravely.

'*You take care of yourself. Tada, love.*'

Thea's hands are shaking slightly as she clicks the screen off at the side. She stares out of the window at the darkening afternoon. Nan's right. She found out before it went any further. Saved herself from an even bigger disappointment when she was invested enough to have memories of him intertwined with her Portland life, or to have started to fall in love with him. One (mainly) platonic night in an airport hotel is not real life.

That's what she tells herself anyway, as Teddy chatters on about how he can't wait to meet Nan in person as he feels they're spiritually very similar. The trouble is, in the brief time she's known Logan, she has already fallen hard.

Chapter Eleven

Why is this guy so available? Thea texts to Teddy, suspicious.

On a Saturday AND on New Year's Eve. That's prime social life real estate. Why is he so willing to give it up for a blind date?

True to his word, Teddy has set Thea up with one of Jake's colleagues. He's some sort of app developer at the start-up Jake works for. Most of the job titles at Jake's place are prefixed with 'some sort' because neither she nor Teddy ever understand what they do.

After he dropped her off yesterday afternoon, Teddy messaged at 10 p.m. saying Jake had suggested Billy, 32, from San Francisco as her palate-cleansing date. Reluctantly Thea agreed to let him pass on her number and almost instantaneously Billy got in touch, asking if she wanted to meet up. As Thea was holding her phone in her hand at the time, willing herself not to Google Logan+Beechwood+Coco, she'd replied yes, purely to distract herself. It was a decision that felt spontaneous and moderately empowering at the time, but when Billy had suggested the next morning AKA New Year's Eve, the feeling congealed into a sickly pit-of-stomach buyer's remorse. The same one she gets from an impulsive online delivery full of directional jeans shapes ordered while kidding herself that she's a completely different type of person than she actually is.

She went with it though, replaying Nan's message about making the best of things and sporadically texting Teddy for reassurance. Now, as she rounds the corner to the coffee cart at the north entrance to Washington Park, the spot they have agreed to meet, she can't stop peppering him with texts.

This feels like a very bad idea. We've barely even exchanged any messages.

The texts between her and Billy have been short and perfunctory. A greeting and a suggestion that they meet, followed up by a time and a place when Thea agreed. Thea's decided he's either efficient enough to rival Nicole or a psychopath. Nicole, obviously, *loves* the sound of him:

Too bad. He'll already be waiting for you. I, for one, admire his get up and go in getting this show on the road. Who needs a pen-pal? Just see if there's chemistry and I'll see you for NYE drinks later.

Thea freezes on the spot as she sees a man next to the coffee cart, holding a cup in each hand. The first thing she notices is that he's hovering awkwardly enough that it can only be someone waiting for a person they're not one hundred per cent sure is going to turn up. The second is that he is *breathtakingly* good-looking. Tall, clean-shaven, with swept-back blondish hair and an overall clean-cut sort of a look that comes down on the side of Abercrombie model rather than normcore. He's wearing a bulky puffer coat and a big, green scarf, above stone-coloured chinos. As she approaches, he smiles widely, showing off teeth so straight and white you could use them to find your keys in the dark. Thea prays that this guy isn't waiting for some *other* date, and her own rendezvous isn't about to step out from the sidelines, puncturing her chance of meeting this – the only correct word for it – *hunk* of a man.

'Hey, I'm Billy.' Billy steps forward as though to hug her, registers the two cups in his hands, and steps back again, shaking them gently in an approximation of a wave instead. He's wearing green gloves that match his scarf. 'Are you Thea?'

'Yes, Thea,' she confirms. She waves back, and he holds out one of the cups. Thea fights the urge to text Teddy and thank him, but he'll only be offended at the suggestion he wouldn't have applied some quality control.

'I got you a vanilla latte. Jake told me that's your drink.' Thea has only ever had precisely one vanilla latte in Jake's presence, but she appreciates the gesture all the same.

'Thank you,' she replies. 'Shall we walk?'

In their scant date arrangements, Billy had suggested grabbing coffee and following the Washington Park trails for as long as they could stand the cold and the exertion, and Thea had agreed. Walking doesn't count as an activity date, as it's a life necessity. She's also grateful he hasn't suggested a bike ride, because that's a distinct possibility in a city like Portland. As someone who won't risk riding a bike in London because she considers it taking her life in her hands, the three-lane roads – on the wrong side – that come as standard over here haven't done anything to convince her that she's wrong.

Billy starts to walk, easy loping steps that he speeds up a bit and matches to Thea's own more-rushed pace. She was only back at home for a few days, but the muscle memory of the London pace has kicked back in. She forces herself to slow down. Once on a level with him, she's grateful she has to look where she's going to stop her gazing at Billy's chiselled profile in disbelief. It crosses her mind that Teddy has hired a male escort to boost her self-esteem and Billy isn't a real blind date at all. Only the fact that Teddy's as broke as she is, and therefore can't afford an escort, convinces her he can't be.

'Do you live locally?' Billy asks, between sips of his drink.

'Pretty much,' she replies. 'Nob Hill.' Six months in, she can just about say it without a childish snigger, followed by an explanation to the enquiring American as to why that word is funny.

If Thea was being specific, she'd say the even funnier 'arse end of Nob Hill', because she lives on the absolute southernmost point you can be and still technically be within the hip Nob Hill region on Google Maps.

When she'd been looking for somewhere to rent, she honed her search into four or five different neighbourhoods that she'd researched online, before quickly realising that she couldn't afford to live in any of them. Then she'd seen a studio in a building on Burnside Street that from the outside looked like the one from *Friends* (without a Central Perk equivalent downstairs – although there's a Taco Bell and a Subway along the same block). She was drawn to it, as well as the price tag, which stood at 65 per cent of her monthly earnings, rather than 120 per cent like everywhere else she'd found. In total, it measures 500 sq. ft – nothing like the spacious *Friends* apartment – has a lone window on one side, a bed that is also the sofa, and a tiny, drab fitted kitchen that runs more to the 'eighties MDF' side of vintage than mid-century modern. But it's only a short drive to iDentity's downtown office, and as she discovered after that first happy hour, Teddy and Jake are nearby, a few blocks north and within the actual, cool bit of Nob Hill. She's also close to Washington Park and its touristy, but lovely, Japanese and Rose Gardens, for when she wants to escape the traffic, mini malls and Irish bars that stretch along her road. Which isn't that often, because everything remotely American is still a charming novelty. Her apartment is kind of crappy, but it's hers and she loves it, and she loves her nascent life here. It feels as though she's just getting started, in the best possible way.

'Whereabouts are you?' she asks in return. 'And do you live alone?'

'I'm in Hawthorne, with a couple of roommates. I moved in after breaking up with my ex last year.'

See, Thea thinks. That's how you casually work your relationship status into conversation. It's a point in Billy's favour, but only serves to remind her who she's comparing him to. She forces herself to concentrate on the date at hand. 'And how was your holiday season?'

They walk and swap Christmas stories. Billy spent the holidays in San Francisco with family before coming back to work a couple of days ago. He asks her about her own Christmas, whereabouts in London she's from, and why she moved over to the States. He tells her he likes *Game of Thrones*, but only as a casual fan. He hardly ever comments on the fan sites he follows.

It's all . . . fine. She keeps stealing little glances at his square jaw as he talks, surprised afresh every time she registers just how handsome he is. He works in tech, only has good things to say about Jake and has no obvious Flaw. He's attentive, respectful and nice – maybe a little earnest from the way he tells her a story about choosing a new surround-sound system for his apartment as though it was a really weighty decision. But is too earnest a bad sign? Probably not, but she can't help comparing him to Logan, who was teasing and warm. As she shuts the thought down, another one bubbles up: even Christian was warm when he wanted to be.

Comparing him negatively to Christian: this is definitely not a good sign.

By the time they reach the rose garden she realises she just doesn't fancy Billy. It feels like a crime considering the way he looks, but while he seems nice enough, for her there's no chemistry. There's nothing wrong with him, but there isn't that undefinable allure either. They wander around some more, under thin cold clouds and sunlight that's struggling to get going. As they wind through different paths, Thea politely answers questions about how long she's been in the US and how long she sees herself staying. She tries to infuse her answers with the personality she knows she has in there somewhere, or even a bit of the candour she showed Logan before Christmas – after all, the questions come from the same getting-to-know-you script – but this time around it feels a bit like a job interview and her responses match her mood. She's wooden and flat, and not worrying *at all* what Billy in turn is thinking about her, which confirms that on her end there's no spark. He's like human morphine, numbing, but attractively so. Although that implies that he's addictive when to her, he's not. Maybe if they went and had an alcoholic drink at, er, eleven in the morning, she might fancy him then? That's when she knows for sure she's clutching at straws.

All of a sudden, she trips on an uneven bit of ground, stubbing her foot. 'Shit!' Her coffee cup flies out of her hand and Billy grabs her arm to steady her. She grabs him back gratefully before righting herself. 'Thanks,' she says. Being on the receiving end of his physical touch hasn't given rise to any change of feelings for her. She could almost cry in disappointment, because she registers next, Billy is still holding on to her arm and looking at her a bit expectantly.

She looks up at all six foot three of him and he has a strange look on his face, sort of pursed-lipped and attentive.

'Say another curse word,' he says, a little smile gleaming on his mouth.

'What?' Thea chokes out a laugh. 'Did I even ... oh, when I fell.'

'I love how swear-words sound in a British accent,' Billy says. He arranges his face into a mouthful of marbles expression. 'Shit. Fuck. Cunt. It sounds so cute, and so—' he flicks a little glance at her – 'naughty.'

Thea tries not to visibly cringe. So, the Flaw is curse word kink. She's embarrassed. Both for him and at the situation. She has nothing *against* swearing and she quite loves a well-chosen F-bomb. She even appreciates Americans enjoying a good old British swear like 'wanker' or 'bollocks', both of which cause hysterics and Dame Maggie Smith impressions when she uses them at happy hour (mainly in relation to Fuchsia). But this isn't enjoyment. It's weirdly pressured. Less, swearing for laughs and more as some sort of – and now she has to stop herself shuddering – foreplay. Does she want to give the impression she's up for that?

Before she can decide what to do, Billy closes in and kisses her, right there on the path. His cheeks are cold, his lips are lukewarm, and his mouth is too wet and too big. It's as unpleasant as putting her jeans on too soon after moisturising her legs. And it's leaving her similarly cold. She couldn't be less in the moment. This is the absolute antithesis of her kiss with Logan on Christmas Eve and the contrast makes her almost teary. She does nothing to reciprocate, thinking that's the quickest way to get it over with quickly, but what feels like hours later it shows no sign of ending. She starts to consider her exit strategy when Billy begins to wind an arm up her back, too polite to just jump away but needing this situation to be over, now.

She hears the thumping tread of a runner coming along the path towards them.

'Excuse me,' a voice says. It gives her the excuse she needs to break away from Billy, and she does it with a grateful gasp, stepping back to let the runner through.

'Fuck!' she exclaims without thinking.

Billy probably thinks she's sworn again to whip him into a passionate frenzy. But she's not looking at him or the creepy, aroused look her cursing has no doubt brought to his face. She's looking at the jogger, who hasn't returned her gaze yet. It's like the moment you realise that you've brushed a nettle, right before the sting kicks in.

The jogger lifts his eyes to hers, and they widen. He stops, stock still.

'Thea?' The word sounds involuntary, as though it has burst out without his permission.

Thea opens her mouth to respond but before she can, before she can even process what she'd say in this situation, Logan's eyebrows rise, and he turns his gaze to Billy before looking back to her again, his blue eyes calcified. He gives her a cold nod of recognition and starts to move again, running through the channel between Thea and Billy and continuing on his way.

Chapter Twelve

Two days later, the moment is still looping in Thea's head like a Netflix preview autoplay whenever she doesn't stuff her brain with a distraction. Sunday promised to be interminable, until the building WhatsApp group asked for volunteers for a neighbourhood 'Sunday Spruce', and she spent seven hours picking litter, assisting with small clear-out tasks for elderly tenants and tidying flowerbeds ready for spring planting: busywork with a side of small talk, all of which kept her away from the post-date message on her phone from Billy that she couldn't even bring herself to open, and the look on Logan's face when he clocked her in the park. The side effect of getting to know her neighbours and feeling as though she's beginning to be part of the community was an added bonus.

Today, her first day back at work after the holidays, she intends to numb herself via Excel spreadsheet before retiring to happy hour with Teddy and the others. All the decorations have been long taken down; and in a few days even the 'Happy New Year' email greetings will taper off.

From the co-working space kitchen comes the sound of banging, before an almighty crash and the sound of Fuchsia screaming, 'FUCK!'

Sitting at their desks in the open-plan workspace around the corner, Teddy, Thea, and the other account executives Maeve, Ernie and Kim exchange quick glances between them, a pentangle of responsibility shifting as to whose turn it is to go and defuse Fuchsia like a bomb. Despite the so-called 'flat hierarchy' floorplan configuration, where they were all supposed to sit together, Fuchsia has had dividing walls erected so that she has her own private office, and she usually stays there unless she wants something. Which suits the others. Because whenever she uses the coffee machine in the floor's communal kitchen – shared with the other businesses and start-ups in their building – someone ends up having to call a technician.

'Thea, would you mind?' Ernie says in the end, against which Thea is in no position to argue as she's the newest and lowliest recruit. Turns out there's no such thing as a flat hierarchy. Teddy shoots her a look of solidarity as she tiptoes around the corner. Fuchsia is pressing every button on the machine with the gusto of a toddler presented with a panel of lift buttons. Steam is shrieking out of the milk-frothing nozzle, dangerously close to Fuchsia's bare arm.

'Fuchsia! I was just going to make myself a coffee,' Thea says in a jolly voice she doesn't feel. Teddy's second rule was never showing you're intimidated, which is nigh on impossible when you spend most of each day on the verge of a boss-triggered nervo. 'Let me get yours too.' She guides her out of the way, ignoring the speckles of milk that have dried down the side of Fuchsia's very expensive short-sleeved polo-neck knitted tank top. Fuchsia's 'signature look' is a leather pencil skirt, fine black knits, with her hair pulled back into a tight mahogany bun and a pair of severe Michael Caine-style glasses frames. It's sort of Elizabeth Holmes meets Jenna Lyons, inspiration-wise. Thea tries not to think about the Elizabeth Holmes part every month when she's holding her breath for payday.

'I don't know who designs these machines,' Fuchsia bitches. 'And the coffee is always terrible.' Everyone else raves about the quality of this machine – the CEO of the e-bike start-up down the corridor personally invested in the brand because he was so passionate about it – but Thea suspects Fuchsia doesn't like it because she is incapable of using it and refuses to download the instruction booklet. She just clenches her lips together and nods in non-verbal agreement. Fuchsia is probably only in her late thirties but she behaves as though she's been around the business world for decades. Thea suspects most boomers would be ashamed of having tech know-how as terrible as her.

'Actually, I'd rather have coffee from Roasters, can you grab me one?' Fuchsia says the second Thea gets the machine working.

Thea inwardly screams. Not only does she now have to head four blocks down the street in the morning's torrential rain, but she knows from experience that Fuchsia will neither offer her any money for the coffee nor pay her back. Thea broached the subject when she was three months and about a hundred dollars' worth of coffee into the job and was subject to her frostiest, most stepped-over-the-line glare. It was as though she'd asked to sleep over at Fuchsia's house.

So instead of 'Get it yourself you lazy incompetent cow' she replies, 'Sure,' snaps off the coffee machine to avoid any other Fuchsia-related damage (and the fallout from the other businesses when it breaks) and turns to go and fetch the rain poncho still dripping on the back of her chair from the dash from the cheap car park that she and Teddy did only thirty minutes ago.

'We've got that new client meeting at ten, so send me the prelim notes,' Fuchsia says, just as she rounds the corner. Thea reverses back into the kitchen.

'What?' Thea is wrong-footed. Again.

'It should be in your diary.'

Another of Fuchsia's organisational black holes is failing to add events to the team calendar. There's every chance she tried and failed, but there's also every chance she didn't bother to start off with, or has added it to Teddy or Maeve's calendars instead. It's 9.30 a.m. now so she needs to fetch coffee *and* make client notes for the mystery client all in half an hour.

'I haven't had any meetings put in for today other than the team catch-up this afternoon,' Thea says. 'I kept checking my inbox over Christmas but I didn't see anything there.' Panic ripples through her. She never gets to go to client meetings and now she's going to one to which she's woefully underprepared. But she doesn't want to lose the opportunity completely. She hears Teddy's voice in her head. 'Just get in the room.'

'I'm of course available to attend though,' she says. 'What's the pitch?'

Fuchsia scrunches her face up and sighs. 'I don't need you to be client-facing, but I want a deck of ideas ready to go. This has been in the pipeline since pre-Christmas, but never mind.' She shoots Thea a disappointed look as though to say 'another ball dropped'. 'I'll pick it up with Ernie.'

'I can work up some ideas right now,' Thea stammers. 'I'm happy to.' She doesn't bother to argue that this is the first she's heard about it (rule #3), and instead scrambles to salvage the situation so that she can contribute something – anything – that might take her away from the admin she's usually tasked with and into a creative pitch.

'What I need right now is that coffee. Especially if I'm the only person with any clear ideas for the direction of this company's marketing and social materials.' She turns on her spike-heel and stalks off back to her office. Thea had thought her so cool at her interview. Which she is. It's just a shame she's also a heinous rage demon.

Thea rushes back to her desk and grabs her waterproof. 'Did anyone get a reminder about a new client pitch this morning?' she hisses. Fuchsia may have constructed her own walls but they're too thin to risk speaking at normal volume.

Four stricken sets of eyes look back at her. Heads shake.

'Well, there is one. I know zero details but apparently I've already messed up, and you, Ernie, are next on the hitlist.'

Ernie starts, a panic flush slowly rising from his neck onto his face. 'What? Did she say the name of the company at least?'

'Nope. She claims it has been in the diary since pre-Christmas if that's any help.'

Ernie wrinkles his face up as he thinks. 'She mentioned an exercise brand back in November but I haven't heard anything since.'

'Or that film guy?' Maeve chips in. 'I definitely had a follow-up flag for that, but it's disappeared.'

'How about the sexual smoothie people?' Teddy adds. 'Did that go anywhere?'

'The what?' says Thea. 'I don't have time to hear about them now. I'll leave it with you guys to work out who the client is as I'm already jettisoned from the project, even though I knew nothing about it. I have to get coffee.'

'Where from?' Kim asks.

'Roasters,' Thea groans. 'Always the one furthest away when the weather is like this.'

'Oh but – but—' Kim scrabbles around in her desk drawer – 'the loyalty card is full for that one, so it's a freebie!'

Kim passes the card full of stamps across to Ernie who passes it to Teddy, who passes it to Thea. It was Kim who came up with the bright idea of pooling loyalty cards for every coffee shop and café in the area, so that they can at least save *some* money when it comes to Fuchsia's freeloading. Recent talk has turned to the establishment of a coffee kitty to be used for Fuchsia's coffees so that whoever she's using as her dedicated coffee monitor at the time – currently Thea – doesn't take a disproportionate financial hit. Thea is aware of how insane this is, and has buried it in a mental file never to be brought up with Nan, who once took her local branch of Costa to task over the price of a cup of tea and vowed never to return.

Thea snatches at the loyalty card gratefully. 'Oh thank God. Hey, did anybody come up short in their pre-Christmas pay packet? Mine was down by about seventy-five dollars, which seems weird, but I double-checked and it definitely is.'

'Yep,' they all chorus back.

'It's like the opposite of a Christmas bonus, having to beg for money we need and are entitled to but is an amount so small to her that she acts as though you're pathetic for asking,' says Teddy.

'I need to get out,' Kim says quietly. As the longest-serving staff member at three and a half years, she says this a lot.

'From what I heard, we all do,' Maeve replies in an equally soft voice. 'A friend at another agency told me she thinks the books aren't balancing here, which would explain why our bank accounts aren't either.'

'How would they know?' Ernie asks.

Maeve shrugs. 'It could be just gossip, but I'm inclined to take notice considering I submitted expenses two months ago for a client lunch Fuchsia told me to go on, and I still haven't received the payment.'

'Fucking start-ups,' Teddy groans as they shoot panicky looks between them. 'See what else you can find out,' he adds to Maeve. 'Meanwhile *you* need to help attract whatever this new business is, if I don't want to have to borrow money from Jake by Valentine's Day.'

Thea glances nervously at Fuchsia's office. It's now 9.40. If she runs, she'll be back before the meeting starts and Fuchsia might even deign to let her 'shadow', as though she's a twenty-year-old student on an internship, rather than a solid second-jobber who has handled plenty of her own clients back in the UK.

She rushes for the stairs that wind through the middle of their shared downtown office space, almost tripping over a vine of devil's ivy that dangles from the top of the open-backed shelves that bisect their area with another creative agency. The rest of the shelves are full of meaty succulents and weighty visual books called things like *Blue* and *St Tropez*. No one ever looks at them. The walls are decorated in pastel hues with large vintage posters on the walls interspersed with framed affirmations telling them to 'Just Fucking Dance'. The whole place is decked out with young, hip people holding standing meetings in areas lit by hanging Edison lightbulbs and with their niche-brand e-bikes propped up against desks in the vicinity as a backdrop.

It looks dynamic and exciting, and she's posted more than one picture of it on her stories, with Nicole always instantly responding with a variation of 'Shall I send you a picture of the red-trouser brigade reading the *FT* with a sad Pret sandwich at my place?'

She pushes out of the glass-fronted doors and pulls her hood up as she runs down the street. Fat drops of freezing-cold rain are bouncing off the pavement in front of her, with rivers of water streaming down the roads. Even in heavy boots and the gigantic khaki rain cape that reaches down to her knees, Thea's jeans are soon soaked, and she can feel her socks starting to squish where water has insinuated itself over and through the laces. January gloom to the nth degree.

Seven minutes later she makes it into Roasters, where thankfully there's not much of a queue, just a smattering of people working on their laptops on the few rickety tables inside. She orders Fuchsia's drink from the barista and stands in front of one of the floor-to-ceiling windows where water is rapidly condensing. Inside the toasty coffee shop, she starts to sweat inside her plastic poncho. Rain drips off and onto the floor and within moments she's standing in a puddle.

'Fee?' he calls shortly afterwards, and Thea can't help but smile. Her East End pronunciation of her own name usually gets mangled in translation. To her eternal shame, Mum never did manage to train her out of saying 'f' instead of 'th' despite her best efforts.

'Here, thanks.' She hands over her loyalty card and the barista hands her the drink. 'Hey, you want an Easter Egg latte? They're free. We're working on some seasonal menu variations so made up a bunch.'

'Sure, why not. Thank you,' she replies. Two free coffees. *Maybe the day is salvageable,* she thinks as she braces for the return journey. An enormous SUV roars through a puddle and splashes her the second she starts back up the block. Maybe not.

Still, she makes it back to the office dead on 10 a.m., sheds her poncho, which is sluicing dripping water, and runs quickly into the toilets to make sure she looks professional enough to materialise in front of a potential client. Her jeans are black so haven't gone two-tone and aside from the front section of her hair, which was poking out of her hood, that's also mercifully dry. She pins the two wet sections back to hide them and brushes her hands down her slouchy sweater before swinging back to her desk, grabbing the coffees and heading to Fuchsia's office. Ernie's desk is empty so she assumes he's been collared. She hopes he had time to work out who he was meeting.

She raps on the door efficiently ('NEVER tentative, Thea,' says her inner Teddy voice) and then enters without waiting for an answer. Ernie is sitting on the yellow velvet sofa across from Fuchsia's desk, while Fuchsia and a man have taken the peach-coloured chairs that run adjacent to it. Fuchsia faces the door, while the man has his back to her.

'Here's your coffee,' Thea says, wending through and handing it to Fuchsia. She sits down next to Ernie without asking if she should stay and throws Fuchsia her most confident smile. 'You mentioned I ought to be involved in this one—' that was not how Fuchsia had phrased it, but what was the point in working with words if you couldn't play with the semantics when it suited you – 'so I'll sit in to get up to speed.' She turns away from Fuchsia before she can register the death glare she knows is coming and towards the client for the first time. She holds out her hand to shake it.

'Oh!' She instantly recognises his swept-back rust-coloured hair and brown eyes from the 'About' video on Logan's website. 'Felix!'

Felix smiles at her, but his eyes wrinkle in confusion. 'Sorry, have we met before?'

Thea feels two bright red spots of embarrassment spreading across her cheeks, and thinks quickly. 'No! We haven't, but I'm obviously familiar with your work having researched Memento Movies in advance of this meeting. I'm Thea, great to meet you.'

Felix smiles and shakes her hand, happy both to place her and that her role in the room is clear.

Out of the corner of her eye, Thea sees Ernie cock his head in a non-verbal question mark.

No one but Teddy knows about her night at The Opulent with Logan, and they certainly don't know that if there's one company's social output she's immersed herself in over the last couple of weeks, it's Memento Movies.

'Thea is a very thorough researcher and analyst,' says Fuchsia smoothly. 'An all-rounder really, as her copywriting and ideas are exceptional, but she has the added benefit of knowing the insights side too.'

It's the highest compliment Fuchsia has paid Thea since she hired her. It's a shame it's all bullshit, as how Fuchsia would know any of this stuff about her, Thea doesn't know. She's rarely allowed to flex any of the skillset muscles Fuchsia is boasting to Felix about. Still, she'll take it if it means she can stay in the room. Wait, though – if Felix is here, doesn't that mean . . .?

Her heart starts to pound and the memory of seeing Logan in the park flashes through her mind again. The way his look grazed over her, as though accepting she was with Billy, and as though he was somehow judging her for it. As though *she*, the non-engaged one in the dynamic, had done something wrong.

'Don't you have a business partner?' she asks, her heart hammering from nerves and reignited outrage. 'From the website, there's two of you, right?' she adds quickly. 'Should we expect him?'

A look Thea can't quite interpret passes across Felix's face. 'He couldn't make it today, so I'm repping us both.'

Shifty, she realises. Felix looks shifty. Her suspicions prickle. Logan doesn't know he's here. Why would that be? He was so positive about their business back at the hotel.

Another question pierces the thought. 'Did you say you work on the insights side of things?'

'Yes,' Thea replies in as confident a voice as she can muster.

'Great, because that's what this prelim is about really. I'd like to know from an external viewpoint where we sit in the market. What do you see as our current positioning?'

Shit.

'Oh-kay,' Thea says, taking a sip from her tooth-achingly sweet Easter Egg latte and playing for time. 'I haven't prepared a deck so it's more of an overview at this stage.'

'Sure. I know this isn't a billable meeting so top lines and overview is fine.'

Thea quickly rakes through the dozens of Instagram captions she read over Christmas. The vibe she got from them and who she felt they were aimed at. She sieves out how she felt about Logan and distils her thoughts into something coherent.

'In terms of the market, you know that you're by no means the only business offering memory-making film packages,' she starts. 'There are plenty of them out there, including some that offer incredibly low rates and can be done remotely.'

'Sure. We can't compete with their rates and nor would we want to,' Felix agrees. He's looking at her expectantly.

'Exactly. That's the DIY end of the market. On the other, there are in-person film-making companies like yours offering what they all refer to as high-quality HD films. I know that you both went to a prestigious film school, *from your website*,' she adds again hurriedly, 'but I don't think you make enough of this on your marketing materials. That's definitely a USP that justifies the price of the films you make, because they're luxury and bespoke, and something I think you should emphasise in any promo we might do for you.'

Felix is nodding in agreement. 'Yeah, sure.' He's one of those people who can't seem to let someone else talk for too long without chipping in. Off-putting in social situations, but a major plus amid her current blag-fest. 'We get a lot of queries and then a lot of people are shocked by our package prices, which is a lot of email admin to deal with when it doesn't convert into new business. The clients we secure are happy to pay though, and that's the demographic I want to make sure we're appealing to. But that's not the only thing I'm interested in. Where do you see us in terms of brand identity?'

Thea thinks back to the night in the hotel, where Logan told her the parts he likes best about his job. 'You're very much a part-of-the-family outfit. Warm, approachable, with an end product that really gets under the skin of the client's needs. I saw the intro about how your partner's grandfather was the inspiration for you to set up the business and I think people really relate to that.'

Did Felix just roll his eyes? Thea ploughs on. 'I'd call it "authentic sentimentality" if I had to categorise it.' Fleetingly, she wishes she'd got to tell Logan this.

Felix nods again, but he looks more brooding than before. 'Yeah, that's what I thought.' She's nailed the assignment, she thinks, relieved. But Felix doesn't look happy about it.

'That's exactly why we're here,' Fuchsia cuts in smoothly, her attention focused on Felix. 'We'll reposition Memento to reach an untapped market and move you away from the same tired customer base. I've got a few initial ideas on here—' she pulls out a tablet and swipes onto a screen before handing it to Felix – 'but if you sign with us, this will all go into greater depth and include a much more detailed insights and strategy package too.'

Thea's eyes dart to Fuchsia. What is happening? There's been an emotional key change in the room, but she can't work out why.

'You're not happy with where you sit in the market?' Thea says. She looks at Ernie, who is making meeting notes on his laptop and nodding as though he knows what is going on. Thea cranes over to see what sort of ideas Fuchsia is suggesting. She's getting a bad feeling about this meeting, particularly Logan's absence from it.

A caught-schoolboy look crosses Felix's face. He breathes out through his nose, as though he's working out how candid to be. 'This all stays in this room, right?' he says eventually.

Fuchsia nods efficiently; Ernie and Thea nod because they have literally no idea what's going on.

'My plan was never to stick to memory films, but we fell into this business and we're making good money. The business is there – more than we can handle without staff expansion, to be honest,' says Felix. 'Hell, we even got featured on that "Where the Heart Is" Instagram feed in November, which is where a lot of new referrals have come from. But have you seen her feed? It's all jam-making, arts and crafts, wholesome pumpkin-patch content.' The way Felix says it, it's as though the goings-on of a bog-standard momfluencer are the activities of an off-duty serial killer. 'I'm creatively suffocating. I can't keep only making hokey home movies about families who all say the same things about each other.'

The derision on Felix's face for their current clients is clear. That he's embarrassed about the subject matter of his successful film-making business is even clearer. He's not holding back, slagging off the company that Logan was so proud of.

'My business partner is all about uplifting films that all have a very similar look and feel. That story about his grandpa gets quoted to us from clients all the time.' *Yep, it's definitely an eye roll.* 'But we're capable of so much more. The way the business looks to the outside world at the moment—' he points to Thea – 'you confirmed everything I thought, by the way. It means we're never going to get those gigs.'

'Which gigs are those?' Thea is confused. She definitely has suggestions about how to target their comms more effectively, but he's telling her that they're making good money, and has a steady stream of new business, so what exactly does he want to change? And why doesn't he like the movies themselves?

She disagrees that they're all the same. Sure, they have a certain *look* about them, but isn't that most film-makers' thing? That you can tell a Tarantino or Spielberg movie from the framing and the cinematography. She's assumed they have their own signature look. And surely that's a creative decision rather than a branding one. Something he needs to talk to his business partner about, not a load of outsiders. And especially not using the word *hokey*?

Fuchsia nods the way she always does when she's brainstorming. She listens to everyone else's ideas and then parrots the best ones back at them as though they're her own. 'I get it. You want to break out from the schmaltz, corner a new market.'

'Exactly,' Felix agrees. 'I'm glad you get it. Creatively I know this is the right decision, but obviously it also needs to make financial sense. My business partner isn't on board with a direction change yet, but with the right stats

I know I can convince him. That's what I want to work towards.'

'We can definitely help you with that.' Fuchsia smiles at Thea, and for once it's a smile that reaches her eyes, so Thea knows she's done well, by progressing the pitch to a point where Felix trusts them. One step closer to signing him as a client.

Signing with their agency so Thea can help him rebrand his business into the polar opposite of the company Logan loves.

Chapter Thirteen

Fuchsia grabs Thea's arm as they show Felix out.

'That was some comeback from not even knowing about the meeting an hour ago,' she says, somehow managing to both compliment and put her down at the same time.

'It's an area I've got a—' Thea stutters over what to say next – 'personal interest in, so I know a little about it.'

Fuchsia nods once, briskly, with a look in her eye that *might* just be a tiny grain of respect. 'I need you to do a full insight report. Everything you said in there today, plus competitor reviews, annual industry turnover etcetera. Include some qualitative surveys from the current users and get Ernie to set up some quantitative surveys about untapped audiences. You heard Felix, he wants to move away from cheesy home movies, so we need to home in on a new customer base. Ernie . . .' Fuchsia looks around to see if he's standing with them at the door. He is, with his head bowed as though waiting his turn for Fuchsia's remarks.

'Yep, I'll start working on the survey.'

'Oh yes, that, sure,' says Fuchsia. 'But what I really need from you right now is another one of these coffees from Roasters.'

Thea tenses. Ernie, who it's clear from this exchange has been handed the mantle of coffee lackey, doesn't react. Fuchsia strides back to her office and Thea squeezes his arm in sympathy. 'Sorry,' she says. She's sorry for both what has just happened, and the fact that she just cashed in the loyalty card so he's going to have to pay for the coffee himself.

'It's not your fault,' he shrugs. 'If you hadn't been there the whole thing would have been a total car crash because I'd barely had time to look up the name of that guy's company, never mind get a handle on the work.' He nudges her hip with his. 'Besides, now you actually get to work on a proper pitch. I saw the way that guy Felix was listening to what you were saying, and Fuchsia was impressed too. You're going to help come up with a strategy to change his whole brand.'

Thea's face creases with worry. 'That's exactly what I'm worried about.'

'What do you mean?'

'It—' Thea can't confess why she doesn't want to be the person to corrupt Memento Movies' entire business model. She doesn't want everyone to know that she fluked this meeting because she was stalking a failed romantic prospect. If she's going to get anywhere at iDentity she needs the opportunity to show off what she can do, and *this* is an opportunity.

So why does she feel so terrible about the prospect of it? She doesn't owe Logan anything. He lied to her about having a fiancée. So what if his business partner is a liar too? She shouldn't feel bad about doing her job. If she can impress Fuchsia and get ahead, then at least *one* decent thing has come out of the whole situation.

That's what she tells herself, anyway.

'It's just a lot of pressure,' she says in the end. 'You know, my first big pitch. If I don't nail it, then I'll be back on coffee duty permanently.' She winces. 'No offence.'

Ernie waves her apology away. They're back in the open-plan room and he heads to collect his wallet. Thea throws herself down in her chair, rebooting her laptop screen and watching for him to leave before she makes another move.

The second he does, she stands up again and meerkats over the desk divider to get Teddy's attention. He catches her eye, and she nudges her head quickly to the left to indicate he should follow, then hurriedly walks to the kitchen, setting the coffee machine going (correctly this time) so that the noise will mask the sound of their conversation.

'What happened?' Teddy asks immediately as he rounds the corner.

Thea glances behind him to make sure none of the others, or worse, Fuchsia, are lurking, and then fills him in. Teddy's eyes grow larger as she explains, and by the end he's holding one hand over his mouth.

'OK, how long do you have before Felix comes back for round two?'

'A week.'

'And she wants all that information in a report by then?'

'Yes. But Teddy, it's not the workload I'm concerned about. It's *who* I'm going to be presenting my findings to. At some point Felix will have to tell Logan about this new business direction and he will be in the room. Am I just going to stand there pretending I don't know him, while decimating everything he's worked towards?'

Teddy nods, his mouth a straight line. 'Yes. You are. Somehow, your crazy-ass sleepover with this guy has opened up the door to a professional opportunity,' he says. 'If you guys were now dating, then absolutely, you should tell him that his business partner is a total snake. But Thea *he's* a snake too. Mr "oh-by-the-way I'm marrying my childhood sweetheart, but sure, let's meet up when I'm back in town".' Teddy's thoughts echo her own. 'All you can do right now, is see what's in it for you. If you tell him, he'll confront Felix, and then Felix will go straight to Fuchsia and tell her you've betrayed his client trust. Which means no more pitch for you, no new client for us – and from what Maeve was saying we *really* need some new clients – not to mention that Fuchsia for once will have a point when she bawls you out. He expressly asked for the conversation to be confidential.'

Thea leans her forehead on the side of one of the plywood cupboards. 'I know. You're right. It just feels so underhand, and really, I was bullshitting so much in there. I don't even know if Felix *should* pursue this rebrand. The whole point of those companies is that they tap into peoples' warm and fuzzy feelings about their families. *That's* the market. What's he looking to do instead – make arthouse documentaries about dysfunctional, toxic families? Who wants to expose all of their skeletons on screen?'

'Doll, you've seen *Keeping up with the Kardashians*, right?' Teddy deadpans.

'Shut up, I'm serious. They get paid *vast* amounts of money to do that. Felix is asking people to pay *him* for these films. People want a sprinkle of Wes Anderson quirk on their movies, not Brian De Palma horror.'

'OK, you've lost me.'

'They *like schmaltz!*' Thea almost yells. 'Why are people so obsessed with cool? Not everything needs a gritty makeover. What does everyone have against happiness?'

Teddy pulls his chin into his neck. 'OK, breathe,' he says, a steadying hand out in front of her. He checks that Thea's outburst hasn't sent anyone scurrying to join in the gossip session. 'I get that that word is triggering for you.'

Thea is still muttering about how cheesy is only levelled at certain things, and it's always things that are considered more female.

'Also,' she adds, 'Felix has Christian energy,' she adds. 'So I don't like him.'

'But this isn't about you, or Christian, or in fact, what the world does and doesn't consider worthwhile. It's a work assignment to rebrand a movie company according to the founder's requirements. Yes?'

Thea busies herself with emptying the grounds from the machine's tamper before lining up enough cups for all five of the content executives. 'Yes,' she says as a sigh. 'You're right.'

'I am,' Teddy confirms. 'This is the opportunity you've been waiting for. To get involved at ground level in a project. Forget how you got in the room to begin with, and forget who *might* be in the room when you present your findings. This is your big break and you're going to smash it. Rule seventeen – no negativity about projects that involve guys you've made out with.'

'That's not one of the rules,' Thea replies, pouring the coffee, and shooting him a look.

Teddy picks up two mugs to carry back to the desks. 'It is now.'

Chapter Fourteen

Voice note from Nan:

Go out there today and impress that snooty boss of yours like I know you can. Or if not her – because there's no pleasing her anyway – then this Felix, because if he likes your work then she'll have to bring you in to the project. You can do it, darling. Nan's thinking of you.

Ernie has booked one of the upstairs meeting rooms, and the conference table is set with pastries, glass water bottles and fruit – bought from the local Trader Joe's and arranged on platters as though they're from somewhere more expensive. Thea and Ernie both arrived an hour early, which is a good job because they're struggling with both the Bluetooth and HDMI cables to connect their laptop to the room's screen.

Thea's nerves are pulsing, knowing that blame for a balls-up will fall at her feet, while any victory will be claimed by Fuchsia. She, Ernie and Fuchsia have been working on the research and presentation all week, pulling late nights and getting to know the material inside out.

Even so, she knows that it's not *just* pre-meeting nerves making her insides feel as though they're on a hot wash. In her job, it's not unusual to have to pitch in front of dozens of stakeholders who are desperate to make sure their opinions are represented. In comparison, this is an intimate and relatively low-stakes situation. It's a pitch for further work, nothing more, nothing less. And there are only five attendees.

But one of them is Logan Beechwood.

And because of that, Thea doesn't just want to nail her work assignment, she wants to show him what he's missed out on, but in a way that makes her look completely indifferent to what he thinks.

'Relax, we still have fifteen minutes,' Ernie reassures her as she looks nervously towards the frosted glass wall that separates them from the corridor. She's done it umpteen times this morning already. 'I will definitely have this screen working by then.'

'I know,' Thea replies. The screen isn't the problem. Well it is, but screens are always a problem and there are few enough of them at the meeting that they can crowd around her laptop screen if it really comes to that. The problem is that she wants to be fully prepared by the time Logan walks into the room. Poised, professional and absolutely over him and his fiancée. She can't let this work opportunity be derailed by the thought of seeing him again.

And she can't let the thought of upsetting him stop her from doing everything she can to toe Fuchsia's party line. Even if her gut is telling her that the work they've been preparing isn't right for this company. Logan's investment in his business being grandfather-approved is already working for them.

After digging into her initial research, she tried to say as much to Fuchsia. She even created a whole alternative PowerPoint presentation that modernises Logan's vision but stays true to the essence of the company. But she bottled out of showing it to Fuchsia when she'd declared that she didn't want any ideas that weren't going to 'disrupt heritage movies as a genre'. Felix wants edgy.

She wonders what Logan has been told. If he knows why he's coming here today, if he knows *who*'s coming, and how he'll react when he sees her. She hasn't been able to sleep properly all week for running through the potential responses, and for worrying that her hurt will somehow betray her and leak out while she's speaking about Q3 projections.

It's not your concern how he reacts, she tells herself for the billionth time. And at least she's had time and notice, so has prepared herself for seeing him.

Although the dizzy sensation she gets when she thinks about meeting his eyes would beg to differ.

She reads over the notes she's made to accompany the slides, standing up straight to allow her to take a few deep breaths. She smooths the sides of her Peter Pan collared blouse back into her skirt where it's started to bulge and picks a stray hair off the calf of her black tights. She's wearing ankle boots and her hair is pulled into a loose topknot, hoping the whole look encapsulates 'professional but not corporate', which is the bullseye in a creative industry like hers. People want a safe pair of hands, but they also want you to look like you understand the clothes they sell in COS. And today Thea also needs to look good enough to give Logan pause. It's a lot of pressure to put on a skirt.

'OK, we're in business,' Ernie says, hitting the laptop keyboard with a flourish. The opening slide, with iDentity's swooshy logo and the client's name, appear on the screen wall at the head of the conference table.

Her phone buzzes on the table. She jumps. Despite all her mental preparation, she's no less jittery than she'd be if she'd run into Logan at a bar.

It's just client nerves, she tells herself as she reads the message from Teddy.

Remember: Girlboss > Girlfriend

She smiles. Aside from Nan, he's the only person who knows about this conundrum. She's relying on the fact that even if Logan is shocked to see her, his relationship status means he won't want to broadcast what their prior connection is, and she won't have to explain herself to Fuchsia. They'll both be in the room, knowing they know each other, but not able to let anyone else know they know each other. The thought that their night, their connection, has been transformed into a grubby secret is profoundly depressing.

She hears Fuchsia's slightly-too-loud small-talk voice tinkling down the corridor and tracks three hard-to-make-out figures through the frosted glass until the door swings open.

She tenses and repeats the phrase 'calm detachment, calm detachment, calm detachment' inside her head.

And then he walks through the door, and her mind blanks of anything but the fact that she wants him to look at her again the way he did at Portland Airport three weeks ago. She doesn't even think it – the concept just arrives in her head unbidden.

Felix wears a broad, friendly grin and says, 'Good to see you again, Thea,' as he settles himself into the room, but she barely notices him. She murmurs some sort of greeting back, her eyes fixed on Logan, who hasn't looked at her, hasn't actually even looked up from where his eyes are trained downwards towards the floor. His forehead is furrowed as he strips off his outside coat – the same one he was wearing before Christmas. He has a brushed-cotton red-and-black plaid shirt on underneath and his beard is shorter, as though he's trimmed it back, but the bristles are still threatening to escape.

He looks good.

Really good.

Too good.

The sort of good that is putting her off her carefully prepared notes. The urge to reach out and touch him makes her wish her skirt had pockets so she has somewhere definitive to shove her hands.

It might not be noticeable to Fuchsia or Ernie, who haven't met him before, but to her it's obvious he's not happy about being here. The Logan she met wasn't afraid to show his feelings. That's who he seemed to be anyway.

And that's why it felt so shitty when his feelings were revealed to be a lie.

There's no sign of the open, goofy and enthusiastic man she had dinner with. His entire body language is that of a person forced into a situation. It's as though he's got a gun to his head as he files to the far side of the conference table, where he'll – thankfully – be sitting at a diagonal to her rather than directly opposite.

Thea forces herself to lean towards him, her hand outstretched.

'I'm Thea, hi,' she says in greeting. Her heart pounds and she hopes he won't blow her cover now. If she can stick to the well-practised structure, she can make it through seeing him again.

But then Logan raises his blue eyes to her briefly, and takes her hand to shake it. The warm clasp of his fingers on hers and the flutter of nerve endings it sets off is all it takes for her to wish that he *would* acknowledge her after all, because that would mean that the night in the hotel was real and she hasn't just built up a one-sided legend in her head. That it meant something to both of them, and he isn't just a chancer with a wife-to-be, looking for whatever he can get away with without said wife-to-be finding out.

'Logan.' With one word, he drops her hand and her gaze, not a flicker of recognition on his face.

Thea is left with her hand in mid-air, wondering if he just felt any of the same emotions she did. There's no way to know. He's looking down at the cover of the printed booklet Thea and Ernie have set at each place, containing the market analysis and research they've put together.

Because, or perhaps in spite of this, Felix is super-chatty, telling Ernie that one of his favourite small-press magazines has its office around here and if he hasn't already he should check it out, because it's what *Kinfolk* *used* to be, before it became too popular (and therefore worse, Thea surmises). He's all charm and chat. Thea has learned from bitter experience that that can be a bad combination.

You don't have to like the clients, Thea reminds herself, forcing herself to concentrate on her notes. You just need to know you can do something for them. And first of all, iDentity needs to land them.

It would be a lot easier if she felt about *both* of them the way she feels about Felix. She steals a look at Logan again and her heart skips. She can't help it, even though he lied about being single, his grandfather's role in the business being established was true. And that makes her feel bad for what they're about to present to him.

'Does everyone have tea or coffee?' Fuchsia says, busying herself working the room. 'We have filter or a selection of teas. Hot water is at the side.' Thea stands up to take care of any drinks orders, but Fuchsia places a cautionary hand in front of her. 'Ernie will see to them, won't you, Ern?'

Ernie – whom no one ever calls Ern, because he hates it – gives a tight smile. 'Of course.' Thea shoots him a sympathetic look and he raises his eyes skyward when Fuchsia isn't looking to show he's not pissed off with Thea, but with Fuchsia's BS.

'Coffee, black, thanks,' Felix says.

Logan just shakes his head with an expression on his face that isn't unfriendly but isn't a smile either.

'You want a tea, Thea?' Ernie asks to show there are no hard feelings over Fuchsia's rotating teacher's pet system. Logan's head jerks up and his eyes connect with hers as though remembering a little in-joke. A full body flush works its way up her body.

She has to focus.

'I'm fine with water for now, thank you.' Logan looks down and thumbs the corners of his booklet, his lips pressed together in a straight line.

Fuchsia glances at her Apple Watch, aware of the time, and starts her patter. 'If we're all OK for drinks, let's get started. Thea, take it away.'

Thea straightens in her seat and hits the return button on her laptop to start the slideshow. She starts with a waver in her voice but hopes anyone who notices will assume it's old-fashioned nerves.

She deliberately looks towards the screen and not at Logan as she talks. She gets herself into the flow state she knows she can achieve with a presentation that's well researched and well practised. Her role is to analyse what's out there and what *can* be done, rather than to criticise or suggest what *should*. That's what she told herself, anyway.

She flicks onto a slide showing two pie charts. 'As you can see, the age bracket with the most spend is the over-fifties, but Ernie's initial research has uncovered that the affluent thirty-five to fifty segment are also "seriously interested" in genealogy and legacy documentary movies

– and they don't feel as though they're being served by the current market.'

Thea sees Felix shoot Logan what can only be described as a triumphant look. Logan's face remains impassive, and he focuses on the screen. It's hard to know if he's listening to all the stats Thea is throwing at them, but Fuchsia keeps nodding, her eyes slightly closed as though Thea is a wise preacher through whom universal truths are being conveyed. 'We're moving away from the schmaltz,' she interjects when Thea pauses to ask if there are any questions at this stage, and it catapults her back to the hotel, when she told Logan that her boss dismissed all her ideas that way, and shared her doubts that Fuchsia knew best. It was around the same time she said that Fuchsia was a tantrum-prone diva.

The memory causes the next line of her presentation to stick in her throat and it comes out as a cough. Logan could bring that up at any moment and completely drop her in it. She takes a sip of water and gets her head back in the zone, concluding with an estimated turnover figure for the newly identified audience. 'Now Fuchsia is going to take over.'

Fuchsia smiles broadly.

Logan gives another of those polite inscrutable nods. She knows she shouldn't care – he's engaged! And he lied about it – but she longs for them to share another secret glance. She tries to concentrate on Fuchsia's spiel as she starts talking through iDentity's vision, along with moodboards for a new web design and logo, and examples of social posts.

The problem is, concentrating on Fuchsia's spiel makes her wince. Projected onto the giant meeting room screen, the work seems even more cynical. She looks again at Logan. As Fuchsia wraps up, his eyes look flat, his face immobile.

Meanwhile, it's clear Felix likes what he sees.

'Fantastic,' he enthuses. 'The whole vision is younger and hipper, sleek and streamlined. I love it. What do you think, Logan?'

Everyone looks at him. He gives a self-conscious laugh. 'Whatever I say now is only going to be taken as me being defensive, or as though I'm some regressive boomer apologist.' He gives a thin smile. 'So, for the record, I have nothing against young and hip.'

'Never said you did, buddy,' Felix says quickly, catching each of the others' eyes in turn as though they're all in on a joke.

'And I have nothing against changing our marketing materials, but this—' he sweeps his arm from the screen and to the booklet, which he flicks through his fingers as he talks – 'basically suggests that everything we've done before is cheesy. Where's the origin story about my grandpa in all this? Is he not cool enough to feature?' Logan's voice is shot through with hurt. 'You might as well call our current customers losers.'

'I wouldn't go that far,' Fuchsia says in a temperate voice.

Thea cringes inwardly. That's exactly what she would have said to Fuchsia and Felix herself, if she'd had the guts.

'You say this new demographic are "seriously interested",' Logan continues, 'but what if we completely change our business identity and they still don't book with us? That will just alienate our current customer base, leaving us with *fewer* bookings.'

Another bingo moment for Thea.

Heat rises to Logan's face as he gets worked up. This man, Thea recognises. Even if he's now talking passionately because he's mad, rather than because he's enthusiastic. This Logan is more like the person she met before Christmas.

'Our business is doing fine and frankly I feel ambushed,' he goes on. 'Let's get a new logo if you want one, Felix, and it was *me* who suggested hiring a social media manager. I have zero desire to spend my time on Google analytics when I could be making films.' He turns to Felix, and Thea can see the hurt etched across his face. 'But why do you want to overhaul our entire brand identity to chase after a bunch of ironic millennials who probably won't be impressed anyway?'

Felix sighs, a weary sound that implies that this isn't their first go-around on this topic. Thea takes another sip of her water to mask the discomfort of witnessing what should be a private discussion. She hovers her cursor over the PowerPoint presentation she has saved on her desktop, the one she couldn't show Fuschia, but that she can't bring herself to delete.

'Companies evolve, Logan. We've been doing this for eight years now and I can't keep making these cookie-cutter films as a tribute to your grandpa. I need something to challenge me.'

Logan reels as though he's been slapped.

'I'm not disregarding that,' Logan responds in a tight voice. His blue eyes are flashing darkly. Even angry, he looks good. 'But you needing to feel challenged is not the same as us needing to overhaul a thriving business. We're making money. Good money. I'm not prepared to risk that just so we can sound more interesting when we tell people what we do.'

Felix's face freezes. 'Is that what you think this is? My ego?'

That's totally what this is, Thea thinks.

Felix shakes his head, then again more rigorously. Logan has hit a nerve, Thea can tell. Two bright red spots have appeared on his cheeks and Thea senses he's about to lash out rather than admit how close he's come to the truth. Felix stands up so quickly his chair tips backwards, clattering to the floor with a series of bangs. 'If that's what you think, then let's forget the whole thing. Carry on as we are, and advertise for a new camera operator, because that's all you think I'm good for. I'm out, Logan. I'm done.'

Felix kicks through the upended chair behind him and storms out, leaving the rest of them sitting at the table in silence.

Chapter Fifteen

Fuchsia shoots Thea and Ernie a look, the meaning of which is impossible to decipher, and then runs after Felix gesturing for Ernie to follow her. Thea and Logan remain at the table, looking down and refusing to meet each other's gazes.

'Did you block me on Instagram before or after you knew you were going to be screwing with my business?' Logan says eventually. His voice is low and weary, but it still has an edge to it.

Thea flinches.

He's going to do this now, Thea thinks, resigned. And then when Fuchsia comes back – with or without Felix – she's going to find out I withheld information, and I'm going to get fired.

'The two things aren't connected,' she says in the most neutral voice she can manage above the sound of her pulse ricocheting around her body.

Logan makes a noise that's somewhere between a snort and a laugh. 'Right,' he mutters. Thea's hackles rise.

'What exactly are you accusing me of?' she asks. 'I work for a company that has been hired to present a brand strategy, and that's exactly what we've done.'

'Even though only fifty per cent of the brand actually knew about it.'

'How is that my fault?' she bursts out. 'Whatever tensions you're having with your business partner are nothing to do with me. I had no idea Felix had approached iDentity until last week.'

He seems to sag. 'You know that *this*—' he throws a hand in the direction of the screen, where the 'Thank You' slide hangs above the table – 'isn't what I want for my company.' Logan looks at her, *really* looks at her, fixing his intense blue eyes on hers. There are little flecks of gold among the blue. 'You know what it means to me. And it's not about clips that look slick on three-second social posts but don't actually tell you anything about the person they pay tribute to.'

Something stirs inside her. She remembers how enthusiastic he was about his films, the clients, *the stories*, the reason why staying true to all of that is so important to him. It's the direct opposite to the derision Felix seems to feel for the clientele that keeps them in business. She had liked the sound of how warm it sounded. And she can't disagree, Fuchsia's vision leaves her feeling hollow too.

'I'm not saying you shouldn't have taken on the project,' Logan says, 'I get it.' His voice is weighted. It implies he knows her. After all, she confided in him about how she was feeling stifled and sidelined. She'd told him that she loved being in Portland but she was still waiting for an opportunity at work to arise so the pieces of her life would fall into place and she could really put down roots here. There's understanding there, even if it's currently swaddled by something else. It's like a pig-in-a-blanket, where the sausage is understanding and the bacon is pissed-off-ness.

Logan inhales deeply, and looks down at the booklet again. 'You could have warned me,' he says. His voice is undercut with defeat.

It would be easier if she didn't agree with him on that point. If she could keep things brisk and businesslike and not acknowledge that even if he's been a shit to Thea, the surprise attack Felix has masterminded today is just as shitty.

'Have you any idea how humiliating it is to be blindsided by someone you thought was your friend?' he says softly.

Thea clamps her mouth shut. He almost had her.

Almost.

The humiliation of why she blocked him resurfaces. How *dare* he play the victim when he knows all about blindsiding people.

'Are you joking?' she says, the words dripping with incredulity. 'Yes, imagine finding out something that made you completely reassess a person you thought you knew. *Imagine.*' She glares at him with the full force of her anger. 'You're one to talk about being duplicitous,' she mutters.

Logan's head snaps up. 'What's that supposed to mean?'

'Oh please,' Thea fires back.

'No, seriously, I'm confused,' Logan says. 'I thought we had a real connection that night at The Opulent. I've never felt so close to someone in such a short amount of time. It meant something to me, Thea. I told you things about my parents that I've never really told anyone, and what I wanted to prove to them with Memento. I thought you understood me. Right up until you blocked me, and the next time I see you you're kissing some nineteen-foot-tall guy in Washington Park. And *then* you turn out to be my business partner's partner in crime. Are you some sort of Memento plant?'

'I'd never even met Felix until a week ago!' Thea shouts. 'And I certainly hadn't been tapping him up for business if that's what you're implying. I'm not even going to dignify the part about Billy with an answer because it's none of your business.' Any vestiges of cool detachment have gone. Thea enunciates every bitter syllable.

'None of my business?' Logan's voice has risen. 'You don't just kiss someone and then—'

The sentence is interrupted by Fuchsia stalking back into the room with Ernie trailing behind her despondently. Thea and Logan jump. Felix isn't with them and Fuchsia scowls at Logan. 'Still here?' she says, her voice devoid of any of the simpering respect she showed to Felix. Managerial Fuchsia has been replaced with the easily vexed Fuchsia that Thea and Ernie deal with on a regular basis. She turns her attention to them, effectively dismissing Logan from the conversation. 'When we get back downstairs, I need you to run through the insights for the brewery prelim we have next week,' she says to Ernie. She looks at Thea. 'And can you be a doll and get me a coffee from the nice place I like?'

Thea nods, trying to quash the rising disappointment that her moment as a full member of a pitch team is over. No Felix means no need of her. That was her shot. On top of all the other reasons she doesn't want to look at Logan right now, she adds the burning sense of humiliation to the pile.

Logan stands up and takes a couple of steps towards the door. He clears his throat. 'I'm sorry this didn't work out the way you guys hoped.' Fuchsia shoots him such a cold look that Thea is impressed when he instead continues rather than scuttling away. But his voice is confident and purposeful. It's Logan in business mode. It's very attractive. 'Your presentation was impressive and if I'd have been consulted beforehand, I wouldn't have been against hiring a rebranding agency to consult with.' Thea is impressed he can even look at Fuchsia when she's beaming such obvious hatred towards him. 'Did you speak to Felix?' he asks.

'Briefly.' Fuchsia looks like she's going to stop there but then can't help herself. 'He said that if your attitude to change is so regressive it has bigger implications for your ongoing partnership than he thought.'

Logan nods. His jaw is set, but Thea can see from the flicker of hurt around his eyes that the betrayal stings. He loiters in the doorway as though he's weighing something up.

'Why don't you send me the deck?' he says, relenting slightly.

Fuchsia's posture stiffens, as though sensing an opportunity. 'I thought it was against everything you believe in,' she says.

Logan gives a small smile. 'Believe me, this is *not* a direction I'm prepared to lean into, but perhaps the points raised are a springboard for further discussion. Let me take another look and talk to him.'

'Ernie, send Luke the deck.'

'It's Logan,' Thea corrects instantly. She can tell it's on the tip of Fuchsia's tongue to reply, 'Whatever,' but she's grabbed a foothold on her professionalism again.

'Logan, apologies.' She grabs Thea's laptop, yanking all the HDMI cables out as she pulls it towards her. She opens up an email window and Thea thanks the universe that she turned off all notifications before the presentation, so there's no chance of Fuchsia catching sight of any of the messages the team exchange about her on a regular basis.

'Do you need me to—' Seeing Fuchsia banging at the keyboard, Thea tries to get her laptop back, but Fuchsia holds up a hand. 'I'll do it,' she snaps, instructing Logan to spell out his email address, which he does, three times before she gets it right. She swipes the attachment from Thea's desktop and hits the return button. They all listen to the swooshing sound of an email departing before a notification rings out from Logan's trouser pocket.

'Thanks,' he says, without taking his phone out. 'I'll take a look later.'

Thea doesn't know what Fuchsia was expecting, but from her pouty reaction, it wasn't this.

'Don't take too long,' she says, dismissive again now. 'I get the impression Felix is impatient for change.'

'I'll keep that in mind,' Logan replies, his eyes lingering on Thea. The look makes her feel as though her insides are swooping across the room along with the email that's just been sent from her account. 'He's not the only one.'

Chapter Sixteen

Date: 12 January, 16.32 PST
To: Thea Bridges
From: Logan Beechwood
Subject: Re: deck
I love this deck!!!
>It's warm and funny – perfect for our audience.
>Can we talk further about it?

Thea's eyes twitch as she reads the message. Has Logan been hacked?

Unless he's being sarcastic, and the three exclamation marks are to ram home how lame he thinks the whole thing is. In which case: why does he want to talk?

Maybe he's changed his mind, she thinks. But to go from unadulterated hatred to thinking it's 'warm and funny'. It's as though he's talking about a completely different—

'Shit.'

Thea buzzes with tension.

Teddy's eyes flick towards her from his desk, widening in a question, and all she can do is fold her lips together and shake her head.

Thea checks her sent items, where the email Fuchsia composed from her laptop at the end of yesterday's disastrous meeting sits. She attached iDentity's Memento deck and sent it. Or, she attached a document from Thea's desktop that she *assumed* was iDentity's Memento deck.

Thea opens the email and scans the attachment name.

Memento Deck Thea version.ppt

Her deck. Not iDentity's deck. The one she'd been too scared to show Fuchsia. The one Fuchsia, and probably Felix, would hate.

A message from Teddy pops up.

What's happening? Your face looks like it did when you scraped your car against the parking lot wall.

This is worse, she replies, feeling sick. But right now, she needs to think about what to do rather than stop and explain what's happened. Tell you later, she types, flipping back to Logan's email.

Be calm, be professional, she tells herself. Her fingers clatter against the keyboard as she hammers out a reply, one that will make this situation – a situation that she cannot explain to Fuchsia – go away. Teddy looks at her again, and frowns, from the noise of her stabbing at the keys and swearing softly each time her fingers race ahead of her brain and make a spelling mistake.

To: Logan Beechwood
From: Thea Bridges
Re: deck

Hi Logan

So sorry – there's been a misunderstanding, the deck attached isn't the finished work we presented. I've attached the presentation from yesterday here.

Thea

She double- and then triple-checks that she's attached the right one, and presses 'send'.

His reply is almost instant.

To: Thea Bridges
From: Logan Beechwood
Subject: Re: deck

I don't care that this is the 'wrong' deck. I much prefer it. There are some great ideas here that move the business along without suffocating who we are.

I'd like to discuss it with Felix and your team. Shall I set up another meeting, or do you want to?

No, no, no, *no*. Fuchsia and Ernie can't discuss this deck, because they don't know of its existence. And as she knows Fuchsia would hate it, she can't now confess she made an alternative presentation that is thematically opposite in every way to the one they showed yesterday. Should she confess to Ernie?

Something tells her that the fewer people who know about this, the better.

She takes a deep breath before suggesting something she wouldn't have dreamed of twenty-four hours ago.

To: Logan Beechwood
From: Thea Bridges
Re: deck
It's tricky to explain. Is there any chance we can discuss this between ourselves in the first instance?

To: Thea Bridges
From: Logan Beechwood
Subject: Re: deck
Sure. You want to jump on a call? Or we could meet f-2-f later?

She can't call him now, with Fuchsia within fake-wall listening distance. And she definitely can't call him with Teddy, Kim, Ernie and Maeve sitting right there.

But seeing him? She saw him yesterday and it made her feel energised and depressed all in one messed-up package. Is there a word for wanting someone you can't have and who lied to your face, while despising yourself for still wanting them – even after they made you feel as though you were in the wrong? Loganfreude? She has a serious case of Loganfreude.

But this is work. Her job. Her career. She needs to straighten this out and stop him blabbing to Felix and Fuchsia. And, if she's honest with herself, she wants an excuse to see him again. For there to be the chance his eyes will rest on her, his mouth pulling into a smile – no matter how small, and no matter how taken he is. Seeing him for work is not the same as arranging to meet him socially, knowing there's a fiancée in the picture.

'I finish at six,' she taps out. 'Let me know where you want to meet.'

She leaves the office and heads east on foot. It's dark and cold with wind rushing at her, and the sporadic snowflakes have turned into a continual, if lackadaisical, snowfall that is drifting down but not settling. The journey would be warmer and shorter on public transport but there's an hour before they're due to meet and she's full of nervous energy. She needs to move.

Her body starts to warm up as she walks, and she adjusts her scarf so that between that and her woolly hat, only the top part of her cheeks is exposed to the numbing elements. Walking is her favourite way to get to know the city, stomping along on her way to a place and taking in what she sees on the way. She passes boutique hotels, countless bars and the looming converted bank that houses the business side of office life in the area. Excitement pricks at her as she goes, just as sharply as the elements. There's so much here for her still to discover.

As long as Fuchsia doesn't find out about this whole mix-up and send her back to the UK.

She huddles over slightly to shield herself from the icy air seeping through her layers and pulls out her phone to start a voice note back to Nan, but she only gets halfway through explaining what's happened today before she has to give up. Her hands are too cold to keep pressing the record button.

Instead she uses her excess zinging energy to concentrate on what she's going to say to Logan when she arrives.

That if he hates Fuchsia's ideas that's fine, but to please not tell anyone about Thea's presentation because it went expressly against her boss's wishes. And Felix will likely be furious if he finds out about it too. More so, if Logan discloses their knowing each other predates Felix's first meeting at iDentity.

Would Fuchsia fire her over this mess? Worst-case scenarios pinball around her brain and her walking pace picks up. She drives herself to getting a little out of breath to try and banish the cortisol spike.

She soon reaches the park that runs the length of the Willamette River, where sheets of freezing wind are blowing horizontally off it. The visible part of her face is now damp with snow, and the parts under woollens are damp with sweat. There's a tiny wooden building to one side of the park with tables outside that in summer are buzzing with cyclists and walkers but this evening are empty and bare. It's a café by day and a cocktail bar by night, and far enough away from the iDentity office that Thea decided it was a safe enough meeting spot when Logan suggested it. Especially because Teddy was suspicious about why she blew off happy hour. She had to tell him she was picking her car up from the shop so will have to find an excuse as to why it's still in the shop tomorrow. Although it wouldn't be the first time that pulling on one mechanical thread loosened something elsewhere. Like when they fixed the handbrake and the central locking stopped working.

After power-walking the whole way, she's fifteen minutes early, but that's OK, as it gives her time to nip to the loo and make herself presentable. She steps inside and the warmth hits her. She hasn't been in before, but interiors-wise, the bar could be described as your grandma's house by way of *Twin Peaks*, which is how ninety per cent of all cool bars can be described. Thankfully, it's more cosy than intimidating.

As the inside of her nose begins to unfreeze, it immediately starts to run. Cold splinters of half-frozen hair dangle in chunks onto her cheeks and everywhere she was previously cold starts to burn hot, while everywhere she was already sweaty gets worse. As she makes her way further inside, she grabs a couple of napkins from the bar to blow her nose on while she locates the toilets.

'Thea!'

Crap, Logan's already here too, nursing a beer in the corner. The sight of him hits her with a thump and the effect adds a dollop of clammy exhilaration to the temperature rollercoaster she's currently riding. He's wearing a chunky sweatshirt, and his face looks several degrees more relaxed than yesterday. His eyes are bright, and his face is fresh from the cold. His smile is like a little volt of electricity, and she automatically smiles back, her heart skipping. She tries to drag a hand through her tangled hair and wipe her nose, without him noticing she's doing either of those things. She sheds her coat, scarf and gloves as she heads towards him and takes a seat opposite, dumping her outside clothes onto the spare chair beside her.

'Hi,' she says, her voice slightly breathless. 'I walked here which is why I'm . . .' She gestures to herself as though to explain why she's such an attractive combination of sweaty, wind-burned and bedraggled.

'It's cold, huh?' he replies, and she nods. There's a pause. They're not here to talk about the weather. She's close enough to him that she can smell the shower gel he uses and something else, a sort of woody, outdoorsy smell. She's nervous now she's sitting down, and she springs right back up.

'I'm going to get a drink. Do you want another?'

'I'm OK, thanks,' he says. She scuttles off, using the moment at the bar to settle herself. Seeing him in a bar environment has brought the memory of their original meeting flooding back, and she has to remind herself that they're here to discuss work. This isn't the meet-up they discussed over Christmas. She picks a mulled wine that the bartender assures her is made from Oregon grapes and the best in the state. She doesn't care as long as it has a kick in it to give her the confidence to straighten this whole thing out.

Back at the table, she clasps her hands around her mulled-wine mug, which has the dual purpose of letting the warmth spread through her fingers and gives her something to do with her hands. She blows on it and takes a sip. Logan has taken a laptop out of his bag, and it sits on the table between them with her presentation up on the screen.

'I need to explain,' she says before Logan can speak. Being around him stirs up too many feelings. She needs to sort this out and then get out again as soon as possible. 'The work Fuchsia sent you was not iDentity work. It was something I was playing around with myself and she attached it by accident. She doesn't know it exists and will go mad if she finds out I sent you something she hasn't approved, especially because she and Felix are so set on a different direction. So you need to delete it, forget about it, and make a decision about what to do based on the work we presented yesterday.'

When she finally stops for breath, Logan is frowning, his eyes crinkled in thought, as though he's assessing her. She squirms under his gaze.

'But the work you sent me is good,' he says. 'Really good. Much better than whatever your boss came up with.'

Thea's ego swells for a moment, enjoying the compliment, but she pulls herself back into the moment where he's still talking.

'You were right about her, by the way. After what you said about her at the hotel—' it's such a casual reference to their previous time together but it takes Thea right back; her pouring her heart out; her thinking he understood her; her thinking they had a nascent connection; then her discovering it was all a lie – 'I'm not confident about her suitability and this just proves it. Why was I shown *that*, when *this* is a possibility? Her instincts are off. I wouldn't want to work with her.'

Thea winces. She told him her doubts about Fuchsia as a friend, as a hopefully soon-to-be-more-than-a-friend.

He's using everything she said as a weapon, and delivering it all as though they haven't met before. He's nailed the exact brand of insouciant professionalism she was going for yesterday. 'Please don't tell Fuchsia or Felix that we've met before,' she pleads, throwing herself on his mercy. 'Or any of what you just said.'

Now he just looks non-plussed. 'But why? There's no way I'm going to approve their work.'

'That's fine,' she squeaks out. 'But you don't need to tell them why. Just walk away from iDentity, sort out your company any way you like, but you have to leave me out of it.'

'Leave you out of it? But you did this! I love the new themes for films you came up with.' His professional veneer cracks. The not-quite-smile he first gave her in the limo is on his face and it makes her automatically lift her eyes to his, where she can see a familiar warmth, and smile back.

She'd loved the *When Harry Met Sally* concept he'd told her about, for couples to talk about how they met. Remembering that had given her the idea for families to be able to choose from a menu of other iconic movies to pastiche in their film.

'And the yearbook idea is also great,' he continues. He scrolls down the document, landing on each idea in turn. The cute, enthusiastic look he got when talking about his work in the hotel is back, and the clipped business owner is gone.

'I was just tinkering around,' she mumbles. 'The ideas are pretty generic.' Where was this cheerleader when she needed someone to champion ideas she'd put together for other pitches? In an alternative timeline, Logan could be her boyfriend, bigging her up to build her confidence at work. Instead, she's in this timeline, where she's having to actively dismiss her work to get the engaged man she can't stop herself being attracted to from doing something that might get her sacked.

He pauses on the next slide, a family tree mocked up in the style of an eighties high-school yearbook. 'Are those photos of your own family?'

'Yes,' she replies, her eyes lingering on the pictures that she's crudely photoshopped onto a template of a yearbook she'd found online. Photos of Nan, Mum, Dad and Kit beam out at her. Nan smiling mischievously, captured just as Thea had showed her a story about Tom Hardy entering a martial arts competition incognito, wrapped in an enormous oversized Stüssy sweatshirt that Kit had got bored of. Mum, in her reading glasses that she's self-conscious about wearing even though Thea thinks they make her look like a cool TV librarian – and Dad and Kit looking more similar than Thea realised until she put a headshot of them next to each other. It's as though Kit's been put through an aging app. The eyes are the same, pale blue and oval shaped, as are their slightly wonky smiles. Kit's 'ironic' fleece is almost identical to Dad's ancient one in their respective photos. But Kit's floppy hair is receded back to thinning grey in Dad's picture, and the deep lines around Dad's eyes where he squints through his cab windscreen day after day mark him as three decades older.

When she'd put together this alternative deck, using examples from her camera roll, it hit her how Logan must have felt putting together a whole movie about his grandpa. It had tugged out memories and feelings that made her feel almost nostalgic for times that weren't even gone yet. And now she wishes she'd had the nerve to at least show Fuchsia what she'd done, because far from dropping it and never speaking of it again, Logan is still effusing about it.

'These concepts felt like a better fit to me and I think you get Memento in a way that Fuchsia just doesn't.'

A new thought crosses her mind. 'You're not expecting me to tell Fuchsia you don't want to work with us, are you? Like I said, please leave me out of it. As far as anyone is concerned, the first time we met was yesterday, and they definitely don't know I'm here now.'

Logan looks at her meaningfully. 'I guess you have your reasons for keeping the night we met quiet.'

'Yes,' she retorts. Her face goes hot just thinking about telling Fuchsia that she knows him because they spent the night together and Thea harboured fantasies of them dating until she found out about his very glossy-looking fiancée. Fuchsia would think the whole thing cheesier than Thea's ideas at work. 'And so do you.' She thinks of the photo again. Of him beaming beside Coco94 and below telling her he loves her, only hours after making Thea feel as though there might be something between them. 'Our prior connection has made things professionally awkward, and as you know, my boss isn't that understanding,' she says briskly, trying to get herself back onto an even footing.

'If you don't want to work with us, that's your decision, but it would help me out if you didn't mention this—' she gestures at the laptop – 'when you break the news to her.'

'I won't,' he replies. Thea's body floods with relief. Fuchsia will be annoyed they've lost the new business, especially if the rumours about iDentity are true, but she makes a pact with the universe: if she gets away with this, she'll be more proactive in finding some leads herself. She lets out a breath she didn't know she was holding and takes a gulp of her wine.

'But she'll probably find out if you agree to the proposal I have for you.'

Thea's wine turns to acid on the way down, her mind still on that ring photo. She shouldn't be grateful that he's not going to grass her up to Fuchsia. She should be mad at him for being a lying, engaged, cheat. 'Great choice of words,' she says deadpan.

'What?' Logan's forehead crinkles. He looks puzzled enough for her to feel a little less foolish about falling for his schtick at Portland Airport. He's a good actor.

'Seems as though you're pretty good at making proposals,' she snorts. Her phone buzzes in her pocket and she pulls it out. 'Hang on,' she says, her eyes widening. 'It's Fuchsia.' It's not unusual for Fuchsia to contact her out of work hours, but because of where she is and who she's with, she immediately prickles with panic, forgetting that she's supposed to be reminding Logan what a creep he is.

'You definitely haven't mentioned me or the alternative presentation to Fuchsia or Felix, have you?' she says, in a voice much less in control than seconds before. She can't answer the call now, with Logan right in front of her, witnessing how quickly she jumps to attention when Fuchsia wants something, even though she told him how little she respects her.

'I haven't. I promise.' He holds his hands up, the picture of innocence. God, he's good. 'But it probably is something to do with all this.' He gestures at the table and the laptop again.

Thea's guts clench. 'To do with what?'

'I told Felix that I'm hiring my own team to pitch for the branding contract with Memento. He's probably just told Fuchsia.'

Her phone registers a voicemail.

'Don't tell me any more,' Thea says quickly. 'It's better if she tells me herself.' *I'm not as good an actor as you,* she adds in her head.

'Well, that's just it,' Logan replies, looking energised. 'I'm going to need to tell you about it, because I want *you* to be part of the other team.'

Chapter Seventeen

'I'm sorry – what?' Thea splutters out.

'I'm serious,' says Logan, looking exactly that. He rubs a hand over his beard and cheeks.

'I want another agency to come up with a second opinion.' He fixes Thea with a look. 'From the work I've seen, that's where you come in. I'm in talks with The Collective—' Thea grimaces as Logan names one of iDentity's biggest rivals in the boutique agency sphere; Fuchsia *hates* them – 'but I want them to lead with your work, so my proposal is that you're part of the team.'

Thea struggles to understand what this means. She swills the wine around in her mug. 'I can't go and work for some other agency, especially when they're a direct competitor to the agency I *currently* work for.' She feels a little surge of adrenaline at the idea of it though. Working for The Collective would be a dream. Their reputation and client list are renowned and they're always winning industry awards.

'I told them I'd spoken to an independent consultant, and they liked the sound of your work, so you could leave iDentity and go freelance. You work with them on this, and then by the time Memento 2.0 is up and running you can use that work as a showcase for other freelance clients. Or I *bet* The Collective will want you to stay on with them.'

'Logan, your belief in me is sweet, but I can't do any of that,' she says stiffly.

'Why not?' He looks confused. 'You told me that Fuchsia never lets you be involved in any of the creative work, so you don't owe her anything.'

'Except my visa,' she says quietly. 'It's sponsored by iDentity. If I quit, my visa gets cancelled. I can't work for another company unless they offer me a permanent position and are prepared to sponsor me. And even aside from all that . . .'

Thea thinks of the photos on Logan's feed of his family home, takes in his confidence as a business owner and as someone who this afternoon engaged the services of one the best, yes, but also one of the most expensive creative agencies in the city. 'I can't jump ship for the promise of one freelance job. Aside from my visa, my health insurance is connected to my job, and I also need a regular salary to pay my bills.' Not to mention the hotel bill that's still festering on Nan's credit card like a stale piece of Christmas cake. Even halved, thanks to sharing the bill with Logan, the interest on the remaining five hundred dollars has already started adding up. iDentity isn't exactly reliable when it comes to wage payments but it's still more stable than a precarious freelance career based on one conversation Logan has had with an eager-to-please potential client. A freelance job she can't even accept without the right paperwork.

'I think you underestimate yourself. You say you just "tinkered around" and made this presentation? Your stuff is good, Thea! And not just on a professional level – you see into the heart of what Memento is all about. You'd easily get more work. You just need more confidence in it.'

'Do I "just"?' Thea spits out sarcastically. She can't help it. 'You wouldn't understand,' she mutters. 'You've probably never had a day's worry in your life about money.'

'I'm sorry,' he says. 'The visa stuff didn't occur to me. That doesn't mean I don't get that you need the security iDentity provides.' Logan frowns. 'But you know why this company means so much to me and why I want to protect it.'

'Your grandpa,' Thea says, nodding.

'Yeah, Grandpa. I didn't tell you that he was the only person in my family who supported me when I said I wanted it to be my full-time job. I love my mom and dad, but they have *opinions* about what constitutes a successful career, and it's not Memento. They went crazy when I invested my inheritance from Hank in it.'

Thea can completely understand the anxiety around the money. Her parents would be just as nervous – if there was any money to invest – but if he's turned it into a going concern, what's their problem? 'Why, if you're earning decent money? Wait, they're not bankrolling the whole thing, are they?'

'No!' Logan yelps. 'I *did* get my start because Grandpa left me some money, but we've been in the black for years. Their disapproval is because I don't earn the sort of crazy money they think is a marker of making it. The kind you get from the real estate investments my parents made their money with, and that's the business they wanted me to join.' He sighs. 'Instead I wanted to do something more creative, that I enjoyed. But it also needs to earn me enough money to prove that Memento isn't just a tribute to my grandfather, but a viable business.'

Thea nods. This whole conversation is taking her back to the hotel room, where they shared stories until they fell asleep about their hopes and fears, lives and families.

'That's why I'm not going to let Felix do what he wants with it on a whim,' he says, determination in his voice. 'I moved here to work on the business and that's what I'm going to do.'

With that sentence, Thea's back in this room. She wonders if Coco94 is still back East, or somewhere in Portland where she could bump into her at any moment? Thea wants to ask why he did it. She'd hoped this meet-up could work as exposure therapy, turn her off him completely. But it hasn't worked. If anything, the proximity, the reasonable talking through of a professional conundrum while he praises her, and the fact that they're both slowly steaming from the wet snow drying inside the warm bar, is making it all worse. She still likes him.

More than likes him.

Engaged, engaged, engaged, she tells herself.

'The Collective are really good. They will come up with something you love that isn't just the tinkerings of a junior member of staff,' she says, bringing things back to safer ground again. 'But will Felix agree to using your choice of agency over his?'

'No.' Logan smiles back, ruefully. Whatever is going on between Logan and Felix professionally right now is hurting him personally too. She can see it on his face. 'Which is why it's going to be a contest between both agencies.'

'A contest?' Thea asks, prickling with nerves again. The only good thing that might have come from this evening was Memento – and Logan Beechwood – going far away from iDentity.

'I don't want to go head to head with Felix, but he's only going to listen to cold hard facts – so each team comes up with a strategy and we test them out,' he says. 'Memento signs with whoever wins.'

'So we're going to be on opposing teams,' Thea says slowly, absorbing the information.

'I assumed you'd be coming over to my side.' Logan at least has the good grace to look uncomfortable, but of course he would make that assumption. His easy confidence, his safety net of money and privilege – he assumed it would all work out in his favour.

Thea feels lightheaded. Under no circumstances must Fuchsia find out that it was her work that gave Logan the idea for this plan. 'I have to stay at iDentity,' she reiterates.

Logan chews his lip, before nodding.

'I understand. But the challenge is happening, with or without you on board. I can't just let Felix rebrand my – our – company without consulting me properly.'

Thea's brain is buzzing. There are too many strands to consider. It would have been hard enough working *with* Logan if Felix had got his way yesterday, but working against him will be no easier. Especially now, knowing she could have been on his team.

At the time, she'd thought that Logan Beechwood coming into her life meant something. That he was going to make an impact. And he has.

Just not the way she hoped.

Chapter Eighteen

Fuchsia is pissed off. Even more pissed off than she was the week she returned from holiday to discover that Teddy hadn't followed up with a potential client that she hadn't told him he needed to follow up with, and then read in the trade press that they'd signed with another agency.

She still refers to it as 'Teddy's failure'.

Her mouth – lined in a dark brown liner that should look terrible but somehow makes her look fashionable – is a thin straight line and her face is arranged in impatient displeasure. She squints at Thea through her glasses. Today's are transparent and rimless with small lenses – the sort someone's dad might wear and look like a dad in, but which Fuchsia pulls off to the point that the observer might be inspired to try it themselves. Only to look like a dad.

'That fucking guy.' She's talking about Logan. Again. Since the official confirmation came through about the agency contest, he's become the lightning rod for all of Fuchsia's ire. Because Thea is a core part of Felix's pitch team, she's been re-promoted from coffee duty, but has spent at least twice the amount of time she *would* spend fetching Fuchsia's coffee orders today listening to all the reasons the whole exercise is a complete waste of time and how idiotic and corny Logan is.

She's standing in Fuchsia's office, beneath the dangling air plants that she became obsessed with two days ago because the company behind them is looking for an agency. They sway gently every time the heating puffs out a blast and their tendrils tickle Thea's neck.

'It's so stupid that we have to go to some challenge kick-off meeting next week with the opponents. Felix is clearly the more forward-looking partner and our idea is bang on for him. Why we have to entertain the other guy is anyone's guess. Probably just has more money than sense and is using mommy and daddy's East Coast dollars to play at being a businessman.'

Thea bristles. Not because Fuchsia is necessarily wrong about the money. Thea feels instantly intimidated when she thinks about how affluent Logan is. But from everything she's heard and seen, Memento means way more to him than a business. His memoir wouldn't exactly be a rags-to-riches story, but he's a savvy operator and he's far more invested in Memento's ongoing success than Felix seems to be. His primary concern is optics.

'If anything, I'd say Felix's plan is financially riskier,' she says, instantly regretting it when Fuchsia stares her down. 'What I mean is, I don't think Felix is short of a few quid either,' she adds hastily.

'Well, his *few quid*—' Fuchsia places heavy emphasis on

Thea's English idiom – 'is paying by the hour for this work, which at least is earning us money now we're being asked to take part in this ridiculous challenge. Of course it would be a fat retainer if they'd just hired us outright like they should have done.' Fuchsia takes a swig of her latest coffee, one that cost five dollars of Ernie's pay packet. 'Felix will be here in ten minutes, so keep opinions like that to yourself. Go fetch Ernie for a run-through.' She swivels on her chair towards her laptop and clicks the mouse track pad, stabbing at it in irritation when it doesn't instantly do what she wants. It's a classic sign that she's about to combust.

Thea starts to hurry out of the room.

'Oh, and Thea,' Fuchsia adds, looking up again. 'It may be a risky plan, but it better be a winner,' she says casually. 'If we fail to secure the business, I'm not going to have enough money to keep running such a large team.'

Thea's heart rate spikes, thinking of Maeve's words about iDentity's financial position. They're constantly pitching but as she's never let anywhere near the clients they land, Thea's unclear on how many companies they have contracts with. Plus they all seem to be start-ups, with precarious incomes. Fuchsia seems so confident, it hadn't occurred to Thea that it wasn't working.

'Are you saying if we don't win the Memento contract, I'm fired?' she says, wanting to be clear before she reports this back to the others.

Fuchsia shrugs. 'Every team member is expected to generate revenue. You've been here almost seven months and haven't won a contract yet.'

'That's because you won't let me into the pitch teams,' Thea gasps out.

'I'm letting you into this one,' she replies, still jabbing at her keyboard. 'So don't let me down.'

'I'd expect to start looking for a new laptop for Fuchsia any day now,' Thea says in a hushed voice to Maeve when she arrives back at her desk.

Maeve sighs. Too tight to engage a proper IT department, Fuchsia latched on to the fact that Maeve had taken computer science courses in college quite early on. She's now treated as both IT support when she loses a document, as well as her personal tech concierge, tasked with seeking out the best deal for new hardware when Fuchsia loses her laptop or breaks it through her impatience and/or aggression. 'At least if I genuinely worked in IT I'd earn good money,' she moans. 'Let's hope she at least keeps it in one piece until Monday. I cannot spend my weekend in Best Buy again.'

'Speaking of which, it's Friday and there are no excuses not to come to Moon Hare this evening,' Teddy says, while looking at Thea meaningfully. '*You* have a lot to fill us in on.'

She hasn't dared to discuss Logan with Teddy yet. He knows about the agency contest – everyone knew about the agency contest after Fuchsia started screaming about it first thing this morning – but not that she met up with the enemy. As far as he's concerned, being on the opposite side to the 'deceitful blowhard' (his words) who lied about being engaged is merely a chance for Thea to take him down a peg or two, and that's before he finds out that landing the contract is key if Thea wants to keep her job. Thea's Slack keeps lighting up with gifs of Joffrey from *Game of Thrones*. Which only reminds her that Billy's messages are still on grey ticks.

'Ernie, Fuchsia wants us both in the office,' she says, not meeting Teddy's eye.

'You guys are going to *nail* those Collective losers,' Teddy shouts, just as Fuchsia breaches the perimeter of her office door to see what's taking Thea so long.

She gives him an approving nod and then glances at Thea as if to say, 'You'd better.'

When Felix arrives, he doesn't waste any time.

'I like what I've seen, but I want to go further before the kick-off next week,' he says, throwing his bag down and manspreading across Fuchsia's entire couch so that she's forced to perch uncomfortably to one side. If a non-client got in her personal space like this, she'd likely turn the couch over Hulk-style in their direction. Not that any of them would want to be anywhere near Fuchsia's personal space. Thea only discovered what neighbourhood she lived in for the express purpose of avoiding it. 'I want something disruptive,' Felix continues, 'something conceptual and edgy.' He's throwing out adjectives without explaining what he means by any of them. 'I want it to architect a brand identity that people are going to talk about.'

Thea suppresses a groan. It's like buzzword bingo.

'Are you looking for attention or for bookings?' she asks, interrupting his flow. 'Because sometimes they're two separate things, and you need to decide which one is more important.'

Felix's shrewd eyes are on her. He's not happy to be pulled out of his monologue. 'What do you mean?'

'Well, as an example, everyone knows that Beyoncé played the opening of that hotel in Dubai and got paid millions of dollars to do it. But how many people can name the hotel, or will book a stay there?'

Fuchsia glares at her. Thea holds the look. It's a valid question. And if they're going to win the contract it's a question they need their client to answer.

'They got a moment of the world's media talking about them,' she explains. 'And if that's what you want – to be in the news cycle in some way – then fine. But it might not be the best money-making strategy.'

Felix chews it over, while literally chewing gum. He snaps it a couple of times and then taps his foot impatiently.

'That's the kind of thing *he* would say.'

'He?' Thea asks, knowing who he means but acting innocent.

'Logan.'

This is clearly not a compliment.

'I'm just looking at this contest from all angles. Due diligence,' Thea backtracks. 'His idea of where to take the business might be different and not to your personal taste, but it doesn't mean it will be a financial bomb.'

She pauses for a second, wondering whether to continue. Logan seemed genuinely sad about fighting with Felix over Memento. She risks it. 'Have you tried—' She stops again. She can feel Fuchsia's eyes boring into her.

'Have I tried what?' She can't work out if Felix's voice is hostile or if he genuinely wants her insight.

'Have you tried working *with* Logan, rather than pitting yourselves against each other?' She says it quickly to get it out. She's holding Fuchsia in her peripheral vision to avoid confirmation of how this idea has gone down.

'He's the one who refused to work with you guys,' Felix says sullenly.

'He's got no vision,' Fuchsia interjects loudly. 'He wants to play it safe.'

Thea nods as though she's absorbing this as a truth, even though she disagrees, and from what Logan said to her last night, he would too. It's not just his money wrapped up in this business, it's his family – both his grandpa's legacy, and his determination to prove his parents wrong.

'I've tried to talk to him, but we have such different ideas about where we want to be. Honestly, at the end of last year I was hoping he'd move back to the East Coast and he could manage the business over there, while I could take it in another direction over here.'

Thea knows she's monopolising the room, but even without being desperate for intel on the guy she currently has such unwelcome feelings for, she'd want to know how he and Felix ended up on such different sides. 'But that's not happening?' she asks in as innocent a voice as she can muster. 'Because I – uh – did some online research about him, when I knew we were working with you, and I thought he had links to someone back East – Claire or Coco or something?'

Felix fixes his eyes on her, but perhaps because she's pulled a load of internet research out of the bag for him once, he doesn't suspect her stalking is anything other than professional. That doesn't stop her thinking he will see right through her at any second.

'Courtney?' Felix says. 'Yeah, they've been on and off forever. They were off all of last year, but I was hoping he'd get back together with her and head home, which would force a natural break and allow for different approaches in our territories – keeping Memento going but separately, like we did before. But Courtney announced she was getting married at Christmas, and he's been weird since he came back from the holiday break. I can't tell if he's upset about her engagement, pissed that she moved on first or pissed about something else entirely. Either way, he's sticking around, which means my easy out has gone.'

There's a silence, one filled for Thea with the sound of adrenaline roaring around her body.

Logan didn't lie? And he isn't engaged?

But what about the photo? The childhood sweethearts caption? The 'love you' comment?

It doesn't make any sense.

She has so many more questions, but none that won't expose her interest in Logan's marital status as being personal rather than professional. Her heart starts thrumming. However he may *feel* about Coco94's engagement, according to Felix he's not an active participant in it.

And if he's not been engaged all this time . . . no wonder he thinks her blocking him on Boxing Day and kissing

Billy was out of order. That she's the one who didn't want to meet up with him.

Shit.

With Thea silent, Fuchsia seizes her moment to stir things up. 'If he's got personal problems in the mix, he's probably not in the right headspace to consider the sort of radical work we can offer you.'

'Damn straight,' agrees Felix. Fuchsia beams. 'And to answer your question,' Felix says, looking directly at Thea, 'it's both.'

'Huh?' She has no idea what he's talking about. Her thoughts are still on last night's conversation. The part where she pounced on the word 'proposal' and tried to use it to shame him. Logan had just looked confused. She wants to disappear from embarrassment or call him immediately and find out the truth. One or the other.

'I want attention *and* I want bookings,' Felix says, before spreading his eye contact to the rest of the room. 'So prove I've backed the right team.'

Friday night happy hour is always busier than early weeknight happy hour, and by the time Fuchsia snaps off her computer at seven – with Maeve breathing a sigh of relief that it's still functioning – Thea, Teddy, Ernie, Maeve and Kim pile downstairs and next door to the bar, which has begun to fill up. Mid-January, they already have posters up for their annual Valentine's Day 'kissing booth' charity event. It's the sort of American cultural touchpoint that gives Thea a fizz of excitement about where she is, even as she thinks how gross kissing randoms for money (even charity money) is and how no one in the UK would entertain such an idea. They scout for a table and even though the big booth at the front, framed by the bar's floor-to-ceiling front window, is free, they head to the back of the room. Despite Fuchsia once declaring that no one with any taste would be seen dead in that cheap-looking bar next door, they have never once, even when Moon Hare was otherwise at shoulder-to-shoulder standing capacity, risked her spotting them there. They find a slightly-too-small table towards the back and, with the help of stools of mismatched heights from other tables, cram around it.

'Don't start until I've got the drinks,' Kim instructs Thea before heading to the bar. She's decided that tonight's first two-for-one cocktail is piña coladas so after a wait long enough to ensure that at least one of them complains that they should have just ordered beers, Kim returns with a laden-down tray.

'OK, spill,' she says, doling out the sickly-cream drinks. 'Ernie said that you and the film hottie have previous but then you thought he was a cheat, but as of this afternoon, it turns out he's *not* definitively a cheat, but he *is* now our professional enemy, so your love triangle has become a business takeover nightmare.' Maeve's eyes gleam in Thea's direction, indicating this too is the version of the story she's heard. Which is basically true.

Thea groans. 'Wait, Logan has only been to one of the upstairs meeting rooms, not the office itself, so how do you know he's a hottie?'

'We looked him up when you were at the meeting,' Maeve shrugs, sucking on the straw in her drink. 'What? You'd have done it too.'

'I actually first looked them up after Felix came in to see us, because he too is a hottie,' says Teddy.

Thea shoots him a look.

'What? He is. Even if he's a douche. You can't blame us for stalking them,' he fires at her. 'Stalking Logan ruined your whole Christmas.' All four sets of eyes fix on her, Teddy's knowing, the rest of them expectant. 'Enough referring to things we don't know about,' instructs Maeve. 'Fill us in.'

Thea takes a sip of her drink. The rum and sweetness hit the back of her throat, and the booze gives her a confidence hit. 'This goes no further, right?'

'Circle of trust,' they all confirm, nodding gravely.

'It started when I was trying to get home for Christmas,' she begins, before giving them the precis of Christmas Eve-Eve. She plays up the mix-up over the room, and plays down how she felt by the end of it. It's OK for Teddy to know how much she pinned her heart on the whole thing – and how much it still hurts to think about what might have been – but her gut tells her that it's best to play this as an entertaining, disastrous dating story, nothing more. She doesn't mention her meet-up with Logan last night or the offer he made her. Not now she knows what's at stake with the Memento contract. 'He DM'ed to ask about meeting up again after Christmas, and I thought "sure",' she says, shooting a little look at Teddy, who flashes her a quick smile to show he won't contradict her.

'But when I had a look at his socials it looked like he had a fiancée so I wrote him off as a player.' She pauses for comic effect. 'And then his business partner walked into our building.'

'Looking like a russet-haired Ryan Gosling,' Maeve throws in, mock swooning.

'And the rest you know from Ernie,' she shrugs. 'Felix came into iDentity and then I saw Logan again at the meeting. So I don't *know* him know him. I just know him more than Fuchsia or Felix think I do.'

'The look he gave her as he left the meeting on Wednesday made me think he *wants* to know you,' Ernie adds in a faux-innocent voice. 'And now we know he's single.'

'Single, and as Kim put it, our professional enemy,' Thea shoots back. 'Fuchsia has made it crystal clear that we have to win this contract.' They all take nervous sips of their drinks thinking about iDentity's precarious financial situation. Maeve announced earlier that she was going to 'dig into some stuff' to see if she could find out how bad it was, and she's seen all of them flicking furtively between job sites when Fuchsia is out at meetings. 'He's not someone I should be dating right now.'

'That part *is* true,' Kim chips in. 'You guys won't remember Gail, but she worked here when I started. We pitched for a client – unsuccessfully – and a few weeks later the company CEO got in touch to ask her out. She wasn't interested and was always going to say no, but she made the mistake of telling us about it in the office. Fuchsia overheard and flipped, saying if she even considered it, she should start looking for a new job.'

Maeve snorts. 'Then why did I have to pretend for *a year* that my roommate was my boyfriend when she wanted to set me up with that data-processing start-up guy?'

'Probably because we won that contract and she wanted to keep him happy,' Kim shrugs. 'No one ever said her rules made moral or legal sense.'

'But it does confirm that I should keep away from Logan – even if he's still interested. Which I doubt, considering all the mad things he thinks I've done since Christmas.'

'A crush on the enemy though,' Teddy says. 'It's kind of sexy.'

'Sexier than being unemployed?' Thea groans. 'I need to impress Fuchsia and I need Felix not to hate me for my sake *and* for the sake of the company if these rumours are anywhere near true.' She stops. 'And I need to not be distracted from either of those things by trying to make Logan like me. No daydreaming about Logan.'

Smiling, Teddy holds his thumb and forefinger a tiny way apart to signify 'maybe a little bit'. 'No!' she says, but laughing now. 'Work only. No illicit crushes.'

Her heart flutters, then freezes, and the sensation sinks.

Chapter Nineteen

Voice note from Nan:

It's been snowing here and your dad's keeping me prisoner in the house [background noise of Dad protesting] ... oh give over, I'm only joking. He's being very sensible, love, it's icy outside so I'm staying in here, even though I'm bored out of my mind. Send me some links to that actor you were telling me about for YouTube, whassisname, the tall, moody one, to keep me occupied.

Anyway, just messaging to wish you luck getting your work done this weekend and for the contest meeting on Monday. I know it's hard but all you have to do is keep your mouth shut and get what you can out of it. Earn your money and think about men later, that's what Nanny says. And I'm old and wise. Hang on. Roy? Are you making a tea? I'll have one thanks—

Crumpled within the sheets of Thea's bed-cum-sofa in her studio flat on Saturday morning, Nan's message cuts through her hangover from the previous night at Moon Hare.

Coffee, she thinks, remembering how many piña coladas they ended up having and tasting the stale tang of pineapple at the back of her throat. She and Teddy got a cab home and she ended up going back to his and Jake's until 2 a.m. while she spilled the uncensored version of the Logan story, over yet more rum. She doesn't even like rum. Her head throbs from both that and the over-sharing.

Her phone buzzes again.

Kit: Sis when are you back in London again 😊
Thea: I'm broke and have no annual leave. So not for ages, why?

A beat. She follows up.

Thea: You lot are supposed to be coming to see me!

Kit is typing . . .

Kit: That's probably not going to happen any time soon though, is it? Not with everything.
Thea: What's 'everything'? Is everyone OK?

Nothing.

Thea: Kit! What does everything mean?
Kit: You know money, time off, that stuff. M&D won't leave Nan either.
Thea: She's coming too though!
Thea: Right?

Flying Home for Christmas

Thea: Kit?

Kit: She'd be there like a shot.

Kit: 'Cept someone maxed out her credit card. 😄

Thea: Ha ha. You're the moneybags of the family, why don't you treat her? Or have you spent it all on hideous jackets?

Kit: I would . . .

Thea: Kit, what's going on? Why are you being weird?

Thea: You want to FaceTime?

Kit: 📍 C U

Kit scarpers, as he always does when she suggests speaking on the phone, leaving her wondering what he's talking about. There's a nervous buzzing in the pit of her stomach.

She opens her thread with Mum.

Mum, is everything OK? Kit made it sound like something's wrong.

She's surprised when her phone buzzes again. Mum's not known for her speedy response times. But it isn't her, it's Teddy.

Do you want to go axe-throwing? (Don't ask and FML) One of Jake's co-workers has organised it as team-building but apparently three of them found it 'triggering' so there's been dropouts. Interested? 5pm at Nordic Punks on Main.

Thea starts to type 'What is axe throwing?' but stops, murmuring 'never mind' to herself. This is what she loves about Portland. That there's always something weird and wonderful happening.

I have no idea what it is. Count me in!

She puts her phone down, but keeps picking it back up to check if Mum has read her message. The rest of the day stretches in front of her and the conversation with Kit has left her unsettled. She's supposed to be spending the weekend on some 'achingly cool, industry-disrupting' ideas to add to their honed Memento presentation by Monday, but the only thing disrupted right now is her brain.

Coffee, she decides. First definitely coffee.

Across the road from Coffee Capers, she sees him through the window. She slows down, reconsidering everything from what she would have ordered if no one she knew was going to see her (a hangover-quelling iced caramel macchiato) and she'll now have to upgrade to something not designed for a toddler, to what she's wearing (leggings and a slouchy jumper with a beanie hat on top of hair that is only half dry because holding a hairdryer in her delicate state quickly became too much effort).

Logan is framed between the bright chalk-pen proclamations that declare everything is better with coffee and that the weather outside might be freezing, but inside they're roasting. She can see him sitting at a table and reading a newspaper – an actual hard-copy paper one – and sipping from a pottery cup. He's all out of context. Here, in her neighbourhood. It's discombobulating. She stops for a second to decide whether to turn back, even though the walk sign is illuminated, so she can take in the sight of him while he doesn't know she's looking. He's wearing a red woollen jumper that looks impossibly soft and clings perfectly to his upper arms. For a second, she pretends she's here to meet him for a date. Saturday-morning coffee with her boyfriend, when they're both hungover, which they will chug down to restore them before going back home to bed . . .

She ought to just turn around and leave. So what if it turns out he's single? No good can come of seeing him while the pitching competition is live – plus, between the kissing and the blocking, he must think she's emotionally unstable.

At the second she decides to go, Logan looks up from his paper and sees her standing – half propped, really – at the crosswalk. He smiles and waves, and the combination dissolves her common sense. It's a coffee shop, she tells herself. She's here to buy coffee. Just because they're on opposing teams doesn't mean she can't be civil and say hi.

She steps into the road and is almost taken down by an e-scooter, the rider of which shouts 'silly bitch' at her, which is a bit rich considering he's both in the wrong and wearing plus fours and a monocle. She scurries across the road.

She pushes the door, which has an old-fashioned bell above it that gives a tinkle as she enters, and throws a semi-awkward wave in Logan's direction. She does a visual sweep of the room, checking for anyone with a vague connection to iDentity or The Collective. The café is miles from the office, as well as Fuchsia's neighbourhood, but in Portland, you can't underestimate how far people will travel for coffee.

'Hey.' Logan's eyes crinkle in surprise as he smiles. 'Do you live around here?' All she can look at are his lips. She has the overwhelming impulse to touch him. Just on the arm, nothing creepy. It's the tactile-looking jumper.

'A few blocks that way,' she says, gesturing back the way she came and ignoring the looping commentary in her head of Felix revealing Logan's relationship status yesterday. 'I came in to grab coffee . . .' She trails off as Logan gives one of his scrunched-up smiles. 'Well, you're in the right place, this being a coffee shop and all.'

She nods down at his empty drink. 'Does it compare to Dunkin' Donuts though, that's the big question?'

Logan chuckles. 'I told you, *nowhere* compares to Dunkin' Donuts.' He gestures to the seat next to him. 'Do you want to join me?'

Heat permeates her body. Her head says no, but before she can stop her mouth, it says, 'Sure. Can I get you another one? Or some cake or something?'

Espionage, she tells herself. *If anyone sees me, I'm here to see what I can get out of him and report back to Fuchsia.* She pushes out the thought that she could have already told Fuchsia everything she knew after her meet-up with him on Thursday if she was really in the market for that.

'I'll have another filter coffee, thanks. And maybe a cookie if you're having something.'

She stands up again, fumbling for her purse. 'Back in a sec.'

Once loaded up, she heads back over to Logan, repeating the words 'covert information' inside her head like an affirmation. Logan looks up from the newspaper again as she crosses the room and the words evaporate. Who is she kidding? The only covert thing she wants from him is of the sort she can definitely never share with Fuchsia.

She slips onto the chair beside his while she pulls off her coat, telling herself it's not a proximity high she's getting, but a wave of dizziness from last night's alcohol leaving her system. Which is a lie. What she's feeling is an electric current that hums like the pincers in Operation do when he's within a certain radius. She can admit it to herself now she knows he's single. Well, pending confirmation is single.

'How's your weekend?' Logan asks as she sits down, sloshing a little of the coffee over the lip of the mug as she fumbles with the plates and cups.

'Good. So far.' Better for finding out Coco94 is off the scene, she wants to say. 'You?'

'Yeah, OK.' He raises an eyebrow at her conspiratorially. 'Work is pretty intense, as you can probably imagine.'

She nods, thinking about everything Felix said yesterday.

'How are you finding working with Felix?' he asks. Her suspicions prick up. Maybe *he* is using *her* for espionage.

'I think you know how I feel about his vision,' she says carefully, 'but he's the client so I'm trying really hard to come up with work that will make him happy.'

Logan nods, rubbing his hand over the bristles of his beard. 'Very diplomatic.'

Thea blows a soft laugh out of her nose. 'Please don't ask me for inside information,' she says, wincing a little. 'Because I can't tell you. I'm under so much pressure with this competition.' She leaves it there. She doesn't want Logan or Felix to know that her job and iDentity's finances might depend on this contract. She suspects it won't make them an attractive prospect. 'I'm already terrified that Fuchsia will find out that the slides you saw ignited this whole pitching contest,' she says instead. 'And then I'll be looking at the first flight back to London. And I don't want to go home. My job's not perfect—' Logan raises his eyebrow even higher this time – 'but I love it here. I'd only ever want to leave on my own terms.'

'I wouldn't do that to you,' Logan says in a way that makes her believe him. 'And besides, I want the outcome of this to be the right one. If Felix's strategy makes good business sense, I'll suck it up and do what he wants, and I hope he'll do the same for me.'

Thea feels the stress in her shoulders dissolve slightly. 'I guess when you reveal your strategy next week then the contest will start and we'll see,' she says lightly.

'I guess we will,' he agrees, breaking his cookie in half. 'Want some?' He holds a piece out to her. It's the excuse she needs to touch him, but Thea shakes her head, gesturing at her own slab of cake. 'I should probably go. I'm not sure how I would explain—' she flaps a hand between them – 'this if anyone saw us together.'

'There's no reason we can't be professionally friendly,' Logan says, fixing his eyes on her.

Her heart sinks at the thought of professional friendliness, the way she is with the person who comes to fix the coffee machine every time Fuchsia breaks it, or the printer (also when Fuchsia breaks it).

'I get it, you didn't want to take things any further after that night in the hotel,' he continues in a matter-of-fact voice, 'so we're not going to date, but this pitching contest isn't personal—'

'Me!' Thea bursts out. 'I didn't just decide to ghost you. I thought you had a fiancée! *That's* why I blocked you.' It's a momentary relief to get it out there, but the second it is she knows there's only one way she could have discovered this (false) information and Logan will soon realise that.

'A fiancée?' A confused look spreads over his face. 'I don't have a fiancée. Why would you think that I did?'

There's a silence as Logan looks at Thea intently, his blue eyes on her grey ones. Thea goes redder and redder until she thinks she's going to combust.

She closes her eyes as she admits it, screwing up her face in embarrassment. 'I was snooping in your social media over Christmas. And that led me to the social media profile of Coco94, and *that* led me to a super-cute photograph of the two of you where she was showing off an engagement ring and referring to you as her childhood sweetheart. Which I took to mean—' She stops, takes a breath. 'I thought you'd lied to me.' *What would Nicole say now? What would Nan?* 'And I wasn't having it,' she finishes.

She opens one eye, chances a look at him. She expects him to get angry or defensive or to accuse her of being crazy. All things Christian had done when she was actually right about him being a liar. In this case, she's the one in the wrong, but so far Logan hasn't accused her of being insane – or, Christian's go-to, paranoid – but that doesn't mean he's not thinking it. He's just looking at her as though that would be a reasonable response to thinking someone is engaged.

'Courtney – my childhood sweetheart, as you rightly identify her – *is* engaged.' He stops, looks her dead in the eye and holds her look. 'But not to me.'

'I know that now,' she admits, buzzing with tension. 'Felix mentioned it in the office yesterday.'

'But that's why you stopped talking to me,' Logan says softly, as if it all now makes sense.

Thea nods, her mouth pressed together in a grimace. 'I'm sorry. There's nothing I can say to make it sound any less weird. All I can say in my defence is that my ex did a real number on me, and when I saw that Christmas Day post, I wasn't about to be taken for a sucker for a second time.'

Logan nods his head as though absorbing the information. 'The guy you mentioned? The one that made you want to leave the country?'

Thea barks out a laugh. Her heart is hammering in her chest. 'Yep, the very same.' She expects Logan is wondering how quickly he can get out of this coffee shop. Between Fuchsia being professionally unstable and Thea being emotionally unstable, he probably can't wait to get far away from her. She chugs her coffee to give him an easy exit. But Logan just sits there, looking as though he's ruminating.

'Courtney and I *were* childhood sweethearts,' he says in the end. 'Our families have lived next door to each other forever and we're the same age, so we started dating pretty much as soon as we were old enough to know what dating was. Everyone thought we were made for each other. Even our parents expected us to end up together.'

'Sounds very Dawson and Joey,' Thea chimes in. The idea of Logan having a teen-drama-worthy pre-determined destiny makes her coffee turn to acid in her stomach. Who can compete with that?

'We went to college in separate states. I stayed in Boston for film school and she went to Michigan for Sport Science. We stayed together, if you can call it that, but we broke up and got back together, broke up and got back together – it was a bit of a cycle. One of us would decide we should have space to do our own thing at college and call it quits, but then the summer would roll around, we'd head home and end up getting back together. Plus, our families always get together at holidays, so Fourth of July, Memorial Day, Christmas – there was no escaping each other.' He takes another pull on his drink. 'I'd see her again and realise that I loved her.'

The sentence winds Thea. It's so matter-of-fact. He was the one that got dumped, then, she concludes, and he's still hung up on her. The little frond of hope that unfurled as he was speaking, snaps off.

'So why aren't you together now?'

'Because while I knew I loved her, it took me a while to work out that I didn't love her like *that*. Maybe because I didn't have anything to compare it to, and our families

231

talked about us like we were a foregone conclusion.' There's a wry look on Logan's face. 'But you also know how I feel about my parents' expectations, so I figured it out in the end. I'd say we should have been siblings, but as I've never wanted to bury her beneath a pile of couch cushions or get her in a headlock like I used to with Jackson and Keaton, I think best friends is the most appropriate label.

'After college we both moved back home and got back together *again*, but really, we were using home as a base while we interned or applied for grad school in other states. We bounced in and out of Boston for a few years. She was someone I wanted to hang out with, and the person who knew everything about me. Our friends used to say how great it was that we had so much freedom within our relationship, to travel with friends, or pick a grad school anywhere in the country, and know the relationship was solid. But the truth is I wanted her to go off and do her own thing, because I wanted to do my own thing too.

'I think if we'd stayed in the same town at the same time long enough, we'd have realised a lot sooner that we shouldn't have been together. Before I moved to Portland, I was back in Boston and she was doing short-term contracts with college sports coaches all around the country, trying to get a permanent position. We were long distance again and barely saw each other. At the beginning of last year, I came out here and we decided to cut out all the contact that kept pulling us back together. We agreed not to speak for a while, and that turned into months, and—' he crumples up his face as though he's slightly embarrassed – 'I was tense about seeing her at Christmas because I was worried she'd want to pick things up again and I'd have to properly break up with her.' He holds his hands up as though he knows it's lame. 'I was scared of having an awkward conversation.'

He pauses, looking as though he's deciding whether to continue. 'And then I met you. We had the sort of connection that felt as though it didn't matter how long I'd known you, because it was there and it was real. Even though I spent less than twenty-four hours getting to know you, rather than the twenty-eight years I'd known Courtney, I knew that it was how I was supposed to feel when I was around someone that—' He stops. 'When we said goodbye at the airport, I knew I had to rip off the Band Aid for good, no matter what she, or our families thought about it.'

He starts crumbling the rest of his cookie into little pieces. 'I psyched myself up to do it when I landed.' He screws up his face as though he's building to a point and Thea can't help but smile. 'And I go to her place and she's engaged!' He barks out a self-deprecating laugh. 'Which hurt my ego a *little* bit.' He pulls his thumb and forefinger an inch or so apart, but he's smiling. 'To some sports strategist guy she met six months ago. And instead *I'm* on the receiving end of *her* awkward rehearsed speech about how this whirlwind romance had shown her how she was supposed to feel around a partner and that she'll always love me, but not like that. I had a moment where I thought "should I pretend to be upset?" before I realised, I'm incapable of hiding my feelings around her and told her about you. She couldn't stop laughing.'

He shrugs. 'I shouldn't be surprised, she figured it all out before I did. She was always much smarter than me.'

Thea feels a tingle in her stomach, because while her brain has obviously locked onto the barrage of compliments Logan has paid this smart, gorgeous, sports scientist woman who sounds like someone she should hate on principle, in the midst of his story, she has also registered: he told her about me. She has visions of them being great friends, like Katy Perry and Miranda Kerr, but where Courtney is Miranda Kerr and Thea is . . . some awkward, barely employed English woman.

'Her fiancé, Chip—' Thea seizes on the name to tell Nicole – 'flew in the day after Christmas. He's a total sports freak, perfect for her, and Courtney kept asking me about you and talking about serendipity. I was thinking how lucky I was to get away without having to be the bad guy.' He screws his mouth up, his rough beard wrinkling across his face. 'And then you blocked me.' Somehow, during Logan's potted history of him and Courtney, they've moved closer together. Thea has started leaning towards him on the edge of her chair. His jeans-clad leg is millimetres away from hers, close enough to feel the heat radiating from him. Her head is cupped in her hand, listening to him talk. 'And the next time I saw you, you were kissing some guy in the park, so I thought you were with him.'

'His name is Billy and *he* kissed *me*,' she clarifies, repressing a shudder. She never did reply to his message after their date. 'There's absolutely nothing going on with us. My friend set me up to distract me.'

'Distract you from what?' His eyes meet Thea's again, a piercing look that makes her chest constrict and her heart thump.

Her breath catches in her throat. Forget playing it cool, he's just told her the truth, so she should too. 'From you.'

Logan's voice is low. 'But you didn't need distracting.'

Thea nods, smiling. 'Guess not. Although it would have still made the pitching contest problematic.' She pushes the thought of unemployment or iDentity's financial downfall out of her mind.

'You have no idea how much I hate this whole fricking situation,' Logan says. 'Why couldn't Felix just—' He stops, making a frustrated, strangled noise.

'Just what?'

'Just talk to me. Instead of going behind my back and potentially costing us our business relationship as well as our friendship.'

'If it wasn't for him, I'd still think you were engaged,' Thea reminds him.

'I guess I can thank him for that. Except I can't tell him. If he even knows I've seen you now, by chance, it'll get you in trouble and he'll probably accuse me of using you to cheat at the contest.' Logan suddenly looks weary. 'God, I can't wait until this is all over. Hey—' He stops.

'What?'

'For today, can we pretend the pitch meeting isn't happening on Monday? And that the last three weeks didn't happen?'

'Why not?' It will all still be waiting on Monday, but somehow when she's with Logan, the real world seems to fall away.

'And if neither of those things exist, maybe I can buy you another cup of coffee and we can get to know each other without thinking the other one has something to hide.'

Thea gives him a genuine smile. 'I would like nothing more.'

Chapter Twenty

'How was the rest of your Christmas?' Logan asks as though he knows about nothing after Boxing Day. 'Was it good to spend time with your nan?'

Thea decides to play along, even though all the bits they're not acknowledging are, for her, simmering in the background.

'*So* nice. Even if it went so fast. And I wasn't on great form because I was bummed out about a guy.' She shoots him a quick look. 'But I loved seeing my family. Nan seemed smaller somehow though.' She stops, realising it's true as she says it. It makes her feel a bit raw and tearful. 'Maybe it's because I'm not seeing her every day, but she seems more frail.'

'She's all right though?' Logan asks.

'I think so.' There's uncertainty in her voice, as now she thinks about it, she's not sure. Thea thinks about the trip to the spa which completely took it out of her, and Kit's texts. 'She got tired easily.' She shakes the doubt away. 'I keep trying to persuade my family to come out and see me, but they won't commit to it. It's a long way I guess.' She visibly straightens as though to stop herself leaning into how much she misses them. 'Have your parents been over?'

'Yeah, a couple of times so far, but it's not so far for them. Both times they've managed to offend everyone they meet.'

'What?' Thea bursts out laughing. 'Why?'

'They're *very* Boston. Direct. People here are much more chilled, so they come across as impatient and cranky.'

'They'd fit in in London,' Thea says. 'Do they hate it when people walk slowly?'

'Yes, but they also walk slowly themselves, so go figure. Maybe they *are* just assholes,' Logan muses. 'I've probably not painted a great picture of them. Aside from the perpetual disappointment in my choice of career, I do love them.'

'I like direct people,' says Thea, thinking of Nicole. And of Teddy. 'What are your friends like?' she asks. 'Aside from Felix.' And Courtney, she thinks. She may not be his fiancée but that doesn't mean she's ready to hear any more about how great she is.

'They live all over the country now, so I feel as though I've started again when it comes to making friends. When I first moved here, I met a lot of people through Felix, which is making this point in my life kind of challenging, but I have a few buddies through a film club I'm in and a hiking group I've joined.'

'What's the hiking group?'

'It's mainly a bunch of old guys who've lived here forever and know all the best trails. We hike for a few hours and then they take me to some bar that's one of the last places to be discovered by the hipsters and tell me stories about all the hiking they've done in the past. I think I'm the youngest by about thirty years, but they've embraced me as a newbie. It reminds me of those camping trips with my grandpa in a lot of ways. I'd like to make a film about them, but am working my way up to asking them. They don't take any BS so I don't want to push my luck. How about you? Have you met a lot of people?'

Thea thinks about how her common interests with her friends here mainly revolve around working their way through Moon Hare's cocktail menu. 'I work a lot, so it's been hard to make friends outside of it, but I'm lucky that I get on with my co-workers. Teddy's my best friend here and I'm seeing him later actually, along with his boyfriend Jake. I hang out with them a lot at weekends.' She laughs self-deprecatingly. 'I'm waiting for them to tell me three's a crowd, but so far, so good.'

Logan looks at her seriously. 'I can't imagine someone not wanting to hang out with you.'

Heat rises to Thea's face. 'Do you want another coffee?' she asks, gesturing at his mug.

'If I drink any more coffee, I don't think I'll sleep again. But I could eat lunch. We could head to the food market if you don't mind a walk?'

'Sounds good.'

Thea tugs on her hat and pulls her coat tightly around her as they leave the coffee shop, heading towards the open-air food market. A blast of crisp January air hits them. It's not quite snowing, but there are tiny crystals of snow falling intermittently. The air is tight with cold, the sort that makes your bones contract and freezes your face until it goes numb. As they walk side by side, the tip of Logan's nose turns red and she imagines hers is the same. They both have thick gloves on, stuffed into their coat pockets.

At the market, the air smells of fried chicken, baked bread and strong cheese. They bustle among couples carrying net shopping bags as they stock up on apples fresh from the orchard and small-batch cider, while sampling tiny cubes of food that are offered at pretty much every stall to entice people to buy. They stop at a vegetable stall. It's all beautifully presented, with homely, handwritten signs that explain the precedence of each item. Even the dirt looks to be distributed in such a way as to make the produce more appealing – and the prices reflect the artistic presentation. Thea imagines Nan comparing the cost of a bowl of veg on Walthamstow Market with what's for sale here. She suppresses a grin. She and Logan wander up and down for an hour, tasting things from the toothpicks offered and filling each other in on the foods they loved and loathed as children.

'I can't believe you don't have Findus Crispy Pancakes over here,' Thea tells Logan when she lists the staple foods she and Kit had after school in the early noughties.

'Are they good?'

'I don't think I've had one since I was about ten and they're probably horrible, but they always remind me of being picked up from school by Nan and having my tea at her place. You must have some food like that.'

'Maybe, Kraft dinner? That's macaroni cheese from a box. Or Lean Cuisine frozen meals?'

'American convenience food always seemed so glamorous to me because it was on TV shows and films, even though it's probably all the same junk. I can't tell you how disappointed I was when I ate Hershey's chocolate for the first time.' Thea mimes a vomit face. 'Your chocolate is *so bad*. Half my suitcase when I came back from England was Dairy Milk bars.'

Logan turns to her, faux outrage emblazoned on his face. 'Hey, that's our candy heritage you're shitting on.'

Thea stops and gives him a serious look. 'Listen, America has created many good things – traffic lights, iPhones, The Rock – but your chocolate is not one of them! It makes me sad for all the children trick or treating that end up with a bucket of Hershey kisses. They sound so good, but they taste so bad!'

'There's a chocolatier in North Portland that makes amazing chocolate bars.'

'Doesn't count,' she says with feeling. 'The British chocolate I'm talking about is cheap, supermarket stuff. If it's made by artisans, it's cheating. I'll prove it to you. Next time I see you I'll bring you a bar from my precious Cadbury's stash. It will blow your mind.'

Logan chuckles. 'An offer I can't refuse. In the meantime, I need to claw back some kudos for my country, so what do you want to eat from this delicious array of local cooks and producers? Thai curry, burgers, hard cider, a crêpe? Will it be as good as a crispy pancake? We'll have to see. Or there's a health food stall selling "longevity lunch tinctures".' He pulls a face at her as she simultaneously pulls the same horrified face.

'If I'm going to have a liquid lunch it's going to be the traditional boozy one. How about curry, cider and then maybe a crêpe for dessert?'

'Sounds good.' They head to a food truck located in an airstream caravan where huge pans of curry simmer on hobs beneath the service window. A moustachioed chef with two full sleeves of tattoos takes their order and another – a woman with her hair in a rockabilly roll – plates them up before handing them over.

Logan's hand brushes Thea's as they both put a card down on the counter to pay. Their eyes lock and there's a palpable crackle in the air. It's as though the atmosphere has been reset. Every nerve in her body is on high alert.

'Half on each?' the server asks, nodding at the cards.

'Yes,' Thea replies decisively. The problem with 'getting to know each other' but with strict boundaries about what they can and can't discuss, means it's unclear what this is. It's not a date, because they ran into each other randomly, and they can't date each other right now anyway. But, like last time, this is starting to feel like the date-iest non-date Thea has ever been on.

They take their plates to a covered area where picnic tables have been set up beneath outdoor heaters, strings of fairy lights hanging above them. Logan sits down on a bench and Thea sits opposite. As is the law in al fresco spaces, the side of her face closest to the heater starts frazzling from the hot air blasting out while the far side remains resolutely freezing.

They eat in silence for a while, people-watching as shoppers come and go from the stalls. A group of women stumble past carrying drinks; from the volume of shrieking, they can't be on their first ciders of the day, and four of them shout to the other about a guy not being worth the aggravation and she should dump him. It jars with the otherwise genteel civility of the market.

'This feels like a date, right?' Logan says in his steady voice, dark eyebrows framing his blue eyes seriously. 'I'm not going crazy.'

Heat floods to Thea's entire face, not just the side being slow-roasted by the patio heater. It's exactly what she wants to hear, just not at the time she wants to hear it. She chews her curry to buy her some time about how to respond.

'Yes, it does,' she admits eventually, putting her fork down and tapping her fingers on the table nervously. 'And I would really like it to be. But it's too complicated at the moment. Right now, I have plausible deniability with Fuchsia. Just about, anyway. If she finds out I know you, I can say sure, we've seen each other around, but there's no conflict of interest.'

'Is that what we're doing? Seeing each other around?' Logan puts down his hand next to hers, and oh-so-gently runs the tip of his index finger along the top of her thumb. The lightest of strokes that takes her breath away.

'For now,' she says.

Her mind starts running through the possibilities.

Fuchsia finds out while they're competing for the Memento contract?

Bad. She can kiss goodbye to her job and her visa.

Fuchsia doesn't find out, but Thea throws herself into this and she gets her heart broken. Again.

Also bad.

There's a third possibility.

But it's a long shot.

She doesn't want to say goodbye to whatever this *could* be, but nor does she want to detonate the life she's building for herself here. A life she's started growing into and a job she needs while she figures out her next move to stay in the US. What if she goes for it, and it all blows up in her face? It's not just about iDentity. The last guy she chose was Christian, which started well and then bit by bit, everything she did pissed him off. Tying herself in knots second-guessing how he wanted her to be only made everything worse. Undermining her and putting her down in front of other people. Cheating on her at least once and making her feel crazy for being upset about it. As she stands there, not finishing the sentence, she can feel an almost physical echo of the misery, small pulsing aftershocks from the emotional fallout. Logan isn't Christian, but she doesn't really know who Logan is yet either. What if he's not as over Courtney as he says he is?

People tell you to trust your gut, but after Christian, Thea isn't sure hers is trustworthy. She wishes she had Nicole's gut instead: solid, reliable, better at filtering out the shit.

Before she decides whether or not she should let today be classed as a date, or even a pre-date date, she needs a second opinion. Nicole isn't here, but Teddy is.

Reluctantly, she pulls her hand away, the sensation of his finger still tingling there like a promise waiting to be fulfilled. And then she says, 'How do you feel about axe-throwing?'

Chapter Twenty-One

Nordic Punk is a mashup of messy references. The heavy wooden door has a skull and crossbones on it, with a snake winding its way through one of the eye sockets. Opening it reveals an enormous bar decked out like a Viking ship, all sturdy wood tables and chunky benches, with noisy voices within, shouting to be heard above the angry punk music playing. A counter runs along one side of the room with shields decorating its lower perimeter, though any adherence to making them look era-specific is cancelled out by having band names like 'Sex Pistols' spray-painted onto them.

'I feel like this is the physical embodiment of what Felix wants to do to our company,' Logan says, his eyes wide as he takes in the scene.

'THEA!' She hears her name screamed at ear-splitting volume during a break in the music and clocks Teddy and Jake sitting around one of the tables with a crowd of people. She notices the half-empty pitcher of beer in front of them seconds before she clocks that the crowd of people contains – oh God – Billy.

'Hi,' she says, approaching them with a small, awkward wave. She gestures to Logan beside her and Teddy's eyes bulge so wide they risk rolling out of the sockets onto the floor. Any second now he will text her to ask what is going on, and Thea will have to admit she doesn't know but she couldn't help but invite Logan along.

'I hope you don't mind but I brought a—' She stops, not knowing how to refer to Logan. 'You said there were extra spaces, so this is Logan.'

Teddy rises from the table and rearranges his face into something resembling a normal human. He shakes Logan's hand. 'Teddy,' he says. 'This is Jake, and then we have—' he turns to Jake – 'actually I don't even know half these people's names, so I'll let Jake introduce you. But I'm Teddy, Thea's friend and—' here he emphasises the word – '*co-worker*.'

'Roger that,' says Logan with a smile. 'For the purposes of all our weekday alter egos, I'm happy to remain out of any response to "how was your weekend?" that you might hear at work on Monday.'

Teddy barks out a cynical laugh. 'You definitely don't know much about Fuchsia if you think that's a question she would ask any of us, but agreed, let's keep this on the DL.'

Jake embraces Thea in a hug, the soft fuzz of his shaved head tickling her as he does.

'Cute,' he murmurs into her ear.

'There's nothing going on,' she whispers back.

'Sure,' he replies, shooting her a cheeky look before pulling away to shake Logan's hand.

'There are about a million people here whose names you'll instantly forget,' he declares to them both, 'but Cameron over there is splitting us into teams for the games so I'll make intros once we've been put into smaller groups. Cam!' he shouts. 'Thea and Logan need to be with me and Teddy 'kay?'

A mild-looking, bespectacled man wearing a T-shirt that declares him to be 'Punk as F*ck' nods and goes back to concentrating on the iPad in front of him. Thea's eyes skim the length of the table. She's the only woman here. The rest of the group contains all the right sartorial elements to indicate that they're hip Portlandians – there's a serious amount of facial hair, plaid and cardigans – but they all exude a slightly goofy, tech-nerd energy. The majority are a little hunched over with the sort of squinty expression you must develop after spending long hours analysing code on screen. Jake has always said that the people he works with are the antithesis to the 'tech bro' stereotype; instead of marching around proclaiming they're going to shake up the industry with their ambiguous moral-compass and rule-breaking inventions, they're the guys who quietly program the inventions using old-fashioned focus and hard work.

And then there's Billy. Folded over one end of the table and looking like a beefy *Men's Health* model, completely at odds with the rest of them.

She catches his eye and smiles in what she hopes is a friendly but vague way. The knowledge she never replied to his message weighs on her conscience in a way it wouldn't if she didn't have to actually face him.

Billy's eyes flick to Logan and narrow. Logan gives Billy a slow nod in return.

'We're playing in teams of six so listen up for your name,' says Cameron, calling the rabble to attention. 'Each team is in a separate room and there's an individual competition within each group, as well as an overall winner, plus a prize for the best-performing team.'

It all sounds very organised to Thea. Cameron, bless him, is clearly the Nicole of Jake's workplace.

'Team one,' he starts to say, calling out six names.

'Team two – Jake, Teddy, Thea, new guy – Logan, was it? – me, and Billy.'

'Shit,' Thea mutters, as Cameron runs through the other teams. Teddy widens his eyes at her, and she mouths, 'FML,' back at him.

Once the rest of the teams have gathered into their groups, mumbling about whether or not they've got a tough draw, Cameron leads the way to their room down a corridor that has been artfully designed to look like CBGB's in the seventies.

The axe-throwing room is sparsely decked out, with two large wooden targets at one end, pocked with indentations from previous competitors' throws, and not much else. There's an interior window looking out into the corridor along one wall, where passing spectators can watch the game, and towards the back of the room there's a thick red line that doesn't fit into either the Nordic or the punk theme, but into the health and safety one. They're told to stand behind it unless expressly permitted to move. A woman in her early twenties is waiting inside for them.

She has intricate facial piercings, a lemon-yellow mohawk and is wearing a Viking tunic over leather trousers with heavy combat boots. She double-takes when Billy enters the room. That's the sort of effect he has.

'Greetings,' she says. 'I'm Bryson, your coach for this evening.' She looks at Billy again, as though she can't quite believe he's real. She shakes her head as though to clear it and get back on track. 'Before I get into it, does anyone have any questions?'

'Yes. Can we order drinks?' Teddy asks instantly.

She smiles. 'Yes, but you can't drink them inside the throwing room and if I think you're drunk you can't play, so take it easy. You can drink them at the table outside there.' She points to a tall round table visible in the corridor through the window. 'But I can order them through this.' She gestures to the tablet dangling around her neck.

'In that case, a pitcher of Pillager Pilsner please,' Teddy says.

'Done,' Bryson replies, tapping it into the screen. 'First the safety stuff. There are two targets, and we're going to be facing off as pairs. The rings on the targets each represent a certain amount of points, least on the outside, more the closer you get to the bullseye. Each person gets five throws per game, and there are three games per match. The most important thing is that no one goes towards the target while the game is still in play. We throw together and then we collect together. Meanwhile, spectators waiting their turn stand behind the red line.'

'Or out there,' Teddy adds, pointing to the beer table.

'Correct.' She picks up a clunky-looking wooden-handled axe in one hand, giving it a little shake to demonstrate grip. 'Now I'm going to demo how to throw.' She plants her stance straight on in front of the target board. 'Beginners will find it easier to throw two-handed, like this.' She holds the handle between both hands above her head with the blade facing forward before throwing and hitting the target. She walks forward and pulls it out, returning to her spot.

She takes her stance again, this time with the axe only in her right hand. 'Now, I'll demonstrate the one-handed throw, which is for more advanced throwers.' She lets go.

'Has anyone done this before?' she asks, retrieving the axe again and scanning the group.

Cameron puts up his hand. 'On a bachelor party a couple of years ago.'

She nods. 'Anyone else?' The rest of them look around and shake their heads.

'Who wants to be the first to have a couple of practice throws?' she asks, brandishing the axe in the general direction of the group.

'I will,' says Teddy. He grabs an axe from Bryson, plants his stance and squints briefly in the direction of the board to focus, before hurling it one-handed. It hits the second innermost ring, landing in exactly the way Bryson has demonstrated.

'Nice!' Bryson calls as the rest of them cheer and applaud. 'Near-perfect form.'

'Teddy!' Thea shouts, impressed. 'Have you done this before? Jake, is he a shark? Are you going to suggest we make things interesting and play for money?'

'I'm good at target sports,' Teddy says dismissively. 'Archery, darts, bowling, probably shooting if I ever tried it, but I refuse to go anywhere the NRA crowd might hang out. It's the only reason I entertained coming. If it had been competitive go-karting, then forget it.'

'It's true,' Jake chips in. 'Teddy only likes games he can win.'

Teddy turns to the group, eyes rolling in scorn. 'No one likes games they're terrible at. Who's next?'

'I'll go.' Thea steps up and tries the two-handed stance. She manages to hit the target, but it bounces off, head first, listing slightly to the right.

Bryson nods encouragingly. 'Good start. Take a step forward next time and spread the weight between both your hands. Next.'

Jake steps up and has the same problem. 'Same for you. People favour their dominant hand, so the axe goes that way.'

Cameron is next and there's a thunk as he hits the board not far from where Teddy's landed.

'Try standing a little more centred but overall, good stance.'

Logan steps up and Thea feels a clench of nerves. This feels like the sort of game that will quickly reveal what sort of competitive personality he has. He takes his time and adjusts his body so he's head-on to the target before throwing two-handed, no attempt to best Teddy. His blade hits parallel to the wood and just outside the circles of the target itself. He turns around and shrugs as though to say, 'good enough'.

Thea feels an inward 'phew'. Joining in, without taking it too seriously. He's passed a test he didn't know he was taking.

'Good start,' says Bryson. She holds an axe out to Billy. 'Now you.'

Billy steps up, getting more into Logan's personal space than is strictly necessary as they cross paths for him to reach the marker. Logan's forehead and mouth crinkle in bemused confusion as he hastens out of his way. Billy pretends not to see, sets his stance and throws hard. When the handle hits the target, the force of the throw causes it to bounce back several feet towards the spectator line.

'Woah!' Bryson shouts as they all jump. Billy looks furious that he's thrown a foul shot. 'You definitely win for brute strength,' says Bryson, in a soothing voice that implies she's used to such displays of try-hard masculinity and is reassessing his good looks in the light of it, 'but you've under-rotated so next time take a step back. And maybe a touch less force.' She picks the axe up and looks at it, as though checking it's still in one piece. 'Let's play! I'll put you into pairs based on equivalent-ish ability, so—' she pulls Teddy and Cameron to one side – 'you and you.' She tugs Thea and Jake out of the line-up. 'You guys together. And you two.' Logan and Billy don't look at each other as they're paired up, and unlike the other pairs, who are joking about how fierce the rivalry is about to get, there's an ominous silence between them.

'Us first,' shouts Teddy, whose enthusiasm for the game has grown in direct proportion to his position as favourite to win. He takes his shots with precision, scoring highly, and then immediately leaves the room to pour himself a drink from the pitcher that has appeared at the table outside. He waves as Cameron takes his, slightly more erratic, but solid shots. Cameron bows to the room and joins Teddy outside.

'Now us. You ready?' says Jake, picking up an axe and handing it to her. Thea nods. She misses her first shot, but gets a cheer when her second hits the board. Logan's voice is among the cheerers, and the low rumble of it distracts her during the third one, which doesn't even make it to the target. The fourth and fifth both hit an outer ring.

'As my only objective at this game is not to shame myself by being terrible, I'm pretty pleased with that,' she declares to the room.

'Team mediocre and proud!' shouts Jake, stepping up. His throws match Thea's, some OK, some complete misses and one fluky but thrilling bullseye that has Teddy banging on the Perspex window and screaming in joy.

They finish and Jake holds out his hand. 'Drink?'

'Definitely,' Thea nods, taking it. Joining a crowd was a good idea. It's diluted the intensity of it being just her and Logan, forcing her to slow things down, and to see him from the perspective of her friends, rather than as someone whose presence has a physical effect on her being. Friends he seems to have slotted in just fine with, she's pleased to note, as he swaps jokes with Jake about how *it's a good job we don't have to chop our own wood any more.*

She and Jake go outside to where Teddy has poured them each a beer, as they watch Logan and Billy. Thea takes a steadying drink from her glass. The situation may have diluted the intensity but it doesn't mean she's not pleased to have a totally legitimate reason to stare at Logan for the next few minutes.

Billy goes first, and after a flick of a look at Logan, he hurls his axes at the board with the same aggression as last time. It makes the spectators outside exchange glances. But there's no under-rotating this time, just a steady thwacking noise beating out a rhythm and a look on Billy's face that implies he's totally in 'the zone'. All but one of his shots pick up some points on the board, and he smiles triumphantly in Logan's direction. Logan holds his gaze.

'Good job,' says Bryson, inputting his score. 'OK, you're up,' she says to Logan, interrupting the charged moment. 'Can you follow that?'

Billy's performance seems to have awoken something in Logan, and the expression on his face tells Thea that he's going to aim for more than good enough this time. She's not the only one who notices. Teddy gives her a nudge.

'I hope they're not going to take it too seriously,' Thea says, wincing slightly. 'That would just make me embarrassed *for* them.'

'It couldn't be more of a hetero-cliché way of fighting over you. Unless one of them is actually going to pee around you.'

'Ew.' Thea focuses on Logan, who has taken off his tactile fluffy jumper to reveal a flannel shirt underneath and is rotating his shoulders as though he's warming them up. That, along with his beard, an axe in his hand and an intense look of concentration, means he is very much pulling off the urban lumberjack look. He catches her eye, and a charge runs through her blood.

'He looks sexy though,' Teddy mutters. 'I hope he's not going to ruin it by being a bad-tempered douche if he loses.'

'Me too,' Thea agrees. 'Although half the reason I brought him here was so you could tell me what sort of a vibe he gave you, so at least if he is, that's our answer.'

'Ah shit,' Logan says emphatically, as his first axe sails past the left-hand side of the board. From the smug smile on Billy's face, he finds Logan's cursing satisfying in an altogether different way than Thea's. But the look is wiped off when the second shot hits with a crack, close to the centre, and the next three follow suit.

'Whew, this one's going to be close,' says Bryson excitedly. 'I love it when I'm right about ability levels.' She consults the scores on her iPad. 'So far, Teddy, Jake and Billy are the winners in each pair, but among the group overall the leader board goes Teddy, Billy then Logan. Let's go again.' Teddy and Cameron return to the room as Billy and Logan file outside.

'Looking good, Billy,' Jake says to his co-worker as he sits down. He pours him a drink from the pitcher.

'I'll wait until after to have a beer,' Billy replies. 'Otherwise I'll be off my game. It's best of three, right, so one more match and I win?'

Thea presses her lips together to hold in a laugh. When she shoots a look at Logan, the competitive look has gone, and he looks like he's trying not to laugh too. Thea's insides fizz. She feels like the us they were at The Opulent before Christmas, sharing a private joke together.

'Ye-es,' Jake says evenly, 'but only within your pair. There's a team league table and an overall one for everyone from work too.' Through the window, he watches Teddy lob another axe one-handed and hit the centremost target. He blows Jake a kiss with his other hand. 'Which I think Ted has a very good chance of winning,' he says proudly. 'I never crush harder than when he's being great at something he couldn't give less of a shit about.'

'Right.' Billy nods, distracted. He seems to still be pondering the league table information.

'We're up,' Thea says to Jake, putting down her glass and re-entering the room. She would rather stay with Logan, but not with Billy there too, killing the buzz.

'Who am I?' Jake holds up his axe and paints a manic look on his face to mimic Jack Nicholson in *The Shining*. 'HEEERE'S JOHNNY!' he shouts. Thea starts giggling, setting Jake off. They both stand there helpless with laughter.

Bryson rolls her eyes. 'You have no idea how many times a day I hear that.'

Bryson's deadpan delivery only makes Thea laugh even more, and all of their throws bomb because they're too busy shouting out film characters who carry axes to concentrate on their form.

'Patrick Bateman!'

'The Tin Man!'

'Thor!'

'That's a hammer,' Billy says, returning to the room with a competitive look in his eye more appropriate for a defending Olympian than Saturday night in a novelty bar. He and Logan throw again, Billy audibly groaning when Logan edges him to the win this round.

'Everything to play for,' Bryson calls.

'I think some of us are too far behind to catch up!' Cameron calls back good-naturedly. Back in the throwing room, Teddy beats him comfortably again.

Thea and Jake return to the room and finish their match. Then Logan and Billy step up again.

Logan goes first. He's concentrating but not overly so, and throws a smile to Thea through the window before he begins.

'He's taking this the exact amount of seriously that you want someone to,' Teddy surmises in approval. 'Like, he's not pretending he doesn't care at all, or that it's lame, but he's not taking *himself* seriously.'

'I was thinking that,' agrees Thea. 'Green flag?'

'Green flag from me. Another green flag for his biceps—' they watch how Logan's arm muscles cause the shirt sleeve to tighten around them as he lifts his axe and it thwacks comfortably onto the outer rings – 'and one more for actually being single.'

'But is he over her? Felix said he was pissed when he came back from Christmas break. That's when he heard the news.'

'Maybe that's because the hot girl he met blocked him for no reason.' Teddy raises his eyebrows. 'Either could be true. No red flag for now.'

'Red flag for being on the opposing side to iDentity though.'

'That's temporary. We just need to win the business, so it's only a red flag *for now*.' Teddy breaks away to down the rest of his drink and shouts through the glass, 'Well done, Logan! Good game.'

Logan bows before Billy steps up, eyeballing him and

then spends an age aligning himself correctly and taking aim, longer still after his first four throws match Logan's, and the final throw will be the decider.

'It's going to be close,' Bryson hoots. Billy releases the axe, and it hits the bullseye.

'YES!' Billy shouts, stepping forward and flicking his chin up mere inches away from Logan's face in a gesture of triumph. Logan simply widens his eyes in response. His expression is neutral but he's *really* trying to keep it like that. There is mirth twinkling in his eyes, which only serves to get Billy more riled up.

'Congratulations,' Logan says, sticking out a sportsman-like hand for Billy to shake. Billy's too busy whooping, his arms aloft in a victory stance, for him to take any notice. He approaches Bryson instead to check his position in the overall league table.

Logan looks down at his disregarded hand, then out through the window to where Thea is at the table with Jake, Cameron and Teddy. He shrugs theatrically and heads out to join them.

'Well, that was ... intense,' he says with a smile as he approaches the table.

'He feels threatened by you,' Teddy says. His voice is tinged with the hint of a slur. 'Because he's into Thea.'

'Shhh, Teddy!' Thea shouts, elbowing him. 'Are you drunk? You shouldn't have been playing intoxicated!'

'Psssh, everyone's better at games after a few beers, it's a universal truth. Now,' he says, grabbing Jake by the hand. 'Let's go back into the freaky main bar. I'd like another pitcher of beer and for Jake to admire my throwing arm.'

He stands up, pulling Jake with him and leading him back down the corridor. Cameron follows, calling out, 'I think the rule should be that the best player buys shots for everyone else. Which is you, Teddy!'

Thea and Logan are left at the table side by side, finishing their drinks. The beer and the high spirits of the game have left her light-headed.

That's a lie.

The proximity to Logan and Teddy's assuaging some of her Logan-related worries have left her light-headed. She fiddles with her glass.

'He *is* into you, you know,' Logan says, fixing her with a look. 'Every time he took a shot, he looked to see what your reaction was.' There's the edge of jealousy in his voice. Thea's not mad about it.

'I told you, I'm not interested in him,' she says. 'Teddy set us up to take my mind off you.'

'And did it?'

Thea thinks back to their date, and how none of it quite fit. How there being nothing wrong with someone – curse kink aside – didn't mean it was right either.

She shakes her head, skin goose-pimpling on her body despite how warm it is in the bar. 'All it did,' she says, looking at him intently, 'was remind me that he wasn't you.'

She wants to kiss him so badly, but it's the wrong place, the wrong time. They should get through the contest and *then*—

And then Logan leans in and kisses her deeply on the mouth and her mind empties of everything other than the feeling of everything being exactly right.

Chapter Twenty-Two

His lips are soft, in contrast to the bristles of his beard, and their mouths fit together with the perfect amount of pressure. They press together hungrily, for how long she doesn't know, but when he pulls away – because it's Logan who pulls away – she gasps out loud from the shock of remembering where she is and why they shouldn't be kissing. Logan leans back and rakes a hand through his hair.

'Sorry,' he says. His smile makes his blue eyes flash. 'But I've wanted to do that all day.'

'Was it my impressive axe-throwing skills that finally tipped you over the edge?'

He laughs softly. 'Totally. I mean, Teddy's were phenomenal but as he's already taken . . .' He grins at her. 'But I shouldn't have done it, I overstepped—'

Thea oversteps right back and kisses him this time, the force of them clashing together knocking them into the table. The smell of him, the taste, leaves her feeling wobbly. A flash of heat hits her and spreads across her whole body, lingering there as his hands clamp around her waist and hers explore his arms. She can confirm his firm biceps were worthy of Teddy's notice.

'Excuse me.' A stormy-faced Billy reaches underneath the table aggressively to grab his bag and gives Logan one last hostile look before stalking down the corridor.

Logan and Thea look at each other and burst out laughing.

'I really want to kiss you again,' Logan says as he winds a hand around hers. The nerve endings in her fingers fire up. She wants to do nothing more than let every nerve in her body ignite. 'But if I do, I don't think I'll want to stop and then all of your plausible deniability is out of the window.'

'I'm not sure I care any more,' Thea replies.

He presses his thumb oh-so-lightly on her forehead, the faintest of touches, but the sensation blisters through her like a burn. 'That's me, pressing pause,' he says, with a crooked, closed-mouth smile that acknowledges how cheesy it sounds. 'On Monday we'll officially launch the contest and then two weeks after that, Memento will either be working with a different agency, or I'll have accepted Felix's strategy and become a well-behaved iDentity client. Then we can do what we like.'

That's not strictly true. If iDentity doesn't win, Thea has everything to lose. It reminds her what's at stake. Reluctantly, she pulls away, a crackle of static energy passing between them as she releases the tips of her fingers from his. It's the sensible thing to do, but right now, she doesn't want to be sensible. She wants to keep kissing him in the hallway of a punk-themed axe-throwing venue and let the rest of the night unfold in the same frenetic way. She tears her eyes from his. 'In that case we're going to have to sit with the rest of the group,' she says huskily. 'Because right now, I don't trust myself to be alone with you and not end up kissing you again.'

Logan nods once in agreement, but the accompanying look feels like the opposite. She feels her resolve erode. He holds up a hand, huffs out a steadying breath, and sets his jaw. 'Agreed,' he says. 'I'll stay for one drink and then I'll go.'

Back at the table, she plonks herself down on a bench next to Teddy, miles from where Logan perches near Cameron, but shooting looks over at him every time she brings her beer glass to her lips. His steady gaze returns her look every time and she can't stop smiling to herself. Having him so close and knowing what's blooming between them, but not being able to do anything about it is both thrillingly hot, and a type of slow torture.

Every time she looks over at Logan, Teddy shoots a suspicious look at her. And then in turn Billy shoots her a wounded one. She's juggling an incredibly complex load of unspoken emotions.

Thirty minutes later, Logan excuses himself, throwing a general goodbye to the table and a very specific, meaningful look to Thea. The air between them could scorch the room. It takes every iota of her willpower to stay where she is and not follow him into the street, but Teddy's hand clamping around her arm grounds her.

'What,' he hisses the second Logan is out of sight, 'is going *on* between you two? It's like watching an episode of *Bridgerton* – all thinly disguised horniness beneath layers of social niceties. Which reminds me, I need you to take me to where they film *Bridgerton* when I come over to England.'

Colour is high in Thea's cheeks. The kiss feels as though it's still in her veins, she can sense it like an occasional pulse at her neck, in her wrists, everywhere.

'We kissed. Well actually, in American lexicon, we *made out* with each other.'

Teddy's hand flies to his mouth. 'Here? Oh my God, you made out with someone at the weird Viking punk bar. I thought only LARPers got off on this whole Cos-Play vibe.'

She pushes him affectionately. 'Shut up.'

'So how was it?' He widens his eyes at her in expectation. 'And why were you sitting the entire length of a longship away from him when you came back to the table?'

'Because we're being sen-si-ble.' Thea draws the word out as theatrically as possible. 'You know my job is at stake with the contest, and you also know what will happen if Fuchsia finds out I'm fraternising with someone on the opposite side. If we win—'

'*Once* we win,' Teddy interrupts.

'Then we can start something. If he still wants to. If he's still speaking to me.'

Teddy grins. 'At least today has taught us that he's not a bad loser, so you can throw everything you've got at him and The Collective.' He frowns and hooks his arm through hers. 'I'm annoyed they got to see your other idea as a starting point though. They get to benefit from seeing something he already liked and then build on it to really blow his mind.'

'The Collective are so good they'll have dozens of ideas to choose from, and it's not about the one that Logan likes best, it's about the one that generates new business for their company. That's the most unfair part. I don't even believe in the idea we're putting forward, yet *I* might get sacked because Fuchsia's idea doesn't work.'

'It's not going to come to that. And like you say, you don't need to love the concept, it just needs to work. Then we win the contract, the team stays intact, and with some money coming in we *might* even get paid on time.'

'Fingers crossed.' Now Logan has left, real life is edging in again, and she's painfully aware of how many things need to go right for it to work out. 'He seems like a good guy, right?' Thea asks, remembering why she brought Logan along to begin with.

'Yes, he seems like a good guy,' Teddy affirms. 'Now we've cleared up the whole fiancée thing, I've downgraded him from no-good cheat to uh-oh . . .' His face is a picture of mock shock.

'What?'

'He might actually be one of those beige-flag nice guys you're so against.'

'Beige-flag nice guys don't kiss like that.'

Teddy raises an eyebrow. 'They do when you like them.' He drains his drink and taps his glass against Thea's. 'Now, as I'm playing the role of your gut this evening, I think you should know it's telling me that we should both drink until we can face doing punk rock karaoke in this God-forsaken place. So top up your beer.'

Chapter Twenty-Three

Today's meeting is on neutral territory with enough space for the iDentity and Collective teams to stand on different sides as they wait for their respective times to present. Thea's attention is fully on Logan as he, along with four representatives from The Collective file in. It's as though he's in portrait mode, the outlines of him sharpening, while everyone else blurs into the background.

The sight of him, and the look he shoots her as he moves around the conference table, is the first contact they've had since Saturday night and is a dopamine hit directly into her system. She's so nervous about what The Collective is going to present and how the next two weeks of the contest are going to go, but if iDentity wins, *then* they can go on a date. A real actual, called-a-date date.

Between the two leads – Fuchsia and her counterpart, Mina, at The Collective – there's *a lot* of statement style jostling for attention. Fuchsia nods at her competitors and addresses them collectively as 'guys', which an outsider might mistake for friendliness, but Thea knows is because she can't be bothered to learn people's names.

Thea's nerves aren't just down to the energy fizzing around her body due to Logan's presence. She, Ernie, Fuchsia and Felix spent yesterday firing tweaks and ideas to each other. They've modified their original presentation, and while Thea still doesn't love it, she knows it's as good as it can be.

Good enough to win the contract and keep her in the country?

It has to be.

Thea, Fuchsia and Ernie present it again now, emphasising the new and refined elements, and the additional 'activations' that Fuchsia is convinced will 'really play to a millennial crowd'. As they finish, Thea heads towards the back of the room on 'their' side before leaning against the wall to take in The Collective's performance. Most client pitches happen individually and behind closed doors, so despite her worry at what they might have come up with, she's interested to have a ringside view of how they work.

As they arrange themselves at the front, Logan turns briefly, catches her eye and throws a quick, nervous smile that only she catches.

Thea turns instantly beetroot, looking away before anyone can see. All she can think about is them kissing two nights ago in the bar and how the sensation of it snakes around her body every time she relives his lips on hers. She forces herself to concentrate.

Clem from The Collective steps up and begins to introduce the team, their challenge and how they've got a confident vision for Memento. Their opening slides are in bold colours, with stats and facts jumping out as animations, and clips of previous client feedback playing as mini reels. Considering the tight time frame for them to get this together, it's slick, rebutting several of the insights that iDentity's team put forward in the original meeting with Felix and Logan. Fuchsia's back is to Thea but she can tell by the set of her shoulders that she's seething about having her work countered.

'Now onto the ideas themselves,' Mina continues smoothly as she takes over. A blank slide hovers for a moment. They certainly know how to build up the suspense. All eyes are on the screen. She, Fuchsia, Felix and Ernie all stand a little straighter in impatient readiness.

Mina flips the slide and Thea flinches as the big idea comes into view.

Or should she say, *her* big idea.

The delivery is more sophisticated than the attachment that was accidentally sent to Logan, and the idea has been slightly refined, but it's still a graphic illustrating her film genre idea.

What is happening? Her heart is pounding with righteous anger. She throws a look at Logan, but his eyes are fixed on the screen.

Mina flips the slide and starts talking through the next new service offering, but Thea doesn't need to listen. It's *her* yearbook family tree idea repackaged into The Collective's style. She feels the colour rising to her chest, her neck, her cheeks, as two more slides flip past, also featuring her ideas.

It's like Christian using her ideas all over again. But this is worse. Back then, she was foolishly pleased that Christian deemed her ideas good enough to use. Now she knows better. Logan has ripped off everything from her presentation – the one that she told him he was absolutely to keep to himself – and it's being parroted back to her as the opposing team's strategy in a contest that will decide whether Thea keeps her job.

So it's not The Collective versus iDentity.

It's Thea versus more Thea.

Yet she can't say a word about this blatant theft, because it will out her as a traitor – and that will also lose her her job.

She was so relieved that the question of Courtney had been resolved that she didn't think that he might still be cheating her, only professionally this time. Was this his plan all along, while they were 'getting to know each other' on Saturday? When he didn't want to talk about anything work-related?

Her eyes bore into the side of his face and she wills him to look at her, to at least acknowledge what is happening, but he doesn't and she can tell it's deliberate. The shared smile earlier wasn't a moment of intimacy, but a poor excuse for an apology.

Her entire body is vibrating with rage. Did he think she wouldn't mind? Or did she not make it clear that he wasn't to use the work that had been sent to him in error? As soon as the questions form, she quashes them. She shouldn't have had to *tell* him not to use it. It's a dick move by any metric.

Another couple of minutes go by and it's over, the 'Thank You' slide looming over the room with The Collective's logo in the corner. Everyone in the room looks at Felix and Logan expectantly to see what happens now. All except Thea, who keeps her glare fixed on Logan, a feedback loop circling in her brain repeating over and over again that she's been shafted.

'Great job, guys,' Fuchsia says, in the fakest voice Thea has ever heard. For once she wants to echo her, if only to command Logan's attention for the moment her sarcastic tone will be heard.

Mina smiles warmly back. 'We added the bells and whistles, but Logan came to us with much of this work fully formed.' At least she's not trying to take credit for it, Thea registers. They're not the turncoats, *he* is. 'We're excited for the next steps.'

'What *are* the next steps?' Fuchsia asks.

'Each team will be given a budget to execute the ideas they've presented,' says Felix, who, far from being annoyed as he was in the boardroom meeting, looks confident and energised by the prospect of the competition. 'We'll test them out on our social channels for two weeks then measure conversions into enquiries and bookings. Whoever generates the most—' he opens his hands out as though to show how simple it is – 'wins. Logan and I have agreed to respect the strategy of the winning team – so when *my* team wins—' there's a smattering of polite laughter from both teams, but not from Thea; and not from Logan – 'we can put all this behind us and get on with making some damn movies.'

'Who's in charge of measuring the data?' Fuchsia barks, ever suspicious.

'Good question,' says Logan smoothly. He's looking everywhere but at Thea. 'We want to make money so there's no point in manipulating it, but we also have an independent adjudicator. A business-school grad student working remotely who neither of us have a prior connection to. He's managing our website metrics for the duration, and they're going to use the contest as part of their thesis so have a vested interest in keeping the data unbiased.'

Felix nods in confirmation. He looks assured, cocky even. But Logan doesn't look worried either. *Why would he?* Thea thinks bitterly. *He has some great ideas to work with.*

Fuchsia nods, and as Mina asks more technical questions, she slides back to where Thea is standing.

'As expected, their strategy is safe and lame,' she whispers. 'But I don't just want to win, I want to show Logan and—' she practically spits it out – 'The Collective that they can't just swan in here and steal a contract that is rightfully mine.'

Thea nods and Fuchsia's eyes flick over Thea's tensed face. 'But if we don't win, remember you can say goodbye to your role here at iDentity.'

The way the sentence is delivered, Thea knows she's supposed to fearfully agree with Fuchsia and promise to do anything in order to hang on to her job.

But instead Fuchsia is left gaping at Thea when her jaw sets, and her eyes flash. 'I want to crush him as much as you do.'

Chapter Twenty-Four

Voicemail from Logan:

Thea, please pick up the phone so I can talk to you about it. It absolutely isn't what you think it is. I know how frustrated you are with your job and I wanted to help. I thought this would be the perfect way to showcase your work to The Collective without you having to give up your job or visa. I didn't warn you beforehand because of your crazy boss – I thought it would be easier if you didn't have to lie to her. I haven't told The Collective it's your idea – yet – because I didn't want them to have that information while the contest is live, but I have every intention of telling them who's behind it when – if – we win. The truth is, they presented me a bunch of other ideas and they just weren't as good as yours, so I told them I wanted them to work with the material I'd sourced from my consultant. Because, like I told you, your stuff is good. Really good. And I just wanted – want – the best for my company. I didn't steal your work, I promise. I did use it, granted, but I don't expect to get it for free.

Thea deletes the message. Like she has the texts and emails Logan has been sending for the past week. She won't let her thoughts veer into the territory of letting him explain. A week after the contest began, with one week to go, and she's still furious. How is using her *own work* against the company she works for 'helping'? If Logan and The Collective win, she's masterminded her own downfall.

Your work was best for his company, that part is true.

She pushes that thought out of her head, and reminds herself that Christian used her ideas for his own career advancement, and she got nothing out of it in the end. She was just the person at his side at work events while people praised him for the campaign that got him promoted – a campaign *she* thought of – and he didn't once acknowledge it, even privately to her. She swore she'd never again make allowances for some guy's bad behaviour. Her career had taken off when they'd broken up and she'd thrown herself into the after-work drinks and networking events that her boss passed on to her when she didn't want to go. Events that were dry – but the drinks were free, and she collected cards and email addresses, dutifully passing on leads, and following the various CEOs and clients she met on social media. It was one of them who in the end had sent her the link to the job at iDentity. This was supposed to be her shot at a 'big' career, away from London and mixers populated by people her ex slept with; somewhere new where she could do things on her own terms.

And now another guy has detonated her trust. Along with, potentially, her life here. She wants – no *needs* – iDentity to win the competition, so that she can stay here.

If it takes Logan down a peg or two at the same time, all the better. He shouldn't have arrogantly assumed she wanted the help – if it's even that, rather than a thinly disguised way of simply furthering his own interests.

For the last week, she's worked even longer hours than usual, volunteering for extra tasks and making herself as indispensable as possible so that if The Collective win, Fuchsia reconsiders her worth. She is definitely not getting distracted by Logan Beechwood's excuses.

Thea rushes into Fuchsia's office with her coffee at 8 a.m., and Ernie is already there, dropping shrivelled-up, neglected air plants into the organic-waste bin. He gives Thea a grim look over the inevitability of the poor plants' demise.

Fuchsia is also already there, absorbed in her laptop screen. She doesn't acknowledge the coffee, which Thea collected from a place twenty minutes' drive from her apartment. There's just the crackling sound of crispy leaves as Ernie retrieves the dead plant stems from the ceiling.

'Can you get Teddy and Kim in here?' Fuchsia says. There's an edge to her voice that makes Thea more tense than usual. She could have discovered that The Collective's idea was hers. Then she'll be fired before she's potentially fired next week. Double fired.

'Sure,' Thea stammers. 'I don't think Maeve is here yet though.'

'I'll get them,' Ernie says quickly. He shoots Thea another, this time unreadable, look.

Thea stands awkwardly in silence as Fuchsia stabs at the trackpad on her laptop and swears under her breath. She's fiddling around with a few things on a PowerPoint presentation. 'Anything I can help with?' she asks. Fuchsia doesn't reply.

Teddy and Kim file in with Ernie, and Thea moves over to accommodate them.

'Maeve has left the company, effective immediately,' Fuchsia says once they're assembled.

Teddy gasps. They were in Moon Hare with her on Friday, and Maeve gave no indication that she was leaving.

'Gone where?' Thea asks, confused.

'Has she been fired?' Teddy asks and is rewarded with a venomous look from Fuchsia.

'Her employment here has come to an end due to a breach of confidentiality,' she says. 'That's all I will say on the matter.'

Thea looks again to Ernie. 'I'll tell you later,' he mouths, the unreadable expression suddenly coming into focus. He knew, Thea realises.

What 'breach of confidentiality' has Maeve committed?

'It's left us completely in the shit at short notice,' Fuchsia continues. 'There's urgent work that she *should* have been working on that I need to share out between you, so clear your social lives because it's going to be all hands on deck.'

Like it isn't *all hands on deck* the rest of the time.

'Will you be recruiting?' Teddy asks. His face is momentarily hopeful.

'You should be concentrating on keeping your own jobs and how you can help the business rather than the personnel structure, don't you think?'

'Right.' He lowers his gaze, so as to avoid being in her direct line of eye contact. It doesn't work, because she seizes on him.

'Teddy, I need you to stay in here to help break down who's doing what. The rest of you get back to your desks.' She dismisses them with a wave of her hand.

Teddy pulls a face as Thea leaves the room. He's standing near the doorway waiting for further orders from Fuchsia. 'Should've kept my mouth shut,' he mutters as she passes by. 'Now part of my extra workload is going to be managing everyone else's extra workload.'

'Stay strong,' Thea replies. 'And let me know if you need help.'

She speed-walks back to the main office. 'I'm sorry I didn't tell you guys,' Ernie apologises to her and Kim in a low voice, 'But Maeve *swore* me to secrecy. According to her, she emailed Fuchsia late on Friday night to say she'd been offered a new position. Fuchsia called her to say she had a three-month notice period but Maeve said she was only working that long a notice period if Fuchsia would guarantee her wages would be in full and on time, and then told her what she'd heard about the company being in trouble. Fuchsia lost it and told her not to bother coming back and then accused her of this breach of confidentiality, which is bullshit because the rumours she passed on were from other people – not from anything she found out here.' He snorts. 'On the plus side, she can start her new job straight away, but she has no idea if she'll get paid for the last two weeks that she's due.'

'Fuck. Is she going to contest it?' Kim asks.

Ernie shakes his head. 'I think she's just glad to be out of here. Her new job has good benefits and amazing ratings on Glassdoor.'

'Good for her,' says Thea, her gut clenching as she wonders what the visa ramifications for her leaving would be if Fuchsia cut her off with immediate effect. Another blast of anxiety to throw into the maelstrom already churning around in her stomach as Ernie talks quietly about leaving drinks. Thea envies Maeve being able to just get out, even if losing two weeks' pay would cripple her financially.

She feels untethered. Her presence at this company, in this country, is conditional, and it's dependent on someone as unpredictable as Fuchsia. Logan has no scruples either and is trying to convince her that he's helping when he's not. He's only thinking of himself.

She suddenly really wants to speak to Nan. She'll reassure her why she's putting herself through all this stress thousands of miles from home.

She walks to the kitchen and fishes around in a cupboard for the PG Tips that she's stashed at the back. She throws a bag into a mug and presses the voice note button while she's brewing her tea.

Hi Nan, it's just me checking in and to fill you in on the next drama here. One of my co-workers – colleagues – has either quit or been fired. Or both. Fuchsia is furious. She's also cancelling all leave because we're so busy – as if American companies even give you any leave to start off with. Meanwhile, you-know-who keeps messaging me. He says he didn't cheat me, but how can that be true when I was in the room when it happened? He stole my work and he knows I can't claim credit. It's Christian all over again. Isn't it? I just don't know what to think, and I can't trust what he's saying—

She hears someone coming and pulls her finger off the button, before pressing it again quickly.

I just wish you were here. Love you. Call me when you get this, okay?

She watches the message load and then send. Grey ticks. It's not as though she expects Nan to snatch up the phone immediately, but Thea looks back at the thread and realises she hasn't heard from Nan all week. Not after her non-date with Logan, and not after the contest kick-off. That's unusual. When Mum called the other day, she said Nan had a cold – or was it an infection? – no, a cold. She said she had a sore throat and wasn't up to speaking much but she was listening to Thea's messages and sent her love. They would have told her if it was something serious.

Wouldn't they?

'Make one for me,' Teddy instructs, coming into the kitchen and collapsing theatrically onto the work surface next to her. 'Ideally with vodka in it.' His head snaps up. 'Don't kill me, but there was no way to split the workload that isn't going to give us all a nervous breakdown, mainly because even *with* Maeve we were under-resourced. So we're all about to drown in work, but I'm afraid, my dear, as the one Fuchsia knows cannot betray her due to your immigration status, she's selected you for all the boring-ass dogsbody work.'

He lifts his head up and looks at her. 'I will help you as much as I can. And if it makes you feel better, none of the extra work is fun. Don't look at me like that, I can't stand it. Don't hate me.'

'It's not that,' Thea replies, finding another mug and making Teddy a tea. 'Well, it's not just that. I've just realised I haven't heard from Nan for days, and I keep hearing from Logan, who wants "to talk".' She tells him about the latest message. Teddy listens, mulling it over, eyebrows raised and nodding as she relays in a hushed voice what he'd said about her work versus The Collective's.

'The plus side is he's acknowledged that it *was* your work and how good it is,' he says. 'But it's not good enough. Using it and then passing it off as his own is messed up on so many levels.' He screws his face up as though weighing up the options. 'Are you going to? Talk to him I mean.'

'I'm too angry,' she replies, squeezing Teddy's teabag so hard with a spoon it's as though that's the thing that's wronged her. 'What am I supposed to say? It's fine? It's not fine! There's no way he could have known that Fuchsia's going to sack me if The Collective win, but if he'd told me what he was planning on doing, I could have explained that it wasn't going to help me – and if he was going to win, could it please be with an original, non-Thea Bridges' idea?'

'Do you think that would have stopped him?'

'I have no idea, and that's the part that's killing me. Was he really trying to help?'

'Or?' Teddy prompts.

'Or would he have done it anyway? Christian used my ideas to get a promotion and then used them against me as evidence that I wasn't cool.'

'He's not Christian,' Teddy replies.

'But is he someone I should trust? Someone I want to date? Every interaction we have leads to complications.'

'And from his side, if we win, will he want to date the person who transforms his company into something he hates?' Teddy replies in a pondering voice. 'What?' he asks, when he catches the look on her face. 'If iDentity wins, that's what's going to happen.'

'You're right.' She slumps against the counter, steaming teabag balanced on top of the spoon. She's only been focusing on why she's angry with him. But if iDentity wins the contest, he has every reason to hate her too.

Chapter Twenty-Five

'Thea, I need you to send over the new social strategy for the men's grooming line pitch. They think moustaches as shorthand for hipsters is tired, so they want a new dynamic idea.'

Thea bites down on her lip to stop her from snapping that the whole moustache thing was Fuchsia's idea, but after four sixteen-hour days working on new business pitches she's not sure she can get the words out. Instead she nods and writes 'eyebrows are the new moustache?' on the notepad in front of her, next to several other prompts that meant something when she wrote them down but now just look like the ravings of a mad woman. 'Go viral – sloth?' is underlined three times. She's not sure which client that's for or where they're going to get the sloth to accomplish it. They're all working constantly but no new business seems to be coming in. Thea fears Maeve was absolutely right about iDentity and got out just in time.

Her stomach rumbles and she looks at the time: 10 p.m. She gets up, stretches and goes to pick up a slice of pizza from the box on Teddy's desk, biting the cold point from it. She can't remember if it was ordered in earlier today or if it's left over from when Teddy ordered in last night, and he's not here now to ask, because he's been ordered to attend an away day for one of Maeve's accounts, who 'vitally need some TLC from us', according to Fuchsia. Teddy's out foraging for herbs in a remote part of the Oregonian forest with just enough phone signal for Fuchsia to keep bothering him. Ernie and Kim are both travelling across the state to meet with clients who are apparently hanging on by a thread, but neither has all the information to hand for when they arrive because of Fuchsia's chaotic system.

'Have you finished that deck?' Fuchsia's voice rings out from her office door.

'Which one?' Thea calls back, rushing back to her desk. 'Vintage Veils is ready for your approval. I'm still working on the one for The Plant Man.' All the decks Thea has created have gone ignored. Fuchsia has exclusively presented her own ideas. Which is probably why none of the meetings have resulted in any contracts being issued.

'I need both. Now. Which reminds me, I need more air plants for when The Plant Man comes in for the meeting. He won't make a commitment and I need something to push him into signing.'

Thea sighs. More air plants to suffocate.

'Thea! Did you hear me? I need air plants.'

'On it!' Her voice is artificially bright. 'I'll do the decks first.'

She pulls up PowerPoint and holds her eyes closed for a moment in an attempt to stop the words swimming together. She's just trying to get to Monday, and the result of the contest. Three more days, until the Zoom call that will announce the results. She's dreading seeing Logan, even on screen. She hasn't replied to any of his messages, and she won't. There's too much at stake – for both of them – to complicate things any further.

Outrage flares again at how helpless she feels. She tries to concentrate on her work, but she has too many tabs open – both on screen and in her brain – and her mind can't settle. She can't think of another word for 'plant' that she hasn't used four thousand times already.

She needs to get out. She'll pick up some warm takeout rather than continue eating the pizza that is solidifying in her stomach in a way that is convincing her it is *not* from today.

'I'm going to grab some food and coffee,' she says, standing up and grabbing her coat. 'Do you want anything?'

Fuchsia comes out of her office and glares at her. The thick rectangles of today's glasses frames emphasise the annoyance in her eyes. 'Now?' she asks, as though the idea that she might want to leave the room again a mere nine hours after she last consumed some food is insane. 'You're getting coffee *now*?'

'And some food, yes.'

'Order in. I need you to help with something that came in this afternoon. Ernie isn't answering his phone.'

'Ernie is currently on Zoom with a client,' Thea replies. She doesn't add, 'He had to cancel his evening plans for it.'

'We've got another pitch?' she asks instead, and instantly regrets it.

'Yes, Thea, we've *got annavva* pitch,' Fuchsia says, mimicking her London accent. It's an annoyingly good impression. 'New business is the only way we're going to grow as a company and as nothing you are helping with is currently bringing that in, I need you to try harder.'

If you presented even one *of my ideas, we might have some new clients by now,* is on the tip of her tongue, but she bites down on it until she tastes flesh. Fuchsia is particularly combative this evening so there's no point, and she hasn't scheduled a meltdown into her working day. 'I'm getting some noodles from across the street. Text me if you want some.'

'I need you back in ten minutes, max.'

Thea nods, and hurries down the stairs, even her moment of peace now on the clock.

The crosswalk on the office side of the road hasn't turned green before Fuchsia messages to say she needs to come back, but the blast of freezing, but fresh, January air that greets her outside after being stuck in the office is too invigorating to surrender. Besides, her stomach is now twisting so hard in hunger that she won't be able to concentrate on anything else until she eats something. If there's no queue, she'll be back in five minutes, less even. Fuchsia can wait five minutes, surely.

But no, her phone lights up again. WhatsApp this time, and she moans, 'leave me alone' under her breath.

Thea sees it's a voice note from Nan, and her heart lifts. Finally.

Mum and Dad had told her the cold was proving hard to kick and that's why she's been quiet, but almost two weeks is the longest they've ever gone without speaking.

She presses play immediately, holding it to her ear as she walks into the noodle bar.

Hello, love, sorry I've not been in touch. I've been a bit under the weather this week, but I'm feeling a bit better now.

Thea's skin prickles as she hears Nan's voice. It's croaky and quiet and the sound of it causes a sharp ache in Thea's chest.

Is she really OK?

She sounds so vulnerable.

She presses pause while she places her order, praying her card goes through as she taps to pay. Today is technically payday, but last time she checked, half an hour ago, her account balance hadn't changed. They've all emailed and messaged Fuchsia about it, but despite her lightning-quick response times to anything client related, these queries remain unanswered. She lets out a breath of relief as the card reader approves her noodles and she hits the play button again while she waits for her order.

I don't know what to say about the work contest and Logan taking your idea. I won't pretend I fully understand it but if he's jeopardised your chance – or even just taken you for a mug – you listen to Nanny and get rid of him. You started over after Christian and you can do it again.

Nan's voice starts to waver and tears spring to Thea's eyes.

You've always wanted to live abroad, so hang on to that job any way you can. I know it's hard to keep trying when you feel like you're getting nowhere, but you are getting somewhere, I promise. It was brave to move to a new country. It meant everything that you came back at Christmas, but it won't be long before the family can come out and see you. You've got all the time in the world to kiss handsome Americans.

Nan yawns.

Anyway, I'm a bit tired this morning, love, but Mum said you'd been worried about me, so I wanted to say hello. I'm going to have a rest now. Don't worry about me, concentrate on you. Find what makes you happy and don't take any shit.

Thea snorts. Nan retired from the pub altogether fifteen years ago but the landlady in her still comes out at times.

I love hearing all about your adventures, so you just keep having them.
  Take care, darling. Ta-da.

Thea's lip wobbles. She's been filling every moment with work, the stress keeping her busy, holding her together, but the kind words from Nan acknowledging it now threaten to undo her.

She's desperate to call, but Thea could hear the exhaustion in Nan's voice. A fragility. It's only 6 a.m. in the UK and Nan should rest rather than have Thea sap the strength she needs to recover from whatever bug she's got. She really didn't sound good, even after two weeks. She should check in with Mum again, see what the doctors have said. Surely they've taken her to the doctor's—

'Order sixteen's up!'

Thea's head snaps up, her attention back in the room. She grabs her to-go bag and rushes on autopilot back towards the office. Her phone rings in her hand as she stands at the crosswalk, on the other side this time.

Fuchsia.

She picks up.

'Where are you?' she practically screams. Thea checks the time. It's been seven minutes.

'I'm walking back now,' Thea replies. 'I'll see you in—' The phone cuts off.

She thinks about Nan again before mentally minimising that tab. All the others jostle for attention, her neurons firing back up as she prepares to re-enter the office. She'll get as much done as she can now and call Mum in an hour once it's properly morning.

The light turns green and she crosses the road.

Chapter Twenty-Six

At noon on Monday, Thea and Fuchsia sit physically in Fuchsia's office and virtually in the waiting room of the Zoom meeting that will reveal the results of the contest. Fuchsia looks stone-faced into the laptop camera, as Thea frantically deals with some other work as they wait – anything to distract her from the fact that she's about to see Logan for the first time in a fortnight, and that the result of this meeting will decide the outcome of her professional career.

There's a writhing knot of anxiety in her stomach. A text from Nicole with the strong arm emoji, saying 'Good luck' pops up at exactly the right time.

Five rectangles flicker to life on Fuchsia's screen. Thea and Fuchsia appear side-by-side – Thea looking tired and hollow-cheeked, with hair that has dried in the contours of the woolly hat she wore to work when she left at 7 a.m. that morning. In the other windows are Felix, sitting in what looks like an airy warehouse apartment, a cluster of people in The Collective's branded conference room, a young and nerdy-looking guy in a baseball cap and enormous noise-cancelling headphones – who must be the grad student monitoring the data – and Logan.

Thea's insides skip as she sees him and she immediately wishes she'd made more of an effort, even though she deliberately hadn't, telling herself she didn't care what he thought of her any more. That all that mattered were the results. He looks scruffily dishevelled against the backdrop of what Thea guesses is the Memento office, as even in the tiny box on screen, she can see complicated-looking camera equipment in the background.

He looks serious, and antsy, and even though she knows he's just looking into his computer lens, it feels as though he's focusing directly on her. If she maximised his window, she's convinced she'd be able to pick up the golden flecks in his eyes from the way the light is streaming through a window to his right-hand side. She hates that she has that thought, even when her job is on the line.

He's moving a little, as though he's jiggling in his seat or tapping his foot, which she takes to mean he's nervous. Both he and Felix – whose knitted eyebrows and set jawline belie the jaunty yellow acid-house-smiley jumper he's wearing – are tense. This result could be the watershed moment for both their business and their friendship.

'Is everyone here?' the grad student, called Deepak according to his on-screen tag, begins, receiving various emojis in the affirmative.

'Great, if you could all mute, I'll quickly run through the data.' He goes into present mode, and quickly recaps the research and objectives that led to the experiment. It's stuff they all know, which only serves to prolong the agony.

Thea can feel Fuchsia radiating impatience beside her, desperate to interrupt and tell him to get on with it. For once, Thea would be glad if she did.

'But now, the results,' he says finally. Deepak pulls up a slide containing a series of graphs. 'The results were close, but still decisive. iDentity's campaign and change of image has been successful, but not as successful as The Collective's strategy. As you can see, it generated more conversions.' There's a rumble of approval from The Collective as they unmute to congratulate Logan.

Thea daren't look at Fuchsia, daren't do anything while she tries to get a handle on how she's feeling. As Deepak witters on about the customer perception and ROI, all she can do is wait, watching their own Zoom rectangle for an indication of how her boss is going to respond to the news. There's a benign look on Fuchsia's face that she knows from experience can be more dangerous than obvious rage.

Thea flicks a glance at Felix to see his reaction to losing. He's squinting as he takes in the insights that The Collective's approach is projected to bring in a third more revenue than iDentity's. Thea looks at Logan's square. It's impossible to know exactly what he's looking at but while he appears quietly pleased, his eyes are also searching, as though he's seeking her out. She glances at herself, ensuring she's poker-faced. 'There are elements of iDentity's strategy that would also be worth incorporating.'

'Worth *incorporating*?' Fuchsia explodes. 'What a fucking JOKE!'

They're on mute, but from the way her face is contorted, it must be obvious to everyone in the meeting that she's furious. Thea swiftly swipes the camera off, as Fuchsia launches into a rant. 'Two fucking weeks to turn around public perception and make headway into new markets? Of course we couldn't do that. This whole contest has been a lame-ass waste of everyone's time.'

Thea wanted to win, but she also understands why they didn't. The other idea – her idea – worked better. Back in London, Thea's old boss had always taught her to be magnanimous in both victory and defeat, and use them as learning experiences. Lost pitches are part of the job, even if it needles.

But learning experiences aren't Fuchsia's style.

She starts stabbing at the laptop to unmute, and Thea knows it's not going to be to offer concessionary congratulations. She sweeps her hands in such a way that Fuchsia can't get to the keys.

'There were some really interesting ideas in the iDentity work,' Mina is saying. 'And the results show there's room for expansion into the market Felix has identified, which I think should form phase two of this project.'

Logan nods firmly. 'I want to make sure you find fulfilment in where we go next, Felix. This never had to be either/or.'

'Except for us,' Fuchsia spits, still reaching for the keys. Thea doesn't disagree, but she knows that whatever Fuchsia has to say right now will benefit no one. It's more likely to build up into a rage spiral so severe that it'll livestream her being fired. She nudges the laptop slightly out of her reach and mutes the audio again. 'Thea, turn the speakers on. I want to give some feedback.'

'I think we should send our thoughts over as a mop-up doc,' Thea replies in as confident a voice as she can muster. She's stalling for time, knowing that the second they're off the call, Fuchsia will sack her. 'We should get a formal breakdown of which parts of our strategy they want to incorporate so we can bill them accordingly.'

'I wouldn't want to work with that bunch of creatively bereft shitheads if you paid me a million dollars.' Somehow Fuchsia manages to unmute for half of the sentence so that 'creatively bereft shitheads' rings out along with the courteous goodbyes the others are exchanging. One by one the other attendees hang up, Logan's face freezing and hanging there last – one last glimpse – before he disappears.

Thea braces.

Chapter Twenty-Seven

Thea hits 'leave meeting' and slowly withdraws her hands from the laptop.

'What happened in there was HUMILIATING,' Fuchsia screams as Thea flinches. 'Your strategy bombed.' In one sentence Fuchsia has handed over possession of the whole thing. 'I had doubts about whether you were ready to be fully involved in a campaign but I took a chance and look where we've ended up.'

Thea's blood starts to simmer. She's been trapped doing drudge work since she started here, and now she's being blamed for a failure that isn't hers to accept.

You know what, I DID win this pitch, she wants to say. *MY idea won. Just not the one our team put forward.*

She chews on her lip to stop any of this spilling out.

Thea's phone buzzes on the table in front of her. It's Logan. All she can see in the preview is Thea, are you OK? I saw your boss shouting.

She flips it over, breathes through her nose.

Fuchsia is staring at her. Hard. Has she seen? Would she know it's the same Logan? Would she even remember Logan's name?

'That guy was a fucking *amateur*!' Fuchsia shouts. It's unclear if she means Felix or Logan, or both. 'Now The Collective think we're amateurs too and we've lost a lucrative contract. Which means you better make damn sure that we don't lose any more. Get back to those other pitches I need you to work on.' She jabs a finger at Thea, colour high in her cheeks. As the bollocking washes over her, Thea processes what she's saying.

So this is all her fault, but she's also not fired? Temporary relief floods through her. Does Fuchsia not remember the threat? Or does she simply want to keep holding it over her, so Thea will do whatever is asked of her, at any time, and for terrible pay, just to avoid getting canned?

Fuchsia's attention is distracted by something on her phone. 'Shit, I need to call them back,' she mutters. She thrusts a finger in Thea's direction. 'I want three new business ideas by first thing tomorrow morning.'

Thea would gasp but the rampaging nervous energy fluttering in her stomach won't allow her to take a deep enough breath.

'But that's—'

'What?' Fuchsia replies, one eye on Thea and one eye on her phone screen.

'Impossible,' is what Thea wants to say. But she realises this is how it's going to be. Traps laid for her, the threat of unemployment constantly hanging over her head. 'You better get back to your desk,' Fuchsia says into the silence. 'You have a lot to do.'

As she scuttles back to the main office, it's empty as it so often has been for the last couple of weeks. The rest of them are rushing in and out all day from meetings around Portland, while Thea is stuck in the office doing what amounts to admin.

She picks up her phone to text Teddy the news, although she's still processing what that is: they lost, but she appears not to be fired. For now.

When she presses the home button, the solid shape of Logan's name is still on her screen, along with a chain of seven or eight messages. It pulls her memory back to Christmas when his one-line updates about his day kept her smiling.

Now, the cubes of text layer on top of each other on the screen, like bricks of pressure on her chest. She swipes her phone open to see what possible explanation he has for the last couple of weeks. What he's saying now that he hasn't said already.

Logan: Thea, are you OK? I saw your boss shouting.

Logan: Now this is over, can we talk?

Logan: You have every right to be mad.

Logan: (Even though you – and I – were right about the strategy)

Logan: My thinking from the start was to pay you a consultancy fee for the deck and the ideas. Then once the contest was over – and your idea won – I was going to introduce you to Mina, with a view to you being on the permanent team.

Logan: But it wasn't something I could do until the result was confirmed and I thought telling you beforehand would put you in a strange position.

Logan: Stranger than the position you're in already, which I realise now was not OK.

301

Does he? Does he really know how deep the betrayal has cut?

And does she believe he's sorry?

Her phone rings.

Not Logan, but Dad.

The second she sees his name, a sense of dread coils its way around her stomach, separate to the stress from Logan's texts and Fuchsia's tasks. He's meticulous about knowing the time difference. He would never usually call her during office hours on a weekday.

Something must be wrong.

'Hello?'

'Thea, it's Dad.' He sounds hoarse.

'What's happened?' she says immediately. 'Who is it?'

'It's—' His voice wobbles. 'It's your Nan. She's had to go to—'

'The hospital? What's wrong with her?' Thea's voice rises, and she senses Fuchsia coming out of her office.

Dad clears his throat. 'Not the hospital, no. She's going to a hospice.'

'What?' Confusion whirls around Thea's head as fear pricks at her insides. Maybe she hasn't heard him properly. 'Mum said she'd had a bad cold. Does she need tests in the hospital?'

There's a pause that stretches out. 'Dad? Are you there?'

Her dad sniffs, a big messy gasp that shows just how close to breaking down he is. 'They did find something, yes, but not since she had the cold. She didn't want us to tell you, love. Swore us to secrecy.'

Thea's world tilts. 'What's wrong with her?'

'Pancreatic cancer,' Dad says, his voice a whisper. 'They found it just after you moved, and when she got the prognosis, she was adamant it shouldn't change anything.'

'What was the prognosis?' Thea asks automatically, knowing as she says it, that Dad gave her the answer at the start: she's going to a hospice.

'There was nothing they could do besides make her as comfortable as possible. They didn't give her long. Months.' Dad blows out a breath as though to steady himself. 'To be fair to her, she's hung in there. It's as though she kept going until Christmas, when you were coming back. But she's taken a turn. They're moving her to Mayfields, and—'

His voice catches. 'You should come. We're not sure how long she has left.'

Chapter Twenty-Eight

The room shrinks to the size of the office chair Thea is sitting on.

She needs to book a flight, now. Cradling the phone between her cheek and shoulder so she can keep talking to Dad, she pulls up Skyscanner, and sees a direct flight at 5 p.m. today. She'll just make it, if she goes home for her passport now.

She hits 'book' without a second's hesitation, only registering the price when she's prompted for her card details. It's a lot. More even than her night in The Opulent.

'Dad, there's a flight later today and I'm booking it,' she tells him while typing the number in. She's trying to hold it together and take in the information Dad has told her. 'Did you say she was going to Mayfields Hospice? I'll go straight there from the airport. Don't collect me. I'll make my own way there.'

Thea's worst fears are confirmed when Dad doesn't insist on picking her up. That's what tells her she might not make it in time. 'Yes, I think that's best,' he says. 'I'm going to go the hospice with Nan now to get her comfortable and settled. I'm ringing now because, well, I wanted to give you enough time to get your ducks in a row.'

'Yes.' Her voice wobbles and she presses her lips together. It's unthinkable that she might not see Nan again. She can't – won't – think about that now. She presses 'confirm booking' through her tears and mentally calculates how many hours it is until she'll be back in London.

'I'd better go,' Dad says. They're sending an ambulance to pick her up and it'll be here any minute. Mum's getting Nan's things together.' Dad's voice has a note in there that Thea doesn't think she's ever heard before. He's scared.

'Yes, you go,' she tells him. 'I love you. Please tell Nan I love her too, and I'm coming.' A sob starts to rise in her throat, and her hands start to shake. Nan can't, she *can't* go without saying goodbye. 'She won't be gone before I get there, will she? Dad, tell her to listen to her voice notes. I'll do one now, in case, in case—' She breaks off before she breaks down.

'I will. Love you, darling. Let me know when you're at the airport and when you land.' Dad breaks down now too. 'Ta-da.'

'Bye, Dad, bye.' The second the call is ended she wishes they were still talking. She looks at the phone in her hand as though it's a mystery, unsure what to do next. Ten minutes ago, Thea had no idea that Nan was even ill. If she lets herself dwell on it, she knows she'll be furious at the thought they all kept it from her.

So she doesn't. She just needs to get home.

The booking is still processing, the wheel still turning. 'Come on,' she mutters as she waits for her confirmation number to come through, so she can leave her desk.

Payment declined.

She must have typed in her card number wrong. Doing too many things while talking to Dad. She forces herself to concentrate, mouthing each number as she types it in, followed by the expiry date and the CVV number.

She hears a cough next to her and looks up. Fuchsia is standing there.

'Fuchsia, I have to leave—'

'I need you to do a deep dive into the Etsy shopping habits of Gen-Z,' she interrupts.

'What?' It's as though Fuchsia is speaking a foreign language. All she can focus on is booking this flight.

Payment declined.

It hits her. They haven't been paid. She doesn't have enough money in her bank account for the ticket. There's a surge of panic now, amid the worry.

'That was my dad on the phone. My grandma—' she can barely choke it out – 'is ill and I have to go back to London urgently. I need to take some leave – unpaid of course – but I also really need you to pay us, because I can't afford the ticket.'

Fuchsia barks out a laugh. 'I can't advance any wages. And I can't approve any vacation right now either, we're snowed under.' She flicks through a pile of printouts in her hand and starts piling some of them on the side of Thea's desk.

'It's not an advance,' Thea says. Her voice feels scratchy in her throat, and the pinch of desperation tightens. Can't Fuchsia tell there's something seriously wrong? She must have heard the phone conversation, or at least her side of it.

'My dad just told me,' she says slowly while trying not to cry, 'that my nan – my grandmother – is being moved to a hospice and I need to go back to the UK. It's not a vacation. She's going to die—' The weight of the word hits her as she says it. 'I need to get there. Today.'

Fuchsia stops what she's doing. Swivels her gaze to Thea's face.

'My grandfather hung on for a really long time when he was supposedly dying,' she says eventually. 'I guess if you get as much done as you can today, you can fly out tomorrow, and then work from the UK for a few days, if you absolutely have to.'

'I need to go now.' She gestures to the screen. Tomorrow's flights are thirty-six hours away. And London is a ten-hour arrival after that. Dad has already impressed how much time is of the essence.

Thea keeps going, justifying, begging. 'I need my wages, Fuchsia,' she says. 'I need you to transfer them right now.'

'All the money is tied up. And besides, if I paid you early, then I'd have to do the same for everyone else.'

'It's not early!' she shouts. 'And you *should* pay *everyone*. You should have paid everyone already. You know what, never mind.' She pulls out Nan's credit card and types in the number.

Payment declined.

'SHIT!' With the hotel room still on there, there's not enough credit.

Think Thea, THINK.

'. . . Oh my God, that client needs to step away from whatever Photoshop course he's been doing online,' Teddy says as he walks into the office, satchel slung over one shoulder and his laptop under his other arm. 'He turned up with a load of images he'd Frankensteined together into a "campaign"—' He stops as he notices Thea and Fuchsia squaring off against each other. 'Is everything OK?' he says, his eyes swivelling between them in confusion. They settle on Thea in alarm. He takes in the sight of her and she shakes her head gently. His eyes widen.

'It's Nan,' she says in a shaky voice. 'I have to go home.'

'No!' Teddy's free hand goes to his mouth. 'What happened? What time's your flight?'

'I haven't booked it yet,' she says miserably, gesturing to the screen. 'We haven't been paid and I don't have enough money. Teddy, could I—'

'If I had it, you could have it. But I haven't been paid either.' He pulls out his phone. 'How much is it? I can ask Jake. Wait – fuck – he's at an all-company team-building day. Which involves an escape room, a sweat lodge and surrendering your phone when you arrive.'

Thea appeals to Fuchsia again, but she's heading back into her office. For a moment, hope rises that it's to go and arrange a bank transfer, but they're left staring at her open-mouthed as she shuts the door.

Thea's phone lights up. It's Logan texting. Again. With another addendum to an ever-growing apology that she can't deal with now. But as she registers his name, a light goes on in Thea's brain and she snatches it up, calling him without reading it.

'Thea, I'm so glad you called me—' he starts, but she doesn't let him get any further. She can't get into it. Not now.

'Logan, I can't talk about the contest – or us – now. My nan is dying, and I have to get home to her. Before, you said you didn't expect to take my work for free, so I need you to prove it. I need you to transfer me that consultancy fee.'

There's a silence and for a moment she thinks he's taken offence and hung up, but she hears a shuffling noise and realises he's put her on loudspeaker so he can get to the phone screen.

'I'm Venmo-ing you right now,' Logan says. She hears the sound of an alert on her own phone while she's speaking to him. 'I'd already asked Mina the going rate and how long she thought this sort of work would have taken, so let me know if it's fair.'

She checks the screen. It's twice what she receives in her monthly pay packet from iDentity and it gives her pause for a second. 'Logan, that's too mu—' she starts to say, reconsidering how ballsy she'd been in demanding money from him. She stops herself. It's the going rate. She earned it. And she doesn't have time to debate it now. Instead she types in her details on the flight site again and hits 'confirm', with everything tensed as the web page reloads.

You're booked!

Her confirmation appears, and she exhales a shaky breath.

'What time is your flight?' he asks.

'It's at five o'clock, but I'm at the office. I have to go and get my passport before I leave for the airport.'

'Give me your address. I'll give you a ride.'

'You don't need to do that,' she says.

'I want to. You shouldn't drive yourself or have to worry about parking.' His voice is firm, and the tone is comforting. It makes it easy for Thea to go along with it.

'Thank you,' she says. 'And not just for the lift. I wouldn't be able to even get there without the money—'

'Thea, the money was always going to be yours. It's not a favour.'

A sob rises in her throat, gratitude and terror mingling together as she squeaks out another thank you. 'I'm at 2100 Burnside,' she manages. 'I'm leaving now. I need to hang up and keep the line clear.'

'I'll see you there in twenty minutes.'

As she ends the call, Teddy is at her desk, picking up her coat. He embraces her, worried tears in his own eyes.

'I'll drive you home,' he says.

'No you won't.' Fuchsia's voice comes through the doorway where she's appeared again. 'I can't be two people down at short notice.'

'Fuchsia, it'll take me an hour to get there and back, max. Besides, we carpool, and Thea drove this morning. I need to pick up my own car.'

She ignores Teddy, speaking to Thea again. 'I haven't authorised this, even though it seems you've already booked a flight, so I'm going to need you to work remotely while you're gone. We *need* to keep working on drumming up new business.'

Thea has a fleeting image of her phone pinging wildly as Fuchsia bombards her with demands, or trying to work with her laptop balanced on her knee and her family gathered around Nan in a hospice bed.

Nan in a hospice bed.

She's bent over backwards to try and please Fuchsia, but this is too important.

'My grandmother is *dying*. I can't commit to that.'

Thea's phone rings again.

It's Kit. Her thumb itches to hit the 'answer' button but Fuchsia is still talking.

'If you can't commit, then why should I consider holding your position open for you?' Fuchsia says coldly.

Her phone rings two, then three times. What if Nan's already gone?

Thea looks hard at Fuchsia. 'Are you saying I'm fired if I leave? Because you've already threatened to sack me once this week.'

'Why don't you try me?' she says in the same tone.

'I'm going to have to, because I have to leave.' She's never spoken to Fuchsia like this before, but she needs to see what Kit wants. She accepts the call before he can hang up.

'Kit, I heard. Dad told me. I'm coming—'

'Stop answering your phone when I need to talk to you!' Fuchsia roars, swatting violently at Thea's hand. Her phone flies across the room, landing hard on the office's polished concrete floor. The glass shatters and the screen blinks off.

'What have you done?' Thea shouts back, lunging for it. 'I haven't even left the voice note for Nan yet. I promised I'd send one, so she has it. In case I don't—'

She presses the home button, but nothing happens. She tries it again, then again, and then frantically over and over, hoping that if she does it enough times it'll miraculously work.

But the screen stays dark.

It's dead.

Chapter Twenty-Nine

Half an hour after leaving the office, Thea's dropping toiletries into a wash bag, locating chargers, and shoving a mishmash of clothes into her backpack. She's trying to occupy her head and her hands to keep thoughts of Nan at bay, but every time her mind settles on something she needs for the trip, the thought slides away again, and only the sensation of needing to get it done remains.

There's a knock at the door, and she opens it to Logan's solemn face.

'Hi,' she says quietly.

'Hey.'

It's sleeting outside and there are drips of water running off his woolly hat, wet tendrils of hair curling out of the bottom.

She hadn't thought about what she'd say to him when he came to pick her up, had forgotten with everything going on that there was unfinished business to address, and the residual anger towards him flits through her mind before falling away again.

She doesn't need to say anything though. He just folds her into a hug. 'I'm so sorry, Thea,' he murmurs as cold water soaks through her clothes from his wet coat. She can feel the warmth of his body beneath.

His solid, reassuring presence is all that matters right now. She's going home to Nan, and he's helping her. The thought quietens her buzzing brain for the first time that day.

'I didn't come up to rush you, just to say I'm ready whenever you are,' he says. 'I was waiting outside, but your phone wouldn't connect when I tried to call.'

'My phone . . . it's broken,' she replies. 'But I'm ready.' Whatever she has in her bag now is fine. She can borrow from mum if she needs to. 'Fuchsia . . .' she starts to explain, before giving up. She'll tell him on the way. 'Teddy gave me an old handset, but I haven't had time to do anything with it.' She grabs her bag, frowning towards the kitchen on the way back to the door. 'I should probably empty the fridge. I don't know how long I'm going to be gone.' It could be permanently, after the way she walked out of the office without a word when Fuchsia broke her phone.

'We should head off,' Logan says, taking control like he did on the phone. 'But is there a spare key? I can come back and do it for you after I drop you off.'

'Teddy has one,' she says.

'I'll talk to him about it,' he replies. He takes her bag and carries it down three flights of stairs and out the front door to where his car is parked on the street. It's a big electric SUV that looks new enough to not spend fifty per cent of its time in the workshop like Thea and Teddy's cars.

Flying Home for Christmas

As they pull away, streets slide past and she can see her pale, washed-out face reflected back in the dark window. Rain is thrashing outside the car; thoughts are thrashing inside her head. She's finding it hard to sit still, full of energy with nowhere to direct it. She's trapped in a forced schedule of steps she needs to follow to get to the person she needs to see before she'll never be able to see her nan again.

Her pulse is drumming like hummingbird wings. *What if I'm too late? What if I don't make it to the airport on time? What if my flight is delayed?*

'The traffic's OK, and I checked that flights are currently running on time,' Logan says as though sensing her thoughts. 'The timings are a little tight, but we'll make it.'

'Thank you,' she says. She's relieved she can relinquish control of the practicalities. She's finding it hard enough to deal with the panic, without having to navigate the route to the airport. There's a pressure against her skull and every time she gets one wave of anxiety under control, another one rises.

'If there's anything you need while you're in London, either sending over or doing here, just let me know. I can easily help.'

Thea nods.

He clears his throat, and there's an intense look on his face that gets illuminated every time they drive past the bright neon lights of a mini mall.

'Now isn't the right time I know, but before you go, I also wanted to say sorry to you properly – for the contest and the way I handled it.' He looks pensive, his lips are crumpled in apology.

'It doesn't matter,' Thea replies in a monotone voice. She means it. It doesn't. Who cares about the stupid contest when Nan is going to die?

His forehead crinkles in thought. 'It doesn't matter compared to this, but it does matter that I hurt you,' he says quietly. 'I was thinking about myself and my business and how it would affect me and I thought because I meant well, it was OK, and it wasn't.'

The sincerity of his apology pulls her from her thoughts, and into the here and now. How Logan has showed up to help when it matters. 'You're right,' Thea agrees, turning it over in her mind. 'It wasn't OK. But if you'd really wanted to screw me over you've had plenty of opportunities to do it. And none of them involve dropping everything to drive me to the airport. Or giving me that money.'

'I didn't give it to you,' he tells her again, his eyes scanning over to her from the road and back again. 'You earned it fair and square.'

'OK, I could have invoiced you and you'd have paid me within thirty days,' she counters. 'But if it wasn't for the money landing this afternoon, I wouldn't have been able to afford a ticket home. That's all that I care about right now.'

Tears slide and then she crumbles. 'I want my nan,' she says softly, before she's taken over by big ugly heaving sobs that she has no control over.

Logan slides one hand from the steering wheel and puts it on top of hers, squeezing gently. His eyes are creased with worry.

'I know,' he says. 'We'll soon be at the airport, and you'll be home by tomorrow. I know this journey must be torture, but remember, your nan knows how much you love her. You've been showing her that your whole life.'

The way he says it makes Thea think he's thinking about his own grandpa as he tries to reassure her.

He removes his hand so he can steer off the freeway ramp, but the warmth and sensation of the pressure remain. Even once her crying has subsided, he carries on talking in a low voice. She can't concentrate on the words, but the tone is soothing, and she holds it in her mind to keep the sadness at bay.

Fifteen minutes later, Logan pulls into the drop-off zone at PDX.

'Did you say you need to fix your phone?' he asks, as he kills the engine and looks at her, clear-eyed and concerned. She never did tell him how she broke it. She doesn't have time to get into it now. She's anxious to get going.

'Yes.' She pulls out her smashed handset and the battered, but functional, one Teddy gave her. Her hands are shaking too much to get the sim tray open, and Logan takes both phones gently from her, swapping the card from one to the other. He turns it on, and follows the on-screen instructions, before flipping quickly through a few screens once it's set up.

'Contacts are there, battery is good,' he murmurs. 'Do you need a charger? You can take this one—' he gestures to the one hanging out of his car's USB port – 'if you need it.'

'I have one, thanks,' she replies. 'I'm all set.'

He passes the handset back to her, registering the time. 'You'd better go,' he says. Logan jumps out of the car to retrieve her bag from the boot, as she unclips her seatbelt. He's waiting for her with it as she steps out of the car and the frigid rain instantly soaks them both.

She starts to thank him, but he interrupts.

'No need. I'm just glad I could help in a small way.' His eyes are tinged with worry. 'I hope you make it in time. Let me know how things are, when you can. No rush.'

She nods. She's incapable of anything else. Her words are stuck in her throat. She croaks out a small 'yes'.

He hugs her quickly, before releasing her, and she heaves her bag onto her shoulder before walking to the terminal. Once inside, she quickly turns back. Through the glass doors she sees Logan's car slowly pull away from the kerb before stopping at a crosswalk for a group of suitcase-dragging travellers. She approaches the check-in desk and stops again abruptly, patting down her pockets to check for her passport, and then opening her handbag to make sure her keys and her purse are in there.

Physically, she has everything she needs, but as she turns again and watches Logan's tail-lights disappear, the sensation that something's missing remains.

Chapter Thirty

Nan's room is as cheerful as you can expect a hospice full of hospital-grade furniture and terrifying-looking machines to be.

The staff are so capable and so warm, the rooms personalised amid the medical equipment, and the food a far cry from clichéd hospital meals.

But it is the place her nan has come to die.

Nan is tiny and sunken in the bed, her cheeks hollowed out and her hair – where before it was a robust white – is almost transparent. Her eyes are closed.

Next to her, Thea hovers, desperate to hold her hand but finely attuned to the fact that she has arrived straight from the airport and is therefore a festering hive of germs, smells and unwashedness that she doesn't want to subject Nan to. She takes another squirt of the sanitiser that is affixed to every second wall and tries not to burst into tears when Nan opens her eyes and rests her gaze – once so shrewd but now dissolved somehow – on her.

Thea breathes forcibly through her nose, trying to smile. She made it in time, that's one good thing.

The only good thing.

She can't be a mess. She has to hold it together for Nan.

'Thea!' Nan's voice is croaky and quiet. 'Have you come all the way from America?'

'Yes. I came as soon as Dad called me.'

Nan tries a little smile, but it looks like an effort. 'That must have been expensive,' she says.

Thea smiles back. Same old Nan. 'I've been freelancing and got paid. I've even got enough left over to pay off your credit card.'

Nan's mouth crinkles into a smile. 'Good girl. I'm so proud of you.'

She pats the bed next to her, her bony hand bruised from where needles have been prodded into it in search of a vein. 'Sit down there and tell me what you've been up to. Was your flight OK?'

'It was fine,' Thea lies.

It had been interminable. Every minute felt an hour long, and the ten hours until she turned on her phone at Heathrow, and got a status update from Dad, were agony. She was waiting for the Elizabeth Line when her service had kicked in and two words from him had flooded her entire system with relief.

No change.

She perches gingerly on the side of the bed. Nan looks too fragile for her to snuggle in and smother her with hugs, the way she wants to.

'Why didn't you tell me?' she bursts out. During the long hours of the flight, she coached herself not to do this,

322

not to have a go at a dying woman, but now she's here, she can't help herself. She's never had any filter with Nan, for better and worse.

'Because you would have come straight home,' Nan says simply. 'And I didn't want you to. It was an opportunity and you would have missed out.' She hisses in a breath as though she's in pain, and Thea's dad, who is dozing in a chair on the other side of the room, starts.

''S all right Roy. It comes and goes.'

A few months' notice wouldn't have made any difference to the outcome, but at least she would have been prepared. Thea thinks about the last few months, the last few days in particular. Working so hard, and for what? 'None of it was worth not getting to see you again.'

'It was to me,' Nan says. Her watery eyes glimmer slightly. 'What an adventure. The furthest I got was to Crystal Palace and I still ended up back in the East End.'

Even through the grief and the jet lag, Thea knows now isn't the time to tell her that if Fuchsia is true to her word, she's going to end up right back there herself.

'Did I tell you about the time I had an egg sandwich?' Nan says, drawing her attention back to the bed.

'What?' Thea's puzzled. What has she missed?

'This started happening a couple of weeks ago,' her dad says with a sad smile. 'Brain confusion.'

Behind her eyes, Nan looks different. There's an alertness but as though it can't settle. Nan is there but also not.

A nurse knocks and comes in.

'Afternoon, Dora. I'm just here to take your obs. How are you feeling?'

'Afternoon, love, still hanging on,' Nan chuckles good-naturedly, seemingly back in the room.

Dad stands up, nervously jangling his car keys in his hand. 'I'm going to quickly take Thea back to the house now, Mum, so she can get changed.'

'I don't want to go,' Thea says.

'I think we should,' her dad insists. 'Mum and Kit are coming back with us, so we'll be quick.'

'You do look a bit of a state, darlin',' Nan says bluntly. 'I'm going to have a bit of a rest now anyway.' Her eyes close and she's almost instantly asleep, mouth open, breathing heavily, as the nurse gently fits the blood pressure cuff around her arm.

'She's on a lot of painkillers,' Dad explains. 'They're zonking her out.'

Thea lets herself be led away and into the car, but her heart and focus are still with Nan. Once she's got him alone, she can't stop firing questions at Dad.

'How do they know there's nothing else that can be done?' she says, getting into the car as Dad turns over the ignition. 'How can they be saying she has such a short time left?' Roads blur past outside the window. The odd crispy Christmas tree still lies sideways on the pavement, waiting to be taken away by bin lorries. People who didn't want the festive season to be over and squeezed as much life out of them as they could. It feels like a metaphor for something, but she hasn't slept so she doesn't know what. 'What if she'd just . . . *gone*?' Her voice is a scratch. 'What would you have told me then?'

Dad waits for a moment before he starts to talk.

'Thea, love. The doctors know. It's pancreatic. Advanced. Brutal. Aside from a couple of experimental trials that Nan was already in too poor health to qualify for, it's a case of making her comfortable. That's what they've been doing for months now. Don't think it was easy for any of us to keep quiet, but she made us promise. Said that's what she wanted.' He shakes his head slightly as he stares hard out of the windscreen at the road ahead. 'The nights that your mum and I lay awake discussing whether to get in touch in secret. But Nan would've known we'd done it the second you arrived back at home, and she'd have been furious. I was just doing what I was told by my mum.' Dad's eyes fill up and he blinks the tears back down. 'You must be able to understand that, even if you don't agree with it.'

He glances at her quickly as he manoeuvres down the High Street and pats her hand. 'But you're here now. And I'm glad. Nan is too, even though she'll give you hell for coming. She kept listening to that message you sent her.'

Thea sniffs. 'Good.' After racing to check in and clear security, Thea managed to fire off a voice note while she waited to board. It was only after it had sent that she noticed that none of the WhatsApp conversation history had appeared on the replacement phone. Her gut lurches again now as she remembers seeing that her thread with Nan now only contains one message. All those voice notes, gone. She's praying that there's some way to retrieve everything from the broken handset.

'Work were OK about you getting away, then?' Dad says. 'Did Fuchsia say how long you could stay?'

'I can take as long as I need,' she replies. She's not going to tell Nan, or Dad, or anyone here, that she's out of a job. Nan doesn't need to know, and the rest of them will find out soon enough.

The whole thing feels a thousand miles away and a million years ago compared to what's happening here and now.

She texts Teddy to say she's arrived, and that Nan is holding on, adding: I hope I haven't dropped you completely in it with Fuchsia and work isn't too awful. Thank you again for the phone.

My pleasure. Aside from anything, you've vindicated me to Jake. Turns out that drawers full of wires and old tech ARE useful.

Just take care, and don't worry about anything here. I'll keep checking in but don't feel as though you have to reply Xxx

She pulls up a new message to text Logan. Every time she thinks about him, her emotions snag, like weeds in a pond.

Without his help, she'd still be in Portland now, begging Fuchsia to pay her, or talking Mum through how to buy her a flight online when she should be sitting with Nan.

He dropped everything to get her here, even though she'd ignored him for two weeks before that, and accused him – again – of cheating her.

Flying Home for Christmas

I don't know how long Nan has got left, but I made it here in time, and that's because of you.

Thank you.

. . . [Logan is typing]

Thea, I can't imagine what you're going through. Please know that I'm thinking of you. You described your nan to me so well that I feel as though I know her too. Sending strength for you and your family. Call me any time.

She looks out of the window, tears blurring her vision. The sensation she's missing something returns and settles in.

She's relieved she's here, right where she needs to be. But if Fuchsia follows through this time, once Nan is . . . she'll be going back to Portland purely to pick up her stuff. That's if they even let you back into the USA with a cancelled work visa.

The life that she's started building will be taken away, which means she'll never get the chance to see if there's something straightforward beyond her and Logan's complicated start.

Coming home could mean facing more than one goodbye, permanently.

Chapter Thirty-One

K it can't stop laughing. Which feels highly inappropriate in the family room of a hospice, but once she'd showered, changed and come back here with Kit, Mum and Dad, they've been taking it in turns to sit at Nan's bedside in pairs while the other two make endless rounds of teas in the kitchen area. She blurted out the whole iDentity mess to Kit while desperate for any conversation that wasn't about Nan disappearing before their very eyes. Instead of worrying about her imminent unemployment, he thinks the whole thing is a hilarious and brilliant distraction.

'Man, this is the best news I've had for days,' Kit says admiringly when she tells him about leaving without Fuchsia's permission. He squeezes the teabags once, twice, three times, wringing every bit of strength out of them. 'Even *I've* never just walked off the job before.'

Guts churning, Thea summons up a smile that she doesn't feel. 'What else was I supposed to do?'

'Sis, I'm on your side. She's a robo-bitch and no job is worth the hassle she was giving you. Miss seeing Nan to work on slogans for some butter brand? No thanks.'

'It's an artisan vegan spread, and that's not all I do, but sure.' Thea presses her foot on the pedal of the bin so Kit can drop the teabags in. 'I'm sure she'll easily replace me,' she adds gloomily.

'You need more faith in yourself. You're *good,* sis. And you got that extra work on the side that paid for your trip, so it's not just me saying it.' The remark reminds her of Logan, how he said the same thing. 'People like her make you think you're not so they can trap you,' says Kit. And that one reminds her of Christian. The difference is glaring. 'Go somewhere else. Prove her wrong.'

'No chance of that now. If she terminates my visa, that's the end of America for me.'

'Don't say that. And definitely don't say that near Nan. She'll lose it if she thinks coming back to see her lost you your job.' His face clouds. 'Well, as much as she's able to lose it right now.'

Nan has deteriorated even in the two hours the round-trip home took her, and since they've been back, her waking moments have been confused, her eyes darting among the people in the room, with only occasional flashes of lucidity amid the drowsiness caused by the illness and the medication.

'I'm not going to do that. I'm not stupid,' Thea retorts.

'She's so invested in you making a go of it over there, and she knows how much you love it. You don't know what it's been like having to keep all this from you. That's why I never want to talk to you.'

'Kit, that's a *lie.* You not wanting to speak to me on the phone is the least likely thing to raise my suspicions ever.

I'm more annoyed with Nan, not telling me, and knowing that I would want to know.'

'If it makes you feel any better, she hit me where it hurts too. She wants me to get better at saving and made me promise that after she's gone, I won't buy any new clothes for a year.' He catches Thea's raised eyebrow. 'Shut up, it's not funny!'

'You think that's the same as being lied to by your entire family?' she says, rolling her eyes. But there's relief too. Messing around with Kit, with Nan in the other room. It's almost normal.

Almost.

'You haven't heard from her, then? The bitch boss,' Kit says, adding a drop of milk to each mug.

She automatically reaches for her phone, before remembering her emails and Slack aren't set up on Teddy's and putting it away again. 'Not as far as I know.'

Kit takes a slurp of his tea, then winces as it burns the inside of his mouth. He stands jiggling from foot to foot.

'When I'm in there, I want to get out, and when I come out, I feel like I should be back in,' he says softly.

'I know,' Thea says nodding. 'It already feels as though it's not quite her any more, but I'm not ready to let this version of her go either.'

They stand, not drinking their tea, tears dripping into the mugs.

'Shall we take these in for Mum and Dad?' Kit says eventually.

'Yeah. Let's go back in.'

⋆　　⋆　　⋆

In the early hours of Wednesday morning, Mum and Dad try to get Kit and Thea to go home and rest, but they don't want to. During the kerfuffle of the family conference in the hallway, Nan dies: her death as efficient and fuss-free as anything she ever did.

It's more common than you think,' one of the palliative nurses tells them in the corridor as they ask how it could have happened like this, with nobody with her, even though they're all *right there.* The nurse squeezes Dad on the arm, gives the rest of them a sympathetic smile. 'It's as though people wait to do it in private when it's time for them to go.'

Shellshocked, they go through the motions of what happens next: a final goodbye with a body that no longer looks like Nan, even so soon after she's gone. Dad is led to an office to sign some paperwork, as Mum ushers Kit and Thea outside.

They stand in the cold car park, stunned and directionless without Nan's bed to orbit around, and wait for Dad, who arrives half an hour later and then announces he's going to walk home. With an almost imperceptible nod at Mum, Kit gives him a five-minute head start before following from a distance.

'I thought we had longer,' Thea says, blinking into the flat, 3 a.m. February dark outside the hospice. Her eyes are dry and sore, and her heart is broken.

'I think she was holding on until you got back,' Mum says gently. 'After Christmas, she went downhill fast.' Thea collapses onto her and inhales shakily. She gets a lungful of mum; the deodorant she's been wearing since

Thea can remember, and her washing powder, plus a top note of the sterile, institutional aroma of the hospice.

She can hear Mum sniffing noisily as though to pull herself together. 'We'll get home, and we'll try and get some sleep,' she says. 'Then I'll start making some calls. Dad won't be up to it.'

'I can help you with that,' Thea says. 'And whatever else you need.'

'Thank you.' Mum kisses the top of her head. 'I don't know how long it will take to get the funeral booked in – from what Barbara told me, there can be quite a wait at the moment.' Thea doesn't know who Barbara is, but now isn't the time to ask. 'Will Fuchsia let you work from here until afterwards?'

'I don't have to rush back,' she replies. Deflecting, not lying, because it's true.

'That's good. I suppose you need to tell her what's going on though, it's only respectful. We'll get going with the arrangements as soon as we can, so we know the dates.'

Mum continues fretting and organising all the way home in the car, where Thea makes her a cup of tea and tries to ignore the silence. Nan's stuff is still all over the place; her boxes of medication, 'her' chair, even an open bag of wine gums next to it, which Thea knows will contain mainly green and yellow sweets because she always leaves them all for Dad to eat.

Thea sees Nan's glasses, lying face down on her side table. She picks them up and turns them over, so as not to scratch the lenses. Not that it matters n—

The realisation threatens to pull her apart.

'First let's get a wash on,' Mum says, getting up again despite her tea being barely touched. Thea can almost see her brain overcompensating for the helplessness she's currently feeling. 'Haven't had time to do any these last few days and you must have stuff to throw in.'

Thea nods, going along with it, even though it's 4 a.m. and no one needs to do a wash that urgently.

Her bag is in her room, clothes spilling out of the top of it where she dragged out what she needed for today and left the rest – she can't even remember what she packed two days ago in Portland, and whether it was clean. There's a pile of T-shirts and underwear on the floor and her laptop is on the bed. She collects some clothes for washing and sweeps Kit's room too, throwing it all into a laundry basket and bringing it downstairs.

'I'll do that,' Mum says, but without moving from the settee.

'You sit there, Mum. Drink your tea.'

The wrongness of Thea looking after her jumpstarts her. 'Calls, yes, I need to make calls. Can you fetch my address book from the hallway?'

'Mum, it's too early,' Thea reminds her.

'But I can make a list. Make sure I don't miss anyone out.'

Thea does as she's told and then ends up facing Nan's shut bedroom door, just off the living room. She can't bring herself to go in, to see all Nan's things, meaningless without Nan there to inhabit them. She ends up back in her own room, too wired to sleep and fiddling with her phone in her hand. Sending messages to tell people Nan is gone makes it too real. She's not ready to see it in black and white.

She flicks back to her one-message history with Nan on Teddy's phone, mourning the loss of their conversation afresh now she knows nothing new will ever be added to it. Then she looks at her laptop again.

Maybe.

Maybe her chat history is backed up on there.

Nerves buzzing, she fires up her laptop, and opens the desktop WhatsApp icon.

Her heart squeezes as the screen fills with the chain of pictures and voice notes they've exchanged for the past six months. They're there. She exhales a breath she didn't know she was holding.

She clicks on one of the voice notes at random and Nan's voice rings out clearly from the tinny laptop speakers. Sobs bubble in Thea's chest as she listens to Nan tell her the plot of *Peaky Blinders*, when she gets to the point Tom Hardy joined the cast.

Well, you know I was a fan of the one that played Tommy Shelby but now there's Alfie too. Oh, he is handsome, even though they're tearing lumps out of everyone in sight.

Thea laughs through the tears, then lets herself cry, clicking on note after note to fill her head up with Nan's voice, one she's already scared she will forget. She clicks on a message from her first week in the States, when she knew no one and was terrified the whole thing had been a stupid mistake.

Thea, you take every chance you're given, do you hear me? Do it all. If someone invites you for a drink or coffee – go! There's no point in being shy or British about it. And I like the sound of this Teddy. Take your opportunities, put yourself out there, wring out every moment, even if just to send your Nan some stories. Get over Christian and even if you don't find love, find some fun.

She thinks of Nan, encouraging her every step of the way. She wouldn't let the small matter of getting fired stop her from trying to get back there somehow. And she never held back when it came to telling people how she felt, for good or for bad.

She pulls up Logan's message again. Suddenly it doesn't matter that she's thousands of miles away and eight hours in the future, or that they might never get to go on a date that's actually a date. After Nan's, right now it's his voice she wants to hear most.

We just lost my nan and I don't know what to do with myself. If that offer of a call still stands, I'd love to hear from you.

The second she sends it, she regrets letting herself be so vulnerable. It's 9 p.m. in Portland. He could be anywhere. He might not even see her message. Or he might not want to spend his evening talking to her about her dead grandmother.

Her phone buzzes in her hand.

'Hello?' her voice wobbles.

'Thea, I know how much your nan meant to you, I'm so sorry.' His voice is low, warm, *there*. 'How are you holding up?'

'I'm a mess,' she admits. 'But trying to stay strong for Mum and Dad. I'm sitting here listening to all Nan's voice notes and wondering how she's just not here any more. It doesn't make any sense.'

'I know how that feels,' he replies. She can imagine his face as he says it. Solemn but creased with kindness. 'I won't lie, I still feel like that sometimes. The world just feels different without them in it.' There's a silence, one where all Thea can hear is her own ragged breath.

'I don't really know how I'll keep going without her,' she says eventually. 'Do you still feel like that about your grandpa?'

'I try to think that he'd *want* me to keep going and hold on to the reminders even when they make me sad. Like, he loved mustard and I can't see it without thinking about him. It's good you have those voice notes to remember your nan by. All those everyday things you talked about that you will always remember.'

'I thought I'd lost them,' Thea bursts out. 'They didn't transfer to the replacement phone, but I found them on my laptop, thank God. Although it's about a hundred years old, so I'm worried they'll disappear if it conks out.' As she says it, the worry grows. It feels urgent to do something about it. 'You'll probably know more about this than me – where and how should I download them, so I don't lose them again?'

'I can help you with that,' Logan says instantly. 'If you forward them to me, I'll make sure they're backed up and you can access them all in one place.'

'There's quite a lot of them,' Thea says uncertainly. She's pretty sure there's stuff on there that she doesn't really want Logan to hear: advice about getting Christian out of her head for good, reassurance about moving thousands of miles from home. What if he listens to them? She'll be mortified.

But how she felt when she thought she'd lost Nan's voice for good was worse.

'If you don't mind, I would really like that,' she says quickly. 'I'll send them now.'

She puts him on speaker and emails them to him from her laptop as they continue to chat.

An hour later, they're still talking. Every so often her mind lands on Nan again and a wave of sadness overtakes her, her voice trembling with tears. Logan lets her talk, and listens as she does.

'Thea!' It's Mum, shouting up the stairs. She clearly hasn't been able to contemplate sleep either. 'Dad and Kit are back.'

'I better go,' Thea says, even though she doesn't want to at all. Going back downstairs means it's all real: Nan isn't coming back.

'Can I call you again?' Logan asks.

'Yes. Please. Any time.' She means it.

'And you can call me any time too. I'm here.'

He's not, but right now it feels like he is.

Until the connection is cut and he's five thousand miles away again.

Chapter Thirty-Two

Every time Thea's fingers hover over the keyboard to start writing Nan's eulogy, she ends up lost in her memories, running over every scraped knee and shared confidence, trying to sift through what's important versus what's important *to her*. As a result, she's barely typed a word on the blank document. She'd told Mum and Dad that she wanted to do it, had known that Nan would have wanted her to be the one to speak, but she's too overwhelmed to write it, and terrified she won't be able to stand up in front of everyone at the funeral and read it out loud without breaking down.

She searches for warmth under the duvet in her bedroom; her hands are freezing cold. The central heating clicked off from its morning timer at around 9 a.m. and despite it being the early days of greyest February and all four of them being in the house, Dad won't entertain putting it back on until 6 p.m., which is still two hours away. He views it as a slippery slope to profligate spending.

Nan would be proud.

Thea sits on her left hand to warm it up while scrolling through what she's got so far with her right:

Tom Hardy obsession
Nicknamed 'Peggy Mitchell' at the pub
Considered Dad's superior tea-making skills her finest
    parental achievement
Would have definitely been a troll towards useless MPs
    if she'd ever worked out how to do Twitter
The most loyal and encouraging person I know

It doesn't seem like much, and yet it's all Nan. She just can't seem to tie it all together. Thea imagines the voice note Nan would be sending her now if this was a work project. *Just get on with it, Thea. The sooner you finish, the sooner you can call that handsome American. I think he's proved he's not a wrong 'un, don't you? And while we're on the topic, what are you even doing in England? You should be back in Portland having adventures. Here for me? Oh no, darling. You work out how to get yourself back to the USA quick smart . . .*

Thea grimaces. Imaginary Nan's voice is as scarily insistent as her real one, and knowing what she'd have to say about all this – including her unemployed status – ingrains a sense of guilt deep into her marrow. She can put off thinking about what's next until after the funeral in two days' time, but then? Mum will be delighted to have her home – at first. But not when she realises it's because she's been fired rather because she's chosen to come back. Then she'll start fretting about Thea's employment prospects.

Thea's already worrying about that too, a little tremor underneath her grief, and while her wearied, late-night

LinkedIn trawls have shown there are jobs out there, decent ones even, the ones she stands a chance of getting are *here*. In London. She doesn't want to come back. Not yet. Not like this. Maybe not ever. Portland is unfinished business, on so many different levels. Her thoughts wander again to Logan, as they so often do when she thinks about drawing a line under the US, admitting defeat and coming home. It would be easier, after all, than going begging to Fuchsia, or seeing if another company is interested in a British citizen with a bad reference.

How do you know it would be easier to live back here? Nan's voice is back. *You haven't even tried.*

She hits return and adds 'always told me to go after what I wanted' to her list of Nan's qualities.

A thought embeds in her mind.

What if she emails The Collective and tells them that she was the consultant for the Memento work? Not with Logan putting a word in like he offered. But on her own terms, making a case for them hiring her. After all, she's already generated them some revenue.

A faint pulse starts beating in the depths of her gut: a prickle of nerves and excitement, with a dash of nothing-to-lose nihilism thrown in for good measure.

Maybe they'll discount her due to the treacherous way she sat on Felix's side of the table having covertly fed ideas to Logan, but her big fear before was Fuchsia finding out – and what does that matter now?

She pulls up her email and before she can change her mind starts typing.

To: Mina Shapiro
From: Theodora Bridges
Subject: Memento Pitch Contest/ Vacancies at
The Collective

Dear Mina

Apologies for emailing you out of the blue. You may remember me from iDentity's pitch team for the Memento challenge.

This is an unconventional email, but in the interests of full disclosure, I think it's one worth sending, because I'm actively job-seeking and if there's a chance of my being considered for a role at The Collective I would like to take it.

I couldn't have been more delighted when it was announced that Memento were going to roll out The Collective's work. It was clearly the stronger pitch and the right direction for the company. However, this isn't just a wannabe employee throwing platitudes to the victor, I genuinely believed in the strategy.

Why? Because your work started as my work.

Due to circumstances I would be happy to explain in person, Logan Beechwood had access to some ideas I was working on for his partner, but that were ultimately not presented. He loved them, but the situation put me in a precarious position with my employer, through whom I have a working visa, so he passed the work on to you anonymously.

As you won the contest, your business must be expanding, and I would like to be considered for a role. Having created work for Memento that was proven to be the right fit for the client, I'm confident I can apply my skills to your other accounts, both existing and yet-to-be-signed.

I have a track record of doing the same thing for many happy clients in the UK and have referees that can provide testimonials to that effect.

I attach my résumé and hope I will be considered for any openings you might have.

Best wishes

Theodora Bridges

As she presses send, she lets herself acknowledge that she's either been brave or stupid and it will only become clear which if and when she gets a response. If Mina goes to Fuchsia then her bridges are well and truly burned, but the alternative is doing nothing, and if she wants to make it back to the States, she owes it to Nan – she owes it to *herself* – to try.

The adrenaline has warmed her up without any need for the radiators to come on. She flicks back to the Word document, fired up now, and starts to type, memories and emotions about Nan pouring out of her. She can't get them down fast enough and the process of typing now keeps her mind off the impulsive email. Pages later, she's interrupted by the buzz of an email arriving, which shocks her back into reality.

Not The Collective, but a file transfer from Logan Beechwood.

Her heart flips. Since their phone call two days ago, they've been exchanging regular messages. Every time, she wants to update Nan, before remembering they're in touch like this *because* of Nan. She opens the email.

> I saved all of your voice notes in a filespace so they're safe. Did you know that some of the words you say sound just like her? 'Nuffink' is my favorite – so Cockney, so cute! I hope you don't mind, but I also put an extra file together for you. I thought it might bring you and your family some comfort (I understand if it might be too hard for right now, and I will not be offended if you don't watch). I pulled a couple of pics from your socials, but if you like it and want to provide pictures and/or clips I can create a longer film for you. I'd be happy to. I still watch the film I made of my grandpa.

Thea clicks on the link, watching as the file slowly downloads and nervous about what to expect. She hits play the second the transfer is confirmed.

The screen is black for a moment before Nan's raspy voice cuts through the darkness.

'I don't regret that liar who left me in the lurch. After all, he gave me your dad, and he gave me all of you.' The screen is overlaid with a shot of Thea's family at Christmas, paper hats on. Kit's looking slightly off camera, towards the wallet Thea bought him, and Mum's elbow is skew-whiff where she was nudging him to get his attention before the timer went off.

On screen, Nan keeps talking, with snippets about Mum, Dad, Kit and Thea that bring tears to her eyes. She makes no move to stop them running into the smile she can't keep from her face.

There's a transition and a montage of pictures of Tom Hardy – red carpets, film roles, a shot of him winning the jiu-jitsu tournament – rush past, accompanied by a composite voiceover of Nan's *many* thoughts about his cheeky smile. Thea bursts out laughing, and the video moves along again. It's not long, maybe three minutes, but for those one hundred and eighty seconds she gets a snapshot of her darling nan.

Some of the audio Logan has pulled out are lines that Thea brushed over at the time: compliments and encouragements she barely heard – or did and dismissed because they came from someone who loved her unconditionally and 'had' to say them. He's put it all together in a way that makes Nan sound familiar, while the arrangement gives a fresh insight, his documentarian's eye focusing on details she wouldn't have herself. It's like a trailer for Nan's life. She already knows she will treasure it, and at the same time, wants to take him up on the offer to do more. She swipes the tears from her cheeks and her hand slides to her phone, so she can tap out a message to say as much. But typing her thanks isn't enough. It won't get across what this film means to her, and she needs to tell him.

'Hey.' She can tell by his voice that he's smiling.

'I got the video,' she replies. 'It's beautiful.' Her voice cracks on the last word and she clears her throat. 'Are you used to people becoming weeping messes when you send them your films?'

Logan gives a low chuckle. 'Does it make me sound like a psycho if I say it's one of the best parts of the job?'

Thea laughs. 'A bit.'

'I wasn't sure if it would be too raw,' he says quietly, 'but some people screen videos or image slideshows at funerals so I thought you might like the option.'

Thea sniffs back a tear and nods, even though he can't see her. 'Dad will really like that idea.'

'I really liked your Nan, from what I heard. She had spirit and she clearly adored you. All of you.'

'I know,' Thea says, letting herself cry now. 'We feel – felt – the same about her. I wish I could show her the film too. She'd love it. Well, she'd love the Tom Hardy clips anyway.' Thea wipes her nose with the back of her hand, glad they're not on FaceTime, where he'd be able to see what a state she looked. 'I'm going to show it to everyone later.' She can hear traffic noises on Logan's end of the phone, and the configuration of it is so specific to her daily routine in Portland that it causes a sharp pang of homesickness for her adopted city. 'Where are you right now? On your way to work?'

'Correct.' She can hear him smiling as he talks. 'I'm meeting a client for coffee near Powell's Books so walking up now. They saw one of the new ads on social and wanted to meet in person. Afterwards, I'm picking up some home-movie reels. Then when I have the footage, I have a couple of days of editing ahead of me.' His voice sounds bouncy and a little breathless as he pounds along the pavement. 'How about you?' he asks. 'You said the funeral is after the weekend, right?'

'Monday,' Thea says. It's Friday now. 'I'm simultane-ously dreading it and wanting to get it out of the way. But

I've been able to finish my tribute now, although that also is probably a couple of days of editing after the amount I've just written.'

'And how are you doing?'

'I'm OK,' she replies automatically. 'Well, not really, but I'm coping.' Her sleep has been thrown out of whack by a combination of the jet lag and the waves of grief, making everything seem sharpened as well as more unreal. At 3 a.m. she's wide awake and oscillating between Nan memories and life decisions and by early evening she feels nauseous and sore-eyed from exhaustion.

'I know you have your family around you,' Logan says, 'but if you need some support, just say the word, Thea. I can fly over.'

The thought of him, here, makes her heart catch. 'If you weren't on a different continent, I would love to see you right now,' she replies.

'I mean it,' he says emphatically. His voice is like being folded into a warm hug. 'I can come. And I'd like to. It's not just empty words. I'll get on a plane this weekend.'

It's dizzying to imagine he's being serious. But his tone *is* serious. Deadly so. She shivers, and not from the cold in her bedroom. No game playing, no trying to figure out what he means. Just: if she wants him to come, he'll come.

She thinks about how chaotic things have been, the rollercoaster of how they met, the agency contest and the complications. But amid it, Logan himself has never been complicated. He's been straightforward when everything else was up in the air. It's one of the things she liked about him when they first met. Before everything got so mixed up. If she hadn't been so busy looking for game-playing and secrets, and instead had been as direct as him, they wouldn't have wasted the last few weeks.

And then she thinks about Nan, who would *love* the grand gesture of it all.

'Come,' she says, being as straightforward as she can. 'I'd really like you to.'

Chapter Thirty-Three

Thea's voice trembles as she starts to talk. She forces herself to project her voice and make sure that every person in the packed crematorium can hear her. There's been a bigger turn-out at the funeral than they were expecting, after news of the former East End pub landlady's funeral spread. Faces Thea's dad hasn't seen since he collected glasses for pocket money as a teenager have shown up, several decades older and from a life Thea's only heard about in stories.

It's not the size of the crowd that's causing her to falter though. It's the coffin, containing Nan, but not Nan, that's in her eyeline. The finality of it threatens to overwhelm her.

Standing at the front in black trousers and a polo neck she thought would be practical for a draughty hall in the dead of winter, it now feels claustrophobic around her neck. Her breathing feels strangled.

She can't even look at Mum, Dad or Kit because it will set her off. Again. Now the practical, organisational work is over, they're all a mess. Kit has been crying since he got up, although it's less active than that, more like he's consistently leaking from his eyes. Dad's eyes are red-rimmed, contrasted against his grey face, and Mum is ninety per cent tissues at this point. Thea looks to the back of the room, and away from her A4 print-out – double spaced and in a much bigger font than you think you'll need, the celebrant had advised – pausing for a moment to gather her thoughts and calm down. As the text blurs through tears, it hits her why the celebrant had been so emphatic on that point.

She blinks a few times and looks around, thinking it might help her to reset if she doesn't settle on one thing. Her eye snags on Logan, sitting in the back row next to the aisle, slightly apart from the three people seated next to him – who Thea has never seen before in her life, but who have the look of sixty-somethings who've spent a lot of time in the pub and are likely former (or current) regulars. Her breath catches again, but because of him this time. He's in a well-cut black suit, with his beard tidied up and his bouncy hair tamed. His face is solemn, without the easy smile she has pictured when she's imagined him at the end of the phone over the past week, but he still looks entirely like himself.

And handsome. He definitely looks handsome. Her blood rises as she thinks how inappropriate that thought is for a funeral, and then it bolsters her, because it would give Nan a laugh.

She didn't see him arrive; he must have slipped in after the hearses pulled up and the family took their seats. He'd texted last night to say that he'd landed and that he'd see her at the venue, no more fuss than that, despite being unfamiliar with most of London and never having been east before. She'd texted back to see if he needed any help with travel or accommodation, and he'd replied that he was all sorted, and she shouldn't worry. Then she'd promptly forgotten all about it in the kerfuffle of calling the pub to confirm numbers for the wake, and fielding texts every two minutes from one of dad's cousins about the parking situation at the crematorium, and if they knew whether his car was liable for the low-emission charge within the North Circular zoning (Dad, of course, knew. It wasn't).

But now Logan is here. Not intruding or making it about him, simply showing up. He gives her a small, supportive smile, just a twist of his lips really, followed by a little nod. A shared moment as he passes on some of his steady strength. She swallows her sorrow, clears her throat, and nods back. Then she begins again.

At the wake, in the slightly tired back room of a pub that was chosen purely for convenience, Thea gets her mum and dad settled into chairs, and then loads up plates of food for relatives that aren't too steady on their feet. She distributes them along with hot drinks, and exchanges a few words with each person, before finding a quiet chair in the corner and collapsing into it.

She closes her eyes, needing a minute, but also maybe an hour. All of her energy was focused on getting her to this point and now she's completely drained.

'I brought you a cup of tea,' a deep American voice says above her. She opens her eyes and Logan is standing there, directing a cup and saucer towards her. She leans up and over to look in the cup.

Dishwater.

She smiles gratefully anyway.

'Thank you,' she says, taking it from him, and balancing it on the table next to her while gesturing for him to sit down. He does, and the chair is so soft and battered that he sinks into it, his knees flying up. He manoeuvres himself into a slightly more dignified pose and moves the chair closer to her. They end up with their legs inches apart, just one small tilt away from being able to press against each other. Thea's skin erupts in goose pimples from the proximity. The abnormality of this whole day, and the feeling that everyone here is playing a part, following the beats of funeral script, has so far stopped her from focusing on how weird it is that Logan is here, in a slightly random pub close-ish to her parents' house. But he is. Not just a tender voice at the end of her phone, but a living, breathing, Logan-shaped person right in front of her, with the gravity pull his presence has always had on her. 'And thank you for coming. I'm not really sure what I was thinking,' she says, shaking her head, 'telling you to fly thousands of miles for a funeral. It's hardly a hot ticket.'

Logan looks around the room and then turns back to her, exaggeratedly raising an eyebrow. 'I don't know, it's kind of jumping in here.' The pub regular crowd has quickly moved on from the teas and coffees provided to stronger beverages, and the noise level has increased in direct proportion.

'I guess so. Nan knew a lot of people.' Thea watches a table of sexagenarians doing shots of sambuca. 'I think Nan would have chucked that lot out by now. Or at least got Derek to do it.' She looks towards former barman and bouncer Derek, who is now pushing eighty. He's sitting in his wheelchair drinking a coffee at the table with her parents, accompanied by his middle-aged daughter.

'Thank you so much for the film,' Thea says. 'It was wonderful. My parents love it too. And you put it together so quickly.'

Logan shakes his head a little and runs a hand through his hair. Under his beard she can see his cheeks have gone a little pink with embarrassment, and it makes her want to brush her hand against them. 'It's my favourite kind of job. Loads of material and a great subject. I'm honoured you showed it at the service.'

Logan had put together a five-minute version of the film he'd sent Thea, based on the voice note reel plus additional photos she'd sent to him. It had caused disproportionate drama among their 'bereavement team' at the funeral home who were in charge of managing their 'event'.

'When I told them I didn't want to use their slide show template and would screen my own film, you'd think I'd asked to pay tribute to Nan through the medium of interpretative dance.' Thea gives a little laugh. 'I think they thought I fancied myself as Steven Spielberg, and then when they saw it, they had to admit that maybe I *was* kind of Steven Spielberg-esque. I didn't tell them I wasn't the film-maker. It was more fun that way.'

'You've got to get your kicks where you can,' Logan agrees, smiling.

'But seriously, it was really lovely. Even though showing it destroyed the room.' Anyone still holding it together was a wreck by the time the screen faded to black and the holding shot of Nan with her birth and death dates flashed up. That included Thea, Kit, Mum and Dad, who had watched it beforehand and knew what to expect.

Thea sniffs, feeling herself get overwhelmed again. 'I really want a cup of tea,' she says, 'but if I cross the room to get one, I'm going to end up having to talk to loads of people and I'm all small-talked out.'

Thea remembers the tea Logan brought over at the same time he does, and they both flick their eyes towards it, hers guiltily.

He coughs out a little laugh. 'That's not good tea, huh?'

Thea wrinkles her face at him in apology. 'You are really good at making films, but you are really not good at making tea, I'm so sorry.'

He holds her gaze. 'Then you're going to have to teach me how to do it properly, or they're going to kick me out of the country.'

'It's true, they will,' she nods gravely. 'And you're on.'

She's been in such regular contact with him, they're talking as though they're carrying on a conversation they were already having. She hasn't asked him anything about his trip, or how he's going to juggle his work with being here. 'How long are you here for? Will Felix wonder where you are?'

'I thought if I was going to cross the Atlantic, I should stay a week or so,' he says. 'And Felix and I don't keep tabs on each other like that.' He gives a wry smile. 'That's probably how he was able to take secret strategy meetings without me to start off with. But we've always worked remotely when we were doing edits. I'll work while I'm here but will have time to hang out too. If you're free, that is.' He lets the sentence hang there.

'A week or so sounds good to me,' she replies firmly. 'And I would like to hang out.' She stands up and holds out her hand to signal he should come with her. 'I also know my parents really want to thank you for the film, so let me introduce you.'

Logan responds by grasping her hand back, firmly, but not tight, and stands up to meet her gaze. A flash of heat pulses through his palm to hers.

'They're going to gush about the film, just to warn you, and my dad will keep trying to pay you for it.' Logan had insisted it was a gift but once Dad had extracted the going rate for one of Memento's movies from Thea, he wouldn't stop talking about ensuring 'the lad wasn't out of pocket'. 'Then he'll start asking about the best rush-hour routes around Portland based on Google Street Map imagery. That's his way of making conversation.'

'It's all about the side streets,' Logan says, deadpan. 'But you need to keep yourself informed about the construction work. I've fallen foul of that one too many times.'

Thea laughs again. 'He'll like you. I'm also going to take an order for a round of teas, and then I'll show you how the Bridges family make it.'

'Deal.'

They make their way over, Thea stopping every few feet to hug someone or trade a few words about Nan, when her phone buzzes. She pulls it from her trouser pocket, expecting another stray guest asking for directions to the pub, but it's a text from Fuchsia. At 8 a.m. in Portland. Her cortisol instantly spikes. Then she remembers she hasn't heard from Fuchsia since she left and the message is likely a formality, laying out the details of her termination. After almost a week of silence, it'll almost be a relief to get it over with.

Thea,
Teddy tells me the funeral is today. I hope all goes as well as it can. If it suits, I'd like you to begin WFH as of Tuesday next week, with a view to returning to the office at a date to be agreed after that. LMK

There is no reference whatsoever to the fact that Thea doesn't work there any more. She rushes over to the tea urn, leaving Logan with a distant relative who wants to know how an American washes up in Leytonstone, while she ponders what to make of it.

She screenshots the email and WhatsApps it to Teddy.

WTF?

He replies instantly.

Do NOT think about this now, today is way more important, but the office, the accounts, everything has been a mess without

you. Plus, Ernie just quit. She knows she can't afford to lose
you, even if she will NEVER admit it.

Which is all to say, whatever her first offer is, don't accept it.
You're in a good bargaining position.

Now get off your phone.

Love you.

Logan hustles over, a slightly alarmed look on his face.
'Who's that lady in the purple cardigan? When she found
out I was American she started telling me a story about a
marine she once met that I'm not sure I can repeat—' He
stops, catching the expression on Thea's face as she stares
at her phone, flipping through Fuchsia's and then Teddy's
messages again. 'Are you OK?'

She doesn't feel how she thought she'd feel at being
un-fired and makes a note to interrogate what that means
later. But not now. Right now, Logan's presence is rooting
her to what's important. Something any dealings with
Fuchsia always seem to throw into disarray.

'That's Doreen,' she says to Logan, clicking off the
screen and putting her phone away. 'And if it's the story I
think it is, she's convinced she's irresistible to all American
men and it's probably for the best that you keep away
from her.' She turns to the tea urn. 'And yes, I'm OK. Ish.
But I'll be better when I have a cup of tea, so I'm going to
give you a tutorial – and then I'm going to introduce you
to the people who mean the most to me in the world.'

Chapter Thirty-Four

'I've heard it all now.' Three days later, at Thea's parents' home, Dad is chuckling, his eyebrows disappearing into his receding hairline as Logan tells him about the hotel he's staying in. 'Who knew there was a *boutique hotel scene*—' even the phrase sounds unfamiliar coming from his mouth – 'in Stratford?'

'I'd heard East London was hip,' Logan replies, confused. 'It always appears on those lists of "coolest neighbourhoods" online.'

'Hmmm,' Roy says in response. 'You should have lived in the East End in the seventies and eighties, mate. Still very hard for me to think of it as cool.' Dad's voice is gruff but he's loving being Logan's fount of London knowledge. Meanwhile, Logan seems genuinely interested in Dad's stories of pre-gentrification, hanging on to his every word.

'That was after the Krays, right?' he asks now, and Dad chuckles again.

'That was the fifties and sixties, Logan, bit before my time, but Mum – Dora – would have been able to tell you about them.'

'Did she *know* them?' he asks eagerly.

'Nah. Knew *of* them, but she ran the pub after that era, thank God. You wouldn't want to be a landlady back then. Protection rackets and gangsters.'

'Dad, we've got to go,' Thea butts in. 'We're due to meet Nicole in forty-five minutes.' She throws a stressed-out look to Logan. 'And she's never late, so we can't be.'

They grab their coats and call out a round of goodbyes. 'Mum, stop doing that now. I'll help you in the morning.' Mum hasn't stopped moving since the funeral, spending every evening sorting through Nan's things and dealing with any residual admin generated by her death. It's as though she knows once she runs out of things to do, she'll have to just face up to Nan not being there.

Dad's different too, but in a quieter, less manic way. He's himself, but slightly deflated, occasionally stopping mid-sentence as a thought comes to him about Nan, his eyes filling up. She's worried about both of them.

As she and Logan leave the house for the tube station, bracing against the biting February headwind, she says as much.

'It's grief,' Logan says, slipping his hand into hers, a gesture that has become familiar over the last few days and comes with a little electrified burst of warmth and energy every time. They've held hands in Leyton, in Soho, in Notting Hill – Teddy was furious about that ('I can't *believe* he is getting the Richard Curtis tour before I am,' he'd fumed over text) – and in every park they've walked through in the winter cold, which is many. Walking, talking, and retiring to a café or pub to do more talking has become their routine.

But so far, holding hands is as passionate as it's got. Which isn't to say Thea doesn't love holding hands, but Logan is due to fly back in three days. She can't work out if he's being respectful to the circumstances under which he travelled to the UK, if he's waiting for *her* to make the first move, or if he *was* interested, but having got to know her better has now mentally friend-zoned Thea and just needs to get through the next three days before he can escape back to the States and never contact her again.

'It's your mom's way of dealing with it. Keeping busy so she doesn't dwell on your Nan being gone, and you leaving again soon too. Remember that she has no idea you were fired.'

As though on cue, another message from Fuchsia arrives.

Thea should be relieved that she still has a job, that she won't have to leave Portland, and hasn't had to confess to Mum and Dad what really happened, and she *is*.

But.

The idea of being back in that office, with Fuchsia's terrible management style and anger issues, fills her with dread. She wants to go back to the States with all her heart, but being dependent on an iDentity-generated visa is a cage she's locked into, with Fuchsia holding the key. She doesn't want a job where she's constantly threatened with the sack. Or where she's doing work well below her skillset for pay that barely covers her rent.

But the alternative is staying in London and building her career here. It means giving up the USA. Which means giving up any chance of seeing where this latest run of not-quite-dates with Logan might lead to.

Kit had been no help when she'd told him about the latest twist; that Fuchsia was pretending everything was fine. 'Sack it off,' he'd shrugged. 'You don't need a boss like that.'

Another buzz, and a calendar invite drops onto the screen titled: New Business Brainstorm. She groans, dread forming at the pit of her stomach. Fuchsia is behaving. For now. But she knows that the second she's actually back at work, all of this civility and respect for boundaries will evaporate.

'Is that Fuchsia again?' Logan asks as her phone goes for the third time in as many minutes.

'Yes. And I don't know what to do. I feel bad enough about leaving Mum and Dad so soon, never mind for a job that I don't even think I like or want. But I can't see a way out, other than resigning and applying for other jobs from over here, and staying with my parents a bit longer. But the chance of a job coming up at a company who will be happy to sponsor me, especially when I've pissed off Fuchsia and she probably won't give me a reference.' She exhales a cold plume of misty air. 'What do you think I should do?'

Logan doesn't reply straight away, just keeps walking, his eyes slightly crinkled at the edges as though in thought. 'I can't answer that question for you,' he says so softly, she can barely hear him above the hum of rush-hour traffic on the High Road. 'You need to do what's best for you, and your career. I interfered on your behalf once before and I shouldn't have.' He presses his lips together before saying. 'But the offer still stands for me to talk to The Collective.'

'I haven't heard anything since I emailed Mina last week,' Thea replies, her stomach twisting with embarrassment at the candid email she sent being met with a wall of silence. 'If you bring it up with them now, it could make your working relationship with them difficult. But thank you.'

They're almost at the tube station when Logan stops abruptly. 'What's your gut saying, right now, about it all?'

Thea tips her head towards the dark sky and groans. 'I want to go back to Portland, but I don't want to work for Fuchsia any more, and I don't want the hard work I've put into my career to be for nothing.' The gap between what she wants and what she has to do is too big. A coil of anxiety zings around her stomach and she brings her chin back down so she's looking at Logan dead on. 'And to be honest, the thing I really can't stop thinking about, amid all this, is are we ever going to kiss each other again and if so, *when*?'

Logan's face looks so serious and stricken that for a second, she thinks she's messed everything up. But then he laughs. A low rumble that disappears into the sound of buses and cars. 'That I can help you with,' he says, using the hand he's holding to pull her closer towards him. 'But first, I have a confession.'

Her chest constricts in case it's something she doesn't want to hear, but the look on his face, windswept and illuminated by the harsh streetlights and headlights crawling down the road is seeking and hopeful.

'I've been waiting for the perfect moment—' He halts 'That's not true. To begin with I was waiting for a *suitable* moment. What if you just needed a friend and I ruined the memory of your Nan by trying to make out with you when the funeral was barely over? Then we started hanging out, and I *think* I was getting the right signals . . .' He raises his eyebrows as though looking for confirmation, which Thea gives with a nod. 'And *then* I started waiting for the perfect moment to kiss you, because the two times we've done it before, it's always been the wrong time or the wrong place.' He lets go of her hands and throws his arms up in exasperation. 'But it turns out there's no such thing as a perfect moment. The next natural silence between us will be on the tube when it starts rattling too loud for us to talk, so I'm probably going to think about kissing you then, and even as a non-Londoner, I don't think that's a great place to do it, for us or for the people trying to commute into the city—'

'The tube isn't a great place to get off with someone, unless you're a teenager, really drunk, or both,' Thea cuts in with a grin. Her heart flutters. She steps closer and brings his still gesticulating arms down so they're standing facing each other, his hands clasped in hers.

'And is it me or does it smell weird in the tube station?' he says. He gently pulls her towards him to close the gap between them. Commuters are bursting out of the station in droves, tutting as they have to move around two stationary people restricting access to the bus stops.

'It does smell weird,' she says. She ignores the commuters and puts the palms of her hands on the front of his coat, leaning in towards him, close enough to feel heat radiating through his jacket and her gloves. 'I'm not sure outside the tube station during rush hour is much better, but—'

She stops talking when he kisses her, soft at first and then harder. His arms coil around her and hold her tightly. Cold noses, hot breath. It's as though they can't get close enough, and Thea's only thought is that she could kiss Logan Beechwood in a noisy East End street for hours, before that falls away. It's as though there's only the two of them, only this moment.

'Does that at least answer one of your questions?' Logan asks, pulling away slightly. There's a cheeky glimmer in his eye.

'Two actually,' she replies, a little breathless. She can't stop smiling. 'I wanted to know if *and* when, so we can tick both off my list.' Her face falls a little. 'As for the other decision, I'd say that it's even more complicated now.' She focuses in on his mouth and eyes, her heart drumming. 'But I'll figure it out.'

Her phone buzzes again.

'Crap, that's either Fuchsia *again* or Nicole saying she's arrived early,' she says, pulling out her phone, 'which she has been known to do.'

She taps quickly at the screen and scans it for a second, before letting out a squeak of disbelief.

'What?' says Logan, his eyes looking from her to the phone and back again.

'It's Mina at The Collective,' Thea squeals, 'I have an interview with her in two weeks' time.'

She turns the phone around so he can read it for himself.

And then she shoves her phone back in her pocket and kisses Logan again. Until one of the tutting commuters shouts 'get a room' and they are definitely, absolutely going to be late to meet Nicole.

Chapter Thirty-Five

TEN MONTHS LATER

Thea scrolls madly through her phone at Portland Airport as Chelsey, the check-in agent, waits patiently for her to locate her boarding pass. She gives a fixed, toothy smile to the enormous queue of travellers waiting behind her, who are getting twitchy about the length of time she's taking at the desk. A family wearing Christmas jumpers with light-up Rudolph noses wrangle a baby in a matching romper into a pushchair, while handing out candy canes to their older children to keep them quiet as they stand by for the next available desk.

'Did you download these ones to your app, or did I download them to mine?' Logan asks, scrolling through his own screen with an increasing note of panic in his voice. 'We did book them, right?'

'Found them!' Thea shouts, thrusting her phone, and their passports, at Chelsey. 'Yes, I booked Portland to London for Christmas,' she reminds him. 'You booked London to Boston for New Year, and Boston to Seattle for Teddy and Jake's wedding after that.'

'That's quite the holiday tour,' Chelsey says as she scans Thea's phone. She swipes their passports in the machine and checks them, before sliding them back over the desk.

'It is, isn't it?' Thea replies, returning her smile. 'I can't wait to see Teddy,' she says to Logan. She misses him now that Teddy and Jake are based in Seattle – Teddy running his own boutique agency while Jake does something at a new app development company that none of them understands.

Her eyes flick towards the airport entrance. Outside, the afternoon is dark, and the sound of pounding rain can be heard above the tinny airport announcements, but inside there are Christmas decorations and adverts for Holiday Cup coffees awaiting them in the food court once they've cleared security.

'The weather isn't due to get any worse, is it?' she asks Chelsey. 'It won't affect today's flights?'

'There are a few delayed departures due to the bad weather on the East Coast but nothing impacting international departures. Don't worry, you'll be home for Christmas Eve.'

'So I don't need to book us a room at the PDX branch of The Opulent?' Logan cracks.

Almost a year later and the word 'us' still gives Thea a tingle every time it comes out of his mouth.

'Maybe for our anniversary,' Thea jokes back, putting her arm around him and nestling in. He's wearing the red sweater that she loves, the bulk of him offset by the softness of the wool. He gives her a little squeeze in return. 'Although maybe not the airport branch.'

'Then I guess we better go to London,' he says with a smile. He hauls their bags onto the conveyor belt as she checks she has all their tickets and documents again. She even splashed out on a new long-haul travelling outfit – one without any takeaway stains on it – in honour of taking her boyfriend home to celebrate Christmas in London.

Her phone pings in her hand and her eyes widen in alarm as she sees a notification from Mina appear on the screen. She left work three hours ago, working right up until the moment that Logan arrived to pick her up, and then a little more during the drive to the airport. The team has been working for a demanding client who doesn't seem to care that Mina has told them The Collective has a seven-day Christmas holiday shutdown policy. They've all winced every time an email arrives from them, and have been frantically working together to make sure everyone gets a break. The volume of work isn't vastly different at the new agency, and there are periods where there's too much work coming in and not enough resources, but Thea's getting to work with clients and Mina's management style is level-headed, which makes a world of difference. After handing in their notices at iDentity, both she and Teddy had had to block Fuchsia on multiple platforms. Maybe this latest task is something Thea can address during the long flight, so she'll be able to switch off once Dad collects them at the other end. And then she can enjoy spending time with Mum, Dad and Kit. And Kit's new boyfriend, apparently, who was a last-minute addition to the guest list. Kit has told Mum not to panic about buying him a present as he'll do it and put their name on it, which is how Thea knows he must really like him – he's obviously out to impress. Thea wants to impress

Logan too. She's booked tickets to a show, as well as broken her 'no Oxford Street on Christmas Eve' policy so she can take him to see the lights. Dad has said he'll drive them there in his black cab to make it even more London-centric and festive. Teddy was seething.

She opens the message and a hand flies up to her mouth as she reads it. 'Mina's given us all a bonus,' Thea says, disbelievingly. She reads out the message as they move away from the desk. '"Everyone's hard work has translated into accounts won, industry award nominations and the prospect of a prosperous year ahead. It hasn't gone unnoticed, and I want to make sure you enjoy this break and come back ready for the New Year."' She scans the rest of the email, which says Mina has put out a company-wide OOO saying no one will be responding to mail until 2nd January and that they should all follow the policy so that she isn't undermined as the CEO. 'She's also given us *two* extra days annual leave,' she bursts out. Even Kit's voice in her head saying, 'Wow, sis, that must add up to what, a whole fortnight now then, eh?' can't drain the pleasure of the moment. She can take the additional days when Mum, Dad and Kit come over next year to do their American road trip.

'Fantastic,' Logan says, picking her free hand up in his and kissing it as they walk away from the desk. 'Something else to celebrate this Christmas. Oh, Courtney asked me if you'd be interested in being one of her bridesmaids. Something about balancing out Chip for asking his *entire* amateur soccer team to be groomsmen.'

Thea's lasting impression of Chip when she met him was of very bright white teeth and lots of muscles. She imagines that multiplied by eleven, and then wonders if his and Courtney's nuptials will be one of those American weddings that escalates to the extent that the guests end up paying thousands of dollars to attend and submitting to all sorts of rules and rituals. A little flutter of panic squirms in her stomach. 'I think I'd prefer to be a regular guest,' she says. 'Is that OK?'

'Definitely. Because it means I can turn Chip down too.' He nods at her to confirm that, yes, an entire football team of groomsmen and there's still scope for more. 'If you think of a way I can also get out of his extreme-sports-themed bachelor party, let me know.'

'You might have to show willing with that one,' Thea commiserates. 'He *is* marrying your best friend. And besides, you like hiking, so an outdoorsy stag do might be fun?'

'You won't be saying that when my white-water raft disappears from some wilderness in Utah,' he mutters darkly.

As they walk down the corridor to security, signs flicker with gate information about the departures. 'Please Wait' flashes up beside the listing for the 16.00 December 23 flight from Portland to London.

'We've got a couple of hours. You want to get something to eat before we board?' Logan asks. Thea thinks of the food she has stashed in her bag. Despite her pay bump at The Collective, old habits die hard. Everyone knows the mark-up on airport food is out of control.

'I brought a plane picnic,' she replies, waggling her bag at him.

'For me too?'

'Of course. For both of us. Turkey and stuffing sandwiches, cinnamon cookies, and I even went to the international supermarket to get some *proper* British chocolate to keep me going until I get home.' She thinks of home with a flash of sadness because Nan won't be there. She can't wait to hug Mum and Dad. They must be feeling her absence even more. 'At least this year I'll be back in time to help with Christmas dinner.'

'Remind me what Yorkshire puddings are again?'

'It's a controversial topic as to whether they should be included in a Christmas roast. You can debate that in the pub when we see Nicole. She's against, but the Bridges family are very pro. My mum makes *the* best ones.'

'Got it,' he says, smiling down at her, his navy eyes twinkling. 'Whatever they are, I'll be sure to compliment them.' She leans up and kisses him, still slightly surprised that she can do that now, whenever she wants. She gives in to the flare of heat that rushes through her veins whenever she does.

They walk towards security to start the first leg of their transatlantic Christmas tour.

Together.

Us.

Acknowledgements

To my mum and dad, who I miss every day, and were the best parents anyone could wish for.

To my brother John, who I wouldn't have got through last year without.

To Ian and Ikey, who I love more than anyone.

Thank you to my agent Sarah Hornsley, as well as Laurie Richardson, my editor Amy Batley, my publicist Kim Nyamhondera, my copy editor Helen Parham (especially for the anus-related save!), Lucy Davey for the lovely cover illustration and to Natalie Chen for the cover design.

Thank you to my friends and cheerleaders who never stop trying to help me reach my dream of becoming a full-time author.

And to everyone who has bought, borrowed, read and reviewed one of my books. I'm very grateful, thank you.

Discover more from Helen Whitaker . . .

After a frosty start, will love thaw them out?

SINGLE IN THE SNOW is available now!